Books in the COLONY Series
QUANT
ARCADIA
GALACTIC SURVEY
SILK ROAD
LOST COLONY
EARTH

Books in the EMPIRE Series
by Richard F. Weyand:
EMPIRE: Reformer
EMPIRE: Usurper
EMPIRE: Tyrant
EMPIRE: Commander
EMPIRE: Warlord
EMPIRE: Conqueror

by Stephanie Osborn:
EMPIRE: Imperial Police
EMPIRE: Imperial Detective
EMPIRE: Imperial Inspector
EMPIRE: Section Six

by Richard F. Weyand:
EMPIRE: Intervention
EMPIRE: Investigation
EMPIRE: Succession
EMPIRE: Renewal
EMPIRE: Resistance
EMPIRE: Resurgence

Books in the Childers Universe
by Richard F. Weyand:
Childers
Childers: Absurd Proposals
Galactic Mail: Revolution
A Charter For The Commonwealth
Campbell: The Problem With Bliss
by Stephanie Osborn:
Campbell: The Sigurdsen Incident

SILK ROAD

A Colony Story

by

RICHARD F. WEYAND

RICHARD F. WEYAND

Copyright 2021 by Richard F. Weyand
All Rights Reserved

ISBN 978-1-954903-05-0
Printed in the United States of America

Cover Credits
Cover Art: Paola Giari and Luca Oleastri,
www.rotwangstudio.com
Back Cover Photo: Oleg Volk

Many thanks to
王睿
for verifying Chinese cultural accuracy.

Published by Weyand Associates, Inc.
Bloomington, Indiana, USA
October 2021

SILK ROAD

CONTENTS

Where To First? 1
Logistics 11
A New Design 21
Personnel 29
Earthsea Departures 40
Earthsea Arrivals 51
Arrival On Playa 65
The Playa Deal 76
Arrival On Tahiti 88
The Tahiti Deal 99
Intermezzo On Arcadia 109
Arrival On Olympia 120
The Olympia Deal 129
Arrival In Aruba 139
The Aruba Deal 148
Shifting Gears 157
Ensuring The Future 169
Colony Flood 178
The Robots Arrive 188
Departure For Amber 198
Star Dancer 208
Gravity And Spin 218
Amber 228
On To Tahiti 239
Tahiti 250
In The Hospital 260
Balance Of Trade 271
Earthsea 281
Home Again 291
Transition In Progress 300
Unexpected 309

RICHARD F. WEYAND

Transfer Of Power 318
Departure 327
Author's Afterword 329
Notes: The Players And The Colonies 331

SILK ROAD

Where To First?

Arcadia City was laid out in a grid, so addresses were easy. The Uptown Market, the multi-story shopping galleria run by the Chen-Jasic family, which was between Fourteenth Street and Fifteenth Street on Market Street, was simply 1400 North Market Street.

The Chen Restaurant on the first floor of the market building at the corner with Fifteenth Street was 1450 North Market Street. The Chen-Jasic apartment building – which also housed the offices of Chen Zufu and Chen Zumu – was in the north half of the block on the west side of the street, across from the restaurant, and it was 1451 North Market Street.

There were four addresses, though, that did not fit this pattern. The administrative building that was delivered with the original colonists was One Charter Square. The other three original buildings were numbered clockwise around the square. The hospital was Two Charter Square, the university was Three Charter Square, and the office building was Four Charter Square.

The four original buildings had been all glass and steel, and pretty spartan when they had been delivered over a century before. Pipes and utilities ran along the surface of steel walls, much like on a ship. But the buildings had been spiffed up over the years, and the interiors were all now well-appointed.

They were also the most prestigious addresses in Arcadia City.

Jixing Trading was in Four Charter Square. The company had options to lease the entire building as it expanded.

Chen ChaoLi, the CEO of Jixing Trading, was now facing the question of which of the six newly discovered colony worlds to make contact with first. Prime Minister Rob Milbank would have to be consulted and agree with any decision, of course. So would Chen Zufu and Chen Zumu, the leadership couple of the Chen-Jasic clan.

But they would likely all support ChaoLi's decision.

A decision she had not yet made.

ChaoLi took the elevator down to the third floor elevator lobby and walked through the pedestrian bridge across Arcadia Boulevard to One Charter Square for her meeting with the prime minister.

She and Milbank were friends, having grown close during their cooperation on the hyperspace project. She was well-known to Milbank's staff, and was waved through the various layers of staff to the prime minister's office.

"ChaoLi! Good to see you. Welcome to the spider's lair," Milbank said, getting up and coming around his desk.

ChaoLi chuckled. Milbank had always come to her offices during the hyperspace project, relishing the opportunity to get out of the office. With as popular as he was now on Arcadia, however, the prime minister's office was no longer a political minefield. Opposing him on any major issue was a mistake a neophyte politician probably only made once.

"It's good to see you, too, Rob. I'm hoping you can shed some light on this little decision we have to make."

"Who do we talk to first?"

"That's the one."

Milbank waved her to the side seating arrangement in his office. There was a pot of tea steeping there, as well as a plate of Earthsea cheese with sesame crackers. It was clear Milbank had set some private stock aside before the cheese-tasting party that heralded the arrival in Arcadia orbit of *Star Runner*. The cheese-tasting party had sold out.

Milbank poured tea, and ChaoLi sipped and nodded. Milbank's favorite of the Chens' premiere teas – Oak, so-called because of the oak wooden box in which it was sold. One of what she called 'the contemplatives,' ChaoLi appreciated its soothing, calming influence in her new position as CEO of Jixing Trading. She knew now why it was Milbank's favorite.

Milbank sipped appreciatively and set his teacup down.

"So what are our options?" he asked.

"We have six new colonies. Olympia, of course. They were number twenty-one to be dropped off, so we could get the seventeen drop-offs between Arcadia and Olympia from them. By doing the parallax analysis on their passenger compartment recordings.

"But we have six to get in contact with right now, so it's not like we have to go there first."

"Do we have enough shuttles to contact multiple planets at once?" Milbank asked.

"Yes, but not all six. We need more orbital shuttles, so we can free up the hyperspace-capable ones. We do have more coming on line. What we need are more trained crews."

"We have four hyper-capable shuttles now?"

"Yes," ChaoLi said.

"Hmm."

Milbank sipped his tea, and his eyes went unfocused for a few minutes. ChaoLi was familiar with JieMin's long pensive moments, and was content to sip her tea while the prime minister considered.

"You know," Milbank said, "when I was talking to the

pilots, they said they used the computer for approach and landing, dismounting and remounting containers, taking off and returning to Arcadia. They relied on the computer for everything."

"Yes, but we still need pilots aboard for backup."

"Maybe not pilots. Maybe just pilot. If the computer is doing everything, the pilot is your backup system. So the co-pilot is a backup on the backup, and we've never even fell back to first backup. Are we overdoing it?"

"I see what you're saying," ChaoLi said. "We have the computer and a pilot. Maybe that's enough. Which would allow me to send all four hyperspace-capable shuttles out to planets, and still have enough crews for the local work fitting out *Star Runner*, *Star Tripper*, and the others."

"Exactly."

"That might work. We still need to decide which four."

"Well, Olympia should be one of them," Milbank said, "or, for the next round, you don't have enough known colony planets to send four shuttles out. There would only be two colony planets left to contact."

"That's right. So Olympia is one."

"What are the other possibilities?"

"Bali, Tahiti, Terminus, Playa, and Aruba," ChaoLi said.

"What have we been able to figure out about them from the flyby data?"

"Bali has a technology focus on endocrinology. All the hormones that affect sexual function, gastrointestinal function, thyroid, adrenaline, diabetes, weight, metabolism, all of that. One group also brought along a whole bunch of different vine cuttings from Earth, and they specialize in excellent wines."

"OK, I like that one right off," Milbank said.

ChaoLi chuckled.

SILK ROAD

"Tahiti has a technical specialty in anti-aging research. Cell senescence and rejuvenation, that sort of thing. One family group there spent all their cubic on bringing seeds of all sorts of heritage apple varieties. They have a couple hundred different varieties of apples."

"Hard to ship apples interstellar."

"Actually, it depends on the variety," ChaoLi said. "And you still have all the products, like apple sauce, apple cider, dried apples, canned apples."

"OK. Fair enough. What's Terminus like?"

"They have a technology specialty in forestry management."

"That doesn't seem that important," Milbank said.

"Think of all the things we use wood for," ChaoLi said, and rapped her knuckles on the wood table between them.

"I stand corrected."

"A colonist group there spent their entire cubic on taking flowers. Seeds and bulbs. The pictures of the planet are incredible. Beautiful gardens and parks. Like nothing you've ever seen."

Milbank nodded.

"What were the others?" he asked. "Playa, I think you said."

"Yes. Playa has a technical specialty in cybernetics. Robots, believe it or not. Also mechanical arms, micro- and macro-manipulators. All that sort of thing. And a family group there brought along hundreds of varieties of edible mushrooms in their cubic."

"There was one more."

"Aruba," ChaoLi said. "Aruba is a bridge planet to the Perseus Arm. They have no technical specialty that JieMin could find. No concentration of people in one specialty. Like us. But a colonist group on Aruba brought along all the varieties of the cocoa plant. There were about half a dozen when we left Earth, but the standard colony stock was all the Forastero variety."

"So they have...."

"Chocolate. Vastly superior chocolate, if my research is right. The standard colony loadout for cocoa was the hardiest plant, not the best tasting one."

"Oh, my," Milbank said.

"Yes. My sentiments exactly."

"And what of Olympia? Besides being number twenty-one, I mean."

"They are close to workable fusion power reactors," ChaoLi said.

"People have been saying that for three hundred years, ChaoLi. More."

"No, they actually have working units in the grid, though they are all one-offs. Perhaps I should better say, they are close to mass-production of a standardized fusion power reactor."

"OK, that makes a difference. Anything else?" Milbank asked.

"Yes. A colonist group there concentrated on distilled spirits."

"Distilled spirits?"

"They have a very competitive market in single-malt whiskeys, as well as brandies and cognacs," ChaoLi said.

"Oh, this is impossible. How do we pick?"

"Olympia is in, you said."

"Right," Milbank said.

"I think Playa should be in."

"The one with the mushrooms?"

"The one with the robots," ChaoLi said. "Robots can work in vacuum. They can do exterior work and repairs on interstellar ships without spacesuits and all that nonsense."

"Ah. Right. OK, I get that. Who else?"

"Probably Aruba, as a bridge to the Perseus Arm, so we can set up a freight transfer station there. Long lead time on that."

"And that gets us much better chocolate," Milbank said.

"That, too."

"OK, and then the other possibles are Bali with endocrinology and wine, Tahiti with anti-aging and apples, and Terminus, with forestry management and flowers."

"Right," ChaoLi said.

"Tahiti."

"Why Tahiti, Rob? For the apples?"

"No," Milbank said. "I'm not getting any younger, ChaoLi. I can wait on the wine."

The last hurdle was to run the tentative decision past Chen Zufu and Chen Zumu. ChaoLi requested a meeting, and got an acceptance for late that afternoon.

"Thank you for meeting with me, Chen Zufu. Chen Zumu."

"Thank you for sending us the background information, ChaoLi. You spoke with the prime minister about this decision?" asked Chen MinChao, Chen Zufu – honored grandfather – of the Chen Jasic family.

"Yes, Chen Zufu. We are agreed."

"And your decision, ChaoLi?" Jessica Chen-Jasic prompted.

"Olympia is one for the first round, Chen Zumu, or else we do not have four colony planets for the second round."

"And how do you solve the pilot shortage problem?"

"The computer is the primary, and the pilot is the backup, Chen Zumu. A co-pilot is a backup of a backup, and we will do without in order to keep everything moving while we train up pilots."

"And you have not fallen back to the first backup yet,

ChaoLi?"

"No, Chen Zumu. I judge it an acceptable risk."

Jessica nodded.

"Please continue, ChaoLi," she said.

"Thank you, Chen Zumu. Playa is in the first round, because robots can work in vacuum without spacesuits, which will be a big help in fitting out and maintaining the hyperspace ships.

"Aruba is also in the first round, as it is one of the two bridge colonies to the Perseus Arm, and will be a good site for a freight transfer station, which is a long lead-time project.

"Finally, given the other three choices, we picked Tahiti because of their anti-aging research. The clock is ticking on everyone, so less delay there seemed worthwhile."

"What are the governments like on these four colonies, ChaoLi?" MinChao asked.

"They are variations on what we have seen so far, Chen Zufu. Parliaments and assemblies, presidents and prime ministers. A couple of the six still have council structures, as the original colonies did, but these have morphed into elected bodies in the time since the colonies were planted."

"And they all have civil rights guarantees, ChaoLi?"

"Yes, Chen Zufu. Curiously, none of these six colonies have reverted to the sort of dreary tyranny all too common in Earth's history."

MinChao and Jessica looked at each other. Jessica gave a tiny nod, and MinChao turned to ChaoLi.

"Very well, ChaoLi. This decision is approved. You may proceed as you have outlined."

"Thank you, Chen Zufu."

"When will the shuttles depart?" MinChao asked.

"As soon as Hyper-1 returns from Earthsea, Chen Zufu. They should arrive there next week. They plan to head here with self-contained QE radios suitable for shipboard use. We can ask Director Laurent to include some of the larger radios for planetary comm links to Olympia and Aruba as well."

"Do we know yet whether the QE radios will work in hyperspace, ChaoLi?" Jessica asked.

"No, Chen Zufu. JieMin thinks they will – the physics seems to predict it – but we won't know for two weeks. The shuttles to Olympia and Aruba will wait until Hyper-1 arrives back on Arcadia, so they can take QE radios with them. One of those will be Hyper-1 itself, so we have to wait until it returns regardless."

"The other two – to Tahiti and Playa – will not take QE radios, ChaoLi?"

"The paths to Tahiti and Playa lie through Earthsea, Chen Zumu. As we go farther into the cluster of colonies, travel times increase. They will stop in Earthsea for a few weeks for gravity reconditioning, then proceed on to Tahiti and Playa. While on Earthsea, they will pick up additional radios, whether they work in hyperspace or not. This will allow them to hook those colonies into the network when they arrive, and also have their own shipboard QE radios on the trip home."

"I see," Jessica said. "Very well."

She nodded.

"I like this plan, ChaoLi. Nicely done."

"Thank you, Chen Zumu."

After ChaoLi left, Jessica and MinChao turned around on their pillows to consider the garden.

"That was an interesting observation ChaoLi had, that it was curious none of the colonies had reverted to tyranny," MinChao said.

"Well, Arcadia almost did. If Madam Chairman had not

intervened through my great grandfather, we would have. Who knows how many other times she has intervened as successfully."

MinChao nodded.

"Fair enough," he said. "At least we don't have to face that issue this time around."

"The devil's bargain? Doing business with a dictator because we really want something he has to trade? No. Not yet. Hopefully it won't come to that, MinChao."

"What do we do if it does, Jessica?"

"Decide then. In the meantime, let's not borrow troubles we do not have."

SILK ROAD

Logistics

"Good morning, Valerie," Rob Milbank said.

"Good afternoon, Rob. How are you today?" asked Valerie Laurent, the director of the planetary council on Earthsea.

"Good. Very good. We're getting ready to send out missions to some of the new colony planets we found, so I thought we should talk about QE radios."

"Sounds like a good idea. What were you thinking?"

"I'm not sure," Milbank said. "When we added Amber to the QE network, it took four radios to create two links. One to Earthsea and one to Arcadia. But the next planet would require six new radios, the one after eight, and so on. That can't be how you're linking your cities on Earthsea."

"No. You're right. That would be untenable, but it's also unnecessary. We have links to all the cities here in Bergheim, and also in Innsbruck, our second largest city. So all the other cities have a link to both. That's four radios per city. The network routes all the messages to where they need to go. When traffic between two other cities gets high enough, they put in an additional link between them to offload the centers. I'm not clear on the details of all of it, but four radios per city as the basic setup I'm sure of."

"So you think four QE radios per planet, Valerie?"

"That's right, Rob. One link to the primary net center, and one link to the secondary net center. So there's actually two radios on each planet, and then one radio for each planet in the two net centers."

"OK, that makes sense."

"And I think Arcadia should be the secondary net center."

"Arcadia as opposed to some other location?" Milbank asked.

"Yes, for two reasons. First, from the colony maps you've put out, Arcadia is a natural transportation hub based on its location. So there will be a lot of net traffic to and from Arcadia, as well as a lot of ship traffic. If we need to replace a radio from here, or ship additional radios from here, it would be simplest to do it to Arcadia, given the ship traffic we expect on that route."

Milbank nodded.

"Makes sense to me, Valerie."

"And second, Arcadia is the one planet I don't expect to try to work around the billing once we start charging for network services."

"You don't think we'll cheat?"

"Compared to that woman on Amber, for instance? No, Rob, I don't expect you to cheat. You've been great partners. And Sal is a big fan of Arcadia. We've talked about it, and he doesn't expect it, either. He thinks the Chen would remove the prime minister if a later government tried."

Milbank nodded. He thought it interesting that Romano had such a good feel for the lay of the land in Arcadia.

"So how do we handle this, then, Valerie? We have two planets we're going to visit who are on the other side of us from you – Olympia and Aruba – and two that are past you from us – Tahiti and Playa. And Hyper-1 should arrive in Earthsea this week from Amber, to drop off Mr. Costa at home and bring the shipboard radios here."

Laurent took some time to think it through.

"The shuttle can take eight containers, is that right?"

"Twelve if they're light enough," Milbank said.

SILK ROAD

"OK, so Olympia and Aruba each get two. You need four for the Arcadia end of a link from each of the four planets. Plus we want to send the self-contained ship radios. You should probably be carrying one on each hyperspace shuttle as it is, so you can do rescues if nothing else. What's that come to?"

"Four, plus four, plus three ship radios, plus one container for personal cubic and water makes twelve, Valerie."

"Huh. I wish we could send more ship radios. They're a lot smaller as far as the radio part, but being self-contained they also have the power supply and cooling, so they're still a full container."

"Well, we could put one on each of the hyperspace shuttles heading to Olympia and Aruba, and save one for *Star Runner*. The other two hyperspace shuttles headed for Tahiti and Playa will stop at Earthsea. They can pick up their own shipboard radios, plus two each for the colonies themselves. They're leaving here soon."

"That'll work," Laurent said. "And if your ships to Tahiti and Playa come back through here with their ambassadors, then we can load them up with more shipboard radios for the leg to Arcadia."

Milbank nodded.

"That'll work. Just make sure the radios are all stenciled with their ultimate destinations, so we get the right ones going to the right places. We'll take care of getting them there, Valerie."

"All right, Rob. That's how we'll do it."

Rob Milbank also met with Haruki Tanaka, his new foreign minister. Arcadia had not needed a foreign minister before contacting other colony planets.

"We need four ambassadors to make first contact with these

colonies, Haruki."

Tanaka nodded.

"I've been considering that as I've been building up staff, Rob. Of course, the problem is that we have no diplomatic service in place. No experience with the sort of issues someone may need to deal with. Our best experience right now lies with Loukas Diakos and Sasha Ivanov, and they're both assigned already, to Earthsea and Amber."

"You have Peter Dunhill as well, who is Loukas's aide on Earthsea. Should we call him home? Assign him to one of the new planets?"

"That's one option," Tanaka said. "He could come back from Earthsea on Hyper-1 once they drop Mr. Costas off at home. By the way, how are we going to bring up all the new radios without Mr. Costas?"

"We have people in the operations group who have been taking training classes over the network. Tying in to the Earthsea technical training. And given multiple links from here to Earthsea already, they can access and debug new radios over the existing links.

"But back to the ambassadorial assignments, I think Earthsea and Amber are in good enough shape we can put new people in those slots, and have Loukas and Sasha open up new planets."

"So Sasha is on the way here from Amber already. Should we send him off to Olympia or Aruba?"

"Olympia, I think," Milbank said. "We need to find out where those other colonies are."

"OK, then Dunhill comes back from Earthsea to here on Hyper-1, and we send him to Aruba?"

"Yes, I think that's the easiest mission of the four. Why wouldn't they want to be a hub planet and have an interstellar freight transfer station?"

Tanaka nodded.

"And we have a backup there in any case," he said, "because there's another colony planet in that two-planet bridge between the Orion Arm and the Perseus Arm."

"Exactly," Milbank said.

"Then we can send a replacement ambassador to Earthsea on one of the shuttles headed in that direction, and Loukas can take his seat for transfer to either Tahiti or Playa."

"Playa, I think. We need robots for servicing the hyperspace ships once we bring *Star Runner* and its sisters into service."

"All right," Tanaka said. "So what I am really looking at is one more ambassador for opening up Tahiti, and two for taking over already-friendly relations on Earthsea and Amber."

"That sounds right to me, Haruki. Oh, and for Tahiti?"

"Yes?"

"Send someone older. Tahiti has those anti-aging treatments. Maybe he can try them out while he's there."

When Hyper-1 dropped out of hyperspace in the Earthsea system, there were mails waiting in their mailboxes.

"So you see we got new assignments?" Justin Moore asked his co-pilot Gavin McKay.

"Yeah. We ain't even home yet. And they're splitting us up."

"Only one pilot per ship. I guess they figure the computer is one, a human pilot makes two, and they don't need three."

"Yeah," McKay said, "but the big problem is there just aren't enough guys can fly the bigger birds."

"Probably so. And we're taking Sasha and Peter back to Arcadia with us."

"Yeah. I guess they have new assignments, too."

"Well, at least the prime minister isn't letting things lie,"

Moore said. "He's keeping things moving along."

"He's keeping us moving along, that's for sure."

"May not be so bad on the way home this time, though."

"How ya figure?" McKay asked.

"We're gonna try out the QE radio on the way home. If that works, we'll have the same access to the network as if we were sittin' on the couch at home.

"Oh, that'll be different. Wouldn't that be somethin'?"

As soon as Hyper-1 dropped out of hyperspace bound for Earthsea, Ivanov checked in with Milbank. The prime minister had news for him.

"A new assignment?" asked Sasha Ivanov, Arcadia's ambassador to Amber. "Rob, I'm not even home yet from the last assignment. And the last assignment is still mine, for that matter."

"I know, Sasha. But I need you to head out one more time. We need to get those colony coordinates from Olympia. That'll open up everything. Then you can come back here and be Haruki's senior guy in terms of giving help to other ambassadors we'll be sending out. He's really got his hands full here, because there's no experience base to draw on. Other than you and Loukas, that is. And Peter, I guess."

"Loukas is moving on as well?"

"Yes," Milbank said. "I need him to go to Playa. They're cybernetics specialists, and we need robots for servicing the big hyper ships in orbit. They can work in vacuum. The hyperspace shuttles we can service on the ground, but the big ships will never see atmosphere."

"That makes sense."

"I worry he'll be disappointed we're moving him away from the mountains, though. Nothing like Earthsea's mountains on

Playa."

Ivanov chuckled, which surprised Milbank.

"Oh, I don't think you need to worry there, Rob. I talked to Loukas over dinner last night, and he misses the Blue Mountains on Arcadia. The mountains on Earthsea were just a bit much, I think."

"For Loukas?" Milbank asked. "That's surprising."

"Rob, pictures just don't do them justice. I think he tried, mind you. Even the locals considered him kind of crazy. But, when all was said and done, the mountains defeated him."

"Boy, that's a surprise. It'll make it easier for him to move on, though. And I have a little extra enticement for you as well."

"What's that?" Ivanov asked.

"In addition to knowing the first twenty-one colony sites, Olympia has fusion reactor technology. All the fusion guys went to the same planet. They actually have something."

"The fusion guys have been saying that for three hundred years, Rob. They're just twenty years away."

Milbank laughed.

"That's what I said, but Chen ChaoLi tells me they're running commercial plants. They're about to go mass production on them. That's not the enticement, though, Sasha. The other thing Olympia has is a specialty in distilled spirits. They make outstanding single-malt whiskeys, brandies, and cognacs."

Ivanov perked up.

"Mr. Prime Minister, you are correct. We should not keep such a deserving planet waiting. I will be happy to be Arcadia's ambassador to Olympia. We need to ensure against a lesser diplomat failing to achieve their entry into our trade consortium. That, sir, would be an interstellar tragedy."

Milbank laughed.

"Thanks, Sasha. I knew I could count on you. And then it's home to Arcadia for keeps. I promise."

It was John Gannet's weekly meeting with his top-level supervisors in the operations department. They met in the conference room at their headquarters, the old hyperspace research facility at the Arcadia City Shuttleport.

"We've got some new marching orders from downtown," Gannet said.

There were groans up and down the table.

"No, I think this is gonna be OK. Better than OK, actually. First, we have four new orbit-capable shuttles coming in this week, and four more four weeks after that."

That got some applause. The operations people were an expressive bunch.

"And Hyper-1 is coming back and will arrive in another six weeks."

More applause.

"The counter to that is we'll be sending all four hyperspace-capable shuttles out interstellar over the next two months. Two of them will leave next week or the week after."

Back to groans.

"How are we going to handle that, John?" one staffer asked. "We don't have the pilots for that level of activity."

"Well, we are bringing people up, starting them on the smaller atmospheric shuttles, and moving the atmosphere boys up into the orbital shuttles. But the other thing we're going to do is go to one-man crews, at least for the hyper-capable shuttles."

"So Gavin, Justin, Minho, and Igor all go out on the hyper shuttles and everyone else stays here?"

"That's right," Gannet said. "The crews of Hyper-1 and Hyper-2 are being split up. They'll take all four hyperspace shuttles, and the other crews stay here."

"How are we going to service the shipyard, John?" another staffer asked. "We need hyper-capable shuttles for that."

"My understanding is they're going to use *Star Runner* to run a massive load of supplies over there, and take a couple orbital shuttles along to offload her. That'll sort of be her space trials. Then she comes back here so we can finish the outfitting. Each ship will do the same in its turn. Make the freight run to Beacon with supplies for the shipyards. Hundreds of containers' worth at a time. That'll free up a lot of shuttle time, too, rather than running containers to Beacon eight at a time."

"OK. That makes some sense, actually."

"It all does," Gannet said. "We're going to have all these big interstellar freight and passenger ships coming on line soon, and they need places to go. If we don't get the hyperspace shuttles out there to open up new planets, we're going to be short of destinations.

"So that's what we're about, everybody. Get the hyperspace shuttles turned and ready for long trips, get the new orbital shuttles up and running, and continue to bring new pilots into the fold as we go.

"We're going to be ramping up for a long time, but this isn't even the worst of it.

"Once those big hyperspace liners are running commercial flights, we're gonna have to load 'em and unload 'em, cargo and passengers. Every single trip."

The meeting ended with another round of groans.

With the short term options in place, and having approved the operations plans of John Gannet and his project manager,

Chris Bellamy, ChaoLi turned her attention to the medium term.

She needed orbital freight transfer stations. At least two of them, one around Arcadia and one around Aruba. Ultimately, as freight traffic increased, every planet would likely have one, while the ones on Arcadia and Aruba would grow huge.

Modular, then.

And they would have to be manufactured in the Beacon asteroid belt and then transported to their respective planets. Assembly in orbit would be required, for which she was planning on using robot assembly workers from Playa.

But first she needed a set of plans.

SILK ROAD

A New Design

When Chen ChaoLi was relieved of the design group and made CEO of Jixing Trading, Denise Peterson took over management of the group. Peterson was also a member of the Chen-Jasic family, a descendant of Jack Peterson and Terri Campbell, one of the original Carolina couples among the colonists.

Like most everyone else in the Chen-Jasic family, Peterson was part Asian, part European through the American Carolina group, and part a mish-mash of other ethnicities. The 'bank baby' program, in which many couples had their second child through artificial insemination from the sperm bank each colony had brought along, ensured the whole panoply of human variety was part of the genetic makeup of the colony planets' citizens.

Peterson had a meeting scheduled for this morning that had her a little nervous. ChaoLi had asked for a meeting with the design group for new designs. While the design group was being run by the Chen for the government, Jixing Trading was the lease customer of the government.

So this was a customer meeting, where ChaoLi, as CEO of the government's current sole customer for their design products, would spell out what she needed going forward.

It was up to Peterson to decide who should be there, but to her the choice was obvious. Karl Huenemann and Chen JieMin, together with Peterson, would meet with ChaoLi.

For his part, Huenemann decided to bring Wayne Porter along.

For a customer meeting, everyone showed up a little early, and the design group people were all in place five minutes before the scheduled time.

"Do we know what the request will be?" Huenemann asked.

"Not for sure. Either new ship designs or designs for freight transfer stations, I think."

Huenemann nodded.

"Well, much of the vision for any new design is going to come from Wayne here, so I thought I would bring him along so he could hear the requirements direct and not secondhand."

"That's fine," Peterson said. "That's a good idea, actually."

JieMin didn't say anything. He knew more of where ChaoLi's thinking was, but offering things his wife and he had discussed over the past several weeks would be talking out of school. Best to let ChaoLi present Jixing's needs herself.

ChaoLi showed up just a few minutes late, which was the prerogative of either a customer or high-level management, of which she was both. It was actually a point of etiquette, letting the other people at the meeting get in place and settled before she showed up, a trick she had learned from Rob Milbank.

"Good morning, everyone," ChaoLi said as she took her seat at the conference table.

"Good morning, ChaoLi," Peterson, as the senior, said for the others.

"What I want to do this morning is lay out the basics for what we need going forward. I'm going to state it all as requirements, but I won't speculate as to how you might meet those requirements. I don't want to tie your hands in terms of coming up with innovative solutions."

Everyone around the table nodded. It was much easier to meet the actual needs if the customer wasn't already fixated on one set of possible solutions.

SILK ROAD

"What we need next is an orbital freight transfer station. We need two initially – for Arcadia and Aruba, the two bridge colonies – but we will probably end up with one at each colony planet as freight traffic builds up.

"The ones at Arcadia and Aruba will also need to get much bigger over time. Or, rather, be able to handle much more traffic. That's the actual requirement, not that they're bigger, but that they can handle much higher traffic levels.

"The medium-term requirement is to be able to service the *Star Runner* class of ships. Over the longer term, I suspect we will come up with new ship designs, and the freight transfer stations will have to be extended or modified to handle those newer ships as well, but no accommodation for those new, unknown ship designs is required at this time.

"And of course I call these freight transfer stations, but in fact they have to be able to handle the passenger off-loading and on-loading, as well as the crews, for both planet leave and rotation.

"The only other requirement is speed. Interstellar shipping is going to be a high-revenue, low-margin operation. Any time the ships spend in dock, rather than under way, is demurrage, pure and simple. It's lease time that is not generating revenue.

"So the final requirement is that all this be done to turn the ship in the fastest way you can while being cost-effective otherwise. It doesn't pay to spend a fortune to save an hour when it's six weeks between planets, but we don't want to spend a week unloading and a week loading either.

"Any questions?"

"I have one, ChaoLi," Peterson said. "Will the freight transfer stations be purchased by the government or Jixing? Be operated by the government or Jixing? That is, where is the administrative boundary between the government and Jixing

Trading with respect to the transfer stations?"

"I don't know the answer to that yet, Denise. I have a meeting scheduled with the prime minister tomorrow, and that will be one of the discussion points."

Peterson nodded.

"I have one, ChaoLi," Huenemann said. "Will the transfer stations be built at the Beacon shipyards and transported to their ultimate locations, or built on the planet and lifted to orbit?"

"I don't care, Karl. That's not a requirement one way or the other. It's up to you. Both the Beacon shipyard and the Arcadia metafactories planetside are available for this project."

Huenemann nodded.

"Any more questions?"

ChaoLi looked up and down the table.

"All right. Thanks, everybody."

With that, ChaoLi got up and left the conference room.

As everyone was heading out of the conference room, Wayne Porter was looking a little dazed. JieMin took his arm, and Wayne stopped and caught his eye.

"Vision, Wayne. Don't force it. Let the vision come to you. And if you want someone to bounce things off of, you know I'm here for you."

"Oh. OK. Thanks, JieMin. I appreciate it."

JieMin nodded sharply, once, and let the gifted designer go.

That night, Denise Bonheur noted that her husband was back to the distracted air he got when deep into a design. Porter told her they had a new project, and Huenemann was relying on him to come up with the design. Bonheur nodded and modified her evening plans to do some quiet reading by herself.

SILK ROAD

Porter sat in the living room the whole evening, looking out the big picture window up into the twilight sky, where ships and shuttles swarmed around a vague shape in his mind. That shape had not yet come into focus.

But it would.

"Good morning, ChaoLi. How are you today?" Rob Milbank asked.

"Good, Rob. Good. Thanks for taking this meeting."

"No problem. It's about the freight transfer stations, you said."

"Yes. I gave Denise and the design group the requirements yesterday, in broad form. So they're off and working on a design."

"Good," Milbank said. "We're going to need them."

"Yes, and they asked an interesting question, which pretty much sums up what I wanted to talk to you about. 'Where is the administrative boundary between the government and Jixing Trading with respect to the transfer stations?'

"I mean, the government is financing them, and we'll be paying docking charges or leases or something. But who runs the stations? The government or Jixing Trading?"

"Jixing Trading runs them, ChaoLi. You just lease the whole station. The government doesn't do things like that very well. The bureaucrat's goal is always more – more employees, more span of control, more waste."

"And when other shipping companies come on-line, Rob? What then? They'll have to pay us docking charges."

"Of course. And you could gouge them terribly on the docking charges, and they would still be cheaper than what they would come to under government control. But I don't expect you will. The total cost of running the station, plus the

25

lease payments, plus a tidy profit should all be equally shared per container and per passenger. Simple enough."

ChaoLi nodded. She knew where Milbank was coming from. The whole hyperspace project almost didn't come about because of government control.

"All right. I just wanted to be sure that's where we were heading."

"Oh, yes. I would expect it to fall under your planetary operations group. You might spin that off at some point. Or not. I don't really care one way or the other."

"And if the government changes?" ChaoLi asked.

"The government can change all it wants. The leases will be in place. And I don't expect the Chen family to change for the next, oh, fifty years or so."

"Really?"

Oh, sure," Milbank said. "Once you and JieMin are Chen Zumu and Chen Zufu, will you suddenly turn larcenous? Or dishonest? Or incompetent? I don't think so."

ChaoLi started at that. Chen Zumu? Her?

Milbank noted her surprise and chuckled.

"I've been around long enough to see the pattern, ChaoLi. How the family grooms and selects its leaders. I think there are probably backups, of course. There always are.

"But you and JieMin have had the inside track for a long time now. I'd thought that for a while, but when you were named CEO of Jixing Trading, I was sure of it. It's the family's biggest project, and the most important to its future."

"But David Bolton and YongLin –"

"Are next, of course. That's why he sits in some of my councils. And then you and JieMin."

Milbank looked at her and shrugged.

"I'm sorry if I let the cat out of the bag."

SILK ROAD

"No. No, that's OK."

It all fell into place now. Chen Zumu's patronage of JieMin. Her pulling strings to get him an appointment with the university. Her arranging things with their families to enable their marriage. The large senior apartment on the top floor of the Chen family apartment building. ChaoLi's two-year leave to finish her education and her progress through the business department. Her being named the head of the hyperspace project.

And now, the head of Jixing Trading.

Chen JuPing – she who was Chen Zumu before Jessica Chen-Jasic – must have identified both her and JieMin as possible candidates twenty years ago and more, and started giving them the opportunities to prove themselves – or to fail.

ChaoLi remembered being invited to sit with Chen JuPing and the then-Chen Zufu, Paul Chen-Jasic, together with the couple-in-waiting, Chen MinChao and Jessica Chen-Jasic, to watch the fireworks at the colony's centennial anniversary. So long ago now, and Chen JuPing had known?

No, ChaoLi realized. It was one possible future. Chen JuPing had nurtured that future – and probably others – to see what would happen. To build their experience base. To ensure the leadership of the family would fall to competent hands in the future.

ChaoLi shook herself out of her reverie to see Milbank watching her curiously.

"I probably should have seen it myself before now."

ChaoLi took a deep breath and let it out slowly. Such responsibility!

But that was all for the future. In the meantime, she had the present to deal with.

"So you're happy with Jixing Trading driving the approvals

on the design of the freight transfer stations and overseeing the construction, all with government financing, and then leasing them from the government and operating them once completed?"

"Yes, ChaoLi. Absolutely. You build them, and I'll sign the checks."

ChaoLi nodded.

"All right, then, Rob. We've got it."

Wayne Porter had an image he couldn't get out of his mind. ChaoLi had said speed was important. Of course, the fastest way to get all the containers off-loaded was to simply push them all out the front of the ship. If you didn't mind three or four thousand loose containers drifting in space, of course.

But the containers didn't just latch down. They latched up as well, to each other or to the shuttle above them.

What had stuck in Porter's mind was containers on a stick, like a lollipop, or, better, corn on the cob. Could he latch all the containers to a central spine and pull or push the whole load in or out of the ship at once?

He couldn't see why not, and he started sketching.

SILK ROAD

Personnel

One thing about using a single pilot on each hyperspace shuttle is that there were now three passenger seats available, not just two. As one of Rob Milbank's priorities was to get interstellar trade operating, he offered any extra seats on the hyperspace shuttles to Jixing Trading.

ChaoLi had to scramble to fill the slots. She needed people who could operate with little support to set up the Earthsea office for Jixing Trading, one with management skills and one with sales and deal-making skills. And they would have to be willing to travel alone, as there just wasn't room for dependents yet. Not until the hyperspace liners started running anyway.

One of the first people ChaoLi had brought on to Jixing Trading was a personnel manager, Naomi Thompson. ChaoLi knew she would be hiring aggressively from the start, and being able to assign all that legwork to someone else was a priority.

So ChaoLi passed this new hiring requirement off to Thompson, who, for as busy as she was, was always upbeat and can-do about her huge task list.

Rob Milbank, too, was scrambling. Without ever having had a diplomatic service before, he had requirements to staff four new ambassadorial positions. Using the experienced Diakos, Ivanov, and Dunhill for new colonies was an easy choice, but that meant he still needed one person who could make first contact with a new colony, and had to backfill the slots in

Earthsea and Amber.

Then again, he had underlings as well, and it was properly Haruki Tanaka's job, as foreign minister, to nominate ambassadorial candidates.

But he got his fourth first-contact ambassador from completely out of left field.

It wasn't everybody who could summon the prime minister to a meeting in the middle of the business day, but then again Chen Zumu wasn't just anybody.

"Good morning, Rob. Thank you for coming to see me," Jessica Chen-Jasic said.

"No problem, Jessica. It's always good to see you."

Milbank sat, and tea was served. He sipped appreciatively. Oak, which Jessica knew was his favorite.

"I understand that you're looking for an ambassador to Tahiti, Rob," Jessica said.

"Yes, Jessica. And backfill ambassadors to Earthsea and Amber. We have good enough relations with Director Laurent and President Dufort that I can put someone new in there to learn the ropes. We're trying to find those people as well."

"Which frees up some experienced talent for new colony contacts."

"Yes, it gives me Loukas Diakos, Sasha Ivanov, and Peter Dunhill, who already have first contact experience, to send to Aruba, Olympia, and Playa. Those are my three highest priorities. On Tahiti, though, I'm stuck."

"There's no one in the government for this position?" Jessica asked.

"There are, sort of. The problem with government people is they're pretty much all bureaucrats. They love to push their papers around in their comfy sinecures. Spending six weeks in a shuttle cabin to go to a foreign planet, away from all their cronies, is not a high priority for them."

Jessica smiled at Milbank's dismissal of his own bureaucracy.

"Doing a little historical research, it seems the position of ambassador to a foreign country on Earth was often held by prominent private citizens," she said.

"Yes, and some of them were more successful than others. I think my research must have been paralleling yours. When the private citizen in question was accomplished, it usually worked out well. When they were famous simply for being famous, it usually was a disaster."

Jessica nodded.

"Well, it turns out I may have some accomplished private citizens for the position of ambassador to Tahiti, if you would be willing to send them both. They've volunteered, if you'll have them."

"Who are they, Jessica? Do I know them?"

"Paul Chen-Jasic and Chen JuPing."

Milbank just stared at her. While he was one of the rare people on a first-name basis with Chen MinChao and Jessica Chen-Jasic, he had never been on a first-name basis with their predecessors as Chen Zufu and Chen Zumu.

Paul Chen-Jasic and Chen JuPing were living legends on Arcadia. In his youth, Paul Chen-Jasic had been the driver of one of the limousines that took the ruling council downtown on the fateful night that Chen Zufu, Matthew Chen-Jasic, had overthrown the Kendall regime. It was he who had released the nerve agent in the administrative building that had killed Kevin Kendall's nascent secret police. And Chen JuPing was Matthew Chen-Jasic's granddaughter. She had actually tallied the nominations for the chair of the constitutional convention.

They had risen to Chen Zumu and Chen Zufu and ruled the Chen-Jasic family for twenty years. But they had retired as Chen Zufu and Chen Zumu over a decade ago, and were very old.

"Jessica, they must be over ninety years old."

"Yes, and in good health for their age. But, Rob, what is the technical specialty of Tahiti?"

"Anti-aging drugs."

And suddenly he saw. Not content to wait for death, Paul Chen-Jasic and Chen JuPing intended to cheat death if they could. Or die trying.

Milbank nodded.

"I see," he said.

"And Chen JuPing is the one person most responsible for there being any hyperspace activity at all. The one who nurtured JieMin's talent, who realized the potential of hyperspace, who fought for the hyperspace project. She dreamt of the stars, and then made it possible. You owe her, Rob. You owe her everything."

Milbank nodded. To the extent any people had been the architects of the present, it was Paul Chen-Jasic and Chen JuPing. From the overthrow of the Kendall regime and the Charter of Arcadia to the opening up of human space through hyperspace travel.

"And they volunteered?" Milbank asked.

"Yes. They are excited about the possibility, but they are not insisting."

Jessica let that settle, then continued.

"*I* am insisting."

"Paul Chen-Jasic and Chen JuPing? Are they still alive?" Tanaka asked.

"Yes. Ninety plus. And they want to be the ambassadors to Tahiti."

"Well, I certainly can't complain about their experience or accomplishments. Assuming they survive the trip, that is. Why would they want to do that, though?"

"Think about it, Haruki. Tahiti's expertise is anti-aging. How much of that is preventing aging and how much is reversing it?"

"Some of both, as I understand it. Ah. I see. They go to Tahiti, and, as soon as they get there, they start some sort of anti-senescence treatment."

"Exactly. And to do that, they need to set up the relationship with the planetary government. You couldn't ask for more motivation than that."

Tanaka nodded.

"Besides," Milbank said, "when Jessica Chen-Jasic insists, it's best to nod sagely and do what she wants."

"Jessica says she's arranged for our appointment as the ambassador to Tahiti," Chen JuPing told Paul Chen-Jasic.

"You or me or both?" he asked.

"Co-ambassadors, I think."

Paul nodded.

"So six weeks in a shuttle cabin?" he asked.

"Actually twelve. Six weeks twice."

"Ouch."

"And what would we do different here, Paul?" JuPing asked. "Plus, it will be in zero gravity, which I'm looking forward to."

"You are?"

"Of course. All the sagging bits will sag less. All the hurting bits will hurt less. That's what I'm hoping for, anyway."

"Ah," Paul said.

He looked out the windows and across the valley in the foothills of the Blue Mountains to which they had retired, then turned back to her.

"You know what this means, JuPing?" he asked.

"What's that?"

"We'll make it after all. To the stars."

JuPing nodded.

"Yes. Imagine. After all this time."

She looked out the window at the valley, then spoke to the air in front of her.

"I'm looking forward to it."

"OK, so what have we got?" Milbank asked.

"Hyper-1 comes to Arcadia with Sasha Ivanov, Peter Dunhill, and the two pilots, Justin Moore and Gavin McKay, plus all the radios they can carry," ChaoLi said.

"All right."

"Hyper-3 goes to Earthsea with pilot Igor Belsky, and takes Paul Chen-Jasic, Chen JuPing, and their caregiver. It then goes on to Tahiti."

"All right."

"Hyper-4 goes to Earthsea with pilot Jeong Minho, and takes the new ambassador to Earthsea, Gregory Prentiss, and his aide, plus the Jixing Trading representative to Earthsea. It then goes on to Playa with Loukas Diakos."

"OK. Good."

"Now this all happens this week. Once Hyper-1 gets back here, it drops all the radios and we do a good servicing on it. It then goes on to Olympia with Justin Moore as the pilot, and takes Sasha Ivanov and any help he wants along."

Milbank nodded.

"And Hyper-2 goes to Aruba with Gavin McKay as the pilot, and takes Peter Dunhill and any help he wants along, as well as a Jixing Trading representative to start setting up for an orbital freight transfer station."

"OK," Milbank said, "that all works for me. And we'll send presents along?"

"Tea to Aruba and Olympia, yes. We can also send cheese along from Earthsea to Tahiti and Playa. We have every container slot spoken for on Hyper-1 coming back here from Earthsea, though. All those radios."

Milbank nodded.

"Can we maybe get some cheese into the luggage container with the personal cubic?" he asked. "I think a dozen or so pounds, so the big shots get a taste, at least."

"That we can probably manage," ChaoLi said, making a note. "Too bad we don't have any Amber coffee."

"Yes, but Sasha had to pull out to seal the deal in taking down this Sellick woman. That all worked out, and their Assembly approved the trade agreement so Dufort could sign it, but we haven't had any way to get anybody back there."

"Not yet. And once we get the other colony locations from Olympia, the shuttles are going to be busy."

"What about *Star Runner*?" Milbank asked.

"As soon as she's available for service, she'll make an Arcadia-Earthsea-Amber-Arcadia loop.

"Which will be when?"

"I'm still hoping by the end of this year," ChaoLi said.

"December, 2369?"

"Yes. They're ahead of schedule, and hopefully they can keep up the pace. It could slip, but right now, that's my best guess."

"Outstanding."

John Gannet looked at the schedule and manifests and gasped. He set up a meeting with Igor Belsky, who had been the co-pilot of Hyper-2 and would now pilot Hyper-3 to Earthsea and Tahiti.

Belsky was pretty far down in the hyperspace operations group to have a meeting with the big boss. He wondered what was going on.

"They have an ambassador for Tahiti now," Gannet said.

"Excellent," Belsky said. "So you have a passenger manifest for me. Who is it, anyway?"

"Paul Chen-Jasic and Chen JuPing."

Belsky shrugged.

"Don't know them."

"They were the last Chen Zufu and Chen Zumu of the Chen-Jasic family."

Belsky's eyes narrowed.

"The previous ones?" he asked. "Aren't the current ones in their seventies? How old are these two?"

"In their nineties. That's why I wanted to talk to you. You need to take it real easy in flying the shuttle. No fancy stuff. No hot-dogging. You'll kill them."

"Why would they send someone that old as ambassador to Tahiti?"

"Think about it," Gannet said. "What we know about Tahiti from the flyby information is their technical specialty is anti-aging treatments."

"Oh, so they go and get the anti-aging things while they're there. I get it. But their aging happened already. It's not like Tahiti can turn back the clock, can it?"

"To some extent, they apparently can, and these two have the clout to wangle the appointment. He was in Matthew Chen-Jasic's overthrow of the Kendall tyranny and she recorded the nominations for the Charter convention chairman. They're planetary heroes. So you gotta try not to kill them with your flying."

"The computer will do most of it," Belsky said, "but I can tweak the flight parameters a bit. Keep the gravities down."

"Whatever you can do. Try to get them there in one piece."

"Am I going to end up nursing them along the way, too?"

"No," Gannet said. "They'll have an aide along who's half nurse, half secretary. He'll take care of all that."

"OK, good, because I don't know anything about that."

"You don't need to worry about that. Just get them there alive."

"OK," Belsky said. "You're the boss."

"I have trade factors for you for Earthsea and Aruba, ma'am," Naomi Thompson said.

"Excellent. Who have we got?"

"For Earthsea, Chen JongJu wants to go. She says Chen MinYan is due to take over the business office."

"Excellent. She knows she's going to be out there alone for six months to a year, right? Before we can get her husband out to her on the *Star Runner*."

"Yes and no, Ma'am. Her husband Bill Thompson and Ambassador Gregory Prentiss know and like each other. Bill is going as the ambassador's aide."

"That could work. Is it going to make things uncomfortable in the shuttle cabin, though? The four of them will be pretty cooped up. It's not exactly fair to the others to have a married couple along if they, you know, act married."

"JongJu brought that up herself, ma'am. She said that after the first week with no showers, abstinence wouldn't be an issue."

37

ChaoLi laughed. Yes, she could see that.

"All right. I think that's an excellent solution, then. What about for Aruba?"

"I asked around, and people suggested Gerardo Perez. He's been in the operations group, and supervised a lot of the construction on the hyperspace probes and shuttles. He's due for a new challenge, too, and Jerry says he's up for it."

"How are his people skills?"

"Good. He always got good marks for that."

"And he knows it'll be a year anyway before he can be relieved?"

"Yes, ma'am. Their kids are out of the house now, and they've been considering taking a break from each other anyway. This fits into his personal life pretty well, actually."

"All right, Naomi. Good job. Let's go ahead and confirm those hires and start getting them ready for their assignments."

"Yes, ma'am."

"And I'll want to talk to them myself before they go. Make sure we're all on the same page."

"Of course, ma'am."

ChaoLi stared out the window of her corner office on the top floor of Four Charter Square, reviewing in her mind all the myriad activities with the shuffling of ambassadors and trade factors, the hyperspace liners, the freight transfer stations. All the little threads that terminated here in this office.

The view was of the Blue Mountains to the north, with the ocean on her right. She looked down Arcadia Boulevard to the Chen-Jasic family complex a mile and a half distant, four city blocks between Fourteenth and Sixteenth Streets. Where she had grown up. Where she had lived all her life.

ChaoLi had the big fancy office, but she knew the really big decisions were being made there, in a pair of small tea rooms that opened onto a beautiful garden.

RICHARD F. WEYAND

Earthsea Departures

Loukas Diakos and Peter Dunhill were waiting at the top of the stairs when Justin Moore opened the cockpit door of Hyper-1 on Earthsea.

"Loukas, how are you doing?" Sasha Ivanov greeted Arcadia's ambassador to Earthsea as he maneuvered through the cockpit door.

"Good, Sasha. Good. You got your travel bags?"

"Yes, we're all prepared."

"Well, let me show you to the showers, then."

"Much better," Ivanov said when they returned to where Diakos waited after freshening up. "The best thing about switching to the hyperspace liners may be the ability to shower on board."

Diakos chuckled.

"I hear you there, Sasha. I'm not looking forward to the trip home. Although it may be a bit better. We're going to try the QE radios en route, and see if they work in hyperspace."

Ivanov raised an eyebrow.

"Really?" he asked. "I had the impression they wouldn't."

"That's not what some of the experts think. And Chen JieMin in particular thinks they have to work."

"I think I would take his opinion over anyone else's."

"Indeed," Diakos said. "Well, let's head on into Bergheim. Director Laurent would like to meet you."

"I am somewhat fatigued, but a short meeting before a good meal would work for me."

"Actually, I think a good meal is what she has planned."

"Ah. Two birds with one stone," Ivanov said. "That sounds good to me. Lead on, MacDuff."

Paolo Costa split off from the party to head for home when they arrived at the administrative building in downtown Bergheim. Diakos had offered to drop him at home, but Costa demurred.

"After zooming back and forth between planets, I'm actually looking forward to something as mundane as a bus ride."

Ivanov laughed heartily. It was a point of view he could understand.

Ivanov and Laurent knew each other from the conspiring they had done to overturn the Sellick chairmanship on Amber. It had been necessary to keep Laurent informed, lest she be concerned Ivanov's recall as Arcadia's ambassador to Amber was more than a political maneuver. But they had never met in person.

"Ambassador Ivanov, I'm so pleased to finally meet you," Laurent said when Diakos led Dunhill and the new arrivals into Laurent's office.

"The pleasure, Director Laurent, is surely all mine," Ivanov said.

They shook hands with real enthusiasm, and then Laurent motioned to the door to her private dining room.

"Come, Sasha. I know you are tired and hungry after six weeks in zero gravity, so let's eat first, and then we can let you go sleep."

They went into the room and sat around the table, and Ivanov pulled a foil package out of his jacket pocket.

"First, Valerie, I have a gift for you from Jean Dufort. They have truly splendid coffees on Amber, and I encourage you to serve this with dinner."

"Thank you, Sasha," Laurent said.

She turned to her head waiter.

"Patrick, can we serve coffee with dinner?"

"Of course, ma'am."

She handed him the vacuum-sealed foil package, and he disappeared into the kitchen as his staff served the salad course.

"I have two full containers of coffee aboard Hyper-1, Valerie," Ivanov said. "Gifts from Jean Dufort to you and Rob Milbank."

"But he didn't know how things were going to turn out on Amber as of the time you left."

"No, he had hopes, but gifts nonetheless. He was pretty sure he would prevail."

"That was some contest," Laurent said.

"Yes, but all three planets are now on board, four more planets are imminent, and two still to get to. I'm told I leave within days for Arcadia, and then on to Olympia."

"Which will locate another twelve planets, assuming you can persuade the Olympia people to tell you where they are."

Ivanov nodded.

"I intend to study what has been found out about Olympia on the way to Arcadia," he said. "From what I can see so far, they would welcome the export market for their fusion plants and distilled spirits. I will entice them with tea, coffee, and cheese."

Ivanov waved a piece of the truly splendid cheese that had been served with the salad course.

"I'm not sure that's going to work, Sasha," Laurent said. "We have eleven radios headed to Arcadia."

"Yes, I saw that. However, I only need enough for the decision makers, as Peter here will for those on Aruba. We've been talking about it, and I think we can squeeze enough into the remaining container to make an impression."

The coffee was served. Ivanov and the pilots, of course, had had it before, but it was new to everyone else.

"This is remarkable," Laurent said after a sip.

"Yes. Enough different in quality to amount to a difference in kind. I am very happy Jean was able to defeat Sellick and sign the treaty."

"Yet it will be a competitor for Arcadia's tea, Sasha."

"With twenty-one planets, there's plenty of market to go around, Valerie."

Laurent nodded.

"It's such an exciting time."

"Indeed."

"Stop fussing us, young man," Chen JuPing said.

"Yes, ma'am. Sorry, ma'am."

Hyper-3 and Hyper-4 sat on adjacent launch pads at the Arcadia City Shuttleport, atop their cargo containers. Eight containers each, loaded with Arcadia tea and spices for transfer to Earthsea, as well as for gifts to Tahiti and Playa. This meant that the shuttle's cockpit hatch was almost thirty feet off the ground.

"You can't carry us up the stairs, so we're best off managing them ourselves."

"Yes, ma'am. Of course, ma'am."

Paul Chen-Jasic and Chen JuPing puttered up the stairs at their own pace. They walked regularly around their property in the foothills of the Blue Mountains, and were mobile for their age, but the stairs were a bit of a challenge, and they took their time.

Chen ChaoLi waited at the top, to say her goodbyes to the woman under whom she had taken her first job more than twenty-five years before. She had become Chen Zumu's tea girl when she turned thirteen.

"Ah, there you are, ChaoLi," JuPing said.

"Chen Zumu," ChaoLi said, with a little bow.

"No, my dear. It's just JuPing now."

"Yes, Che– JuPing."

JuPing nodded.

"All these years, and you have made it come true after all, ChaoLi. We go to the stars."

"Have a good trip, JuPing."

"Thank you, ChaoLi. You take care. We'll be talking to you soon."

JuPing hugged her, then held her at arm's length and nodded. She patted ChaoLi on the shoulder, and touched her cheek, then turned to the cabin door. JuPing and Paul climbed into the cockpit and sat in the rear jump seats. JuPing looked around with approval.

"They said it would be cramped. This is quite roomy."

"I imagine we'll get tired of it in six weeks, JuPing," Paul said.

"Of course, Paul. But six weeks is not a long time, after all."

JuPing made a little wave to ChaoLi, and ChaoLi waved back, ignoring the tears in her eyes.

Their caregiver, Stuart Reynolds, was next, climbing into the co-pilot's seat. He would probably spend most of the trip with the seat rotated around, away from the controls and facing his charges.

As Igor Belsky was ready to enter the cockpit, ChaoLi caught his arm. They had never met, but Belsky certainly knew who she was. ChaoLi for her part had checked his flight records and recordings, and picked him for this trip over Jeong Minho, who was a bit more of a hotdog.

"Gently, Mr. Belsky," ChaoLi said.

"Oh, I understand, ma'am."

ChaoLi nodded and released his arm, and Belsky climbed into the cabin of Hyper-3.

ChaoLi went down the stairs and over to Hyper-4 to say goodbye to Chen JongJu, her successor as JuPing's tea girl when ChaoLi moved to the reception desk where she had met Chen JieMin. JongJu had also come up within the family's business office, often as ChaoLi's trusted lieutenant.

"Have a good trip, JongJu."

"Thanks, ChaoLi. We'll talk to you soon."

They hugged, and then JongJu went up the stairs to the cabin hatch of Hyper-4 together with her husband, Bill Thompson, the new ambassador to Earthsea, Gregory Prentiss, and the pilot, Jeong Minho.

ChaoLi withdrew to the headquarters building and watched through the observation window as the stairs were withdrawn and final flight checks were made. The air traffic control channel was playing on speakers in the observation room.

When all flight checks had been performed, and takeoff clearances granted, Hyper-3 and Hyper-4 launched, one after the other, gained altitude, and set off for the hyperspace limit and Earthsea.

A similar scene played itself out on Earthsea with Hyper-1. Loukas Diakos was wishing bon voyage to Sasha Ivanov and Diakos's aide for the past several months, Peter Dunhill.

Ivanov had managed to get several thousand pounds of cheese and coffee aboard the one container that held their water tank for the shuttle cabin as well as their personal cubic.

The shuttle cockpit hatch was almost forty feet off the ground with a four-wide, three-high stack of containers below it. The other eleven containers were all QE radios, including one standalone unit they would try using while in hyperspace.

"Congratulations on being named ambassador to Aruba, Peter. Good luck with your new assignment."

"Thanks, Loukas. Thanks for everything."

Dunhill had hitched his wagon to Diakos's rising star years before, and they both knew it. And now, with a diplomatic personnel shortage, it had paid off.

"And you, Sasha. Have a good trip. Say hi to home for me on your way through," Diakos said.

"Yes, well, I won't be on Arcadia long. I'm off to check out the cognac on Olympia almost immediately."

Diakos laughed.

"Don't forget to get the locations of the other twelve colonies while you're there," he said.

"Oh, yes. There is that other little matter, isn't there?" Ivanov asked with a twinkle in his eye.

Then Ivanov, Dunhill, Moore, and McKay made their way up the tall stairs they needed to get to the shuttle on that pile of containers. Diakos withdrew to the observation lounge of the hangar where Hyper-1 had been serviced to watch the takeoff.

With the full load it had, Hyper-1 was slow off the pad. They had to focus the thrust of the engines more than normal to get liftoff, and then the shuttle and its heavy load were gone, heading to the hyperspace limit and Arcadia.

Two days after Hyper-3 and Hyper-4 departed for Earthsea, Rob Milbank received a video call from Sasha Ivanov.

"Sasha, I thought you had left Earthsea by now."

"We left two days ago, Rob, and are now in hyperspace."

"Really? Excellent!"

"Yes, the QE radios work just fine in hyperspace, as Chen JieMin had concluded they must."

"Never doubt that young man on something about which he is sure."

"Indeed. So let ChaoLi and JieMin know, if you would."

"Absolutely, Sasha. I'll do that. And you're on your way back now?"

"Yes, and, despite carrying eleven containers of QE radios, I managed to sneak some thousand pounds of cheese and coffee aboard in the personal cubic container."

"You did? That's stupendous. Now we'll have gifts for the high and mighty on Aruba and Olympia. Well done."

"Thanks, Rob. So I'll see you in six weeks or so. Probably hang around for a week or two before heading on. Sitting in this cockpit for weeks at a time, journey after journey, is getting tedious."

"No problem at all, Sasha. And at least now you'll have access to the network while you travel."

They were sitting in the living room after dinner. The boys were in their rooms doing homework.

"You were right, JieMin," ChaoLi said.

"Apparently so. You know, I looked at it, and I just couldn't see how the physics would work out if QE radios didn't function in hyperspace. I could have been wrong, but it would have meant doing some serious rethinking on some parts of the mathematics."

"No need now. They work."

"Yes. There are some interesting ramifications," JieMin said.

"Oh, yeah. People can now be in touch while they're

traveling."

"Yes, of course. But think beyond that for a moment. If we can be in touch with the deployment vehicles in hyperspace, there's no weeks- or months-long trip back to Arcadia to report their data. We can send them out, have them take some measurements, report their findings and move on. We can steer them while they are in hyperspace."

"I don't see the importance of that," ChaoLi said. "We can have them report from wherever they are now, if they take radios along."

"Let me give you a for instance. We know roughly where a lot of the other colonies have to be now, right?"

"Generally, yes. But not their actual locations."

"Right," JieMin said. "But we could send the deployment vehicles out now, get them heading in the right direction, and when Ambassador Ivanov gets their actual locations from Olympia, they will be mostly there already."

"Oh. Oh, my."

ChaoLi's eyes got wide, then narrowed.

"But we don't have enough shipboard QE radios. All the radios coming back with Hyper-1 are committed."

"Yes, but many of the colonies lie in the Sagittarius Arm, past Earthsea. We could have the deployment vehicles stop at Earthsea and pick up radios, then head out in more or less the right direction. Short-circuit the wait. By the time Ambassador Ivanov arrives on Olympia in fourteen weeks or so, they would be in the right neighborhood."

"And we can send the deployment vehicles instructions on where to go over QE radio. The delay would be maybe a week or two after Ivanov gets the locations, instead of twelve weeks or more from here."

"Correct. And then the prime minister could contact their

governments over QE radio. We don't need to wait for manned missions to set out from here and travel two or three or four six-week hops from here."

"Oh, JieMin, that's brilliant. Not least because we have the probes now. Six of them, anyway. And they aren't otherwise committed at the moment."

"All right, you guys," John Gannet told his next staff meeting. "In the middle of everything else going on, we have new orders."

Expressive as always, the operations group responded with groans.

"No, this one's not so bad. We need to send out the deployment vehicles we have – all six of them – and send them to Earthsea. They'll mount these shipboard QE radios on them, and then we'll talk to them from here and get them started out to where we expect new colonies to be. By the time we actually do get the locations of other colonies, they should be pretty close already."

"Do we send them with RDF satellites, John?" a staffer asked.

"One each, I think. First thing they do is a standard flyby. We pick up all the data, but now they can just send it here right away. Everybody here studies that data for a week or so, and learns what they can about them. Then we send it back into the system from where we parked it for a week, and the prime minister can call them up and say Hi."

"That's pretty slick," another staffer said. "Who came up with that idea? Not some government type."

"No. I hear it was Chen JieMin."

"OK, well that makes sense."

"It will sure speed things up, that's for sure," Gannet said.

49

The six deployment vehicles whose RDF satellites had found the six new colonies were sitting out at the hyperspace limit in a long slow orbit of Arcadia. They were a bit down on fuel for their maneuvering thrusters from the close-in maneuvering required to pick up the RDF satellites for the return to Arcadia, but it was decided, since the pickups would occur on another trip, that refueling them could wait.

They each detached three of their RDF satellites where they were. They then shoved off from them with a minimum push from their maneuvering thrusters to open up the distance a bit.

That done, they spun up their hyperspace fields and disappeared, destination Earthsea.

SILK ROAD

Earthsea Arrivals

Rob Milbank discussed the plans with Valerie Laurent before the deployment vehicles set out for Earthsea.

"The idea, Valerie, is that we can get these unmanned ships to do flybys and drop QE radios at each colony before we send manned missions out to them. We have four manned shuttles, and six of these unmanned ships, but the big hyperspace liners aren't operational yet.

"Using the unmanned ships greatly increases our ability to contact other colonies and the speed with which we can do so, because we can have them set out in more or less the right directions from Earthsea now. Between them, they could carry enough of the self-contained QE radios to get an initial link up to every other colony out there."

"I understand, Rob. What do you need from us?"

"Eighteen of the self-contained QE radios, three for each unmanned ship. We don't really need to deploy eighteen for the twelve remaining colonies, but we may be a little off here and there about where the colonies are."

"That's not a problem. These unmanned ships, will they land here?"

"No, they don't have the engines for that. They just stop at the hyperspace limit and get serviced there."

"We're going to need help with that part of it. We don't have any experience going that far out, or transferring containers in space. Can your people on Hyper-3 and Hyper-4 take care of that before they head back to Arcadia?"

"Absolutely. Both of our pilots have a lot of experience with that sort of work. It will take two trips to carry eighteen QE radios out there. Probably one trip with both shuttles, actually. Then they can head back here with more of the shipboard radios for the other liners as they come into service."

Laurent was nodding.

"That works for us."

"Are you going to have enough of the self-contained radios?"

"Not on hand at the moment. We have maybe half what we need, but we'll ramp up a bit on this end. We'll have them by the time we need them."

"Excellent. Thanks, Valerie."

"No problem, Rob."

"There's one more thing I wanted to mention. Our ambassadors to Tahiti are in their nineties. I think they're planning on seeing just how good Tahiti is with their anti-aging technology. But a normal 'Welcome to Earthsea' meeting is probably not the best approach."

"I can handle that, Rob. We'll probably transfer them directly to a hotel suite downtown, and have medical people standing by if there are any issues."

"They have a caregiver along."

"A two-bedroom hotel suite. Got it."

"Thanks, Valerie."

"Thanks for the heads-up, Rob."

When Hyper-1 arrived in the Arcadia system six weeks later, Moore and McKay set the computer for automatic landing. With twelve containers aboard, and running close to the shuttle's mass limit, it wasn't the time to practice their flying skills. And with six-week transits and long planet stays, they were getting rusty.

SILK ROAD

"Hyper-1 to Arcadia Air Traffic Control."

"Go ahead, Hyper-1."

"Requesting expanded clearance for landing. We are four-wide and three-high. Hyper-1 over."

"Roger four-wide and three-high, Hyper-1. You are cleared to land on shuttlepad two-seven. Take your time. Over."

"Cleared for shuttlepad two-seven. Hyper-1 out."

"We gonna be OK, coming in this heavy?" Ivanov asked.

"Yeah, the computer's done it before," Moore said. "Heavier. Still, I like to have some extra room and to keep a close eye on things."

"It's still got the glide path of a lead brick, though," McKay said.

"That's why we keep an eye on it," Moore said with exaggerated patience.

"Geez, she's coming in hot."

"Yeah. They're way heavy."

"I hope they don't leave a big hole in the ground."

"The computer's just saving fuel for when it really needs it."

"We're on the upper edge of the velocity envelope," McKay said.

"We over?" Moore asked.

"No."

McKay looked back and forth between displays and gauges.

"Not yet," he added.

"Just keep an eye on it," Moore said, but his hands were on the controls now. "If I need to take over, let me know."

"Oh, it's close. She's riding the edge."

Then the shuttle's engines went to full power, braking hard

against the gravity well, fighting against her momentum.

"She's bleeding oxygen into the feed now," McKay said. "Thrust is up against the wall."

The g-forces in the shuttle had spiked and were still climbing.

"Backing off the velocity limit now," McKay got out through gritted teeth as the shuttle began to shake. "I hope the cargo stays put."

"You and me both," Moore said.

Ivanov and Dunhill weren't paying much attention to the conversation now. They were concentrating too hard on being uncomfortable as the computer fought to keep the shuttle within the flight envelope.

Then the engines started to throttle back a bit as it picked up ground effect, the g-forces fell, and the shuttle settled onto shuttlepad twenty-seven.

"Fuck me, what a ride," McKay said.

"You got that right," Moore said.

"How's about next time we don't go twelve heavy. You know. Eight heavy, or twelve light, whatever. But not twelve heavy."

"You got my vote," Moore said. "Then again, look at the fuel gauges."

"Geez. I take back everything I said about computers. If it had taken it easy—"

"Then the way too fast part would have been at the end instead of the beginning."

"I like it this way better," McKay said.

By advance arrangement with Milbank, they eschewed any celebrations or greetings for the moment. The prime minister sent two cars out to the Arcadia City shuttleport to take Ivanov, Dunhill, Moore, and McKay, haggard and smelly as they were, directly to their respective residences.

After months of hyperspace and alien planets, it was good to be home.

When Hyper-3 and Hyper-4 arrived in Earthsea space within an hour of each other, the query came up from the planet about the health status of Paul Chen-Jasic and Chen JuPing. In truth, they were in good health and high spirits, and Igor Belsky reported that to Earthsea Air Traffic Control.

"Oh, I hope they're not planning any celebration or anything of that kind," JuPing said. "I feel OK, but I'm very tired. I need a decent night's sleep to feel my best."

"Me, too," Paul said.

"That's the plan Earthsea Air Traffic Control sent me, ma'am," Belsky reported from the pilot's seat. "They will have a car waiting to pick us up, and it will take you directly to a hotel suite where you can get food and go to bed, in whichever order you prefer."

"Oh, good."

Belsky saw a raised eyebrow from Stuart Reynolds, their caregiver.

"It's a two-bedroom suite," the pilot said softly.

Reynolds nodded back.

Belsky turned his attention back to his rear seat passengers.

"I'm going to dismount from the containers before you debark, ma'am. Very short stairs, then directly into the car to your hotel."

"Wonderful," JuPing said. "That's very thoughtful."

The two pilots, Belsky and Jeong MinHo, had talked to Moore and McKay before they set out from Arcadia. The Hyper-1 pilots had recommended computer approach and landing, given that the shuttleport systems were compatible and especially given the mountains ringing Bergheim.

As they came in on their approach, Belsky was glad he had taken their advice.

"Just look at those mountains," Belsky said.

"They're very beautiful," JuPing said. "What a lovely planet."

Their approach and landing was uneventful. After Belsky had the computer dismount the shuttle from the containers, a limousine pulled up at the foot of the short stairs from the shuttle cockpit door to the ground.

"And there's our car, ma'am," Belsky said.

"Thank you, Mr. Belsky. Nicely done."

"You're welcome, ma'am."

As JuPing and Paul moved down the stairs, she called back to their hovering caretaker.

"Come along, Stuart."

Hyper-4 landed several minutes after Hyper-3. Jeong Minho also instructed the shuttle computer to dismount from its container stack and settle the shuttle on the adjacent parking pad.

Jeong, Chen JongJu, Bill Thompson, and Gregory Prentiss all found they had logins in the local computer network. Checking them once they had landed, they found a mail from Director Laurent welcoming them to Earthsea and offering to get together for lunch tomorrow, after they had dinner and a good night's sleep.

The arrangements for Paul and JuPing had struck Valerie Laurent as a good idea for everyone. A second limousine pulled up at Hyper-4 to take them all downtown to hotel rooms already booked for them.

SILK ROAD

Paul Chen-Jasic and Chen JuPing slept in, which for them meant seven hours. Longer than that gave the aches and pains of old age too much time to creep up on them. They ordered a simple breakfast of toast, some chicken soup, and orange juice from room service.

After breakfast, JuPing opened the drapes in their penthouse suite and looked out over the city to the tall and jagged mountains beyond.

"What a lovely planet."

They got dressed for the day in the soft fleece loungers that were now their preferred dress. Stuart Reynolds came in with their morning medications, and they took those.

They sat in the comfy armchairs in the living room of the suite and napped off and on until lunch. It would take them a while to catch up on their sleep.

Bill Thompson and Chen JuJong also slept in. After showers and eight hours of sleep, they woke to find themselves in a bed, in normal gravity, and without the strictures of etiquette enforced on them by the presence of their shuttle cockpit-mates. They took quite a while to reacquaint themselves with each other before heading to the showers again.

They followed that with a hearty breakfast. Aware of the quality of Earthsea's cheeses and dairy products, they had omelets, with sausage and toast on the side, coffee, and orange juice.

After breakfast, they logged into the network in their heads-up displays and started catching up on the news, both from Earthsea and Arcadia.

In their mail, they got advice from Arcadia that the QE radios worked in hyperspace, as Chen JieMin had predicted.

Gregory Prentiss awoke to find a mail from Loukas Diakos offering to brief him over breakfast. Prentiss invited him over to the hotel suite to have a room service breakfast so they could speak in private.

There was a knock on the door and Prentiss opened it.

"Greg, how are you?"

"Good, Loukas. Come on in."

Diakos walked into the suite and Prentiss closed the door.

"We should probably order first," Prentiss said.

"Good idea. I would recommend the omelets. The cheeses here are superb."

They both ordered in their heads-up displays, with Diakos using Prentiss's room number. They sat down in the living room to wait for delivery.

'So what's the most important thing I need to know? Has that changed since the last time we talked?"

"No. Director Laurent is a true partner, and is now friends with the prime minister. Rob for his part has bent over backwards to include both Earthsea and Amber as full partners. No 'our contribution is more important than your contribution' nonsense."

"Well, it is the Arcadian discovery and mastery of hyperspace travel that makes any of this possible. And our astrography ensures that we will be a major freight hub."

"Yes, and everybody knows both of those things, so Rob is careful to never bring them up. We're partners. Period. Partners in making life better for everyone through interstellar trade."

Prentiss nodded, and Diakos continued.

"So the only mistake you could make here is screwing up the relationship between Laurent and Milbank. Your biggest job is to make sure nothing else comes up that could do that without it being dealt with properly. If you see some concern developing, you need to let Rob know."

"OK. I understand. And I also understand that the QE radios have been found to work in hyperspace."

"Yes, and that's a very big deal. It really opens up the interstellar passenger business. Now instead of being out of touch for six weeks, or twelve weeks, or eighteen weeks between planets, you are in touch the entire trip. You can hold business meetings, keep up on the news, respond in real-time to events happening thousands of light-years away."

"Wow."

"Exactly. It means that decision makers can go interstellar without ever being out of touch. People who otherwise couldn't travel through hyperspace because of their need to be in constant contact. And Director Laurent has been providing QE radios like potato chips. Anything Rob wants, he's getting."

"Earthsea controls them though, right?"

"Of course, and at some point they'll start charging traffic fees, just as Arcadia will start charging cargo fees. But for this expansion period, Laurent's been providing QE radios and bandwidth at no charge. It's a big help to opening up these planets."

"OK, so they really are a partner in Rob's grand vision. I can see that."

"Good. It's something you can never forget. We're not the senior partner here. Not in our boss's eyes, anyway. We're all equal partners, and everybody is bringing something to the table. That's very important for the future of this whole effort."

Their food showed up, and they ate breakfast talking of lesser things, mostly the latest political gossip from Arcadia.

Valerie Laurent was also getting briefed, by her ambassador

to Arcadia, Salvatore Romano, over QE radio.

"The Chen – more properly the Chen-Jasic family – is an extended clan that has a dominant role in Arcadian politics and business. The family and their allies have a say in every major and most minor activities on Arcadia.

"As a small example, their trade factor for Earthsea is a member of the family, as is the ambassador's aide. Rob Milbank is a family ally and was groomed and mentored for prime minister by the family's current leadership. And Sasha Ivanov, Loukas Diakos and Gregory Prentiss are family allies as well.

"And it's not by accident that they're so influential. The family began with an alliance between a Chinese peasant family and a group of North American suburbanites before the original colonists had even left Earth. The Chinese family was organized under their patriarch, while the North American group was united by all their children having intermarried. They amounted to a family group as well.

"In addition, they had both made smart choices in what they brought in their personal cubic, combining their resources to fill up the group's cubic with items that gave them a significant head start in Arcadia's economy.

"The union of these two family groups resulted in a technologically savvy, agriculturally savvy powerhouse united under a single couple as head of family. Personal and cultural loyalties to that ruling couple have led them to grow in power and influence since.

"For their part, Arcadians generally have been happy with the Chen's influence. The colony has done very well due in large part to the family's efforts. It was the head of the Chen family seventy-five years ago who overthrew a nascent tyranny and gave Arcadia the most freedom-oriented government of any colony we have seen so far, including our own.

"And it was the Chen family who discovered hyperspace and pushed the project through to success when the government botched it. Rob Milbank made a major move there when he hired the Chen, with government funds, to complete the project."

"And this couple, Paul Chen-Jasic and Chen JuPing?" Laurent asked.

"I told you about my interview with the current ruling couple, which are always called Chen Zufu and Chen Zumu. They came up with the solutions to the calendar and nudity problems."

Laurent nodded. The Arcadians' lack of a nudity taboo had been an issue with opening up the news wires between the two planets. Requiring opt-in to the feeds had defanged the issue without triggering censorship concerns on either planet.

"Well, Paul Chen-Jasic and Chen JuPing are the immediately prior Chen Zufu and Chen Zumu. They retired from the leadership over a decade ago. But more than that, they are planetary heroes here.

"Paul Chen-Jasic played a critical role in the overthrow of the previous government, that nascent tyranny, while Chen JuPing is the granddaughter of the Chen Zufu who overthrew that government. She actually tabulated the nominations for chairman at their constitutional convention.

"When they were Chen Zufu and Chen Zumu, they recognized the potential of the mathematical hypothesis of the existence of hyperspace and personally funded the research for years to get to where they are now. They are, more than anyone, the reason we have hyperspace travel today."

"Wow. So why are they heading to Tahiti as Arcadia's ambassadors?" Laurent asked.

"Tahiti's specialty is anti-aging research. I think it's clear they are going there for therapy as much as for their role as ambassadors. That said, though, they are extremely savvy people, used to mixing it up with the powerful, and will have no problem negotiating the trade agreement with Tahiti."

"I can see that," Laurent said.

Romano nodded.

"So any deference you can pay to Paul Chen-Jasic and Chen JuPing is not only well deserved, but will redound to Earthsea's benefit in its relationship with Arcadia. They are planetary heroes here for their roles in the revolution, but they are humanity's heroes as well, for their pivotal role in the development of interstellar travel."

When she got off the call with Romano, Laurent looked at the time. No time for working through channels. She called the manager of the upscale hotel where the crews and passengers of Hyper-3 and Hyper-4 were staying.

Needless to say, when the director of the Earthsea planetary council called, she got through right away.

"Yes, Madam Director. What can I do for you today?"

"I have invited the recent arrivals from Arcadia to lunch with me today. Two of them are in their nineties, and it occurs to me that it is much easier for me to attend them there than for them to come here. Can you accommodate a luncheon for twelve in a private banquet room today? You only have three hours, I'm afraid."

"Of course, Madam Director. I'll be happy to take care of it personally. I would suggest one of our rooftop rooms. The views of the mountains are splendid."

"Excellent. Thank you."

"It is my pleasure, Madam Director."

SILK ROAD

Laurent sent an update mail to everyone, telling them she would be hosting them for lunch in the rooftop banquet rooms of the hotel.

"The director of the planetary council is coming here for her lunch with us?" Paul asked when he received the mail.

"How very considerate of her," JuPing said. "We need travel no farther than the elevator."

Valerie Laurent, her aide, and her chief of staff got off the elevator on the top floor of the hotel fifteen minutes early. The hotel manager himself was waiting for them.

"This way, please, Madam Director."

He waved them on into one of the rooms branching off the elevator lobby, one of half a dozen banquet rooms of various sizes at the top of the hotel.

Laurent walked into the room. A single rectangular table was set for twelve. There were two chairs at both the head and foot of the table, and four along each side. Beyond that, the room was glass on three sides, with unobstructed views of the mountains all around.

"This is splendid. Thank you. Please make sure my guests find their way here as well."

"Of course, Madam Director."

Everyone else was in place and chatting around the table when Paul Chen-Jasic and Chen JuPing came into the banquet room. There were place cards around the table, and Laurent had left the two chairs at the head of the table empty.

When they entered, Laurent stood and perforce so did everyone else. Laurent applauded the ancient couple, dressed in their fleece loungers, and everyone else joined in. She waved them to be seated at the head of the table.

Paul and Jessica sat, while Laurent remained standing for several seconds more, she and the others applauding.

Laurent finally sat, and the others took their seats as well.

"Good heavens, Madam Director. What was all that about?" JuPing asked Laurent, sitting to her right.

"For hyperspace, Chen JuPing. I know very well that, but for the two of you, we would not be here today, at the beginning of this interstellar Renaissance, and I, for one, am grateful."

"We dreamt of the stars, Paul and I."

"And you made it happen. For everyone."

SILK ROAD

Arrival On Playa

The mission to Playa left Earthsea first. Loukas Diakos had been on Earthsea for almost a year by this point, and did not need time to recover from an inbound flight. For his part, Jeong Minho was young, and had a lot of experience working in zero-gravity by this point. His own recovery requirements were much shorter than those considered safe for Paul Chen-Jasic and Chen JuPing.

For this trip, it was just Jeong Minho and Loukas Diakos, so they had much more room in the small shuttle cockpit. Loukas sat in the back row, which allowed them both to stretch out across the seats for sleep. Somehow it felt more natural to be stretched out 'horizontally,' even in zero gravity.

For this trip, Hyper-4 carried four containers – one with personal cubic and water, and also containing tea from Arcadia, coffee from Amber, and cheese from Earthsea; a standalone shipboard radio for Hyper-4; and two of the big multi-channel QE radios to remain in Playa.

During the trip, Diakos studied up on Playa. Their technical specialty was cybernetics, and they also had a lot of different varieties of mushrooms.

The data collected in the flyby of Playa was curious, in that it included a lot of communications streams with a human identifier on one end and a machine identifier on the other. It wasn't the central server farm of the colony's network, however. Every colony had one of those. This was a lot of different machine identifiers. Thousands upon thousands of them.

The other thing Diakos noted in the imagery in the data stream is that most of the prominent people on Playa appeared to be overweight, in a way that was seldom seen on Arcadia, for instance. Not the average man in the street so much, but the rich and powerful were, by and large, on the heavy side.

That was curious.

Given that they had QE radio while in hyperspace, Diakos talked it over with Rob Milbank.

"So what do you think, Rob? Why are they all overweight?"

"Maybe they have the robots do all the work, and sit around all day," Milbank said.

"But if a robot was doing the work, wouldn't you go out and play golf or go climbing or something? Compared to sitting at a desk job, you would get more exercise, not less."

"I don't know, Loukas. I guess you'll have to find out. One caution, though."

"What's that?"

"If all the wealthy and powerful are overweight, they might think a wiry, skinny guy like yourself must be a nobody."

"But that's because I'm a climber, Rob. You know that. You often end up supporting yourself or pulling yourself up with one hand. If you're heavy, it's much harder to climb."

"Just saying, Loukas. Watch out for it."

"Playa Air Traffic Control, this is hyperspace shuttle Hyper-4, inbound from colony planet Arcadia. Estimating arrival in twenty-two hours. Request instructions. Over."

"Hyper-4, this is Playa Control. Repeat your transmission. Over."

"Playa Air Traffic Control, this is hyperspace shuttle Hyper-4, inbound from colony planet Arcadia. Estimating arrival in twenty-two hours. Request instructions. Over."

"Roger, Hyper-4. Maintain profile. Radio when two hours out for landing clearance."

Jeong turned to Diakos.

"Well, more sit back and wait," Jeong said.

"If they run true to form, they'll ask for more information within about an hour."

"What was that?" Planetary Chairman Oliver Nieman asked.

"They said they were a hyperspace vessel inbound to Playa from the colony planet Arcadia, sir," Nieman's chief of staff, Reginald Field, repeated.

"An interstellar vessel? How extraordinary."

"Yes, sir."

"I would have expected this to happen much earlier," Nieman said. "I had decided it wasn't going to happen at all."

"Nevertheless, sir."

"Yes. Yes, quite. Hmm."

First interstellar contact, for Playa at least. Arcadia had been the third drop-off, and Playa had been thirteenth. So the Arcadians hadn't known where Playa was from the viewscreen recordings of the original drop-off. Which meant the Arcadians had to look for them. They had probably contacted at least a few others already. The first two, for sure.

"Reg."

His chief of staff turned back toward him in the display.

"Yes, sir?"

"They must have an ambassador or some such aboard. Have traffic control ask if they have briefing materials for me."

"Of course, sir."

Field cut the display, and Nieman sat back to think about interstellar contact.

Field was his chief of staff, but Field wasn't actually in the same location with Nieman. The powerful didn't go into the office, at least not on Playa. Field was at home, as Nieman himself was. He seldom left his home and gardens these days.

Contact with other planets was interesting, though. How much would the colonies have drifted apart from a more or less common start a century and a quarter before? Call it six generations.

And what would the implications be for Playa?

"There it is, right on time, The request for briefing materials," Jeong said. "You want me to send the video recording?"

"Yes, go ahead and transmit it," Diakos said.

"Did you have a chance to watch that video, Reg?" Nieman asked.

"Yes, sir. And I've read most of the accompanying materials."

"I'm surprised they sent such a junior person as ambassador. Then again, perhaps no senior people wanted to go on such a long trip."

"I think that may be a misreading of the situation, sir," Field said.

"Really? Why so?"

"Loukas Diakos was actually a senior member of the lower chamber of their legislature, called the House, before moving into the ambassadorial role. He had been there fifteen years, after making his fortune in business by his early forties."

"He made a fortune by his forties, and was in the legislature for fifteen years?"

"Yes, sir. Now, their House has ninety members, so it's

larger than our Council, but even so. He's a senior government guy, and a savvy businessman, both."

"Hmpf. Well, he certainly doesn't look it. He looks half starved to me. Makes me hungry just to look at him."

Nieman shifted his bulk in his chair to grab another cookie, then thought better of it. He returned his attention to Field, in the three-dimensional display that took up the entire wall in front of him.

"I understand, sir, but they have a very different culture. From the video, it appears that even their rich and powerful people go into the office every day. You saw those shots of their legislature in action. They were all physically present in a large auditorium."

"Yes. Remarkable. Why not just call in from home? All that running about. And the time wasted in travel."

"Like I said, sir. A very different culture. Part of that may be because they have little or no automation compared to us."

Nieman nodded. He had seen no robots anywhere in the video recording, on any of the three planets, Amber, Earthsea, and Arcadia. Did they do everything themselves?

"And they have all joined this agreement of theirs. All three planets. Apparently we would be the fourth," Nieman said.

"Yes, sir. It looks as simple as they said. Arcadia discovered the hyperspace drive, and they knew where Earthsea and Amber were, so they just went there. They had to look for the others, and have found some of them, including us."

Nieman nodded again. That all sounded right. Whether by design or chance, they had found Playa.

"What do you think this agreement of theirs is like, Reg?"

"They say it is an open fair-trade agreement, sir, and that all trading partners have equal status."

"Which is what I would expect them to say."

"Of course, sir. Without having seen the actual text yet, it's hard to say."

"Well, we shall see. Let's put their delegation up in the hotel downtown."

"Do you want me to meet them at the shuttleport, sir?"

"No, I shall meet them."

"Very well, sir."

Nieman cut the connection and signaled his major domo. His primary robot came into his living room several minutes later carrying his dinner on a tray. He fixed it across the arms of Nieman's chair.

"Will there be anything else, sir?" the robot asked.

"Dismissed."

The robot nodded its head once and left the room.

After dinner, once the major domo had returned and removed the tray, Nieman maneuvered his powered chair out through the powered sliding patio door into his gardens.

He looked up into the darkening sky as the stars started to come out, one by one. Which one was Arcadia, he wondered?

Then again, he could probably not see it from here, even in full dark. A G2 sun – like Earth's, like Playa's – from six thousand light-years distant would be lost in the cloud of nearer and larger stars in the Sagittarius Arm.

To have crossed such vast distances, finally. It was a remarkable achievement.

Of course, Janice Quant had achieved the same thing over a century before, but that was different. The massive artificial intelligence Bernd Decker had constructed had solved space travel in a most elegant way.

But Playa's engineers and scientists had never been able to duplicate what they called the Decker Breakthrough, Bernd Decker's unpublished and undocumented architecture for

SILK ROAD

Quant. All such efforts had resulted in failure. The Decker Architecture that did get published was solid computer design, an advancement of the field, but it was not artificial intelligence.

And Quant was long gone. At least, Playa's scientists and engineers thought the odds of her having survived so long were slim to none. For one simple reason if no other.

If Janice Quant had in fact survived, where was she?

So Playa had not solved the artificial intelligence problem. Playa's robots were mechanical devices, not artificial beings. They were task-oriented, not self-directing.

Oliver Nieman thought that was probably a good thing.

"Hyper-4 to Playa Control. We are two hours out. Requesting landing clearance. Over."

"Roger, Hyper-4. You are cleared to shuttlepad 3. Playa Control out."

"Huh. No other traffic warnings," Jeong Minho said.

"Maybe they don't have a lot of other traffic today," Loukas Diakos said.

"I suppose. Well, the computer has lock on shuttlepad 3 and there's a standard approach that comes with that. Keep your eyes open."

But the computer put Hyper-4 down on shuttlepad 3 with no problems. A stairway drove up to the shuttle, and someone was coming up the stair. All good.

Jeong opened the shuttle cockpit hatch to find a mechanical man standing at the doorway. He was a bit taken aback by that, and looked at him curiously.

The robot was humaniform, more or less, about average height and build for a human. It did have two arms hanging from each shoulder, but was otherwise much like a human. It was covered in a plastic flexible skin that was colored blue like a coverall, but was flesh-colored on face and hands and black on scalp and feet, which had no toes. Like it was wearing boots.

"Welcome to Playa, gentlemen," it said.

"You're our welcoming party?" Jeong asked.

"I am the planetary chairman's aide, sir. I am to take you to the hotel for your stay here."

"Well, lead on, MacDuff."

"I will lead you, sir, but my name is Fred."

Jeong looked back to Diakos, who shrugged and motioned Jeong forward.

"Very well. Lead on, Fred."

"Yes, sir."

Fred led them down the stair and a short distance to a car. It opened the rear passenger door for them to get in, and closed it behind them. It then walked around to the driver's door, got behind the wheel, and headed toward town.

Jeong and Diakos were used to self-driving vehicles from Arcadia, so they weren't unaccustomed to vehicles driving themselves, but having a mechanical man drive a car was new.

They looked around curiously on their way into town. There were very few people about, at least compared to Arcadia or Earthsea. There were a lot of robots, though, each walking purposefully. On some sort of mission, they supposed. Maybe just to go get groceries. With four hands, they could carry a lot of grocery bags.

There was much less vehicle traffic than on Arcadia as well. Most of those vehicles – all of them that Diakos could see – were being driven by robots like their own.

"Not many people out and about, Fred," Diakos said.

The robot's head spun around to face into the rear seat.

SILK ROAD

"No reason to go anywhere, sir. We can bring you anything you need."

"Uh, shouldn't you be watching where you're going?"

"I use the car's sensors, sir. I normally face forward only because people seem to find it more comfortable."

"I would find it more comfortable as well," Diakos said.

"Very well, sir."

The robot's head turned to face forward again.

"So you'll bring us anything we need."

"Yes, sir."

"What about meetings and the like?" Diakos asked.

"People just call each other. Meetings are all held in the displays. There's no need to actually travel to get together."

"How do people meet each other? You know, young people. How do they meet someone to marry?"

"I'm not sure, sir. They seem to manage."

Fred spun his head around again.

"They prefer that we not be around, sir. So we don't really know."

The robot spun his head back forward again.

"Well, I can see that, I guess," Diakos said.

There was no check-in process at the hotel. The robot led them past the clerk to the elevators and up to their room.

"Small hotel," Diakos remarked.

"People don't travel much, sir. There's not much need."

"I see."

"Very good, sir. If you need anything, just let the front desk know."

"When do I meet with the Chairman?" Diakos asked.

"The Chairman would be pleased to have lunch with you tomorrow, sir. After you've had a chance to recuperate from your travel."

"Very good. And do we go to him or does he come here?"

"I'm sorry, sir," Fred said. "I don't understand."

"Do we eat here, or at his place, wherever that is."

"Oh. I see. You suffer from a misapprehension, sir. You will eat here, and he will eat there, and you will eat together, via the display."

Fred waved at a large display.

"I see. OK, thank you, Fred."

"You're very welcome, sir. Have a good rest period."

With that the robot left. When he did, Diakos and Jeong both laughed.

"Wow. What a planet," Jeong said.

"Now we know why they're overweight."

Diakos looked around. The room seemed OK if a little stuffy. Like it wasn't used very often. There were two bedrooms off a common living space. There was the large display in one wall, in front of which sat two large armchairs.

Diakos sat in one. It dwarfed him.

"Clearly made for a larger ass than me," Diakos said.

Jeong laughed, then pointed.

"Loukas, it's on wheels."

"What?"

"The chairs. They're on wheels. I think they're motorized."

"Huh. I can go out on the balcony without even getting up."

Jeong just shook his head.

"Another hundred years and they won't be able to walk at all," he said.

"Maybe the robots will just carry them around, like in sedan chairs or something."

"How strange."

"Yeah," Diakos said. "Takes all kinds."

SILK ROAD

Jeong had left the shipboard QE radio on when they left, and patched into the ship's radio system. Diakos tried to patch through to Arcadia, and got a call through to Rob Milbank. It was morning on Arcadia, though it was early evening here.

"Loukas, did you arrive on Playa?" Milbank asked when he saw the hotel room background.

"Yes, we're in a hotel here. Or, I should say, the hotel. Apparently they only have one, and it's a small one at that."

"What?"

"People here don't travel."

Diakos brought Milbank up to speed on what they had learned since their arrival.

"So having lunch with the chairman means eating on a call with each other?"

"Apparently so. Nobody goes anywhere. The streets are deserted by Arcadia or Earthsea standards. I guess everybody stays home all the time. And look at the size of this chair. It's more of a loveseat. You and I could both sit in it. and it's on motorized wheels so I don't have to get up to move around."

"Remarkable," Milbank said. "Absolutely remarkable. Well, that's one I didn't see coming. Of course, in the late Middle Ages being heavy was considered attractive. It meant the person wasn't starving or diseased."

"Yeah, I understand, but I don't think the possibility of interstellar travel is going to be a big selling point here. They don't even leave home. I'm going to push the gourmet imported foods angle. That sounds like it would be a winner."

RICHARD F. WEYAND

The Playa Deal

The next day, Diakos ordered breakfast from room service. A robot showed up with the tray. The robot laid out his breakfast by the simple expedient of clipping the large tray to a pivoting apparatus on the arm of the chair in front of the display.

"Hi, Fred," Diakos said. "I have a question."

"Actually, my name is George, sir."

"You look just like Fred."

"Yes, sir," George said. "We are the same model."

"Then how does anyone know who is who?"

"Most people do not use our names, sir. Quite unusual."

"So what do they call you?" Diakos asked.

"They don't, sir. What is your question?"

"I have some gifts for the planetary chairman. How do I get them to him?"

"I can take care of that for you, sir," George said.

"All right."

Diakos gave the robot the wooden tea box, the drum-shaped box of cheese, and the foil-wrapped package of coffee. As an afterthought, he included the official document naming him ambassador to Playa.

"I'll see to it, sir."

"Will he have them before our lunch?"

"Yes, sir."

"Excellent. Thank you."

"Of course, sir. Would you like to order lunch now as well?"

"Do I call that in as before?"

"You can do that, sir, or you can just tell me what you'd like. I can make suggestions as well."

"Why don't you just bring me whatever you consider appropriate? It will be both me and my companion, Jeong Minho."

"Of course, sir."

About ten minutes before the meeting with Planetary Chairman Oliver Nieman, George came back and brought dinner for a family of six, arranged on two trays. He connected the trays to the two chairs in front of the display, uncovered the dishes and departed without a word.

"My word," Jeong Minho said. "Are we expecting company?"

"Yes. Rather extraordinary, isn't it?" Diakos asked.

Diakos looked at the time in his heads-up display.

"Well, I guess we should be seated."

They swung the trays out, took their seats, and swung the trays back across their laps. It wasn't long before the display lit up with an incoming call.

Diakos accepted the call and the display lit up in a split screen. The man he recognized as Oliver Nieman was on his left, directly in front of him, with another fellow on his right in front of Jeong. Both were very big men, and sat in large chairs with meal trays in front of them. Both had as large a meal on their trays as Diakos and Jeong had.

"Good day, gentlemen. It is good to meet you, Mr. Ambassador."

"It is good to meet you as well, Mr. Chairman."

"This is my chief of staff, Reginald Field," Nieman said, waving to the other side of the screen.

"Hello, Mr. Field. This is my pilot for the trip here, Jeong

Minho."

"It's Mr. Jeong, isn't it?" Nieman asked. "Family name first?"

"That's correct, Mr. Chairman," Jeong said.

"Hello, Mr. Jeong. Welcome to Playa."

"Thank you, sir."

Nieman nodded.

"Well, let's eat, shall we, Mr. Ambassador?" he asked. "We can get acquainted over lunch, and discuss business later."

"That will work splendidly, Mr. Chairman."

With that, Nieman nodded and began to demolish a whole chicken on the plate before him. He began with a leg, cleaning it off in one move by sticking the whole thing in his mouth and pulling out the central bone.

Diakos tried not to stare as he began work on the substantial fraction of a cow that had been placed before him. It was perhaps eight inches of the whole filet mignon. He might manage to eat a quarter of it.

"You've come from Arcadia, Mr. Ambassador? By our reckoning, that is some six-thousand light-years away."

"Yes, Mr. Chairman, though I was recently Arcadia's ambassador to Earthsea, and have just come from there."

"A mere thirty-two hundred light-years. Mr. Ambassador. Yet still a tremendous journey. How long did that take?"

"Six weeks, Mr. Chairman."

"In that little ship, Mr. Ambassador? And in zero gravity?"

"Yes, Mr. Chairman."

"Remarkable. I'm surprised you could pack enough food for such a lengthy trip, Mr. Ambassador."

"We ate special low-residue foods, Mr. Chairman. It did not take much to sustain us, as we were not moving about at all in that small cockpit."

SILK ROAD

"Even so."

The conversation was continuously interrupted by eating, as Nieman continued to wreak havoc on the bird before him.

"And what do you think of Playa, Mr. Ambassador?"

"I find the robots fascinating, Mr. Chairman."

"Yes. They are a boon to us, Mr. Ambassador. They tend the fields, they tend the animals, they process our food, run our errands, maintain our homes and gardens. We've created abundance for ourselves while eliminating the need for humans to do manual labor."

"I am surprised they are so human in form, Mr. Chairman."

"It is the most efficient form for our use, Mr. Ambassador. All the myriad tools and methods that humans have invented over the millennia are designed for someone of our stature and layout. Robots of the same stature and layout means there is no need to redesign all of human technology for their use."

"Ah. Of course, Mr. Chairman. That makes a lot of sense. Yet four arms?"

"Have you never wished you had an extra pair of hands, Mr. Ambassador, when doing some manual task? To hold both this and that in place, while assembling them with this other? We've found four hands to be the most effective."

Diakos nodded. He actually did get that. An extra pair of hands would make all sorts of things a lot easier to do.

"And you've finally solved the artificial intelligence problem, Mr. Chairman."

"Actually, we haven't, Mr. Ambassador. The robots are all task-oriented. If you don't tell them something to do, they simply sit there. They are not self-dispatching. We have never managed to achieve something like Janice Quant."

Wait. What?

"Janice Quant, Mr. Chairman?"

79

"Yes, Mr. Ambassador. A stunning achievement. Bernd Decker was the da Vinci of computer science."

"I don't understand, Mr. Chairman."

"You are, of course, familiar with Janice Quant, Mr. Ambassador?"

"Yes, Mr. Chairman. The Chairman of the World Authority who directed the colony project."

"More than that, Mr. Ambassador. Janice Quant *was* the colony project. She invented the interstellar displacement technique that made it all possible."

"I thought that Anthony Lake and Donald Shore invented the Lake-Shore Drive."

Nieman chuckled, a deep rumbling sound.

"Artifices, Mr. Ambassador, artifices. And a bit of a joke as well. Janice Quant was a massive artificial intelligence that ran the whole colony project, through thousands of avatars, all with meetings via displays. A massive achievement in parallel processing we have not been able to duplicate."

Diakos felt dizzy. Could Nieman possibly be right? Had no one else ever figured this out? It was certainly the first he had ever heard of it.

Nieman went on.

"Janice Quant picked the names Anthony Lake and David Shore so she could call her interstellar displacement technique the Lake-Shore Drive. Imagine. A computer with a sense of humor, albeit a somewhat rudimentary one.

"As for me, Mr. Ambassador, I'm just as glad that we have not been able to replicate Mr. Decker's accomplishment. Janice Quant took over the Earth's government to drive the colony project to completion, and I quite like being planetary chairman."

"But if Janice Quant was an artificial intelligence, Mr.

Chairman, she should, or at least could, be immortal. Where is she now?"

"Indeed, Mr. Ambassador. That is the fundamental question. We have concluded that she is no more. Perhaps Bernd Decker shut down the machine once the colony project was completed. Perhaps, left without purpose, she shut herself down. It is likely we will never know what became of Janice Quant."

Diakos was just beginning to think through the implications of Nieman's incredible assertion when they finished lunch. Despite a herculean effort, Diakos and Jeong had merely dented the array of food placed before them. Nieman and Field had done much better.

Robots cleared away Nieman's and Field's trays, and Diakos signaled to George to clear his and Jeong's as well. With four hands, George took both trays at once, one above the other.

With the trays gone, Nieman settled down to business.

"So, Mr. Ambassador. What is your mission to Playa?"

"After more than twenty years of work from the initial conceptual breakthrough, Mr. Chairman, Arcadia has managed to build interstellar ships that travel through something we call hyperspace. We can manage about three light-years per hour.

"We have used this technology to travel to the planets whose locations we knew, those before us in the drop-off queue, Earthsea and Amber. And we have concluded a multilateral fair trade agreement among the three planets.

"We also managed to find half a dozen additional colony planets."

"How did you do that, Mr. Ambassador?"

"We sent out probes to listen for the radiation of their power grids, Mr. Chairman. By now, those radiations are almost two hundred and fifty light-years in diameter. With twenty-four probes, we found six colonies, including Playa."

"I see, Mr. Ambassador. Please, continue."

"Yes, Mr. Chairman. So we are now approaching four of the six new colony planets we found."

"You chose Playa as one of the four out of six, Mr. Ambassador?"

"Yes, Mr. Chairman."

"Your mission is to conclude a trade agreement with us as well, then, Mr. Ambassador?"

"No, Mr. Chairman. My goal is to install quantum entanglement radios on Playa, so the principals can negotiate the trade agreement directly."

"Ah, yes. I believe your Mr. Milbank mentioned the QE radios in his video introduction, Mr. Ambassador."

"That's correct, Mr. Chairman."

"I understand you brought these radios with you, Mr. Ambassador?"

"Yes, Mr. Chairman. We brought two large multi-channel radios suitable for planetary interconnect with us. That gives redundant channels to hubs located on Earthsea and Amber. We also have a self-contained radio to the Earthsea hub on our shuttle. That's operational now. I was able to patch through it to Arcadia last night."

"You spoke to Arcadia last night, Mr. Ambassador?"

"Yes, Mr. Chairman. I advised the prime minister we had arrived."

"Six thousand light-years away, in real time. That's remarkable, Mr. Ambassador."

"Yes, Mr. Chairman."

"Were we to conclude a trade deal, Mr. Ambassador, what do you imagine we would trade?"

"That's very interesting, Mr. Chairman. First, an analysis of the colonist records of the planets indicates that most colony planets had a concentration of people in one technical discipline. On Playa, for example, it was cybernetics. On Earthsea, quantum entanglement researchers. On Amber, medical nanotechnology experts. That appears to have been organized by the colony project itself."

"By Janice Quant," Nieman said, nodding. "Yes, I see, Mr. Ambassador. Go on, please."

"In addition, Mr. Chairman, all the planets we have gathered data on have something additional. Something that was brought along by the colonists themselves, that supplements the colony's original stock. Earthsea makes the most astounding cheeses. Amber has varieties of coffee that are truly outstanding, and not in the standard colony supplies. Arcadia has spices and teas, as well as silk.

"My understanding is that Playa has dozens of varieties of mushrooms."

"More like hundreds, Mr. Ambassador. But yes, it is a fascination for some part of our population. I believe there was a mushroom gravy with that beef you had for lunch."

"Yes, Mr. Chairman. It was wonderful."

Nieman nodded.

"I had some of the cheese from Earthsea you sent over before lunch, Mr. Ambassador. It was delightful. As were the tea and coffee, which were served with my lunch."

Wait. He ate Earthsea cheese before that lunch?

"All the planets we have data on so far have something similar, Mr. Chairman. Olympia has distilled spirits, including excellent brandies and cognacs. Aruba has chocolate, of premium varieties of the cocoa tree not available anywhere else. Tahiti has hundreds of apple varieties. Bali has fine wines, from grape vines they brought as cuttings. Terminus has flowers and ornamental plants not in the standard colony stock."

"It seems that together we have an embarrassment of riches, Mr. Ambassador."

"Indeed, Mr. Chairman. Trade between and among the colonies promises to make life better for us all."

Nieman nodded. Diakos painted a compelling picture. But were mushrooms enough?

"As for our contribution, we have mushrooms, but we also have the robots, Mr. Ambassador. Since we had the cybernetics people among the colonies, am I correct to assume you don't have robots? I didn't see any on the video."

"That's correct, Mr. Chairman."

"So while Arcadia has the technical contribution of hyperspace travel that makes all this possible, we also have QE radios, and medical nanotechnology, and now robots in the mix."

"Yes, Mr. Chairman. And from the other colonies, we have anti-aging medical technology, immunology, endocrinology, plant genetics, animal genetics, fusion power. It goes on and on."

"Would your people have an interest in robots, Mr. Ambassador?"

"Yes, Mr. Chairman, for one great need if nothing else."

"And what would that be, Mr. Ambassador?"

"Servicing the big hyperspace liners we are building, Mr. Chairman."

"The big ships I saw in the video, Mr. Ambassador? Those are real, then?"

"Oh, yes, Mr. Chairman. That was not a simulation. But they will always be in space. Robot workers who could maintain and service them in vacuum – rather than humans in space suits – would be a big help."

"I see, Mr. Ambassador. Yes, I can see where that would be a very big help."

Nieman looked down at his hands in his lap for a moment, then looked back up to Diakos.

"Very well, Mr. Ambassador. Let's get these radios you brought along installed, and then I will be able to speak with Prime Minister Milbank, Director Laurent, and President Dufort myself."

"Of course, Mr. Chairman."

"What do you think, Reg?" Nieman asked Field after the meeting had adjourned.

"It sounds very good, sir, that is if it's a truly free-trade arrangement."

"Diakos sent me the text of the actual agreement. Against my expectations, it is exactly that. An agreement for fair and open trade, in very simple terms. Here, let me send it on to you."

Field looked at the agreement in an inset in his display.

"That's it, sir? One page?"

"Yes. That's the entire agreement."

"Some domestic producers will probably complain, sir."

"Of course," Nieman said. "But the cost of interstellar shipping is barrier enough to protect them, I think. And it will open a huge export market for us."

Field nodded.

"Besides, Reg, I want those medical technologies. Our lifestyle is very comfortable, but it is not without its medical implications, and I'm not getting any younger."

"I understand, sir."

It was barely a week later that Ambassador Diakos had a

short meeting with Planetary Chairman Nieman. It was, as always, over the display in Jeong's and Diakos's hotel room.

"Well, Mr. Ambassador. I wanted to thank you for making the trip all the way out here, and wish you a good journey home."

"Are you dismissing me as Arcadia's ambassador to Playa, Mr. Chairman?"

"No, Mr. Ambassador. Anything but. You've done a splendid job, and we have had a most productive relationship so far. I am looking forward to continuing it."

"Then I don't understand, Mr. Chairman."

"How have we communicated, Mr. Ambassador?"

"Via display, Mr. Chairman."

"Correct, Mr. Ambassador. With the QE radios operational now, can you not do the same from Arcadia? While in transit, for that matter? How would it change our relationship?"

"Ah. I see, Mr. Chairman. We can continue as we are."

"Yes, Mr. Ambassador. I very much appreciate you bringing us the QE radios, but there is no benefit at this point in you remaining here. Why should you not be comfortable at home?"

"That's very considerate, Mr. Chairman."

Nieman waved it away.

"And I have something for you to take with you, Mr. Ambassador. A container of mushrooms – our finest varieties – as reciprocal gifts for Arcadia, Earthsea, and Amber."

"I'll be happy to see them delivered, Mr. Chairman."

"Excellent. And I have one more little surprise, Mr. Ambassador. My gift to you personally."

"That's not necessary, Mr. Chairman."

"Nonsense, Mr. Ambassador. I very much appreciate your efforts to put this trade agreement together. My personal gift to you will be delivered to the shuttle before your departure."

SILK ROAD

The shuttle had been turned, including being fueled, refilled with fresh water, and thoroughly cleaned. The containers containing the multi-channel radios for Playa had been removed and installed in a building at the shuttleport. The container with gifts to Planetary Director Nieman had been reloaded with Nieman's reciprocal gifts to Milbank, Laurent, and Dufort.

They were all ready to leave, but there was no sign of any gift from Nieman to Diakos. Diakos shrugged and entered the shuttle cockpit.

Sitting in one of the back seats was a robot.

"Good day, sir. My name is Bob."

RICHARD F. WEYAND

Arrival On Tahiti

"Tahiti Air Traffic Control, this is hyperspace shuttle Hyper-3, inbound from colony planet Arcadia. Estimating arrival in twenty-two hours. Request instructions. Over."

"Roger, Hyper-3. Maintain profile. Radio when two hours out for landing clearance."

"Did that guy say what I thought he said?"

"Yeah."

"So what did you do?"

"Remember that part in the ATC training manual where it said if an alien spaceship comes on your screens and asks for landing instructions, what do you do?"

"Yeah. 'Give him a landing clearance within the parameters of existing traffic.' But that was a joke."

"It's not anymore."

"No shit."

Tyler Massey knocked once on the door of the president's office then opened it.

"Sir, we just got a message from Tahiti Air Traffic Control that they received an incoming arrival announcement of a ship from Arcadia."

"Arcadia? That's a colony planet, isn't it?" asked Henry Wang, the President of Tahiti.

"Yes, sir."

"A ship?"

"They call themselves hyperspace shuttle Hyper-3, sir."

"Well, well, well. Someone has finally done it. Created an interstellar drive."

"Apparently so, sir."

"Make sure the prime minister knows. I would be interested in his take on all this."

"I'm sure he knows, sir. Is he not in authority over this matter?"

"No, Tyler. Do not forget that the Constitution of Tahiti establishes foreign policy as the province of the head of state."

"But we've never had need of a foreign policy, sir."

"Yes, and that situation has now abruptly come to an end."

Massey's eyes grew wide.

Wang called Prime Minister Jacob Keller half an hour later.

"Hi, Jake."

"Hi, Hank. What's going on?"

"I wanted your input on what I should do with regard to this hyperspace shuttle that has come calling."

"What *you* should do?"

"Of course. Foreign policy is the sole discretion of the presidency under the Constitution."

"Hank, the presidency has been a purely ceremonial role for over a century."

"Yes, that's correct. Until now. But I wanted to get your input before I contacted this shuttle."

"Hank –"

"Do not fight me on this, Jake. I'll fight back, and I'll win. You have parliamentary elections coming up, whereas I'm in mid-term. Now let's just abide by the Constitution, shall we? I won't act without your input – that's why I'm calling – but I will by God act. And I can make it stick."

Keller had always had a good relationship with Wang, and

had never seen him so assertive. He held up his hands in a warding-off gesture.

"All right, Hank. All right. No reason to get pushy about it. I was going to contact them and see if they had some sort of background information for us. Whether this is an exploration mission or a diplomatic mission, they ought to have some materials along."

"That's a good idea, Jake. I'll contact them and ask them. And whatever materials they share with me, I'll copy them to you and then we can talk about them. We good with that?"

"Yes, Hank. I'm good with that."

"All right, Jake. I'll let you know."

"Would he really do that, sir? Cause a stink?" asked Frank Janko, Keller's chief of staff.

"Yes, he would," Keller said. "Don't ever underestimate Henry Wang. He didn't get to be president without having lots of friends in high places. And he can sidestep most of the heavy lifting that goes along with day-to-day political wrangling, which means his popularity is always going to be much higher than mine. If he wants to cause trouble, he can."

"But, sir, the presidency has always been a man without a job, in some sense."

"Yes, Frank, but that's not how it was designed. The writers of the Constitution always thought there would be contact with other human planets. They just thought it would come about much sooner than it did. Earth had interstellar transport, after all. The president was to be outwardly focused, and the prime minister inwardly focused. It just didn't ever happen."

"Until now," Janko said.

"Until now, which Hank just reminded me of."

Keller sighed before continuing.

"And we're going to have to play it his way. For now, at least."

"And then, sir?"

"We'll see how it goes, Frank. If we don't win the parliamentary elections, I'm out of a job, and I'm not willing to risk that by taking on Henry Wang right now."

Keller drummed his fingers on his desk for several seconds.

"And, when you get right down to it, he's right, you know."

"They're requesting the transmission of any background materials we may have."

"Transmit the video and its attachments, Mr. Belsky," JuPing said.

"Yes, Ma'am. Transmitting."

"Did you get a chance to view that video, Jake?"

"Yes, Hank. Thanks for sending it on. And I've taken a look through the attachments as well. One question for you. You're Chinese, ethnically at least. What do zufu and zumu mean?"

"My Wang ancestors were in North America for generations, so I looked it up to be sure I remembered correctly. But zufu means 'honored grandfather' and zumu means 'honored grandmother.'"

"The biographies implied those were important positions."

"Yes, Jake. Family is very important among Chinese. This Chen family is a financial and political powerhouse on Arcadia. They're running the entire hyperspace effort for the government there. If they've stuck with Chinese tradition, the zufu and zumu of the family would be the decision makers for the whole clan."

"Wouldn't it be important for them to stay on Arcadia then, Hank?"

"If they were the current leaders, yes. But they stepped down over a decade ago."

"Some sort of scandal?"

Wang chuckled.

"That's what a politician would think, Hank. But it's simpler than that. They stepped down due to age."

"But they're only in their nineties, Jake."

"Two things there, Jake. Arcadia's year is about four percent longer than a solar year. Paul Chen-Jasic – Chen Zufu – is a hundred years old, and his wife Chen JuPing – Chen Zumu – is ninety-seven.

"The second thing is that Arcadia did not have anti-senescence scientists among their original colonists like we did. They probably don't have juvie."

Keller's eyes grew wide. If they didn't have the juvenalis drugs, that would be their natural age.

"Yeah. That would make a difference. A big difference. But why is someone that old going into hyperspace?"

"One guess, Jake. Arcadia would have the listings of the various colonies' technical specialties as well."

"They're here for treatment, Hank?"

"Not exclusively, I wouldn't think. But at least partially."

Keller nodded.

"So what are you going to do?"

"Welcome them. See what they want. Get them treatment as long as they're here."

"That all makes sense to me, Hank."

"All right, Jake. And when we get down to substantive discussions, I'll include you."

"Thanks, Hank. I appreciate it."

"No problem, Jake. You have elections coming up, as I noted before, and, push come to shove, I prefer you – a lot – to the other guy."

"Hyperspace shuttle Hyper-3 to Tahiti Air Traffic Control."
"Go ahead, Hyper-3."
"Tahiti Control, I am declaring a medical emergency. One of my passengers is in medical distress. Over."
"Roger, Hyper-3. What is your loadout? Over."
"Tahiti Control, I am four-wide and one high. Over."
"Roger, Hyper-3. If you can divert, you are cleared directly to shuttlepad H-1. Over."
Igor Belsky cast a nervous glance over his shoulder, and entered H-1 into the computer.
"Roger, Tahiti Control. Diverting to shuttlepad H-1. Over."
"Roger, Hyper-3. We will advise to have medical personnel standing by. Tahiti Control out."

The flight computer modified Hyper-3's glide path to overfly the shuttleport and head out over downtown Papeete. Hyper-3 came down on the roof of the hospital building, one of the four original buildings delivered with the colony. It was now one of a complex of buildings stretching off to the northwest in the capital's downtown.

Medical personnel raced up the mobile stairway as it approached the shuttle. Belsky opened the cockpit hatch, and got out. He had rotated the front seats around to give them more room.

Paul Chen-Jasic was laid out on the back seats, Chen JuPing and Stuart Reynolds attending him. She looked up at the first EMT into the shuttle.

"Apparent myocardial infarction. First onset under one hour ago. Powdered aspirin and nitroglycerin three times so far."

"Excellent. We're going to move him directly to the cardiac

ER unit. Age?"

"One hundred solar years," JuPing said.

The EMT gave her a quick surprised glance, and then they were moving. The stair had a motorized stretcher on one handrail. They maneuvered the semi-conscious Paul into it, then ran him to the bottom, moved the stretcher to a gurney, and wheeled him into the elevator bay, JuPing and Stuart Reynolds following along behind.

Igor Belsky stood on the platform at the top of the stairs watching the grim procession pass into the hospital's rooftop elevator bay, unsure of what to do next. He was called back into the cockpit by the radio.

"Tahiti Control to Hyper-3. Come in, please."

Belsky re-entered the cockpit, swung the pilot seat around to face forward and took the pilot's position.

"Hyper-3 here, Tahiti Control. Over."

"Hyper-3, we need you to clear that emergency shuttlepad. Advise when ready for transfer to shuttleport. Over."

Belsky had left one engine idling, so he had on-board power to restart the others.

"Hyper-3 ready for transfer to shuttleport now, Tahiti Control. Over."

"Roger, Hyper-3. You are cleared for transfer to shuttlepad one-four at altitude one thousand feet. Over."

"Transfer to shuttlepad one-four. One thousand feet. In progress. Hyper-3 out."

Belsky had been restarting engines while he was talking. The stairs had receded when he shut the shuttle's cockpit door. With all engines nominal, he throttled up and the shuttle rose from the hospital roof.

SILK ROAD

Hyper-3 came down on shuttlepad 14 at the Papeete Capital Shuttleport. A mobile stairway approached the shuttle, sitting twelve feet off the ground on its payload of four containers. A man walked up the stairs.

Igor Belsky opened the cockpit hatch and stepped out through the door to the platform.

"Hello, I'm Tyler Massey. I'm President Henry Wang's aide."

"Igor Belsky. Pilot of Hyper-3. Good to meet you."

Massey craned his head to look into the shuttle cockpit.

"I was under the impression there were passengers," he said.

"I had to drop all my passengers at the hospital. Medical emergency."

"Is everyone OK?" Massey asked.

"I don't know. They wheeled the ambassador into the hospital. His wife and caregiver are with him."

"Oh, my. I do hope he'll be OK."

Massey looked helpless for a moment.

"Um, I'm supposed to take everyone to meet the president."

"I'll be happy to go talk with him if I can have a chance at a quick shower and change first."

Massey looked Belsky up and down. His six-week growth of beard, the fleece lounger and booties – and his six-week accumulation of body odor was becoming more than apparent.

"Yes. Yes, perhaps that's best. This way, Mr. Belsky."

Belsky grabbed his small bag and followed Massey down the stairs.

In less than an hour, fate had whittled down the four-man Arcadian delegation to Tahiti to one middle-aged shuttle pilot.

Tyler Massey showed Igor Belsky into the president's office

in the administrative building in downtown Papeete.

"Ah. Mr. Belsky," Henry Wang said, coming around from behind his desk. "It's good to meet you."

"It's good to meet you, too, Mr. President."

Wang waved to a side seating arrangement in his office.

"Please, have a seat, Mr. Belsky."

"Thank you, Mr. President."

They all sat, including Massey, who sat off to one side.

"The first thing I have to tell you is that I have made inquiries at the hospital. Mr. Chen-Jasic is doing well. They have stabilized him, and he is resting comfortably pending further treatment. Madam Chen JuPing has also been admitted for treatment."

"That's excellent news, Mr. President."

Wang nodded.

"Indeed, Mr. Belsky. But it leaves us with something of a quandary. It is clearly not yet time to engage the ambassadors with business discussions, so it is up to you and I to continue as best we can."

"Well, I'm just a shuttle pilot, but I'll do the best I can."

"Excellent, Mr. Belsky. Excellent. So I have some questions, and have made some surmises, and let's start with those."

"Of course, Mr. President."

"Clearly Arcadia has developed interstellar travel, and you know something about that."

"Yes, sir."

"How does it work, generally speaking, Mr. Belsky?"

"We get a certain distance away from the planet, Mr. President, then we transfer into hyperspace. We travel in hyperspace until we get to within a certain distance from our destination, then we drop out of hyperspace and make the last bit of the journey in normal space."

"And how fast do you go in hyperspace, Mr. Belsky?"

"It's about three light-years per hour, Mr. President."

"And how far did you come to get here, Mr. Belsky?"

"Thirty-one hundred light-years from Arcadia to Earthsea, Mr. President, and then another thirty-two hundred light-years or so from Earthsea to here."

"So you did it in two trips, Mr. Belsky?"

"Yes, Mr. President. We stayed over on Earthsea for three weeks so Mr. Chen-Jasic and Madam Chen could have recovery time."

"Recovery time, Mr. Belsky?"

"Yes, Mr. President. Each leg was about six weeks, and it was all in zero gravity."

"I see."

Wang thought back over the video that they had sent him from the shuttle on its way to the planet.

"So your trip in this shuttle was to set up a relationship between Arcadia and Tahiti, Mr. Belsky?"

"Well, that and to bring QE radios along, Mr. President."

"You have QE radios with you, Mr. Belsky?"

"Yes, Mr. President. The shuttle itself has an onboard QE radio system for itself back to the network hub on Earthsea, and we brought two multi-channel planetary radios that are paired with QE radios on the network hub on Earthsea and the secondary network hub on Arcadia."

"So you can contact Earthsea from here in real time with the shuttle's radio, Mr. Belsky?"

"Yes, Mr. President. With any of the planets, actually. They're all linked already, and I can contact anyone on Earthsea, Arcadia, or Amber. I've also had training on how to hook up and start the big planetary radios, which would give Tahiti redundant interconnectivity to the other colonies."

Wang sat back and thought about that. With the radios in place, he could contact the Arcadian prime minister directly, and not disturb the Arcadian ambassadors during their hospitalization. Belsky, though, was clearly fatigued, both from the trip and, Wang surmised, from the adrenaline crash from his handling of the recent emergency.

"Can you patch me through to Arcadia now, Mr. Belsky? From here, using the shuttle's QE radio?"

"Yes, Mr. President. I can do that."

"Please do that, Mr. Belsky, and then I can have Mr. Massey here show you to a hotel room where you can get dinner and some sleep."

"I would appreciate that a great deal, Mr. President."

SILK ROAD

The Tahiti Deal

It was about eight o'clock in the evening when Rob Milbank got an interstellar call. He normally diverted most of his calls to a switchboard when out of the office. He had a white list of friends and important politicians who could reach him at home. But he had also white-listed interstellar calls for the time being.

Milbank excused himself from his evening at home with his wife, Julia Whitcomb, and headed into his home office to take the call.

Milbank found himself facing someone he didn't know. His caller had a typical colonial mixed ancestry, and was a mix of European and Oriental backgrounds. Perhaps some African ancestry as well. He was perhaps forty-five years old.

For his part, Wang found himself facing a big man in some sort of loudly patterned wrap-around garment and naked from the waist up. He looked to Wang to be about a hundred years old. Correcting for the lack of juvenalis drugs on Arcadia, he figured Milbank to be approaching seventy.

"Rob Milbank here."

"Good evening, Mr. Prime Minister. I am Henry Wang, President of Tahiti. I'm sorry to disturb you at home."

"No, no, Mr. President. That's fine. How are you? I take it our mission to Tahiti has arrived."

"Yes, Mr. Prime Minister. Not without incident, however. After the second six-week leg of their journey in zero gravity, Ambassador Paul Chen-Jasic suffered a heart attack with the reimposition of gravity on deceleration into Tahiti's atmosphere."

"How is he doing, Mr. President? Has he survived?"

"Yes, Mr. Prime Minister. Your Mr. Belsky handled the situation admirably, declaring a medical emergency, and we diverted the incoming shuttle directly to the shuttlepad on the roof of the hospital here. Mr. Chen-Jasic has been stabilized, and is resting comfortably pending further treatment. Madam Chen was also admitted to the hospital pending treatment."

"That's very good news, Mr. President. They are among our most prominent citizens."

"Yes, I'm aware, Mr. Prime Minister. However, that leaves us to work out the details of any arrangement between our planets by ourselves, for the moment at least."

Milbank nodded.

"Very well, Mr. President. Do you have any questions for me?"

"Yes, Mr. Prime Minister. I suppose the first one is obvious. What is your mission here on Tahiti?"

"We hope to implement a free trade agreement between Tahiti and the other four planets who have signed up, on an equal basis for each."

"Four planets, Mr. Prime Minister? That would be Arcadia, Earthsea, Amber, and whom?"

"Playa, Mr. President. Our mission to Playa left Earthsea a couple of weeks before our mission to Tahiti, and Playa has already joined the agreement."

"I see, Mr. Prime Minister. May I have a copy of the text of this agreement?"

"Of course, Mr. President. Transmitting now."

"Thank you, Mr. Prime Minister. I will review the agreement with our people here and we will discuss it in a later call."

"Of course, Mr. President."

SILK ROAD

"My next question is about the QE radios, Mr. Prime Minister. On what basis are those being provided?"

"Earthsea is donating QE radio service for the period of our negotiations, Mr. President. If you join the free trade agreement, QE radio service is one of the things Earthsea has to trade. Pricing is yet to be determined, as is pricing for freight shipping on the hyperspace liners we will be bringing into service late this year."

"How will those prices be determined, Mr. Prime Minister?"

"In a competitive free market, Mr. President."

"Those things would be relatively price inelastic, though, Mr. Prime Minister. They are both monopoly positions."

Milbank nodded. Wang was clearly not a lightweight, though he looked young to be a planetary president.

"Yes, Mr. President. But all the colony planets have similar monopoly positions in some technology product or service. Amber has medical nanotechnology that successfully treats some very difficult diseases. Playa makes robots that can perform many manual tasks, freeing up people for more inventive and creative tasks.

"I see, Mr. Prime Minister. And Tahiti would fit in how?"

"How old do you think I am, Mr. President?"

"Without any age-delaying drugs, Mr. Prime Minister? I would say approaching seventy years old."

"And on Tahiti, Mr. President? How old would you guess I was, if I were on Tahiti?"

"More like a hundred years old, Mr. Prime Minister. I myself am seventy years old."

"So you see, Mr. President. We are the same age, yet you clearly have the advantage of me. And Tahiti has just as much of a monopoly, price-inelastic position in that area as Arcadia does in hyperspace shipping or Earthsea has in QE radios."

Wang nodded.

"And the protections, Mr. Prime Minister?"

"The only protections are those of a free market, Mr. President. Each planet agrees to provide their products and services at the same price to their foreign trade as to their domestic customers. And each planet agrees to impose no taxes or customs on their imports that they do not impose on their domestic sales."

"That's it, Mr. Prime Minister?"

"That's it, Mr. President. Clean and simple."

"There will be those who try to cheat, Mr. Prime Minister."

"Of course, Mr. President. But in the end, they will only hurt themselves."

Wang nodded.

"Very well, Mr. Prime Minister. Mr. Belsky tells me he is prepared to hook up and activate the QE radios they have brought along, and we will get that under way. We will also review this agreement and get back to you."

"Thank you, Mr. President. Our mission to Tahiti brought other gifts as well, and Mr. Belsky can deliver those to you with our compliments."

"Thank you, Mr. President. And thank you for your time this evening. We will keep you informed as to the health condition of Mr. Chen-Jasic and Madam Chen."

"Thank you, Mr. President. I appreciate that."

"Good evening, Mr. Prime Minister."

"Good evening Mr. President. Thank you for calling."

Chen JuPing woke up in the hospital bed in Papeete. Yesterday had been a nightmare. After all these years, she had almost lost Paul. Her sleep had been disturbed by nightmares in which they had not made it in time. In which he had been

SILK ROAD

DOA at the hospital, or he had slipped away before they could stabilize him.

JuPing looked over to the other bed in the room. He looked a lot better this morning, and was sleeping soundly. She sighed.

So close.

But they had made it. Made it to the one hospital in all of human space that could treat the deadly medical condition from which they both suffered.

Old age.

Stuart Reynolds padded into the room. He had a little pot of tea and a tea set on a tray. He poured a cup for her and set it on her lap table. Walnut. What had been a gift for the president of Tahiti, she guessed.

It was like a taste of home, and relaxed her immensely.

She looked her gratitude to Reynolds, and he nodded.

"What do you think of the agreement, Jake?"

"I can't believe how simple it is, Hank. I expected pages and pages of legalese and mumbo-jumbo. You know, protections for this and exemptions for that. There's none of that."

"No. None at all."

They were sitting in Henry Wang's office enjoying a cup of the coffee that had been part of the gifts to Tahiti that arrived with the shuttle. Belsky had seen them unloaded when he dismounted the shuttle to free up the planetary radios for installation. That should get done today.

Meeting in Wang's office was symbolic of Keller's acquiescence of the foreign policy role to Wang.

"Of course, you know people will try to cheat," Keller said.

"Yes, Jake, but the agreement does deal with that."

Keller nodded.

"Yes," he said. "Reciprocal sanctions. If you put a ten

percent surcharge on my goods, I can put a ten percent surcharge on yours."

"Which reduces trade to and from that one colony due to the increase in prices. That's pretty simple microeconomics. And reduced trade hurts the colony doing it. Over the long haul, it hurts them a lot."

"I understand, Hank. I think it may even work."

"So you think I should sign it, Jake?"

"Yes. That's my advice. Sign it, and I'll take it to the legislature for approval."

"Will the legislature approve it?"

"Yes. My majority is pretty good at the moment, and I'll push it. I'll pick up a few people on the other side of the aisle, for that matter."

"Then I think we have a deal."

It was about two weeks after their arrival on Tahiti that Henry Wang stopped into the hospital to visit Paul Chen-Jasic and Chen JuPing. They were wearing fleece loungers, and relaxing after their latest treatment.

Stuart Reynolds, ever-present by their side, stood when the president entered the room, but Wang waved him to sit.

"Good day, Mr. President," JuPing said.

"Hello to both of you. It's good to meet you at last. I would have stopped by sooner, but we've both been busy."

JuPing chuckled.

"Yes, Mr. President. I think we present something of a challenge match for your anti-aging people. They haven't dealt with someone our age without your juvi drugs for a long time. They're falling all over themselves to try this or that treatment."

Wang smiled.

"Have they given you any prognosis, Madam Ambassador? Any idea of what is possible?"

"My understanding is that your technology slows the aging process to about fifty percent of what it would normally be after age twenty-five. You look to be in your late forties, Mr. President, so I would guess your actual age to be about seventy."

"Yes, Madam Ambassador. That's correct."

"Now that's with treatment beginning at age twenty-five, Mr. President. For someone like us, for whom the aging has already occurred, they can get perhaps half the benefit, and then hold it to half the rate going forward."

"That's my understanding as well, Madam Ambassador."

"If that's the case, Mr. President, at a hundred years old, they can back us up perhaps nineteen or twenty years. To the early eighties. But it will take us nearly forty years to get to an apparent age of a hundred again."

"After that last treatment, I feel like I'm only ninety again," Paul said, and JuPing and Wang laughed.

"Have they said how long the treatments will take, Madam Ambassador?"

"Perhaps three months, perhaps six. They're in uncharted waters, Mr. President. They just don't know."

Wang nodded.

"Well, then, Madam Ambassador, I think you'll want to send Mr. Belsky back to Arcadia with the shuttle. You can go back home yourself on a hyperliner once passenger traffic starts."

"Send Mr. Belsky home, Mr. President?"

"Yes, Madam Ambassador. One reason I stopped by today was to inform you that your mission was a success. I have signed, and the legislature has approved, the free trade agreement you came to negotiate."

"Those were the easiest negotiations I've ever participated in, Mr. President."

"Mr. Belsky was instrumental in putting me in touch with your prime minister, Madam Ambassador. Mr. Milbank and I had several fruitful conversations. We are the same age, and have much the same viewpoint on many things."

"Rob's a good man."

"Indeed," Wang said. "I've also opened up the QE radio system to public use, Madam Ambassador, so you are free now to call friends back home and tell them how you're doing. I have been assuring people, but they are very worried about you both."

JuPing nodded. She reached across the gap between the beds and took Paul's hand.

"We're fine, Mr. President. But we just made it. To the one place in human space that could treat old age itself."

"I understand from Mr. Milbank that it is by your own hand, Madam Ambassador. If you hadn't been so instrumental in bringing about hyperspace travel, you wouldn't have."

JuPing nodded, and Paul spoke up.

"We were lucky," he said.

"Stuart," JuPing said.

"Yes, ma'am."

"Stuart, you should go back to Arcadia with Mr. Belsky."

"But, ma'am, my place is here. With you."

JuPing shook her head.

"No, Stuart. You're place is on Arcadia. You're a young man, and have a life to live. We are being well cared for here, and will not need a caregiver once we are discharged. You've been very good to us, and we appreciate your service, but it's time for you to move on."

"Well, if you're sure, ma'am,...."

"Yes, Stuart. We're sure. And Mr. Belsky needs some company on the long trip home. First to Earthsea, then on to Arcadia. Twelve weeks total. Even with QE radio, he'll go mad without some company."

"All right, ma'am. Sir. As long as you're sure."

JuPing nodded.

"And we've given you a separation payment, Stuart," Paul said. "Regular payment through your trip back home, and a separation payment in gratitude for your service."

"Thank you, sir."

"Do stay in touch with us, Stuart," JuPing said. "QE radio means we can chat now and again."

"Of course, ma'am."

"Well, Mr. Reynolds. Are you ready to depart for home?" Belsky asked.

"Yes, Mr. Belsky. At your convenience."

Belsky nodded.

"Hyper-3 to Tahiti Air Traffic Control."

"Go ahead, Hyper-3."

"Hyper-3 requesting takeoff and clearance to space. Over."

"Roger Hyper-3. You are cleared for takeoff and departure to space on heading zero niner. Over."

"Roger, Tahiti Control. Cleared for takeoff and departure to space on heading zero niner. Over."

"Good spacing, Hyper-3. Tahiti Control out."

Belsky throttled up the engines and waited for them to spool up. When he had RPMs, he focused the thrust and Hyper-3 and its two pendent containers lifted off shuttlepad 14 of the Papeete Capital Shuttleport.

Once under way, Reynolds had a question.

"I meant to ask you, Igor. What's in the other container?"

Belsky turned to Reynolds and grinned.

"Apples."

Reynolds nodded. The apples on Tahiti were incredible. As was the apple sauce, the apple cider – everything apple.

"Makes sense."

"Oh, but it gets better, Stu."

"Yes?"

"I brought apple pie."

Chen JuPing heard the shuttle pass overhead. She turned to look out the east-facing window of their hospital room and watched it go.

"Good spacing," she whispered.

She turned her attention back to her dessert.

They really did make the best apple pie here.

SILK ROAD

Intermezzo On Arcadia

It was a busy time for Rob Milbank.

First, Loukas Diakos completed the deal with Playa. They had actually sent him back to Arcadia, maintaining he could be the liaison to them as well here as there. Since they didn't hold meetings in person, Milbank couldn't argue the point. Hyper-4 was en route back to Earthsea, then home to Arcadia.

Then Paul Chen-Jasic had a heart attack while arriving at Tahiti. Unexpected that, and it could have thrown a wrench in the works. But Henry Wang really wanted a deal – perhaps for his own political reasons as much as anything else – and Milbank and Wang had put it together in several QE radio meetings. Paul and JuPing were staying on Tahiti for treatment, but Hyper-3 was now on the way back to Earthsea, then would come home to Arcadia.

Meanwhile, Sasha Ivanov, Peter Dunhill, and a bunch more QE radios had arrived on Arcadia from Earthsea aboard Hyper-1. After some time to accustom themselves to gravity once again, Ivanov and Dunhill had set out in Hyper-1 and Hyper-2 for Olympia and Aruba, respectively. They should arrive in about a month.

The six deployment vehicles were en route to Earthsea, where they would each be equipped with three self-contained QE radios by the returning Hyper-3 and Hyper-4 shuttles. They would drop those radios in orbit around colony planets that had not yet been contacted.

In Arcadia, there were now three big hyperspace liners orbiting Arcadia – *Star Runner*, *Star Tripper*, and *Star Gazer*. *Star*

Dreamer was almost done at the Beacon shipyards, and *Star Rover* and *Star Singer* were under construction. When *Star Dreamer* was pushed off, construction would begin on *Star Dancer*.

The design group was also working on the plans for the interstellar freight transfer stations for Arcadia and Aruba. Milbank hadn't seen the plans yet, but he heard they were going well.

Wayne Porter would not have offered the same assessment. He had the actual freight transfer portions done – unloading ships, sorting and staging containers, loading ships – but he was having a heck of a time with crew quarters. He had asked Chen JieMin to stop by.

There was a knock on the door frame. Porter turned around from the display, and it was JieMin.

"Hi, JieMin. Come in. Have a seat."

"Thanks, Wayne."

JieMin took a seat on a side chair and looked into the display. Porter was working in wireframe view. He triggered a rendering, and the station came to life in simulation.

"So what have you got, Wayne?"

"OK, so here's the unloading and loading mechanism."

A skeletal device with an extended arm approached a ship docked to the station. The arm passed down the length of the cargo portion of the ship. A close-up view showed cam-driven rails being extended out from the sides of the arm to engage and latch to the upper tier of containers all along the forward freight cavity of the giant ship.

The latches of the bottom containers to the ship released, and then the cam-driven rails pulled back against the arm, clearing a gap all the way around the thousands of containers in the freight cavity of the ship. The skeletal device pulled back from the ship, extracting all the nearly four thousand containers in one pull. It looked like a gigantic ear of corn, the outer containers being the kernels.

"Wow. Nice," JieMin said.

"Watch."

The skeletal device now rotated around, and brought another skeletal arm into view. This one was covered with containers as well. It inserted the huge mass of containers – over three hundred feet in diameter and five hundred feet long – into the freight cavity of the ship. The same cam-actuated rails pushed the containers out just a bit – a few feet – against the latches of the ship and the containers latched into place.

The latches on the skeletal arm's rails then released, the rails retracted, and the skeletal device backed out and away from the ship. The ship released from the station and was on its way.

The view switched to an overhead view, and JieMin could see there were six such arms radiating out from the skeletal device, which he now realized was a gigantic bridgework structure. Cargo shuttles were taking containers off one arm – the one that had just been pulled out of the ship – and putting containers on other arms – the ones being loaded for ships to arrive.

"That's really nice, Wayne. They build up the cargo independent of the ship, and then just shove the whole thing in at once."

"Yeah, it really speeds up the time the ship is on the station. And we can just keep extending this design."

The view pulled back, and JieMin saw six such bridgework structures along a long central spine.

"So what's the problem, Wayne? You sounded desperate."

"I just can't figure out where the people live. The

maintenance people. The shuttle pilots who shuffle the containers around. I can't have people up there for extended periods because of zero gravity, unless of course I build in gravity somehow.

"I can't spin the whole station, though. The structure is too large, the stresses would tear it apart. If I spin part of it, I have to design a whole new habitat. That would be all one-off parts and that sort of thing. Or else I have to cycle people down to the planet every several weeks.

"I just can't figure it out."

JieMin looked back at the drawing. There was something there. Something....

"Wayne, look at it a second. What do you see?"

"The model of the transfer station."

"What else?"

"The shuttles working the containers."

"What else?"

Porter stared at the drawing.

"Well, the ships, of course. The hyperspace liners."

"Aren't those designed to spin while in hyperspace?"

"Well, sure, but–"

And then Porter saw it.

"I can just use the ship design! Don't put hyperspace drives in it, don't include the freight rails and some other minor stuff. Just permanently mount it on the station – like with a track around the front edge – and spin it in place. A few airlocks, and I'm there. And the design is done already. That's brilliant, JieMin."

"And it already has all the connections on the back side, away from the station, for food and water and reactor connections. The whole thing."

"Of course. You would probably have to slow it to a stop to

service those things, and counter the angular momentum transfer to the station with some thrusters, which you could do if you went slow enough, and then re-spin it...."

JieMin chuckled. Porter was staring into the display and muttering to himself by this point. JieMin put his hand on Porter's shoulder.

"I'll leave you to it, Wayne."

"Thanks, JieMin. That's a great idea."

"You would have gotten there, Wayne. And it was your ship design that made it possible in the first place."

A week later, Mikhail Borovsky, the project manager for the design group, reported to Karl Huenemann, the head of the design group, that the interstellar freight transfer station design was complete.

"How the hell can it be complete?" Huenemann asked. "Even Wayne can't go from no clue on the staff quarters to complete in a week."

"Wait until you see this. You're gonna shit."

Borovsky brought up the design on the display in Huenemann's office. They watched through the loading and unloading of containers.

"Yeah, I seen all this before," Huenemann said. "All good stuff, but what about staff quarters?"

"You're looking at it, you're just not seeing it. What's different about that one ship?"

"It's spinning on its axis. The rest are just sitting there."

Comprehension dawned.

"Wait. That's the staff quarters? Of course! That's all designed already. And it's made for spinning and shit. Oh, Mikhail, that's fuckin' brilliant."

"Told ya."

"It's too bad we're not the military or something. I could give that boy a medal. We need to give him a bonus or somethin'."

"Well, you know he's consulting with JieMin. Some of this is probably from him."

"Yeah, but it's Porter's responsibility, and I know JieMin wouldn't push himself on him. If he's consulting JieMin to get his job done, that's a plus, not a minus."

Borovsky nodded.

"How about Senior Staff Designer, then? One level promotion."

"Yeah, let's do that."

Huenemann looked back at the simulation on the display.

"That's fuckin' brilliant."

Denise Bonheur noticed her husband Wayne Porter's mood the moment he walked in the door. He had been getting increasingly moody and distracted until a week or so ago. then had brightened up. He had gotten happier and happier over the last week, but tonight he was positively ebullient.

"Wayne, what's going on? What's happened?" she asked.

"Last week, I had a breakthrough in that design I've been banging my head against. Chen JieMin came over and looked at it with me. He had a great idea, and I ran with it."

"And?"

"So I finished the design and turned it in this morning. And this afternoon Karl Huenemann himself came over to congratulate me on it."

"Wow."

"It gets better. He promoted me to Senior Staff Designer. That's along with a twenty percent increase in pay. He said he didn't want me leaving to go off and design toaster ovens or something."

"Denise laughed.

"Congratulations, Wayne."

"So, you think your sister could watch the kids tonight?"

"Probably. Where we going?"

"Chen's, of course."

"Oh, my. Let me call her quick and make sure it's OK."

It was, and they went up to Fifteenth Street for dinner.

It was wonderful.

It was also Chen JieMin's and ChaoLi's weekly night out. Chen JieMin noticed Wayne Porter and his wife eating at the Chen family restaurant that night. He pointed them out to ChaoLi.

"That's Wayne Porter, Karl's top designer. I heard he turned in the design for the interstellar freight transfer station today, and Karl Huenemann promoted him."

"Is that the design Karl sent us this afternoon, with the staff quarters based on the ship design, spinning in place on the station."

"Yes. That's the one."

"You helped him with that, didn't you? You mentioned it to me last week."

"Yes, but he would have gotten there. He's very talented."

They left before Porter and his wife, and ChaoLi made it a point to stop by their table. When Porter saw her, he jumped to his feet.

"I don't want to interrupt, Mr. Porter, but I had to stop and tell you how impressed I am with the design you submitted today. It's brilliant. Congratulations."

ChaoLi shook his hand.

"Th-thank you, Chen ChaoLi," Porter said.

"You're very welcome, Mr. Porter. Keep up the good work."

ChaoLi nodded to Bonheur and left.

Wayne sat down as in a dream.

"Chen ChaoLi," Bonheur said. "She's the head of Jixing Trading."

"Yes. One of the most powerful people on Arcadia."

"Wow," Bonheur said. "That's something."

She turned to Porter and took his hands.

"What do you know? I'm married to a big shot."

At the Beacon shipyard, *Star Dreamer*, her hull finished, was pushed off by the three factories that had built her. She fired her thrusters briefly to back away from the asteroid of her birth. When she had gained enough separation, *Star Dreamer* would space for Arcadia.

The three factories that had made her, though, did not immediately start in on *Star Dancer*. Instead they each started building a clone of themselves. When those factories were finished, they would find another asteroid and start building the beams and girders and machinery of the Arcadia interstellar freight station.

The last cargo shuttle pulled out of the front freight cavity of *Star Runner*. They had filled her with containers of supplies for the Beacon shipyard. As the stack on each of her sixteen interior sides was finished, *Star Runner* pulled them further into her freight cavity. The stacks were made in her first container position on each facet of her interior, to reduce the amount of tight maneuvering the shuttles had to do, then pulled deeper into the ship.

When all six stacks of forty containers each was loaded on each of her sixteen interior facets, *Star Runner* headed for the

SILK ROAD

hyperspace limit with thirty-six hundred containers of supplies. She was now QE-radio equipped, and could be remotely piloted, even in hyperspace.

Arriving at the Beacon shipyard, *Star Runner* unloaded herself by the simple expedient of pushing each facet of two hundred and forty containers out the front of the ship. They drifted off toward the waiting factories, who would dispatch small container tugs to nudge them into position.

The days of delivering containers eight or twelve at a time with hyperspace shuttles were over, and the Beacon shipyard kicked into high gear.

Star Runner completed her space trials without any crew.

Sasha Ivanov and Peter Dunhill had conversations and briefings with Rob Milbank while they were on their way to their destinations of Olympia and Aruba.

"I think the big takeaway from these negotiations is that they get easier as we go along. The more planets that sign up, the more compelling membership is. Who wouldn't want anti-aging drugs from Tahiti, or robots from Playa, for example?

"So each one we sign gets easier. The first couple were kind of dicey at times. If Director Laurent and President Dufort weren't so positive, it could have gotten difficult. But these last two were easy."

"I'm not sure we can count on that, though, Rob," Ivanov said. "I don't want to get complacent."

"Agreed, Sasha. But the other thing I just learned is that Planetary Director Oliver Nieman on Playa has given Loukas the coordinates of the colonies they know about. We're nailing them down now, but we think we can find Samoa, Hawaii, New Earth, Westernesse, Fiji, and Nirvana."

"Good," Ivanov said. "That takes a little pressure off. So the ones we are looking for from Olympia are Endor, Dorado, Tonga, Spring, Numenor, and Atlantis."

"That's right, Sasha."

Milbank turned his attention to Dunhill.

"How about you, Peter?"

"I'm good, Rob. The plans for the interstellar freight station will help a lot, I think. Jerry Perez is looking them over now, but I think it's a splendid design and will help sell the whole thing."

"Excellent. All right, gentlemen. Any questions come up, you can always get a hold of me."

Chen JieMin had the coordinates from Loukas Diakos – the results of the parallax analysis of known stars from the six colony planets dropped off before Playa that they didn't already have locations for. He mapped them in his bubble map of the colony worlds, and fixed their positions.

The unfixed bubbles moved around, maintaining the distances to possible colony locations that were still at least three thousand light-years from any other human planet.

JieMin added in the pre-programmed routes of the six deployment vehicles they had sent out. All of them would be upgraded with QE radios on Earthsea when Hyper-3 and Hyper-4 arrived back from Aruba and Playa, and would leave Earthsea headed for probable colony locations.

JieMin stared into the display a long time, rotating it this way and that. He had locations right now for eight colonies that had not yet been contacted, and where the other nine would likely be was becoming more apparent from his bubble map. He projected routes for each of the six deployment vehicles, each stopping at multiple colonies to drop their QE radios, and sent their first stops on to the operations group.

SILK ROAD

Selecting those routes, though, got JieMin thinking. One of the things his wife ChaoLi would have to come up with is the best least-time route to make her freight runs. It was the traveling salesman problem, a mathematical puzzle which had never been completely solved.

Maybe now was the time.

RICHARD F. WEYAND

Arrival On Olympia

"You realize Olympia is ten weeks in hyperspace, one way," Sasha Ivanov said. "There is clearly another layer of colonies between us and them that we just don't know about."

"Yes, I know, Sasha," Milbank said. "As I said, I do appreciate the effort. But we need the locations of the other colony planets."

Ivanov sighed.

"I hope after ten weeks in zero gravity, I have the muscle tone left to left to be able to walk when I get there."

"It may not hurt to ask for assistance when you arrive."

"That's probably a good idea."

"Just think of it this way," Milbank said. "You'll have plenty of time to read books on the way. And the libraries of Earthsea, Amber, Playa, and Tahiti are now available."

"Read books? I intend to write a book. With that amount of time, I should be able to complete a book en route."

"There's an idea. What's it about?"

"My adventures. I was thinking of calling it 'Ambassador to Alien Worlds.' Or do you think that's too sensationalistic?"

"You and Mr. Moore will be the first people to set foot on four different planets. I don't think that's sensationalistic at all."

"Well, we'll see how it comes out. I need something to do for ten weeks. But I think I'm going to wait for one of the big hyperspace liners to show up to bring me home. We're close enough now, and ten weeks of zero-gravity is not my idea of fun."

"Hyperspace shuttle Hyper-1 to Olympia Air Traffic Control."

"Go ahead, Hyper-1."

"We are inbound from colony planet Arcadia. We estimate arrival in twenty-two hours. Requesting instructions. Over."

There was a pause of several seconds before Olympia ATC answered.

"Roger, Hyper-1. Maintain profile. Call in when two hours out from Olympus City Shuttleport. Over."

"Roger, Olympia Control. Call when two hours out. Hyper-1 out."

Olympia had a tri-partite executive, the politics of which were as convoluted as one might expect. In practice, one of the three nominally equal members of the executive committee was dominant, and, allied with one of the others, could make most decisions.

Of course, the dominant member of the committee was restrained by the ability of the other two members to unite to outvote him. Similarly, one member could find themselves out in the cold if the other two remained united.

The members of the executive committee served staggered nine-year terms, and the politics was further complicated by who was facing election next and who was safe from the electorate for several more years.

Currently Lars Swenson was the dominant player on the executive committee, and it was he who received first notice of the incoming visitors.

"Sir, Olympia Air Traffic Control has received a message from an incoming shuttle claiming to be from the colony planet Arcadia."

Swenson raised an eyebrow.

"Indeed."

"Yes, sir," said William Monroe, the chief of staff for the executive committee. "In the message, they called themselves hyperspace shuttle Hyper-1. They will arrive in about twenty-one hours now."

"Now that is interesting."

Swenson looked up the colonies in his heads-up display. Arcadia was the third colony planet to be dropped off by the interstellar transporter that had planted all twenty-four of the colonies, while Olympia was the twenty-first. The map of the colonies showed Arcadia to lie in a less dense part of the galaxy between the Orion and Sagittarius Arms.

"Yes, sir. What do you want me to do?"

"Let me talk to Olivia and Roger. I'll get back to you."

"Yes, sir."

Olivia Monet was Swenson's natural ally on the executive committee. Roger Steadman had run as an outsider, with big plans to shake things up.

Of course, that was one of the reasons the founders of Olympia's current government, in place now for almost eighty years, had specified an executive committee. It kept government policy from whipsawing back and forth every election, as it had prior.

Steadman was facing reelection in another year and a half. Continuously stymied in his more outlandish ideas by the other two members of the committee throughout his term, he had settled down to a grim fatalism, and would probably not run again.

Swenson had recently won re-election to the executive committee, and, as the one most recently to have been chosen by the electorate, he was considered the senior of the three. Considered to most accurately reflect the current mood of the electorate, he presided as chair when they met.

Nevertheless, something of this magnitude required that the entire committee be involved, in Swenson's opinion, and he requested an immediate meeting of all three members.

As expected, Olivia Monet was first to call in.
"Good morning, Lars."
"Good morning, Olivia."
"Should we wait for Roger, or just start in?"
"Let's wait. I think this is pretty major and we all should be involved."

That got a raised eyebrow from Olivia, but she was content to wait. She continued to work on something out of view in the display.

After several minutes, Roger Steadman joined.
"Yes, Lars. What is it?"
"Good morning to you, too, Roger. Something's come up, and I think we all need to be involved in it."
"Really."
"Yes. Olympia Air Traffic Control received a message about an hour ago from a shuttle coming in from outer space. They claim to be from the colony planet of Arcadia."
"Oh, that's exciting," Monet said.
"Well, it was bound to happen sooner or later," Steadman said.
"I agree with both of you," Swenson said. "The question is, What do we do about it?"
"Do we know anything more than that?" Steadman asked.
"Just that they'll be here about ten tomorrow morning. I guess they have a ways to come yet. Oh, and they call

themselves a hyperspace shuttle, so that gives a clue to how they got here."

"They probably can't turn off their interstellar drive too close to the planet or something, so they have to come in the regular way," Monet said.

Steadman grunted, and Swenson said, "That's my guess."

"We should probably ask for more information," Steadman said. "They should have some advance information for us. Some sort of packet or something. From whoever sent them. I'm assuming they didn't just blunder onto us."

Swenson nodded.

"So we should request more information?" he asked.

"Oh, I would think so," Monet said. "If you get something more, will you call us back, Lars?"

"Of course. I'll probably speak to you again in an hour or so. Keep an eye out for mail from me."

"All right. This is so exciting," Monet said.

"Goodbye," Steadman said.

"They've requested additional information. Time to send the video and attached files?" Moore asked.

"Yes, please transmit them, Justin," Ivanov said.

Ivanov checked the time.

"Two hours. That's a bit long."

It was worrying as well. Ivanov had not been impressed with what he had read in the captured data about their three-man executive committee. It sounded cumbersome.

Their delay in asking for more information seemed to back up the point.

"Have we all viewed their video?" Swenson asked.

"Yes, of course. And I've been reading the attachments,"

SILK ROAD

Monet said.

"Yes, I watched the video," Steadman said.

"My reaction is cautious interest," Swenson said. "If they put together a trade consortium of all the colony planets, that would open up markets for our fusion powerplants, as well as our luxury goods, such as the distilled spirits group."

"We would also get access to the other colonies' products," Monet said. "The medical products, the technology products. I think it's an exciting opportunity."

"Yes," Steadman said. "I'm sure the wealthy will be much better off. Immortal to boot, or next thing to it. But all this will be out of the reach of the common man."

"We don't know that, Roger," Monet said. "There is no pricing yet. But they have to charge the same as they charge to their domestic markets, plus the shipping costs."

"And Arcadia will control the shipping costs," Steadman countered. "They have a monopoly on hyperspace."

"Did you watch the interview with the CEO of this Jixing Trading Company of theirs, Roger?" Monet asked. "She assumes there will be competition in shipping."

"A likely story," Steadman said. "You don't think they're going to cheat on the agreement?"

Swenson sat back and let them pound on each other a bit. With Monet, it was always the upside opportunities, driven by markets and technology. With Steadman, it was always grim possibilities, driven by the nameless, evil 'they'.

Swenson sighed.

At a gap in the current variation of their perennial argument, he got in a question.

"So what is our move at this point?" he asked.

"We should talk to them, clearly," Monet said.

"I want to see this agreement they brag about," Steadman

said.

"All right. So we're agreed that we meet with this ambassador of theirs – Mr. Ivanov – and talk to them about the agreement?"

"Of course," Monet said.

"Yes, but that's all I've agreed to," Steadman said.

"I understand, Roger."

The return to full gravity after ten weeks of zero gravity was as hard on Ivanov as he had expected. Moore seemed less affected, but then he was a decade or more younger. Moore's legs were still pretty rubbery when he opened the shuttle cockpit hatch to greet the man who came up the stairs to welcome them.

"Hello," Moore said.

"Good morning, sir. I am Brian McCabe. I am an aide for William Monroe, who is the chief of staff for the Olympia Executive Committee."

"Good to meet you, Mr. McCabe. My name is Justin Moore, the pilot of this shuttle. Can I ask if we can get some assistance for Ambassador Ivanov? He's having some trouble getting used to being in gravity again after ten weeks of zero-g."

"Of course, sir. Let me call for some help."

It was about ten minutes before two big baggage handlers came over from the terminal complex. They had a wheelchair as well. They brought the wheelchair up the stairs with them.

"Let us help you out, sir," one of the baggage handlers said to Ivanov.

"Thank you very much," Ivanov said. "I'm just very weak against the gravity at the moment."

"I understand, sir."

The two big men helped Ivanov out of the shuttle and into

the wheelchair. Ivanov looked down the stairs with dismay.

"All well and good, but how do we get down?" he asked.

"Just sit still, sir. We have it."

With that, the two men each grabbed a big wheel of the wheelchair in one hand, reached across their bodies with the other to stabilize the wheelchair, and walked down the stairs side by side with Ivanov between them. They placed the chair on the ground at the bottom.

"There you are, sir."

"Why, thank you, gentlemen. You are most kind."

"No problem, sir."

They walked back off to the terminal, and Moore got behind Ivanov and leaned on the assist handles of the wheelchair.

"And now, Mr. McCabe," Ivanov said, "if we could trouble you for someplace we could shower and shave, we would be most grateful."

"Of course, Mr. Ambassador. This way, please."

McCabe led them out to a limousine parked on the other side of the hangar for this shuttlepad. Ivanov balked at the door of the car.

"A shower and a shave, Mr. McCabe?"

"We're taking you directly to your hotel room, Mr. Ambassador. Mr. Swenson – he's on the executive committee, sir – when advised of your fatigue, insisted."

"Ah. Most kind. My thanks to Mr. Swenson, please, Mr. McCabe."

"Of course, sir."

Ivanov ordered a breakfast designed to be kind to his mistreated stomach, but he did order a cognac with it. He then took a shower and changed while waiting for room service.

The breakfast was nicely prepared, and the cognac served

appropriately, in a warm snifter, which was covered for the trip to his room. When he finished breakfast, Ivanov removed the cover from the snifter and inhaled a wonderful bouquet.

A sip was enough to tell him that this was a truly outstanding cognac, yet not the most expensive – by far – on the hotel's menu.

"Perhaps it was worth ten weeks in transit after all," Ivanov said as he toasted the room.

When he finished his cognac, he crawled into bed and slept for ten hours.

Waking near midnight local time, Ivanov ordered a late dinner, complete with a small bottle of a single-malt scotch whiskey. After dinner, he settled down with the delightful beverage and reviewed materials on Olympia for several hours, retiring at his normal bedtime.

When he woke, Ivanov found that he had a mail account on the local system. He checked it and found a mail from Lars Swenson inviting him and Mr. Moore to join the Olympia Executive Committee for lunch. He accepted, then sent a mail to Justin Moore asking him to join him for breakfast.

As his long-underused muscles adapted to the gravity once again, Ivanov was finding it easier to move about. He walked over to the window drapes and opened them to look out on Olympus, the capital of the planet.

Unlike Amber or Bergheim, Olympus was much like Arcadia City, a modern city snuggled into the corner where mountains and the sea bounded a great plain.

Moore showed up and they had a wonderful breakfast out on the balcony, with a sea breeze on a warm day and a view out toward the mountains.

SILK ROAD

The Olympia Deal

"Mr. Ambassador, it's good to meet you," Lars Swenson said as Moore wheeled Ivanov into the private dining room in the administrative building.

"It's good to meet you as well, Mr. Councilor."

"We were concerned about your health after yesterday."

"It is already much relieved by a good night's sleep and the passage of time, Mr. Councilor. I continue to use the wheel chair you most graciously provided so as not to tire quite so quickly."

Ivanov turned to the other Councilors.

"Mr. Ambassador," Olivia Monet said with a nod.

"Hello, Mr. Ambassador," Roger Steadman said.

"And our chief of staff, Mr. Ambassador. Mr. William Monroe."

"Hello to you, Councilors. Mr. Monroe. And allow me to introduce my shuttle pilot and traveling companion, Mr. Justin Moore."

Nods were exchanged all around, and Moore wheeled Ivanov up to the chairless place that was left for him opposite Swenson. Everyone sat down, with Swenson in the middle of his colleagues, and Moore to the right of Ivanov, opposite Steadman.

"Mr. Ambassador," Swenson said, "I propose we eat first, and hold business for over coffee."

"I agree, Mr. Councilor, with the caveat that there is one piece of business we should probably conduct immediately."

Ivanov withdrew his commission from his pocket and

passed it across to Swenson. He glanced at it, then passed it to Monet. She glanced at it and handed it behind Swenson's back to Steadman.

"Very good, Mr. Ambassador," Swenson said. "Duly appointed then, and installed properly as Arcadia's ambassador to Olympia."

"Yes, Mr. Councilor. And that being done, I bring gifts from the three earliest signers of the trade agreement. Tea from Arcadia, cheese from Earthsea, and coffee from Amber."

Ivanov set them on the table before him as he announced them – a wooden presentation box of the Chens' Walnut tea; a gift-wrapped drum-shaped box of Earthsea cheese, and a vacuum-packed, sealed-foil package of Amber coffee. He pushed them across to Swenson, who nodded.

"Thank you, Mr. Ambassador."

Swenson turned to the head waiter standing nearby.

"Franklin, can we work these into lunch in some way?"

"Of course, Mr. Swenson."

The head waiter took the gifts off to the kitchen, while his staff served the soup course.

"Our maps show Arcadia to be some five thousand light-years away, Mr. Ambassador."

"Yes, Mr. Councilor. That is correct."

"And you covered this distance in ten weeks, Mr. Ambassador?"

"Yes, Mr. Councilor. Our means of propulsion in hyperspace travels at about three light-years per hour, which, as fast as that is, makes it a journey of some seventy days."

"Remarkable, Mr. Ambassador. And you were weightless this entire time?"

"Yes, Mr. Councilor. Which has taken a toll on my person, in the form of a weakening of muscles relieved for so long of gravity's burden."

The head waiter returned with a large teapot, and served all six of them.

"Thank you, Franklin," Swenson said.

He lifted his cup to Ivanov and sipped his tea, then looked at the cup in wonder.

"How extraordinary, Mr. Ambassador."

"The Chen family on Arcadia grows wonderful teas, Mr. Councilor."

Monet sipped hers as well, and seemed well pleased. Steadman sipped too, and even his perpetually irritated expression seemed to ease a bit.

"For all that, though, Mr. Councilor," Ivanov said, "Olympia's cognacs are superlative. Even a modest selection from the hotel menu last night would be the superior offering on any of the three worlds I have had occasion to inhabit in the past year."

"Truly, Mr. Ambassador?"

"Oh, yes, Mr. Councilor. And a later sampling of a single-malt Scotch last night confirmed that your expertise with distilled spirits is not confined to the cognacs. Your export market awaits you."

The wait staff exchanged empty soup bowls for entrees. It was a fish dish, served over a rice pilaf, with blanched vegetables and a lemon caper sauce.

"We move perilously close to business, Mr. Ambassador. Let me ask you instead, what is Arcadia like?"

"From what I have seen, it's very similar to Olympia, Mr. Councilor. Our capital is, like yours, nestled against the mountains, with the sea attending, and a great plain stretching off on the other two sides. The climate is similarly welcoming. Why, Mr. Moore and I ate breakfast on the balcony this morning. Very pleasant. And very much like home, for that matter."

"What are the people like on Arcadia, Mr. Ambassador?"

"Young, for the most part, Mr. Councilor. Honest and hardworking. Fun-loving, too. We love parades, and the beach, and street parties. From what I've seen of the data our probe past your planet gathered, we are not so different than Olympia in those respects."

"And the government, Mr. Ambassador?"

"Also like you in one way, Mr. Councilor. We changed our government seventy-five years ago or so. For a different reason, though. Where you put in place an executive committee for stability, we overthrew a budding tyranny. The system we put in place is a parliamentary system, with a prime minister."

"Mr. Milbank."

"Rob Milbank is our current prime minister, yes. Has been for some time now, Mr. Councilor."

The dessert course came out. Apple pie, with cheese wedges, and coffee. The cheese and coffee were the Earthsea and Amber varieties.

"Oh, this is wonderful," Monet said after nibbling on the cheese.

Steadman took a sip of coffee, then a deeper drink. His stolid and somewhat pained expression truly softened at last.

"One thing I can appreciate is a good cup of coffee," he said. "And this is a great cup of coffee, Mr. Ambassador."

He saluted Ivanov with his cup, then held it out to Franklin, the head waiter, for a refill.

"Well, I think we've come to business at last, Mr. Ambassador. So let me ask you. What is your mission? To sign us up for your trade agreement?"

"No, Mr. Councilor, not really."

SILK ROAD

Swenson looked surprised, and Ivanov continued.

"Oh, I certainly wouldn't mind if you signed up for the agreement straight away. I'll send you the text right now, so you can consider it at your leisure.

"But that's not my purpose on this mission. I have two goals really. The first is to install QE radios on Olympia, so that you can have instantaneous communications with the other planets so equipped. Five so far, including Playa and Tahiti. You can discuss the agreement directly with Prime Minister Milbank, or Director Laurent of Earthsea, or President Dufort of Amber."

"You brought these radios with you, Mr. Ambassador? That's what the video said."

"Yes, and traffic over them is free for now while we get everything set up. Eventually, Earthsea will charge for their use. That's one of the products and services they have to trade, Mr. Councilor, like you have your distilled spirits and fusion powerplants. We brought multi-channel planetary QE radios to hook Olympia up into the network."

"And your other purpose, Mr. Ambassador?"

"To learn where six more colony planets are, Mr. Councilor. Endor, Dorado, Tonga, Spring, Numenor, and Atlantis. The rest up through number twenty-one we know."

"So you can hook them up into the network and offer them the trade agreement as well, Mr. Ambassador?"

"Yes, Mr. Councilor. They each have their technology concentration, and I assume they each have their other special interests as well."

"You will reassemble the diaspora, Mr. Ambassador. Bring all the pieces back together."

Ivanov nodded.

"I think of it a bit differently, Mr. Councilor. We are establishing, once again, the Silk Road of antiquity. Each planet remains itself, but all benefit from the specialties of the others."

Swenson nodded.

"We are an executive council, Mr. Ambassador. We must of necessity meet privately to consider your proposals. We will be in touch."

"Thank you, Mr. Councilor."

Ivanov nodded to the others as well.

"Councilor Monet. Councilor Steadman."

When they got back to the hotel, Moore helped Ivanov to his room.

"What will you do now?" Moore asked.

"Meet with Councilor Steadman."

"You mean Councilor Swenson."

"No," Ivanov said. "I will meet with Steadman. An executive council can be carried with a two-to-one vote, but they will try not to do that. I need at least Steadman's acquiescence for a binding decision. And I think I can get that."

"Really? He looked sort of intractable to me."

"Perhaps. Perhaps not."

Ivanov shrugged.

"But that is the way forward."

"Ah, Councilor Steadman. Come in, come in. Thank you for meeting with me."

"Everyone calls me Roger," Steadman said.

"And you must call me Sasha. Please," Ivanov said, gesturing into the living room of his hotel suite.

"You met with Swenson and Monet already?"

"No, Roger. I wanted to meet with you."

The doors onto the balcony were open, and Ivanov led Steadman in that direction.

"I thought we might have coffee on the balcony."

"That would be fine."

Ivanov's personal cubic had been delivered from the shuttle during the day, and Ivanov had taken full advantage. He had a burr coffee grinder, a chemical flask, filters, and a heating pitcher, all set out on the table.

"Some setup, Sasha."

"In my personal cubic, brought from Amber. I hand-ground the beans an hour ago, so they could properly bruise before brewing."

Sasha fussed the coffee before serving them both. Steadman sipped the coffee, then sat back with a sigh.

"I thought the coffee at lunch outstanding, Sasha, but this, this is superlative."

"Amber's finest whole-bean coffee, medium roast, hand-ground, allowed to bruise, and brewed at precisely the right temperature. Details make a difference, Roger."

Steadman nodded and sipped again. He closed his eyes as he savored it.

"Truly wonderful. And you're right, Sasha. Details make a difference. Such as with this trade agreement of yours."

Ivanov simply nodded.

"People are going to cheat," Steadman said.

"Of course, Roger. But it won't avail them."

"Why not?"

"Because then other people will raise barriers to them, too. We'll end up with a weird sort of mish-mash, of barriers of different height between different planets, all across human space."

"And this is OK with you, Sasha?"

"Of course not. But it's the best we can do, Roger. The world is imperfect. Human beings are imperfect. But we'll do the best we can, and it will work out. Not as good as it could work out, perhaps. But better than being without such an agreement."

"So we do as good as we can, and what we get is what we get, Sasha? Do I detect some Russian fatalism there?"

"Yes, Roger. I cannot escape the emotional baggage of my forebears. But it's true, as well."

"Huh."

Steadman sipped his coffee, then paused with the cup below his nose as he appreciated the aroma. Finally he lowered his cup.

"This whole scheme is just a way for the rich to make more money, Sasha."

"Of course."

"And you're OK with that?"

"Yes. Because in a free-market system, the only way for the rich to make more money is for the middle class to willingly trade them money for goods and services. They have to offer value, or no more money. In any other system, the rich can just take the money, without providing value."

"You believe that, Sasha?"

"Yes, Roger, I do. As long as the consumer has a choice, he can vote with his wallet. You, rich man, don't get my money. I would rather buy this other thing from this other rich man over here. In such a system, the rich have to compete with each other for the consumer's money."

"And the rich get richer."

"The rich always get richer, Roger. Let's make them work for it."

Ivanov raised a conspiratorial eyebrow to Steadman.

"Hmm," Steadman said, and sipped his coffee.

Lars Swenson was not looking forward to this morning's

meeting of the executive committee. The one item of discussion was how to proceed with the Arcadia mission and the issues it raised.

Swenson expected Roger Steadman to be a pain in the ass. But on this, he was prepared to vote him down and proceed on a two-to-one vote if he had to. Then again, Monet might not be willing to do that on something this important.

Swenson just didn't know.

Everyone was on time for once.

"Good morning, Lars," Monet said when she joined the call.

"Good morning, Olivia."

"Hello, everybody," Steadman said when he joined seconds later.

"Hello, Roger."

Swenson took a deep breath. Well, here goes.

"All right, let's get started," he said. "Our topic today is the visitors from Arcadia. What do we want to do? Roger, why don't you start?"

"Very well. I think we should do this whole thing. The radios. Tell them where the other colonies are. Sign the trade agreement. The whole shebang."

Monet and Swenson stared at him.

"What?" Steadman asked, looking back and forth between them.

"That's not what I expected, Roger," Monet said.

"Oh, I have my misgivings," Steadman said. "And I don't think it's all going to be a bed of roses. Or rather, it will be a bed of roses. There'll be thorns. But we're probably better off with it than without it. And if it turns out we're not, we give them our regrets and pull out of it. But I'm not willing not to give it a try."

Swenson looked to Monet.

"Agreed," she said.

"I am also agreed," Swenson said. "I also have my misgivings, which may not be the same as yours, Roger. But if we don't join, we can't possibly know. If we do, we can assess as we go along."

Steadman nodded.

"Exactly my point," he said.

Monet nodded.

"I'm excited about it," she said.

"Very well, then," Swenson said. "We're decided."

"Hello, Sasha. How are things on Olympia?" Rob Milbank asked.

"Good, Rob. Excellent, in fact. We have the QE radios hooked up. And they've given me the coordinates of the other six colony planets they know about."

"Excellent. Great job, Sasha."

"What's more, they've signed the free-trade agreement."

Milbank stared for a moment.

"Really? I worried about that executive council of theirs. How did you get unanimity there, or did they split?"

"Nope. Unanimous. Three to zero. I wined and dined the troublemaker. Actually, I made him a cup of coffee."

"Well, however you did it, that's tremendous news. And the more colonies that join, the easier it gets to sign them up."

Ivanov nodded.

"And wait until you get a taste of their cognac, Rob."

"That good?"

"No. Better. Much better."

SILK ROAD

Arrival In Aruba

Aruba was also five-thousand light-years from Arcadia. Peter Dunhill's trip was directly across the Orion Arm, however, whereas Sasha Ivanov's trip to Olympia was diagonally into and along the Orion Arm from Arcadia's position between the Orion Arm and the Sagittarius Arm.

Five thousand light-years made for a long trip either way, but the much younger Dunhill was not so debilitated by ten weeks in zero-g as Sasha Ivanov was. Pilot Gavin McKay and Jixing Trading representative Jerry Perez also fared pretty well on the trip.

"Hyperspace shuttle Hyper-2 to Aruba Air Traffic Control."

"Go ahead, Hyper-2."

"We are inbound from colony planet Arcadia. We estimate arrival in twenty-two hours. Requesting instructions. Over."

"Roger, Hyper-2. Maintain profile. Call in when two hours out from Barcelona Shuttleport. Over."

"Roger, Aruba Control. Call when two hours out. Hyper-2 out."

"Did you just give landing clearance to some guy from another planet?"

"No. I told him to call me for clearance when he's two hours out."

"Now what do we do?"

"When in doubt, notify higher authority. Not my problem."

"What do you mean, not your problem?"

"It's not. Our job is to have people land and takeoff safely. Who it is and why they're here is above our pay grade. Once they're on the ground, we're done."

There was a knock on Aruba Prime Minister Mildred Plakson's office door and her chief of staff walked in.

"Madam Prime Minister," Sanjay Patel said, "something has come up."

"Lovely. Now what?"

"Aruba just received a request for clearance for a shuttle from Arcadia, ma'am. That's another colony planet."

"Excuse me?"

"Yes, ma'am. They identified themselves as hyperspace shuttle Hyper-2, inbound from Arcadia. They'll arrive tomorrow."

Plakson sat back in her chair. Now that was interesting. Hyperspace, eh? There'd been speculation among the science types for centuries about such a thing, and now here it was. Someone had figured it out and was using it to get around.

Plakson pulled up a colony planet map in her heads-up display. Aruba was the eighteenth drop-off, and Arcadia was third. Interestingly, they were both colonies in the 'gaps' – the less dense volume of stars between arms of the galaxy.

Plakson had long noted Aruba's strategic location. They were a natural bridge from the Orion Arm, where the Earth was, to the Perseus Arm. Arcadia was similarly situated between the Orion Arm and the Sagittarius Arm. They were natural centers for shipping between colony planets.

If, of course, anyone ever figured out how to get around at interstellar distances.

But now, apparently, someone had.

It came at an interesting time. Parliamentary elections were coming up, and Plakson's party was in the middle of a nasty dogfight with the minority. They were pushing hard on the notion that there wasn't anything the government couldn't do, no service it couldn't provide, if only the government had more enlightened leadership.

And of course it would all be free.

It was hard to argue with free, and most Arubans knew better, but the minority was making inroads.

How could Plakson spin this in the run-up to the elections?

She needed more information.

"See if you can get more information, Sanjay. Anything they have on who they are, how they got here, and what they're up to."

"Yes, ma'am."

"Request for more information just came in," McKay said.

"Send them the video, Gavin," Dunhill said. "And the attachments."

"OK, Peter. Transmitting."

"Did you watch the video, Sanjay?"

"Yes, ma'am. I'm working my way through the attachments now."

"So they have six planets signed up to this trade agreement of theirs. All six of those they've managed to contact so far. That's pretty impressive."

"Yes, ma'am. We haven't seen the trade agreement yet, however."

"No. They say it's a free-trade agreement, without any set-asides or exceptions."

"I'm not sure how true that is, ma'am. It doesn't seem likely. Surely every planet would have some reservations about such an arrangement."

Plakson nodded. Patel was one of the most savvy political operators she had ever met. He was too hard-edged to be a popular politician, but she had grabbed him for her staff early in her career, and he was a big part of why she was where she was.

"What do the attachments look like, Sanjay? I haven't gotten very far there yet."

"There is a map of all the colony planets through the twenty-first drop-off, Olympia. It rather puts point to what you once told me of Aruba's strategic position, ma'am."

Plakson nodded, and Patel went on.

"There is a list of what they call the technical concentration of each colony. Apparently, colony headquarters concentrated colonists of certain specialties on specific planets."

"What's our specialty?"

"We didn't have one, ma'am. Neither did Arcadia or Numenor."

"The bridge planets. The ones in the gaps."

"Yes, ma'am. There is also a recorded message from each of the planetary leaders. In addition to the main video by Arcadia Prime Minister Rob Milbank, there are also videos from Earthsea Director Valerie Laurent, Amber President Jean Dufort, Tahiti President Henry Wang, Playa Planetary Chairman Oliver Nieman, and Olympia Councilor Lars Swenson."

"Councilor? That's a new one on me."

"Olympia has a three-member executive council, ma'am. As the councilor most recently elected or re-elected, Lars Swenson is apparently considered slightly senior among equals."

"Closest to the electorate."

"Yes, ma'am."

SILK ROAD

"What else is in there, Sanjay?"

"There's also the video of an interview with Chen ChaoLi, the head of Jixing Trading on Arcadia. She says they intend to provide competitive shipping services among the colony planets. She expects there to be competition for the shipping business on the medium term."

"Not a monopoly, then."

"Apparently not, ma'am."

Plakson nodded.

"What else?"

"Well, in addition to the technical specialties, they have apparently been discovering that each colony planet has some other item or items at which they excel. These were apparently brought along by the colonists themselves, ma'am. For Arcadia, for instance, it's tea and spices. For Earthsea, cheese. For Amber coffee. That sort of thing."

Plakson nodded.

"We may not have a technical specialty, Sanjay, but in addition to our strategic location, we have one other expertise."

Patel nodded as Plakson's eyes lit up.

"Chocolate," she said.

"Premium chocolate has historically been a good export item, ma'am. High value density."

"Start thinking about how this plays for the election, Sanjay. It would be great if we could trap the minority on the wrong side of this issue."

"Yes, ma'am. Which side is the wrong side?"

"I haven't decided yet."

"Yes, ma'am."

"OK, we have communications established with the transponder for shuttlepad twelve," McKay said. "Gonna be an easy one."

"Easy is good," Perez said. "I like easy."

As the shuttle descended, the combination of braking and lift started adding gravity back to the cabin. After ten weeks in zero gravity, being subjected to two and three gravities on their descent was brutal.

But their velocity gradually came down, and the gravity with it. They descended through wispy late afternoon clouds to make a precise landing on shuttlepad twelve of the Barcelona Shuttleport.

"Oh, that was rough," Dunhill said once they were down.

"I thought it was pretty smooth," McKay said.

"It was. The gravities were rough."

"Ah."

McKay looked out the shuttle window.

"Well, it looks like our greeting party is here."

The mobile stairs drove up to the shuttle. Two somber men waited, then one of them mounted the stairs. McKay opened the shuttle cockpit hatch.

"Hi. I'm Gavin McKay."

"I'm Trevor West. I'm on Prime Minister Plakson's security detail. If you would all come with me, please."

"Of course. Just let us get our things together here."

"Yes, sir."

"Are we being arrested?" Perez asked.

"Escorted, I would think," Dunhill said. "If that's Mildred Plakson's security detail, she must have come out here to the shuttleport."

"That makes sense," Perez said.

They gathered their small travel bags and maneuvered themselves with some difficulty out onto the platform.

"Are you all right, sir?" West asked.

SILK ROAD

"We've been ten weeks in zero gravity, Mr. West," Dunhill said. "We're a little wobbly."

"Let me arrange a cart, sir."

"That would be most appreciated, Mr. West."

It was only a couple minutes until an electric cart pulled up to the bottom of the ramp. McKay and Dunhill made their way down the stairs while standing, but the older Perez first sat on the top stair and then went down the stairs one step at a time, like a toddler.

"Better than falling," he said.

They all got into the back seats of the cart, with the security detail in the front. The driver pulled the cart away from the stairs and drove it into the terminal annex that stretched off down the lines of shuttlepads.

They were let off the cart in an inside corridor and ushered into a meeting room. Mildred Plakson and Sanjay Patel waited inside.

Plakson didn't know what to expect, but it certainly wasn't this. Three scruffy, dirty, smelly men, with several months' growth of beard and wearing fleece loungers and booties, hobbled with difficulty to the meeting table. Without further ado, they sat down, nearly collapsing into the chairs.

The youngest one, perhaps in his mid- to late-thirties, spoke first.

"Pardon us, Madam Prime Minister, but we've spent ten weeks with no showers, no shaves, and no gravity to come to see you. I'm afraid we're a little the worse for wear, and being back in a planet's gravity is really affecting us right now.

"My name, by the way, is Peter Dunhill. I am the duly appointed Arcadian ambassador to Aruba."

"I see, Mr. Ambassador. Ten weeks, to go what? Five

thousand light-years?"

"Yes, Madam Prime Minister."

"That is truly remarkable, Mr. Ambassador."

Plakson looked them up and down.

"Perhaps what we should do is put you gentlemen up in a hotel for tonight and take this conversation up over lunch tomorrow."

"That would be most appreciated, Madam Prime Minister."

"Sanjay, can we take them downtown to their hotel? And perhaps we should use a meeting room at the hotel for lunch tomorrow, to limit their need to travel."

"Yes, ma'am."

"I will see you tomorrow, Mr. Ambassador."

With that, Plakson and Patel left with her security detail. The driver of the cart remained.

"If you would come with me, please, gentlemen."

They were driven out to a waiting car, which took them to a hotel in downtown Barcelona.

Dunhill woke in the middle of the night after eight hours of sleep. He found himself laying on the top of the big hotel bed, still unshaven and unshowered, still in his smelly fleece loungers. He had simply collapsed there the night before.

Dunhill got up and went to the bathroom, stripped down, and climbed into the tub. He lay back as it filled with very warm water and sighed. The water itself was a relief, as it buoyed him and mitigated, to some extent, the gravity.

After half an hour in the tub and a shave, Dunhill felt much better. He checked, and the hotel had round-the-clock room service, so he ordered a small snack.

He ate the snack when it came, then checked the time, shrugged, and got into bed. Under the covers this time.

SILK ROAD

Dunhill woke at something like a normal hour, and found he had a mail account on the local system. There was an invitation to lunch with the prime minister in a private banquet room in the hotel.

Dunhill sent a mail to Perez and McKay, inviting them to breakfast with him in his room.

"So what's the plan?" Perez asked Dunhill as they waited for room service to bring their breakfast.

"I will do the normal things like giving them gifts, trying to get the radios installed, giving them the text of the trade agreement. All of that. Then I will try to get you together with their engineers to discuss the construction of the interstellar freight station."

"Do you need anything from me?" McKay asked.

"If I mention you, a sentence or two about the difficulties of loading containers piecemeal in space with shuttles compared to using a freight station would be in order."

"Gotcha. Loading one of those big freighters without would take weeks."

"Exactly. Which should impress upon them how important having the freight station will be to their status as a natural freight transfer hub."

Their food showed up, and they ate heartily. Ten weeks of low-residue food with water had left them with an appreciation for even a mundane breakfast, and the high-end hotel's room service did much better than that.

RICHARD F. WEYAND

The Aruba Deal

"Madam Prime Minister, it's good to see you again."

"It's good to see you again as well, Mr. Ambassador. I must say, you are looking much more rested than yesterday."

"Yes, ma'am. It's difficult for me to get a good night's sleep in zero gravity. And I was remiss yesterday in introducing my companions. Mr. Gerardo Perez is the representative to Aruba for Jixing Trading Company, and Mr. Gavin McKay is our pilot."

"It's good to see you again, gentlemen. And this is my chief of staff, Sanjay Patel."

There were hellos and handshakes all around, and then they all settled into their seats at the table.

"Before anything else, Madam Prime Minister, allow me to present my credentials."

Dunhill passed the document naming him the duly appointed and confirmed ambassador to Aruba to Pakson.

"Thank you, Mr. Ambassador."

"I also have gifts for you from your counterparts on Arcadia, Earthsea, and Amber."

As he named each, Dunhill produced a wooden presentation box of the Chens' Walnut tea, a gift-wrapped drum-shaped box of Earthsea cheese, and a vacuum-packed, sealed-foil package of Amber coffee. He pushed them across the table to Plakson.

"Why, thank you, Mr. Ambassador. How thoughtful of them."

She turned to the head waiter standing nearby. He was an employee of the hotel, but the Prime Minister was the Prime

SILK ROAD

Minister.

"Could you please see to it these are served with our luncheon?" Plakson asked.

"Of course, madam."

He handed them off to an assistant and remained.

"I think business can wait until after lunch, Mr. Ambassador. Is that OK with you?"

"Of course, Madam Prime Minister."

Plakson turned to the head waiter and simply nodded. Wait staff brought in the salad course, accompanied by bread and spreads. The conversation continued between mouthfuls.

"So Arcadia discovered hyperspace, Mr. Ambassador?"

"Yes, Madam Prime Minister. We have been working on first the theoretical framework and then the actual hardware for over twenty years. Mr. Perez had a hand in constructing the hardware."

"I supervised the construction of the vessel we arrived in, ma'am," Perez said.

"And for five thousand light-years, it took ten weeks, Mr. Ambassador?"

"Yes, Madam Prime Minister. We can manage just a bit over three light-years per hour in hyperspace. That seems extremely fast – and it is – but long distances still take time."

"All in zero gravity, Mr. Ambassador?"

"Yes, Madam Prime Minister. Although we have solved that problem in the vessels we are building now. The vessel itself spins while it travels, providing some semblance of gravity during the voyage. I believe it is planned for about half a gravity. But that vessel is four hundred feet in diameter. Our shuttle is too small to use such a mechanism."

"I see, Mr. Ambassador. I saw the ships in the video you sent us. Very impressive."

"And they're real, Madam Prime Minister. Those video shots were camera images, not a simulation."

The salad plates were whisked away and the entrees appeared. Some sort of beef cut, very tender, with fried potato wedges and a vegetable medley on the side. Served with them was a small plate of cheese wedges for each, as well as a cup of tea.

Plakson nibbled on a wedge of cheese and her eyebrows shot up. She closed her eyes and concentrated on savoring it.

"This cheese, Mr. Ambassador, is wonderful."

"Yes, Madam Prime Minister. I believe Earthsea is gearing up its production capacity now in anticipation of the export market."

Plakson took a sip of the tea.

"And as well for the tea, Mr. Ambassador. I have never been much of a tea drinker, but that may have to change."

"Indeed," Sanjay Patel said. "Very tasty. Both of them."

The conversation died away as they set to the entrees. The beef was very good, even if the sauce was a little bland by Arcadia standards. The Chens' spices would be welcome here as well, Dunhill thought.

When they were finished with the entrees, dessert was served. It was a chocolate layer cake, with chocolate frosting, served with coffee. Dunhill took a bit of the cake and sat stunned. He loved chocolate, but this was extraordinary.

"And now you show us your export specialty, Madam Prime Minister. I was a chocolate lover already, but this cake raises that to a whole new level."

Dunhill sipped his coffee, as did Plakson. He had had Amber coffee once before, on Earthsea, from Sasha Ivanov's private stash. It was Plakson's first time.

"And this coffee is superlative, Mr. Ambassador. Chocolate

cake with coffee may become an Aruba staple if coffee of this quality becomes available."

Dunhill simply nodded and applied his attention to the cake. Plakson chuckled.

Finally, with dessert dishes swept away and coffee cups refilled, Plakson folded her hands on the table before her.

"And so we come to business, Mr. Ambassador. You spent ten weeks in a closet with no gravity to get here. Why? What is your mission?"

"It is actually three-fold, Madam Prime Minister. The first is to install quantum-entanglement radios on your planet, to tie you in to the rest of the colony planet network. This will enable zero-delay communications between you and the other six colony planets we have already so equipped."

"The video said you were bringing these radios with you, Mr. Ambassador."

"Indeed, Madam Prime Minister. They occupy two of the containers on our shuttle. This will allow you to discuss matters with regard to the trade agreement with Arcadia Prime Minister Rob Milbank and your other peers.

"The second goal of my mission here is to introduce you to the trade agreement which has already been signed by those six colony planets, and which we will offer to the other colony planets as we make contact with them. I would expect that actually signing on to the trade agreement, were you to do so, would come after you had a chance to discuss it with your peers."

Plakson nodded. Sensible.

"The third goal of my mission here is to put Mr. Perez in contact with your engineering people, Madam Prime Minister. He has brought along the plans for an interstellar freight station which we would hope to build in Aruba orbit."

Plakson's eyebrows rose.

"You have offered such a station to the other planets as well, Mr. Ambassador?"

"No, Madam Prime Minister. On the medium term, we anticipate two such stations. One here at Aruba and one at Arcadia. I don't know if you're aware, but an examination of a map of colony locations, strung as they are across three arms of the galaxy, reveals that Arcadia and Aruba have unique astrographic advantages."

Plakson nodded.

"Yes, Mr. Ambassador. We sit between the arms, a natural waypoint for arm-to-arm traffic."

"Correct, Madam Prime Minister. And a natural hub for hub-and-spoke freight traffic. Hence a freight transfer station. Such a station makes loading and unloading ships much faster, and demurrage on the ships in port is a major cost in the slim-margins business of interstellar shipping.

"Mr. McKay can speak to the difficulties of loading and unloading ships with shuttles."

Plakson turned to McKay.

"Yes, ma'am," McKay said. "The problem has three aspects. One is that a shuttle can only carry eight or twelve loaded containers at a time. So a limited number of shuttles takes a very long time to transfer several thousand containers to orbit."

"Several thousand containers, Mr. McKay?"

"Yes, ma'am. The hyperspace liners have a capacity of thirty-eight hundred containers."

"I see. Continue, Mr. McKay."

"Yes, ma'am. The second thing is that openings on the ship must be created before outbound containers can be loaded. So one has containers floating around loose in orbit that have to be maneuvered around until one can get the outbound containers loaded, freeing up the shuttle to go chasing after the loose ones.

"And third, one simply can't add more shuttles to speed up the process because they get in each other's way. Only so many shuttles can simultaneously maneuver around the ship without a major incident."

"I see. And you have personal experience of this, Mr. McKay?"

"Yes, ma'am. I've flown hundreds of missions up to the hyperspace liners being outfitted in orbit around Arcadia. Ferrying workers and supplies. A much less intense effort than unloading and loading, and we had to be very careful not to get in each other's way as it was."

"I see. Thank you, Mr. McKay."

McKay nodded and Plakson turned to Sanjay Patel.

"Sanjay?" she asked.

"I think we should begin all these things, ma'am. Installing the radios, looking at the specific wording of the agreement, and reviewing Mr. Perez's plans."

"Agreed," Plakson said, and turned to Dunhill. "All right, Mr. Ambassador. Let's get things under way."

"Of course, Madam Prime Minister. I'm sending you the trade agreement text now."

"What do you think, Sanjay?" Plakson asked.

"The trade agreement is as simple as advertised, ma'am. Which is something of a shock, to be honest."

Plakson nodded.

"And the freight transfer station?"

"That would be a tremendous coup, ma'am. It is the sort of thing we might build ourselves, to attract the freight traffic. But Jixing Trading proposes to build it themselves, with loans from the Arcadia government, and pay the loans off from freight revenue."

"Of course, a lot of the potential expense is being born by their automated construction capability in their shipyard, wherever that is."

"Yes, ma'am. You noticed, of course, that they're being a little cagey about where that is located, but I can make some guesses. In any case, to turn them down on building it here, at their own expense, would be, in my view, a major mistake."

"It will be controlled by them, though, Sanjay."

"It will be controlled by Jixing Trading, ma'am, which will become an interstellar company very quickly. This CEO of theirs – Chen ChaoLi – is pure business, as was clear from her interview."

Plakson nodded. That was her view as well.

"So how do we induce Mr. Stanford and his minority to jump the wrong way on this, Sanjay?"

"Rob Milbank here."

"Hello, Mr. Prime Minister. Aruba Prime Minister Mildred Plakson here."

"Yes, Madam Prime Minister. It's very good to speak with you."

"Let's drop all the titles, Mr. Prime Minister. Mr. Dunhill and I have already done that on this end. Call me Milly."

"And I'm Rob, Milly."

"Very good, Rob. I'm calling to advise you of our status here on Aruba."

"Very well, Milly. Peter said there was some hold-up on your end."

"Not really, Rob. We're in the middle of an election here. I'm sure you appreciate the implications of that."

"I do indeed, Milly. I've been through a few of those

myself."

"Yes, Rob. Peter told me. So we've managed to get the other side to jump the wrong way on this whole interstellar trade agreement. They're bleating the whole nine yards now, about Arcadian imperialism, and foreign control of Aruba's freight station, and squandering our natural advantages of location."

"Oh, they've jumped in with both feet, haven't they?"

"Yes, and I've waited for them to commit hard enough they can't reverse themselves. We're about to begin the counter-offensive now."

Milbank chuckled. He'd played enough of these games over the years to appreciate Plakson's strategy.

"What's your big play, Milly?"

"Two-fold. I'm going to open up the QE radio network to universal access here. Turn the big, scary Them the minority is declaiming into 'those nice people on the other planets.'"

"That should help, Milly."

"I think so, too. And then I'm going to have a big tea, coffee, and cheese party."

"Do you have enough of them for that, Milly?"

"Rob, you sent us a hundred and forty thousand pounds of cheese and almost four thousand cubic feet of both tea and coffee in that one container."

Milbank nodded.

"I had a cheese-tasting party to great effect here last year."

"Yes. My chief of staff saw that in your news archives and pointed it out to me. That's where I got the idea."

"One thing about opening up the network, Milly. Will Arcadia's lack of a nudity taboo be a problem?"

"Not really. On Aruba, all our beaches are clothing optional, and most Arubans do without swimming suits when at the beach. That isn't everywhere, like Arcadia, but it's not shocking. I wonder you haven't had problems with that on other planets, though."

"We actually did, Milly. A little at least. So you think you'll come out on top in the upcoming elections?"

"Yes. I expect to expand my majority, actually. Our private polling indicates the public will break for free trade, not against it."

"Excellent. Please keep me informed."

"I will, Rob. I just wanted to let you know why there might be a little delay. It's tactical, on my end. We're already decided."

Plakson's tea, cheese, and coffee party was a huge success. They closed off traffic in the downtown area of Barcelona and the streets were full of people. They actually ran out of cheese about three hours in, though the coffee and tea flowed throughout the afternoon and into the evening.

Public opinion swung heavily toward free trade, and Terry Stanford's minority party took a drubbing at the polls. Plakson extended her majority in both houses of the parliament, and signed the free trade agreement with Peter Dunhill in a public ceremony that was carried on the news wires.

Peter Dunhill was in heaven becoming an aficionado of Aruba chocolate, and Gerry Perez was up to his elbows planning the interstellar freight station with Aruba's civil engineering community. They had some good ideas about minor enhancements to Wayne Porter's design, which they were enthusiastic about. Perez sent those ideas back to the design group on Arcadia.

When it was time for Hyper-2 to leave for Arcadia, Gavin McKay found himself sharing the cockpit with Aruba's new ambassador to Arcadia and his aide for the ten-week transit.

SILK ROAD

Shifting Gears

The same morning Mildred Plakson called Rob Milbank, Chen ChaoLi asked him for an appointment, and he sent back an invitation to join him for lunch in his private dining room.

"I had good news this morning, ChaoLi," Milbank said. "The prime minister of Aruba told me they were going to approve the trade agreement and the interstellar freight station. It'll just take them a while because they're in the middle of election season over there."

"Which just puts point to my reason for this meeting. Rob, we need to get this show on the road. We're not moving fast enough. We've got seven planets now in this trade agreement, we now know where fourteen of the others are, and I have a total of four ships in outfitting and three more under construction."

Milbank nodded.

"We have a serious ship shortage. And a shuttle shortage. And we're not moving fast enough to catch up."

"What do you suggest, ChaoLi?"

"Triple the number of ships under way. At least. Have all the factories in Beacon duplicate themselves, then have those new ones duplicate themselves. Maybe a couple rounds of that. We desperately need more hulls."

"Can you outfit them that fast, ChaoLi? Can you crew them that fast?"

"No, but I can speed that up, Rob."

"How?"

"First is not to outfit them to quite as high a standard as we are now. Rob, the cabins don't all have to be to the standards of a five-star hotel room. But the second thing is I've changed my original idea as to the first destination of *Star Runner*."

"Where does she go first?"

"Playa."

"Ah. Robots. Of course. For outfitting, or for crew?"

"Both. Much of what needs doing is just the sort of thing they can do."

"Is that going to cause you trouble with your employees, ChaoLi?"

"I don't think so. I'm already hiring pretty much anybody who shows up at our offices with a pulse. The humans will all end up supervisors of a robot work crew."

"So how does that work? They come back here as cargo?"

"And as crew. And as passengers. We'll pack 'em in to the deckheads, Rob. They don't eat and they don't generate biological waste."

"What about the exchange rate?"

"I've been talking to Oliver Nieman about that. For the time being, we'll carry them on the books as robots of type XYZ, in exchange for so many tons of this tea, that tea, the other tea. Same thing with Earthsea cheeses. Once exchange rates and pricing stabilizes, we'll square the books."

"Does that work? Carrying it on the books like that?"

"I've already talked to the Bank of Earthsea about it."

Milbank nodded.

"So you run out to Earthsea because it's on the way, full of tea?"

"And spices. Right."

"And you drop, say half."

"Or two-thirds. Right."

"And fill back up with cheese, and go to Playa, and unload

the rest of the tea and half the cheese."

"Then come back here with cheese, and a can-full of robots. Right."

"So what do you need to make the trip?"

"A skeleton crew, and some of the orbital shuttles."

"A skeleton crew?"

"It'll be a full crew on the way back, Rob."

"Right. Of course. Full of robots."

"Exactly."

"Who can then start fitting out new ships."

"But to a lower standard of luxury," ChaoLi said, nodding.

"So we need to expand the shipyard, generate new hyperspace shuttles, and start rolling out many new hulls."

"One of the first jobs of which will be to bring back here the components needed for the interstellar freight transfer station."

"How are you going to get those big crew quarters here, ChaoLi?"

"Fly them here, then pull the engines as spares. And they'll be full of parts for the trip. The robots can weld it all together, then fly a second one to Aruba."

"Wow."

"Like I said, Rob. We need to get this show on the road."

Chen JieMin had previously worked out the locations of the six new colony locations they had learned from Playa: Samoa, Hawaii, New Earth, Westernesse, Fiji, and Nirvana.

The deployment vehicles had been sent out without knowing where exactly they were going. They had each been diverted in hyperspace onto a course to their destination using one of the self-contained QE radios they were all carrying.

Now JieMin had the other six colony locations from Olympia: Endor, Dorado, Tonga, Spring, Numenor, and

Atlantis.

JieMin added those six new colony locations to his bubble map. The last three unfixed bubbles moved around. There were actually quite a few locations where those might fit, on the edges of the existing clusters.

JieMin worked out new minimum-distance routes through all the remaining colony locations using his nascent routing algorithm.

It would take six months to drop a self-contained QE radio into orbit around all the colony planets, but it was what it was. With every hop being six weeks, and without routes that were all adjacent colonies, it would take what it would take.

JieMin sent the new routes on to John Gannet and Chris Bellamy in the operations group.

They were laying on the surface of the salty water in the lagoon of their secluded cove, arms locked so they wouldn't drift apart from each other. They had brought a picnic lunch, then made love on the beach. In the afterglow, they lay nude in the warm water in the sun.

"ChaoLi."

"Yes, JieMin."

"When you send *Star Runner* to Playa? You're sending a skeleton crew and few or no passengers, right?"

"Right. Maybe a few passengers. Maybe none. Couple of dozen crew, because there's no passengers to take care of."

"So you don't need as many container positions in the rear cargo compartment of the ship, is that right?"

The rear cargo compartment wasn't for cargo at all, but for supplies. It was only one container deep, not six like the forward compartment. It included water, food, and waste storage for the trip, plus the passenger transfer containers.

"Yes, that's right," ChaoLi said. "Lots of empty positions available."

"Fill them all with containers of fitting-out supplies."

"Fitting-out supplies?"

"Sure. The robots can start their work fitting out the ship on the way back from Playa. You can do that with all the ships. As soon as they have enough compartments completed for the skeleton crew, send them out on freight runs and have the robots finish them out during their trips."

"Oh, JieMin, that's brilliant. I can send most of the ships we have out to colonies now."

"Well, once the first batch of robots gets back, anyway. It's probably worth waiting for that."

ChaoLi nodded.

"And Loukas Diakos is on the way home from Playa with one of the robots. Maybe we should ask if we can borrow it, JieMin. Have his robot observe all the fitting out processes on *Star Runner*, then go with her to Playa."

"Well, I assume the robots know how to do painting and carpentry and wood finishing and electrical and things like that. But having him see the way we're applying those to the ship is probably worthwhile."

"I'll give Loukas a call tomorrow."

ChaoLi would have to get project planning and operations to rebuild all their schedules tomorrow.

Everything was going to move up.

"Sure, ChaoLi. You can borrow Bob for six months or a year. I'm not quite sure what to do with him anyway."

"Well, as this all proceeds, I'm sure there will be a six-month lease rate on robots, so Jixing Trading will compensate you. We'll carry it on the books that way for the moment."

"OK. I won't turn it down. I'm just glad it's going to be a help, though."

"Loukas, a question for you. Bob is there, right?"

"Sure."

"Can you ask him if he and the other robots know things like carpentry, hanging drywall, electrical wiring, painting, and wood finishing?"

Loukas turned to Bob, sitting next to him in the rear seats of the shuttle cockpit, and repeated the question.

"Yes, sir. On Playa, houses and office buildings are constructed entirely by robots from plans. These skills are part of one of our software modules, which we swap in and out of our memory at need. As long as we have access to the software library on Playa, it won't be a problem."

Diakos turned his attention back to his heads-up display.

"Yeah, ChaoLi, they know all that stuff. One of their standard modules. Bob says on Playa they build entire houses from the plans by themselves."

"What about flying cargo shuttles and delivering containers to orbit, Loukas?"

Diakos repeated the question to Bob.

"Flying cargo shuttles is no problem, sir. Delivering containers to orbit would be new to us, but if there are complete flight recordings of human pilots performing those operations, I can process those and build the required enhancements to the software module."

Diakos repeated the information to ChaoLi in his heads-up display.

"I'll send you access to the flight recording data, Loukas. We've made extensive recordings as we went along so we could do post-mortem analysis and program the flight computers. Why don't you give Bob access to those and let him

SILK ROAD

build his software enhancement on the way?"

"I'll do that, ChaoLi. We're just sitting here anyway."

"That's great, Loukas. OK, thanks. Have a good rest of the trip."

"Thanks, ChaoLi. See you in a couple-three weeks."

John Gannet just stared at the wall for half an hour after he got off the call with ChaoLi. She had sent out her planning document, then called him about it.

Now he sat stunned.

He shook himself and called in his project manager, Chris Bellamy.

"Hi, John. What's going on?"

Seeing the look on his face, she grew concerned.

"John, what's the matter?"

"ChaoLi just threw the schedule in the trash. We're going to be sending out *Star Runner* in a month."

"What? How can we do that?"

"Skeleton crew. No revenue passengers. She's going to Playa via Earthsea, to pick up several thousand robots."

"Several thousand?"

"Yup. And when they get back here, they're going to be set to outfitting work and ferrying containers."

"John, can we even use that many without them getting in their own way?"

"ChaoLi is also going to double and re-double the size of the Beacon shipyards. They're going to start rolling a hull every month."

"We don't have the shuttles for that, John."

"The eight new orbital cargo shuttles we're getting, Chris?"

"Yeah?"

"Make that forty-eight."

163

"We don't have the pilots."

"The robots are going to be the pilots."

Bellamy stared at him.

"ChaoLi is getting impatient," he said.

"Boy, I'll say."

"So throw everything out and start building a new project schedule. Assume one new hyperspace liner a month, fifty-six orbital shuttles, robot pilots, and robot outfitters. The robots work twenty-five hours a day and have no food or waste requirements."

"That'll kick things into high gear."

"Oh, and robots will go along on the initial flights. They can do the outfitting while the ship is under way."

"Hello, Oliver."

"Hello, ChaoLi," Oliver Nieman said. "It's good to speak with you again."

"And with you. I wanted to see if we could nail down how many robots we could bring back with the *Star Runner* when she arrives in Playa in four months or so."

"When quiescent, they do not take much room, ChaoLi. They can literally stand shoulder to shoulder in the ship's passenger spaces. Fifty will fit in a ten foot by ten foot space without problem."

"That would be thousands of them, Oliver. Do you have that many to spare?"

"We have millions of robots on Playa, ChaoLi. We normally keep an inventory of twenty or thirty thousand new robots on hand. In case something comes up. You know. Like the desire for a new building complex or something."

"So you could send me ten thousand robots in four months, Oliver?"

SILK ROAD

"I could send you twenty thousand today, ChaoLi."

"That's amazing."

Nieman shrugged.

"It's sort of what we do here."

"I see. Well, let's plan on ten thousand, Oliver."

"Very well. And we'll carry them on the books in kind until exchange rates get sorted out, is that right?"

"Yes. I think it's going to take a while for prices to settle out. There are a lot of other colonies still to come on line, and we just don't know where things are going to settle out."

"Understood. But in the meantime, let's not let that keep us from forging ahead, ChaoLi. We need to get this interstellar economy going, to the benefit of all."

"Thank you, Oliver. I agree completely. Let's get it done."

The first eight new orbital shuttles came on line in the nick of time. They spent two weeks loading *Star Runner* with two thousand containers of tea and spices bound for Earthsea and Playa.

Despite the relative inexperience of the new shuttle pilots who had moved up from atmospheric shuttles, there were no accidents. They had each spent the prior month co-piloting with the existing pilots in orbital operations.

While this was under way, *Star Singer* showed up from the Beacon shipyards. *Star Runner*, *Star Tripper*, *Star Gazer*, *Star Dreamer*, *Star Rover* and *Star Singer* were all now in orbit about Arcadia. The open factories in Beacon were now duplicating themselves.

When Hyper-4 showed up in Arcadia space with Jeong Minho, Loukas Diakos, and Bob, ChaoLi had an assignment for them on the way to Arcadia: drop Bob off on *Star Singer*. That completed, they made re-entry and landed at Arcadia City

Shuttleport. Jeong and Diakos went straight home and to bed.

Following instructions, Bob walked about *Star Singer*, inspecting the interior spaces of the big ship. This was the way the ship arrived from the shipyard, with outfitting not even begun yet. He was then shuttled to each hyperspace liner in orbit in turn, inspecting their interior spaces through the process of outfitting, ending up on *Star Runner*.

During the shuttle transfers from one ship to the next, Bob inspected the outside of the ships.

When his inspection tour was completed, he reported to ChaoLi, as he had been instructed to do by Diakos.

"Do you understand the outfitting process now, Bob? What it is we are doing at every stage?" ChaoLi asked.

"Yes, ma'am. It is straightforward construction and detail work, of the type we already know how to do."

"And have you worked out how to fly one of the orbital cargo shuttles? How to do orbital pickup and delivery of containers?"

"Yes, ma'am. The flight data was complete, and I was able to add the appropriate portions to our existing shuttle flight programming."

"So you would be comfortable doing surface-to-orbit and orbit-to-surface delivery?"

"Yes, ma'am."

"Very well, Bob. You should remain on *Star Runner*, and you will go with her to Earthsea and Playa. You will be flying an orbital cargo shuttle taking containers to the surface and back on both stops."

"Yes, ma'am."

"So we're sending four orbital cargo shuttles along with *Star*

Runner?" Bellamy asked.

"Right," Gannet said. "And three pilots."

"Three pilots?"

"The fourth cargo shuttle is going to be flown by the one robot we already have."

"OK," Bellamy said.

But she didn't sound sure.

Once loaded, her skeleton crew transferred aboard, and the three shuttle pilots camped out in mostly completed cabins, *Star Runner* accelerated forward in her orbit, leaving her companions behind. It took two days for the massive ship to reach the hyperspace limit.

Then her crew turned on her hyperspace field generator, and *Star Runner* disappeared from normal space. She made her turn in hyperspace, and started for Earthsea.

The crew was running her hyperspace field generator in screw-drive mode, and the counter-torque started the big ship spinning. As she spun faster, the internal apparent gravity gradually came up to one-half g. The captain switched the hyperspace drive to ripple-drive mode.

Star Runner had entered hyperspace for the trip to Earthsea on Thursday, October 23, 2369, two months ahead of ChaoLi's most hopeful estimate.

Then again, *Star Runner*'s interior spaces were not yet complete. She had dozens of containers of outfitting supplies in her aft containers, though. The containers that were accessible during the journey. With short staffing and no passengers – without the need to carry a full complement of food and waste containers – there were plenty of container positions for supplies.

During the trip, Bob worked on completing *Star Runner*'s

outfitting. In twelve weeks, even working twenty-four hours a day, he would not finish the work by the time they reached Playa.

With ten thousand robots on the way back, however, they would probably finish the work in a day or two. The biggest issue would be not getting in each other's way.

Finishing *Star Runner* would be satisfying. Bob liked to work, and he liked finishing a project.

It was good to be useful.

After six weeks in hyperspace, *Star Runner* appeared in the Earthsea system and made her way toward the planet, using her thrusters to brake the big ship all the way.

Blazoned along her bows was her name, and under it, two Chinese characters:

Star Runner
吉星

Ji Xing.
Lucky Star.

SILK ROAD

Ensuring The Future

Jessica Chen-Jasic's display in her tea room had become her window onto the wider world beyond her gardens. She increasingly communicated from here rather than from her desk.

In one such call, she spoke to Chen JuPing on Tahiti.

"Hello, JuPing. You are looking well."

"I'm feeling very well, Jessica. My apparent physical age is going down with the treatments here."

"When do they say those will be completed?"

"Another month or two. I would be happy to be done with them. I would like to go back home. Back to the mountains."

"How is Paul doing?"

"Also very well. His heart is strengthening as well."

"All this is good news, JuPing, and has relevance to me as well."

JuPing nodded in the display.

"Yes. You and Paul are almost eighty now, Jessica. They could take perhaps fourteen or fifteen years off your apparent age, to sixty-five or so. You would then have seventy years before you were a normal hundred years old."

Jessica nodded.

"That was the direction of my thinking, JuPing. But I think David Bolton and Chen YongLin should go to Tahiti first. Slow down their aging first, before they become Chen Zufu and Chen Zumu. They will not be able to travel during that period, as the Chen should be here. Once MinChao and I retire, we can go."

JuPing nodded.

"Do not wait too long, Jessica. You're aging now at twice the rate you need to, and only half that difference can be clawed back. That said, you are probably correct on the best course."

"Unless you would wish to step back into the leadership, JuPing?"

JuPing shook her head.

"No, Jessica. I was happy finally to set such responsibilities aside. I am pleased to be able to consult from time to time, but the leadership role belongs to someone younger. There is something you might do, however."

"Yes, JuPing?"

"Encourage JieMin and ChaoLi to come here. They would not get much younger, but they would age much more slowly going forward. They can conduct business from here as well as there."

Jessica nodded.

"That would allow them to play an active role in the family business for a much longer time."

"It would preserve what has been a valuable resource for the family well into the future. See to it, Jessica. Perhaps they can come with David and YongLin, on the ship that takes Paul and me home."

"I will take care of it, JuPing."

"I spoke to JuPing this morning, MinChao."

"How are she and Paul doing, Jessica?"

"Very well. Their age is being reduced to an apparent eighty years old. They will have forty more years before they reach one hundred again."

"Amazing."

"Yes, and it brings up an issue we need to address. I would

do the same, you and I, but we must transfer leadership to David and YongLin first. The Chen belong here."

"That means David and YongLin should go first, Jessica."

"That is correct. They go, they come back, and we retire. Perhaps on the one hundred and twenty-fifth anniversary. Then we go. On Tahiti, they can reverse us back to perhaps sixty-five, and we then have seventy years to an apparent age of one hundred."

MinChao nodded.

"And without the responsibilities of leadership."

"That would be welcome at this point. And I think JieMin and ChaoLi should go with David and YongLin."

"She will resist that. She will think she must stay here."

"Yes. I may need you to help me with that, MinChao."

MinChao nodded.

"I will put in a word once you have hit her resistance."

ChaoLi continued to report to her superiors periodically. She met with Chen Zufu and Chen Zumu every two weeks. They usually met in Chen Zumu's tea room. These meetings were usually routine.

The meeting ChaoLi had with MinChao and Jessica the week after *Star Runner* left for Earthsea and Playa most definitely was not.

"I noted the departure of *Star Runner*, ChaoLi."

"Yes, Chen Zumu. She will stop at Earthsea on the way to Playa, where she will pick up ten thousand robots so we can outfit ships faster."

"And the Beacon Shipyard is now gearing up for faster production, as you mentioned last time?"

"Yes, Chen Zumu. We will soon have a dozen hulls under construction at once. We may speed it up further in the future, but I want to take it a step at a time. As it is, we are speeding up production four-fold with this one move."

Jessica nodded.

"The robots are a critical step, then," MinChao said.

"Yes, Chen Zufu. Without them, we simply cannot outfit ships fast enough. With them, outfitting will be at least six times faster, plus they can finish outfitting ships while under way. The passenger spaces take the most work, and passenger traffic will likely build up slowly."

"Six times, ChaoLi?"

"Yes, Chen Zufu. They work twenty-five hours a day, plus they do not need food service, which takes additional manpower and shuttle services, to bring up food and remove waste containers for emptying."

"They do not need time to, I don't know, charge up or something, ChaoLi?"

"They use fast-charge batteries, Chen Zufu. It takes about five minutes for a twelve-hour charge."

MinChao nodded.

"I see," he said.

"The early ships will be able to handle passengers, however?" Jessica asked.

"Yes, Chen Zumu, just not at their full capacity. But we do not need to push their full capacity right away. I expect passenger traffic to grow slowly. Freight traffic will be as large as we can carry from the very start."

"I see," Jessica said. "Well, I have to say, this is all going very well. Using robots from Playa for outfitting and piloting work was a splendid idea."

"JieMin's idea, Chen Zumu."

Jessica nodded.

"But that ability to carry passengers has brought some long-simmering decisions to a head, ChaoLi. I need to bring you up to date on those."

"Of course, Chen Zumu."

"MinChao and I will retire next year, ChaoLi, at the one hundred twenty-fifth anniversary of the colony. David Bolton and Chen YongLin will become Chen Zufu and Chen Zumu."

ChaoLi nodded. As expected.

"Yes, Chen Zumu."

"At that point, MinChao and I will go to Tahiti for anti-aging treatments. In the meantime, the Chen belong here."

"I understand, Chen Zumu."

"Similarly, David and YongLin cannot go to Tahiti after becoming Chen Zufu and Chen Zumu, so they must go before we retire."

"That makes sense to me, Chen Zumu."

"You and JieMin will go with them, ChaoLi."

ChaoLi's mouth opened, but no words came out. She shut it. How could she explain that she couldn't possibly go to Tahiti now, with everything going on?

"I cannot possibly go now, Chen Zumu. There is too much going on."

"You expect things to slow down, ChaoLi, with ships coming off the line four times faster, and with QE radios being delivered to another fourteen colonies in the next several months?"

"No, Chen Zumu, of course not, but how can I possibly go now?"

"You can conduct business all the way there and back via QE radio, ChaoLi. How much of your business do you do now on your display rather than in in-person meetings?"

ChaoLi was thinking furiously, running through scenarios in her mind. This couldn't work.

"Consider, ChaoLi," Jessica said. "You are coming up on forty years old. You are actually forty-two in solar years, due to the mismatch in calendars. On Tahiti, they can set back your apparent age to thirty-eight, and you would then have a hundred and twenty-four years until you turned the apparent age of a hundred. You would live to a hundred and sixty."

"But how do I do everything that needs doing now?"

"To mortgage the future in the name of the present is not a winning strategy, ChaoLi," MinChao said. "We must ensure the future."

"How?" Jessica asked. "You will plan. You will delegate. You will challenge people within your staff to step up. In short, ChaoLi, you will manage."

"You and JieMin will ultimately become Chen Zumu and Chen Zufu, ChaoLi," MinChao said. "To be able to one day handle such responsibility, you must learn the subtleties of power. This is your assignment."

Chen Zufu had spoken. There was no argument. ChaoLi bowed deeply in turn to MinChao and then to Jessica.

"Yes, Chen Zufu. Yes, Chen Zumu."

After the morning meeting with Chen Zufu and Chen Zumu, ChaoLi went downtown. Not to her own office in Four Charter Square, but to JieMin's office in the Chen Hall of Science at 100 North Arcadia Boulevard.

"Hi, what's going on?" JieMin asked.

"JieMin, we need to talk."

ChaoLi closed the door behind her and sat in one of JieMin's side chairs. She related to him the conversation with Chen Zufu and Chen Zumu.

When she completed, JieMin nodded.

"All of this makes sense to me," he said.

SILK ROAD

"But how can I possibly do this, JieMin?"

"As Chen Zumu said. Plan, delegate, challenge your staff, and do it all by display rather than in-person meetings."

JieMin thought about it, and ChaoLi waited.

"You know, you have an advantage in that it's still several weeks off," JieMin said. "Start delegating more. Use the display to attend meetings more. Smooth the transition, so there is less of a jolt when we depart."

"So you're on board with this whole plan?"

"Sure. Why not? Sounds like fun."

"What about Chen Zufu saying you and I will become Chen Zufu and Chen Zumu some day?'

JieMin shrugged.

"I've known or suspected that for a long time, ChaoLi."

ChaoLi felt like she was the only one who hadn't known, at least until recently.

"You have?"

"Of course. Who sat with Chen Zumu and Chen Zufu at the centennial fireworks."

"That was twenty-four years ago. You've thought this that long?"

"Yes. That we were on the short list, at least. I became certain when they made you head of the hyperspace project. That was always very important to both JuPing and Jessica. Regaining the stars."

"So we go to Tahiti?"

"Yes. Of course. Would you defy Chen Zufu?"

"All right. I better start training people to be more independent."

"Much as Chen Zumu did with us."

ChaoLi started at that, but then she nodded.

"Yes. Yes, I see that now."

ChaoLi sighed.

"I'm going to need you to put together a freight route that runs through Tahiti and still makes a profit. Running tea and apples back and forth won't cut it by itself."

"Of course. Probably through Earthsea in one direction and Amber in the other. I'll work on it."

Once *Star Runner* arrived in orbit around Earthsea, it was time to begin transferring containers in both directions. They had a thousand containers of tea and spices to go down to the surface and twelve hundred containers of cheese to come back up. While the tea and spices weren't very heavy, the cheese was.

They unloaded the tea and spices and transported it to the surface a dozen containers at a time, but only brought the cheese up eight containers at a time. This opened up the cargo area a bit as time went on, and made it easier to maneuver in the shuttles.

They didn't unload and reload the forward half of the forward cargo compartment. Instead they emptied eight of the sixteen rails all the way to the back of the compartment, with the ship pushing the stacks of containers forward. They then filled those rails back up, with the ship pulling the stacks back in as they filled. The result was that they could unload either cheese or tea at their next destination, not just the last thing loaded.

After eighty-four trips down and back, the tea was all delivered, but they still had sixty-six more trips to make, deadheading down and bringing cheese up.

The three human pilots managed four round-trips in a twelve-hour day. They could handle that because most of it was being done under complete computer control.

SILK ROAD

Bob ran twenty-four hours, making eight round-trips a day.

Between the four shuttles, they managed to make all one hundred and fifty trips in eight days.

With all her cargo transferred, *Star Runner* set out for the hyperspace limit. With the trip to the planet, the cargo transfer, and the trip back out to the hyperspace limit, she was in normal space-time twelve days before transitioning back into hyperspace and setting off for Playa.

"I don't know about this robot guy."

"Why?"

"The guy works twenty-four hours. He's back to doing outfitting now. Carpentry and shit."

"So?"

"Flies the shuttle twenty-five hours a day when we get here. Works around the clock on outfitting. All the guy does is work."

"I still don't get it. He seems to enjoy working. What's the problem?"

"Is he gonna replace us entirely?"

"Not hardly. You ever talk to him? It's like talking to a flight computer."

"Yeah, but still."

"I don't get you. You might as well be jealous of a washing machine. The question still comes down to who decides. Who decides what he works on? We do."

"Yeah. So far, anyway."

RICHARD F. WEYAND

Colony Flood

While *Star Runner* was still under way to Earthsea, the six deployment vehicles had made their first drops of standalone QE radios into orbit around new colony planets. The radios had patched into the news wires on their respective planets, and forwarded those transmissions to the operations group on Arcadia.

After a month of collecting the news wire feeds, and the operations group and others analyzing the data, briefing materials were prepared for Rob Milbank.

Arcadia Prime Minister Rob Milbank scheduled a meeting with his first allies in the colony trade project, Earthsea Director Valerie Laurent and Amber President Jean Dufort.

"Valerie, Jean, thanks for attending this meeting," Milbank said.

"Sure, Rob. What's going on?" Dufort asked.

"We have standalone QE radios now in orbit around six new colony planets. My people have been analyzing the data we're getting, and I have briefing books on them all."

"Oh, my," Laurent said. "A flood of new colonies."

"Exactly, and there's still eight more to go," Milbank said. "So now what do we do?"

"Can we call them?" Dufort asked.

"Yes," Laurent said, "but it will come in without a local identifier. So it will probably go to a secretary or something."

"Probably best then would be to have a secretary try to get through. You know, 'This is colony planet Arcadia calling. I'm placing a call for Prime Minister Rob Milbank. Could you put me through to President Smith's office, please?'"

Milbank nodded. He hadn't thought of that angle.

"Maybe we can alias the identifier," Laurent said. "Get it to show planet name followed by local name on that planet. That would probably help. I'll look into it."

"Thanks, Valerie," Milbank said. "What I was wondering is, Can we split these up among us? Each take two?"

"Spread out the workload? Sounds good to me," Dufort said.

"Not just that. I also want to make sure Arcadia is just one among equals. No leadership role. Down that road is trouble. We've all hung together so far."

Laurent and Dufort both nodded.

"Sure, Rob," Laurent said. "Makes sense to me. And when the next eight come on-line, we can probably get some of the others involved, too."

Milbank nodded.

"I think that would be a good move, too," he said.

"Let me talk to Bali and Nirvana," Dufort said. "They're both in medical sciences with endocrinology and anti-cancer research. I speak the lingo better."

"Let me talk to Hawaii and Fiji," Laurent said. "Hawaii is big in comm and crypto, so that works."

"Fiji's technical specialty is immunology, though, Valerie."

"Yes, but they also reportedly have excellent beers, Rob. Beer and cheese. Can't beat it."

Milbank laughed.

"OK, so that leaves me with Terminus and Samoa," Milbank said. "We're all agreed, then?"

"It's good with me, Rob," Dufort said.

"Me, too," Laurent said.

"OK. Thanks. I'll send you both the latest videos, including the ones we have now from Aruba, Olympia, Playa, and Tahiti. Let's see where we get."

For all that having a shuttle call in for landing clearance at your shuttleport – a shuttle claiming to be from a different planet – was disorienting, it was more believable than a video call from someone claiming to be on a different planet.

The shuttle, after all, was a physical thing. It was there. There was no denying it. And it clearly wasn't one of yours. The design, the markings, were mute testimony to the truth of what the visitors claimed.

Not so with a video call.

As Rob Milbank found out.

"Mr. President, I have a video meeting request from someone claiming to be the prime minister of the colony planet Arcadia."

"Hmpf. I've told you not to bring me prank calls, Emily."

"I'm not so sure on this one, sir. It doesn't sound like a prank call to me."

Samoan President Jasper Tilden sighed.

"Very well. Pass it through, Emily."

"Yes, Sir."

A man in his late sixties appeared in Tilden's display.

"President Tilden, my name is Rob Milbank. I am the prime minister of the colony planet Arcadia."

"A likely story. You came in on our network, like you're calling from somewhere down the block. I've had prank calls before. This one isn't even very creative."

Milbank didn't know what to say to that at first. He hadn't expected somebody to just plain not believe him. Then he had

SILK ROAD

an idea.

"President Tilden, would you allow me a few moments to prove my claim to you?"

"Sure. Go ahead. This I gotta see."

Milbank got up from his desk and walked out of his offices to the elevator bank, and took the elevator down to street level. He walked out into Charter Square. It was early afternoon, and there were a lot of people about in the square. It was a beautiful day, and about ten percent of them were nude.

Milbank switched his transmission from his own face to a view of the square.

"Does this look like Samoa, Mr. President?"

Tilden looked at the imagery. It could still be faked. How could he tell for sure if it wasn't?

"Stop those three young women there, and ask them what flavor of ice cream they have," Tilden said.

"All right," Milbank said. Then louder: "Excuse me, miss."

Three pretty girls about sixteen, walking through the square eating ice cream, stopped when Milbank addressed them. All three were nude.

"Yes? Oh, Mr. Prime Minister."

"Could you tell me what flavor of ice cream you have?"

"I have chocolate."

"Me, too," a second said. "I love chocolate."

"I have butter pecan, sir," the third said.

"Thank you," Milbank said. "I was just curious."

"Of course, Mr. Prime Minister."

They walked on, and Milbank turned so Tilden could watch them walk away. The view was just as fetching – and just as impossible on Samoa – from this angle.

"Does this look like Samoa to you, Mr. President?"

No, it doesn't, Tilden thought. The buildings were all wrong, for one thing. Samoa had a very different architecture, enabled by its advances in materials science. They had no downtown park like this square his caller was walking around in. And they certainly didn't have people just walking around nude in public. Topless on the beaches, yes, certainly. But not completely nude, and not in the middle of town in any case.

At the same time, it couldn't just be a simulation. He had picked those girls himself, and he had framed the question. Besides which, it was mid-morning in Samoa's capital of Apia, and the morning rain had just moved through. Milbank's square had been dry.

"I'm sorry, Mr. Prime Minister, but your claim was so incredible on its face...."

"I understand, President Tilden."

"And your name again, Mr. Prime Minister?"

"Rob Milbank."

Tilden saw people waving to Milbank, or saying 'Hello, Mr. Prime Minister' or even 'Hi, Rob' as he walked back across the square to the building his office was in.

Milbank waited until he was back in his office, behind his desk, before he switched the view back to himself. He was mopping his forehead.

"Sorry, Mr. President. It's a little warm today to be running around outside in a suit at the height of the day."

"I understand, Mr. Prime Minister, and thank you for offering proof you are who you say you are. It is something of a shock, though."

"Oh, I understand, Mr. Prime Minister. We have been getting in touch with the other human colonies as fast as we can find them and get a quantum entanglement radio out there. We just managed to get a radio to you."

"That's why we can speak in real-time, Mr. Prime Minister?"

SILK ROAD

"Yes. There's a little time lag, because our probe dropped the radio in orbit, but that's why we can speak over thousands of light-years, Mr. President."

Tilden nodded.

"So now what, Mr. Prime Minister?" Tilden asked.

"I have a package of videos and background material I would like to send you, Mr. President. When you and your people have reviewed those, we should speak again."

"Very well, Mr. Prime Minister. Until next time, then."

"What do you think, Mark?" Tilden asked his chief of staff. "Did you get a chance to look at the videos?"

"Yes, sir, and the supplementary materials," Mark Wegner said.

"What do you think? Is it real?"

"I did a little leg work on that, sir. I sent the videos over to the computer types at the university. They don't see any artifacts of a simulation. Now they were quick to caution they could be simulations, they just don't see it. And I would expect them to see some slip-up somewhere, in a package that big."

"I think so, too," Tilden said. "Especially the real-time video of Milbank in the plaza."

"Yes, sir, and the fact it was real-time, and you selected the girls and the question, means a simulation would have had to have been constructed or modified in real-time, and they just don't see that happening.

"There's one other big thing, though, Mr. President."

"What's that Mark?"

"I had the astronomy guys check for a new satellite, and they found one," Wegner said. "It looks like a shipping container, sir, and it says EARTHSEA COMMUNICATIONS along the side."

183

"Damn. That tears it then."

Wegner nodded.

"We certainly didn't put it there, sir. And it wasn't there the last time they looked at that location. A month ago."

"QE radio links have to be manufactured together, right? I mean, the two ends of the link," Tilden said.

"Yes, sir. You have to produce a pair of entangled particles, then capture them both, and take one of them to the other location."

"So the other end of that link is going to be on Earthsea."

"Probably, sir," Wegner said. "They could have taken the other end somewhere else, I suppose, but there was no reason to if they have a redundant interstellar network among the other planets as they claim. Milbank can talk to you over his link to Earthsea and that link to here."

Tilden nodded.

"So the question is, Now what do we do?" he said.

"Do we want to be a part of their trade network, sir?"

"What do we trade?"

"Our materials science," Wegner said. "That's one thing. The alloys, the compounds, the machines, like the extrusion machines and the fusing machines, the machine tools. A lot of products there, sir. The impact on building, manufacturing, civil engineering – all infrastructure, really – is hard to overstate. Plus we have architecture."

"Ship out architects, Mark?"

"No, sir. That's a brain drain. The architecture can be done here. That's cash flow. Interstellar balance of payments stuff."

Tilden nodded.

"The bigger question, sir," Wegner said, "is, Do we want to be a part of it?"

"I think so, Mark. Some of those other products look

compelling, and fit well with ours. Imagine the building boom, with our materials and Playa's robots, for example. We can bid buildings complete."

"The robots won't know how to build using our machines and methods, though, sir."

"No," Tilden said, "but if you teach one, they all know. Think about the implications of that."

Wegner's eyes grew wide.

"I see, sir. I do see, indeed."

"Good afternoon, Mr. President," Rob Milbank said.

"Call me Jasper, Mr. Prime Minister. We have enough titles floating around. It's not like you and I don't hear it all the time already."

Milbank chuckled.

"Indeed, Jasper. Call me Rob. What can I do for you today?"

"Well, the videos and background materials paint a compelling picture, Rob. All the desirable products, all the profitable markets. I guess it comes down to what the agreement is like. You say in the video that it's free trade, but that's always been a catch-all for a lot of things that aren't."

Milbank nodded.

"But in this case it is, Jasper. Let me send it to you."

Tilden looked off to one side of his display, then turned back to Milbank.

"I only got the first page, Rob."

"That's it, Jasper. One page. That's all there is."

"One page? Really?"

"How hard is it to say, 'Equal treatment for imports, exports, and domestic products,' Jasper? That's all it comes down to really. Oh, and the bit about, 'If you don't, I can retaliate the same way. Fair's fair.' That's about it."

185

"I guess I've been in politics too long, Rob. When somebody tells me something, I no longer expect it to be true. In fact, I expect it will usually be false."

"Oh, I understand that feeling, Jasper. But not this time."

"In that case, Rob, we're in."

"Really?"

"Oh, yes. I have to run it through the parliament, but my majority there is strong and this will be an easy case for me to make."

"That's terrific, Jasper. It's good to have you aboard."

It went similarly with the other five colonies of this round. Milbank used Arcadia's peculiar lack of a dress code to prove he was who he said he was. Valerie Laurent used Earthsea's stupendous mountains and their outré taste in furnishings and interior decoration, something called Gothic Baroque. Jean Dufort had the hardest time of it, but eventually proved his bona fides with tours of Amber's medical nanotechnology facilities, unparalleled in human space.

Samoa's parliament signed off and they officially joined. Terminus, with their expertise in forestry management and decorative plants, signed up with Milbank as well.

Hawaii signed up with Laurent, bringing in their crypto and communications expertise as well as their varieties of citrus and pulpy fruits. Laurent also signed Fiji, who offered immunology and expertise in multiple varieties of beers.

Bali signed up with Dufort, contributing their expertise in endocrinology to the consortium, as well as a fine selection of wines from their work in viniculture. Dufort also brought in Nirvana, whose anti-cancer research had resulted in cures to many previously intractable forms of the disease, along with their interests in interior design and fashion.

SILK ROAD

In the weeks they worked those six colonies, the deployment vehicles moved on, continuing to drop radios. It wasn't long before Milbank, Laurent, and Dufort had six more planets to contact.

"All right, so that went really well, I think," Milbank said.

"Agreed," Laurent said.

Dufort nodded.

"Though I had a much harder time proving I was who I said I was," he said.

Milbank nodded.

"So now we have six more coming up," he said. "The two deployment vehicles with the longest initial hop have dropped their first QE radios, and the other four have dropped their second. Our people have had a chance to collect data and prepare briefing books."

"Who have we got this time?" Laurent asked.

"New Earth, Westernesse, Endor, Tonga, Spring, and Atlantis."

They all looked over their lists of the technological specialties and extra interests of the various planets.

"Let me take Tonga and Spring," Dufort said. "They specialize in animal genetics and human genetics, and that's a medical specialty."

"I think I should take Westernesse," Laurent said. "They have direct neural virtual reality, and how we hook that in to the QE radios will be interesting. And probably Endor. They do water management, and that's a big issue for us with these mountains."

"That's fine," Milbank said. "That leaves me New Earth, with plant genetics, and Atlantis, with fabrication technologies. Let's meet up again in two weeks and see how we did."

RICHARD F. WEYAND

The Robots Arrive

When *Star Runner* got to Playa, The first shuttle trip down to the surface was with a passenger container. It was built on the model of the passenger containers that Colony headquarters had used to transport the colonists to their respective colony planets over a century prior. There were three levels, each holding up to a thousand passengers.

ChaoLi had ultimately decided to embark fifteen thousand robots for the trip back to Arcadia. Oliver Nieman had been most accommodating in this regard.

"If you need them, you will have them. If you don't need them, don't use them. They will remain our inventory, located remotely on Arcadia. No charge. But I think you will need them, or at least find them useful."

ChaoLi couldn't argue with a zero-demurrage backup inventory, and so the shuttle with the passenger compartment made six trips, with Bob piloting, the first day.

The robots simply got on the passenger container on the planet, and got off once they got to the ship. They made their way – in zero-gravity, using handholds along the walls – to the nearest passenger compartments. The compartments nearest the passenger entries were not finished yet, and the robots stood shoulder to shoulder and heel to toe awaiting an assignment.

That wouldn't come until gravity returned, on the trip home.

Three of the robots relieved the human shuttle pilots, who had started running tea, spice and cheese containers down to

SILK ROAD

Playa, and mushroom containers back. There were a thousand containers of tea and spices to go down – the other half of their initial load from Arcadia – and six hundred containers of cheese – half of their load from Earthsea. The other six hundred containers of cheese would go on to Arcadia.

Five hundred containers of mushrooms came back up, but the biggest part of the Playa cargo coming back to Arcadia would be the robots.

It took almost a hundred and sixty trips to the planet and back to load and unload cargo. With four robot pilots flying twenty-four hours a day, it still took six days.

After ten days in the Playa system – two to the planet, six to transfer cargoes, and two more to the hyperspace limit, *Star Runner* re-entered hyperspace for the direct run to Arcadia. Cutting the angle on the Earthsea route, it would take nine weeks.

When the gravity came up in *Star Runner*'s interior spaces, as she used the screw-drive to get the ship spinning, five hundred of the robots taken on board in Playa started working on finishing her outfitting. They worked all day, around the clock.

As they gained a better idea of how many robots could work at once without getting in each other's way, that number inched up to a thousand.

They were everywhere. Unpacking materials from the containers in *Star Runner*'s rear cargo compartment. Carrying those supplies to the correct places in the ship. Cutting or shaping or finishing those materials. Fitting and fastening them to the interior of the ship.

The ship had been almost complete after months of work in zero gravity in orbit. Under way, with gravity, and a thousand robots working around the clock, the ship was complete in two days.

Bob was supervising the process, and he reported in to ChaoLi on the third day of the trip back to Arcadia.

"*Star Runner* is finished, Bob?" ChaoLi asked.

"Yes, ma'am."

"That was quick."

"Thank you, ma'am," Bob said. "In truth, it was almost complete. Also, the work was expedited by the apparent gravity. It would have taken much longer to have done the work in zero gravity."

"So working to outfit the ships in Arcadia orbit was a mistake in retrospect."

"I wouldn't be able to make that assessment, ma'am. I am lacking the knowledge of the options available at the time. But finishing the ships under way certainly appears to be the best option now."

"And how many robots were working at the same time, Bob?" ChaoLi asked.

"Close to one thousand, ma'am. I think much more than that would add little. We would always be in each other's way."

"So the best bet would probably be to put a thousand robots on each new ship coming in from Beacon and send it off on its first cargo run immediately."

"If sufficient outfitting supplies are available, ma'am, that would appear optimal."

"I know what supplies we used on *Star Runner* up to the point you took over completing it, Bob. I can send that to you. Would you prepare an as-used list for me, so we can pack enough on the other ships?"

"Of course, ma'am. Do you want me to build in a customary allowance for variance?"

SILK ROAD

"Yes, as long as you make it a separate line item from the actually-used totals."

"Of course, ma'am."

ChaoLi sent the supplies inventory list from *Star Runner* to Bob, and received back a recommendation for loading new ships less than thirty minutes later.

Star Runner should drop out of hyperspace in the Arcadia system on or about March 12, 2370. By then, there would be seven hyperspace liners in Arcadia orbit, six of them needing fitting out, either partial or total.

Star Runner would need no more outfitting work. *Star Tripper*, *Star Gazer*, *Star Dreamer*, *Star Rover*, *Star Singer* and *Star Dancer* would all need work. ChaoLi would use six thousand robots right off the bat.

In the meantime, she needed cargoes of tea and spices, and either a full or partial complement of outfitting supplies for them all.

ChaoLi stopped outfitting work on the hyperspace liners in orbit, and put everyone to work assembling and loading containers with cargoes and supplies.

In April, 2370, the big hyperspace ship hulls would start showing up in Arcadia from Beacon on one-month intervals.

They were in their secret cove on the beach, laying in the sand after a picnic lunch and sex on the beach.

"JieMin?"

"Yes, ChaoLi."

"I have a schedule now. I know when we can go to Tahiti."

"When is that?" JieMin asked.

"March 15."

"That seems very specific."

"Oh, it is," ChaoLi said. "*Star Runner* will get back from

Playa on March 12, then has two days to Arcadia. We distribute robots to all the other ships in orbit and send all the ships out."

"The very next day?"

"Yes. The ships will be all loaded – cargo and outfitting supplies – and ready to go. We just transfer a thousand robots aboard each ship, and away they all go. Three thousand robots per trip with the passenger container, and the robots will all be in orbit already."

"Wow," JieMin said. "So what you really need is a schedule of port calls for seven ships, all departing on different routes on March 15th."

"Right."

"And you need to tell everyone along each route when to have cargo to ship."

"Right. And one ship should go to Aruba with the first bunch of freight station parts."

"That should probably be *Star Runner*."

"Why?"

"Because she's all fitted out already, so you have cabin space for the work crews who will be doing the assembly."

"Oh. OK, that makes sense. We can have her run over to Beacon and pick up the parts on the way."

JieMin nodded.

"There's one thing about leaving on March 15th, though," ChaoLi said.

"What's that, ChaoLi?"

"We won't be back in time for the anniversary. Neither will David Bolton and Chen YongLin, for that matter. It's minimum ten weeks each way. Call it five months round trip. Another four to five months there for treatment, and we can't be back before December sometime."

JieMin nodded.

SILK ROAD

"Probably best to let Chen Zufu and Chen Zumu know."

"Do you think that will change their timetable or their decision?"

"No. The anniversary was an artificial constraint, not a real one. They'll preside over the anniversary, and then retire when David and YongLin return."

"OK. Well, I'll let them know anyway."

"Yes, they need to know. David and YongLin, too."

"Of course."

"And don't forget Paul Chen-Jasic and Chen JuPing. That's their ride home."

"Ten weeks minimum, ChaoLi?" Jessica asked. "That is direct to Tahiti from Arcadia, is that right?"

"Yes, Chen Zumu, and that is not the best way."

"I wouldn't think so. Tahiti is between Earthsea and Amber, and beyond them."

"Yes, Chen Zufu."

"So it seems to me you should space via one on the way out, and via the other on the way back. To have the route be profitable."

"Yes, Chen Zufu. But that will be fourteen weeks out and fourteen weeks back. Together with four to five months in treatment, David Bolton, Chen YongLin, JieMin, and I will be gone almost a year."

"As may be, ChaoLi. We do not have so many ships yet that we can deadhead ferry service, even for such passengers."

"You will not be able to retire by the anniversary, Chen Zumu."

"Also as may be, ChaoLi. We will be here for the anniversary, and a few months later, we will retire. Then we will also go to Tahiti. Also on a profitable route."

"Yes, Chen Zumu."

"And by the time you return, there will be almost twenty hyperspace liners in service. That is remarkable."

ChaoLi sat stunned, but Jessica was right. With one a month rolling out of Beacon, that would make a total of nineteen by the time they came back.

"Yes, Chen Zumu."

"Looking at a calendar, ChaoLi, that would put you in Tahiti sometime about the third week of June, and the ship could leave by the end of June, beginning of July, I think."

"Yes, Chen Zumu. I believe that is correct."

"Very well, I will let Chen JuPing know. I will also let Chen YongLin know of their expected departure date."

"Thank you, Chen Zumu."

The operations group and the outfitting group were all still busy, even though outfitting had stopped. The issue now was getting outfitting supplies together for six ships and getting them up into orbit.

The Chen family was also busy. They had been expanding their fields as the magnitude of the export market became clear. That was one thing. Getting as many as fifteen thousand containers of tea and spices ready for transit was another.

The one nice thing from the operations group's point of view – and Chris Bellamy's point of view in particular – is they had the best part of two months to get seventeen thousand containers to orbit.

Call it almost two thousand round trips. Four round trips per day per shuttle. Sixty days. So eight shuttles. Hmm. If she made it twelve shuttles five days a week for eight weeks, she had it.

That was good. Everybody could still take the weekends off.

SILK ROAD

That is, assuming there were loads ready to go. She started looking at the delivery schedule for the tea, the spices, and the outfitting supplies.

Oh, great. Everybody was acting like they could drop everything at the shuttleport the night before departure and have it get loaded.

Well, *that* wasn't happening.

Bellamy sent out a number of mails correcting people's mistaken impression with regard to delivery times.

Oh, and each one of those liners would be taking four of the heavy orbital cargo shuttles with them.

Bellamy rechecked the delivery schedule on the other cargo shuttles she was expecting.

This just might work.

Bellamy did make it work. She hectored suppliers until deliveries began showing up for lift to orbit. A dozen shuttles ran non-stop during daylight hours all week long.

Bellamy set up bedrooms for her shuttle pilots at the operations group's shuttleport headquarters so they didn't have to commute home overnight during the week. She brought in gourmet meals for them for breakfast and supper. Anything to make the grind easier on them, to keep their flying skills sharp.

Yes, the shuttle's flight computers were doing a lot of the work, but things could get cramped once they got up to orbit and were loading the big liners. Being on your toes was necessary to avoid disaster.

They had two close calls, but no disasters, and the ships were all loaded and waiting when *Star Runner* transitioned out of hyperspace on March 12th.

As the way out of orbit when leaving Arcadia was to thrust in the orbital direction, and *Star Runner* would be leaving last because it had to be unloaded and loaded, the new arrival took up last position in the string of ships orbiting in formation above Arcadia.

When she arrived in orbit, Bob took one of *Star Runner*'s cargo shuttles and used the passenger container to transfer a thousand robots to each of the loaded liners in turn.

Skeleton crews came aboard and started preparing for departure. For right now, without their cabins finished, they were hammocking in an open compartment. In zero gravity, they tied the hammock closed when they slept.

"You're taking *Star Dancer* rather than *Star Runner*, ma'am?" Naomi Thompson asked.

Thompson had moved up from the personnel position to be ChaoLi's trusted lieutenant in running Jixing Trading.

"Yes, Naomi," ChaoLi said. "I want to see the whole process. The outfitting, setting everything up, the whole process. As long as I am going, I want to learn as much as I can."

"Well, good spacing, ma'am."

"Thanks, Naomi."

ChaoLi and JieMin had talked about the kids, specifically the boys. Did they take them along or not?

The twins, YanMing and YanJing, were now sixteen years old and had other things on their minds than spending a year off-planet. Mostly girls. YanMing in particular would probably be married before they got back. They would have to attend his wedding in the display.

JieJun was now twelve, and he was a different matter altogether. They couldn't leave him to his own devices for a year, but would he really want to come along?

As it turned out, JieJun and their eldest, ChaoPing, had already worked out the problem by the time they asked about it. Their eldest daughter, now twenty-two, had long been their baby's favorite sibling, and she and her husband would take him in for the year. They had plenty of room, and he could help with ChaoPing's and JuMing's three-year-old boy, LingTao, especially since ChaoPing was pregnant again.

That also would happen while they were gone.

With all that settled, ChaoLi and JieMin, without children for the first time in twenty-two years, prepared to set out into space, in a ship whose design and construction she had overseen, traveling in the hyperspace he had discovered.

RICHARD F. WEYAND

Departure For Amber

There were a number of items, large and small, to take care of before leaving Arcadia.

Bob expressed a desire to return to the service of Loukas Diakos.

"It was very satisfying, ma'am, to complete the outfitting of *Star Runner*. But you will be well served aboard *Star Dancer*, and Mr. Diakos currently has no assistance."

"I understand, Bob," ChaoLi said. "Thank you for all your help."

"It was my pleasure to serve, ma'am."

Bob would come down in the shuttle passenger container that would take them and the rest of the crew up to *Star Dancer*.

ChaoLi and JieMin also took their leave of Chen Zufu and Chen Zumu.

"We will be gone a year, Chen Zumu," ChaoLi said. "More or less."

"Not so long, ChaoLi. And we will be in touch. I will expect your progress reports as before."

"Of course, Chen Zumu."

"Good spacing, ChaoLi, JieMin," MinChao said.

"Thank you, Chen Zufu."

The day of departure arrived, and ChaoLi and JieMin watched the shuttles come down at the Arcadia City Shuttleport. Six shuttles with passenger containers, one for

SILK ROAD

each of the six hyperspace liners that would be leaving today. They would all be taking on the rest of their crews. With six ships, several hundred crew filled the hangar space at the operations headquarters.

"All right, everyone. Make sure you get on the correct shuttle so you end up at the ship you're assigned to," the speakers in the observation lounge, meeting rooms, hangars and shuttlepad aprons announced.

Headquarters crew were servicing the shuttles, mostly running from shuttle to shuttle with fuel and oxygen trucks. Baggage crews were also filling the baggage space on the passenger compartments with everyone's personal cubic.

All ChaoLi's and JieMin's family came out to the Arcadia City Shuttleport to see them off: ChaoPing and JuMing, with LingTao and JieJun; LeiTao and her husband, DaGang, and their children, XiPing and GangLi; and the twins, YanMing and YanJing.

There were lots of hugs and well wishes in both directions. They held back until everyone else was aboard. ChaoLi's heart was in her throat as she and JieMin turned and walked out to the shuttle for *Star Dancer*.

As they walked to the shuttle, JieMin took ChaoLi's arm. She looked at him and he pointed up into the sky. Sunlight glinted off the string of hyperspace liners orbiting Arcadia every ninety minutes. Seven tiny glinting jewels, strung out across the blue of the sky.

As they approached the shuttle, a robot walked down the short stairs from the passenger container. The first robot to set foot on Arcadia. He walked up to ChaoLi.

"Hello, ma'am. I am Bob."

"Well, hello, Bob. Thank you again for all your help."

"Not a problem at all, ma'am. I enjoy being useful."

Bob looked around, at the shuttles and the hyperspace headquarters complex.

"I am somewhat at a loss to know how best to find Mr. Diakos."

"Do you know where he lives, Bob? His address?"

"Yes, ma'am. And I have located it on a map of Arcadia City. Should I walk there?"

"Overlay your map with the map of bus routes for Arcadia City, Bob. I think you can take a bus to get much closer, and walk from there."

Bob hesitated for perhaps two seconds.

"I see, ma'am. The bus stop should be right there," Bob said, pointing, "on the other side of these buildings."

"That's correct."

"Excellent. Thank you, ma'am. And good spacing to you both."

With that, Bob set off for a path through the hyperspace headquarters complex.

JieMin watched him go, then turned to ChaoLi.

"Will Arcadia be the same when we return?" he asked.

"No," ChaoLi said, looking after Bob.

She turned to JieMin.

"Nothing will."

When they got on the shuttle, there was a robot at the door that scanned their communicators and checked them against the manifest.

"This is the shuttle for *Star Dancer*," he said. "You may take a seat anywhere."

There were fifty or so crew aboard, both men and women,

and half a dozen robots stood across the back wall. ChaoLi and JieMin took seats up front, by the forward display, next to David Bolton and Chen YongLin. Once they were aboard, the robot at the door shut the hatch and checked it.

The robot at the door turned to everyone in the shuttle.

"We will be taking off soon," he said. "We will have gravity from lift and acceleration until we approach *Star Dancer*. At that point, we will lose gravity and be in freefall for approximately two days. It is my understanding that for many of you this will be your first time in zero gravity, all your training having been completed on the planet in simulation.

"You should have a bag ready in case you lose the contents of your stomach when we go into zero gravity. Having those contents floating about the cabin would otherwise be unpleasant for your fellow crew members and passengers. I will announce when this period approaches. We also have medications aboard that can help if you have problems.

"During the two days we are in freefall, you will all likely need to void your bladder and bowels. There are facilities aboard for that purpose. It resembles a regular toilet, but operates more like a vacuum cleaner. We stand ready to assist you in the use of these facilities. You should not be embarrassed to request our assistance, as we have no interest in human biological functions other than to be of assistance to you.

"We will also be distributing meals and drinks during these two days. Their content and packaging has been designed for use in freefall. We can instruct you if you have any difficulties in their use.

"To use your time most effectively while restricted to the shuttle, you will find that we will maintain contact with the planetary network. All the entertainment and business materials and resources you are familiar with will remain available during this period. We ask that you remain belted into your seats during this period, particularly while sleeping, so you do not float about the cabin.

"If you need anything, at any time, please do not hesitate to ask any of us. My name is Tom.

"We will now begin our takeoff procedures. I hope you enjoy your flight."

With that, Tom and the other six robots took seats and strapped themselves in. The speakers started playing the tower communications channel, and they could hear the pilots of the shuttles checking in with Arcadia Air Traffic Control.

As *Star Dancer* would be the first hyperspace liner to depart Arcadia, their shuttle would be the first one off the pad.

"Shuttle Jixing-14 to Arcadia Control."

"Go ahead, Jixing-14."

"Jixing-14 requesting takeoff clearance and departure clearance to *Star Dancer*. Over."

"Roger, Jixing-14. You have clearance for takeoff on a departure heading of nine-zero to *Star Dancer*. Heading nine-zero. Traffic to the north does not intersect your flight path. Over."

"Roger, Arcadia Control. Takeoff and heading nine-zero to *Star Dancer*. Traffic to the north does not intersect. Jixing-14 out."

ChaoLi noted it was a robot's voice for shuttle Jixing-14.

She wondered how long it would be before it was a robot's voice for Arcadia Control.

ChaoLi watched the takeoff in her heads up display, accessing the shuttlepad viewing cameras at the hyperspace headquarters complex. It was strange feeling the takeoff as the shuttle shook around her, while watching it from the outside.

The sensation was that of riding on a very fast elevator. She watched the shuttle clear the pad and head east out over the southern part of Arcadia City. The forward display, in the upper part of her vision, showed the view forward, and she watched as the city fell below and behind them.

Then they were out over the ocean. The shuttle continued to gain altitude quickly even as it flew east.

Five minutes later, she watched a second shuttle take off, then a third. Six in all, at five minute intervals, the shuttles headed to orbit to meet up with their parent ships. The shuttles themselves were each part of their ship's complement of four, to be used to load and unload ships at their destinations.

Each of the hyperspace liners, plus *Star Runner* – which would be leaving in another week or ten days, once she was unloaded and loaded – were heading to different planets, each running its own route. Between them, they would hit every one of the twenty other colony planets.

Rob Milbank, Valerie Laurent, and Jean Dufort had by now contacted all the remaining colonies. All had eventually signed up for the trade agreement, some with more handholding and persuasion than others.

So JieMin's routing of the seven liners had been designed to cover all the colonies, getting each of them some immediate benefit to reinforce their joining the trade consortium.

Of course, each colony would not receive imported goods from all the other colonies at once. All would get Arcadia tea and spices. Some would get imports from other, earlier planets on their route. They would all have the opportunity to export their own goods, though, and sooner or later they would all see all the other colonies' goods showing up in their imported items.

The ultimate solution to the problem of being able to send anything anywhere would come with the hub and spoke system ChaoLi envisioned, which would have to wait for enough hyperspace liners to be available and the construction of the interstellar freight transfer stations on Arcadia and Aruba.

Two years, perhaps. In two years it would all be in place.

In the meantime, everybody got something from some other planet, and the other planets' products would gradually move around the trading network.

Sooner or later, everybody would be importing everyone else's export goods.

The forward display showed a truly amazing sight. All seven hyperspace liners, strung out in a line, as the shuttle came up from behind and below them. They were trading velocity for altitude now, and the shuttle was slowing as it approached the front of the line, passing under each in turn.

Apparent gravity in the cabin was only a portion of one gravity now, and dropping, but they were not yet in freefall.

Tom stood up and faced the cabin.

"Prepare for free fall. Less than five minutes now," he said, and then sat down and belted himself back into his seat.

People sought out their plastic bags in case they got sick.

A warning bell sounded, and then they were weightless. A couple of people got sick. ChaoLi swallowed hard a couple of times, then imagined herself swimming, and she was OK.

She looked over to JieMin. He didn't seem discomfited very much.

"Like swimming," ChaoLi said.

"Yes. Of course."

SILK ROAD

David Bolton, on JieMin's other side didn't look particularly discomfited by zero gravity, but YongLin looked a little green. She closed her eyes.

"Like swimming," she said. "Oh, that works. Thank you, ChaoLi."

It was another twenty minutes of a thruster push here and a thruster push there before the pilot hit his mark and latched onto the *Star Dancer*. That was the last piece of the puzzle for her captain.

"*Star Dancer*, ready to depart Arcadia. Thrusters at full power."

ChaoLi felt quite a bit of gravity back into her seat as the *Star Dancer* left orbit. That was initially, as a dozen JATO bottles were used to get the big ship moving. Time to the hyperspace limit was highly dependent on how fast you could build velocity early on.

When the JATO bottles had burned out, the ship continued thrusting at a lower level as it steadily built velocity and altitude.

Using the bathroom was interesting. ChaoLi did ask for assistance. She had had five children and any body modesty around medical professionals had been lost long ago, much less around robots.

JieMin similarly asked for assistance, as he seemed to treat his body as just the thing he rode around in. Like a vehicle. If the mechanic wanted to look under the hood, that was fine.

Most of the crew did not request assistance, as they had all had crew training before being assigned to *Star Dancer*, and had used identical equipment before, albeit not in zero gravity.

The meals were palatable if not particularly memorable. The

drinks, though, were very refreshing.

Two days to the hyperspace limit was what it was, and everybody tried to make the best of it.

ChaoLi spent most of the time doing paperwork. She also had one business call with Naomi Thompson, just to make sure things were going fine.

Finally the time came for transition to hyperspace. JieMin was very interested in this part. It was his first personal experience of what he had postulated so long ago.

As it was, it was nearly a non-event. The captain of *Star Dancer* announced the transition, and then announced it was over. The front viewscreen went blank. That was about it.

JieMin, though, selected the unblanked view of hyperspace in his heads-up display.

"Hmm."

"What, JieMin?" ChaoLi asked.

"It looks nothing like I imagined."

"What does it look like?"

"It's formless. Your eye keeps trying to see something that isn't there, which is disturbing to some people, I guess. But it's featureless."

"Are you surprised?"

"I wasn't sure what to expect. I thought I would see something, but it's just too alien."

The real benefit of the transition to hyperspace was that *Star Dancer* could use the screw-drive. As the ship's rotation increased, gravity came back slowly. When it got to a quarter gravity, Tom stood up at the front of the cabin.

"We now have enough gravity for people to find their way to their cabins aboard *Star Dancer*," he said. "You should have your interim assignments in your mail accounts. These will be upgraded in the next few days as the interior spaces of *Star Dancer* are fitted out. Your baggage will be delivered to your interim cabin within the hour.

"Please let us know if you need any assistance."

With that, Tom and one of the other robots opened the cabin hatches in the front of the passenger container, on either side of the forward display.

ChaoLi and JieMin got up from their seats and queued at the hatchway. While they were in line, they accessed their mail accounts and found their assignment as well as a map of the ship indicating where their cabin assignment was and how to get there.

They stepped across the hatchway into *Star Dancer* and followed the map down the corridors.

RICHARD F. WEYAND

Star Dancer

Star Dancer was fresh from the Beacon shipyards. None of her interior spaces were finished. Piping and electrical conduits ran along the steel walls, which were still unpainted and without finish coverings like drywall. Here in the passenger spaces, the corridors would ultimately be finished out, trimmed, and carpeted, but right now there was nothing.

ChaoLi and JieMin walked through the corridors in the direction the map indicated. The gravity was still growing toward one-half g as the ship continued to spin faster. There was also a slight push toward one side of the corridor from the acceleration of the spin, so apparent down wasn't straight down. It wasn't hard to compensate for, but one did have to keep it in mind, especially when turning corners.

They reached their assigned cabin, which opened with a button in their heads-up displays. It was a bare steel room with two armchairs in the center, which were tack-welded to the floor. There were hammocks strung across the two far corners, hanging from hooks tack-welded to the walls.

ChaoLi walked over to the door on one side. Beyond was a bathroom. All the fixtures were installed, but had a temporary look. There was no finish work done in here either.

ChaoLi walked back out into the main room.

"Home sweet home," she said. "For the time being, at least."

"All the way to Tahiti, like this?" JieMin asked.

"No. Obviously they threw this together for us so we would have a place until they finished our stateroom. With a thousand robots on board, how long do you think that will take?"

SILK ROAD

"I don't know. When will they start working?"

"Listen," ChaoLi said.

JieMin listened closely. He could hear noises of someone working. The sound of power tools, the banging of doors, footsteps in corridors.

"They're already working," he said.

"Exactly. We'll likely have a stateroom tomorrow or the next day. They're probably working other areas of the ship, then they'll move us, then they'll do this area."

"It's kind of exciting," JieMin said. "Seeing them finish the ship while it's spacing."

ChaoLi nodded.

"I want to see some of the work being done. It's important to me to see the actual process, I think. To know what it takes, see how they do it, all that sort of thing. Helps with managing."

JieMin nodded. He went over and sat in one of the armchairs.

"Well, the chair is comfy. No display yet, but we have our heads-up displays."

ChaoLi nodded.

"Good. I have paperwork to do."

They were getting hungry and were beginning to wonder how they might get supper when there was a knock on the door. ChaoLi opened it in her heads-up display, and a robot entered, carrying two trays, one above the other, one in each pair of its arms.

"I have dinner for you, sir, ma'am."

"Oh, good," ChaoLi said. "We were wondering where the mess was."

"We would prefer you eat here, ma'am. There are a lot of us about, and a lot of heavy construction going on. If you remain here, you will not be in our way, and will not be potentially injured in some mishap."

The robot came over and set one tray across the arms of ChaoLi's chair, and one across the arms of JieMin's chair.

"In any case, ma'am, you can buzz me for anything you need. You should have that button in your heads-up display. My name is Bert."

"OK, Bert. I do have one question for you. When will our cabin be completed?"

"Tomorrow, Ma'am. We can only go so fast. There are some delays we cannot avoid, such as the time for tile adhesive to set up."

"Understood, Bert. And you'll let us know when our cabin is ready?"

"Yes, ma'am. And I have your baggage here, if you would like it now."

"Yes, please."

Bert set their bags in the room, just inside the door.

"You can just buzz me when you want your trays removed, ma'am."

"All right, Bert. Thank you. That is all."

Bert nodded to her, nodded to JieMin, then turned and walked out of the room.

"Well, what's for dinner?" ChaoLi asked as she removed the cover from one dish.

"Well, dinner was good," JieMin said later, after the trays were removed by Bert.

"Pre-cooked and warmed up. I don't think they have the kitchens running yet."

"Yes, but it was still good."

ChaoLi nodded.

SILK ROAD

"Yes, but after all the preparations, the excitement, and zero gravity, I'm exhausted. Could you sleep, or is it too early?"

"No, I could sleep," JieMin said.

"Oh, good."

ChaoLi looked behind her at the two hammocks.

"Together or separately?" she asked.

"Together."

They climbed into one hammock, still in the fleece loungers and booties in which they had left Arcadia, then laced the hammock closed so neither of them fell to the floor.

They cuddled up, and both were asleep within minutes.

When ChaoLi woke nine hours later, she found JieMin awake and watching her.

"Good morning," she said.

"We probably look ridiculous. Like some kind of bizarre cocoon."

"Well, this butterfly is ready to get out. How about you?"

"Oh, yes," JieMin said. "I'm good."

"We have our baggage, we have a shower, and there are towels. Who goes first?"

"First for bathroom, second for shower."

"Deal."

They unlaced the hammock and got out gingerly so neither would fall. After bathroom and shower, ChaoLi buzzed Bert, with a note they were ready for breakfast. Fifteen minutes later there was a knock on the door. ChaoLi opened the door in her heads-up display, and Bert came in carrying two trays.

When he put the trays in front of them, across the arms of the armchairs, ChaoLi lifted one of the covers. Eggs, sausage, toast. There were pancakes under another.

"Fresh breakfast this morning," she said.

"Yes, ma'am. We got the short-order stations running in one of the kitchens last night. We should have one full kitchen operational for dinner. Our other concentration is to get cabins finished for everyone aboard. That will be done today."

"Oh, my. Then what will you do?"

"It's a big ship, ma'am. Occupancy is currently at a small fraction of capacity. But by the time we get to Amber, we should be close to finished."

"You fellows are amazing, Bert."

"Thank you, ma'am."

Bert nodded and left and they dug into their breakfasts.

"They sure do know how to cook," JieMin said with appreciation as he set about demolishing a stack of pancakes.

"Yes. What the impact will be on society is another whole question."

"I would think it would make it much more efficient."

"Yes, but how much do people need, JieMin?" ChaoLi asked. "Do we all end up overweight and under-exercised?"

"With cooking like this, perhaps so."

When they were finished with breakfast, ChaoLi summoned Bert to pick up the trays. When he arrived, she had orders for him.

"Bert, I need to have a tour of the construction. I want to see one of the kitchens under way, and several cabins in various stages of completion. I want to observe the work being done."

"I don't advise that, ma'am. Any construction area can be dangerous to visitors."

"Bert, I am the Chief Executive Officer of the company that leases this ship, that employs everyone aboard, that purchased you and the other robots from Playa. I need to see the work being done in order to perform my function."

SILK ROAD

Bert just stopped for three whole seconds. ChaoLi thought that 'perform my function' would hit the robot right in his own priorities.

"Very well, ma'am. I understand."

"Chen JieMin as well, Bert."

"What is his function, ma'am?"

"Adviser to the CEO. But that is not your affair, Bert. My orders are binding on you. I should not have to explain myself to you. And in the future, I will not."

"Of course, ma'am. I will make arrangements."

Bert nodded to her and left with the breakfast trays.

"Wow. Quite a bit of pushback there," JieMin said.

"Yes," ChaoLi said. "But they need to understand that I am the one who gives the orders. I'm not a passenger on this ship. I'm the owner."

Bert came back two hours later.

"I have found suitable areas to tour, ma'am."

"And we'll see construction under way?" ChaoLi asked.

"Yes, ma'am."

"Very well. Let's go."

Bert led them around the ship. While the hallways leading fore and aft were straight, the hallways running around the belt of the ship were curved. The floor was always 'down', but the floor itself curved in a great circle around the ship.

The turned the corner into one hallway under construction. That is, the steel hallway was there, but the hallway was being finished. The hallway they turned into was finished from the intersection, but, looking down the length of it, they saw all the steps of the finishing process.

At the far end, robots were welding metal U-channels as studs on the steel walls. Not continuous welding, but here,

here, here down the length of the stud. The next team was painting the walls with spray painting equipment, covering the bare steel with an anti-rust coating. This was much easier in a space-going ship than a sea-going ship, because there was no salt air or spray to contend with.

After them came the drywall hangers. Robots carried sheets of drywall in a continuous stream to the crew here, who laid the drywall sheets against the studs and screwed them on. The robots carrying in the drywall were coming in through a side aisle, so ChaoLi, JieMin, and Bert were not in their way, which was probably why this location was selected. Similar activities were no doubt happening all over the ship.

After the drywall hangers came the tapers and finishers, finishing the seams and screw heads. Behind them a team was spray-painting a sealer coat, followed up by a team spraying the finish color. The team after that was rolling out carpeting, seaming the sections together as they went, and fastening it down with adhesive.

The final team, right in front of them, was applying crown moldings, floor moldings, and hand holds for use in zero gravity.

The entire assemblage was moving down the hallway at better than one foot per minute.

"Well, I have to say that's pretty amazing, Bert. And they just keep moving down the hallways?"

"This team, yes, ma'am. Similar teams are working up kitchens, crew cabins, and passenger cabins. Moving from room to room. All are working twenty-four hours a day."

That phrase still sounded odd to ChaoLi, no matter how many times she heard it, given Arcadia's twenty-five hour day, but she understood what Bert meant.

"Take me to a corridor where they are working on cabins,

SILK ROAD

Bert."

"Yes, ma'am. Crew cabins or passenger cabins?"

"Whichever is most convenient, where we won't be in the way."

"Of course, ma'am."

Bert led them back around the ship to another corridor. This corridor had not been completed yet. They walked down the corridor, peaking in the rooms as they passed, and trying to stay out of the way of the steady stream robots who were delivering supplies to each room.

Here the teams were similar, but each team was in a separate room, performing its part of the task. There were additional teams for installing electrical connections, finishing out the bathrooms, and installing furniture.

When they got past the teams, they looked into a completed cabin.

"Very nice, Bert."

"Thank you, ma'am," Bert said, then paused. "Actually, if you watch the corridor now, we have a shift coming up."

They turned and looked down the corridor. All at once, the robot team in each room walked out into the hallway, carrying all their equipment in their four arms. They moved down the hallway one room and entered the next room to begin again.

"OK, that was interesting to see. How often do they shift like that, Bert?"

"We have it down to about ninety-five minutes now, ma'am."

"So a thousand cabins, more or less, is fifteen hundred hours, Bert? Call it sixty days?"

"This is not the only team working cabins, ma'am."

"Ah. Of course. So you have teams on corridors and teams on cabins. What else?"

"There are teams on the kitchens, ma'am, and the dining rooms. There are teams on all the other rooms, like the exercise rooms, the crew and passenger lounges, and the meeting rooms. There are also teams on unloading the materials from the containers, mixing paint and finish materials, cutting the materials to size, finishing the wood trim pieces, and delivering the materials to all the teams' work locations."

"Cutting the materials to size is separate, Bert?"

"Of course, ma'am. There is no benefit in transporting excess material to the work location, then transporting waste back."

"So the drywall is all cut to size at one central location and delivered in the size required?"

"Yes, ma'am. There is constant radio chatter between the teams on requirements. Measurements and the like."

"Amazing," ChaoLi said, and meant it. "All right, Bert, we've gotten in your way long enough. Back to our cabin, please."

"Of course, ma'am. This way, please."

Bert led them back around the ship. ChaoLi couldn't keep track of all the corridors, but it didn't seem like they were going back to where they had started. They finally ended up in a finished hallway, and Bert opened the door of a cabin and waved them into the room.

It was a finished passenger cabin. More, it was one of the staterooms, for high-roller passengers. ChaoLi and JieMin walked in and looked around.

"Very nice. This is our cabin, Bert?" ChaoLi asked.

"Yes, ma'am. For the rest of the trip. I took the liberty of having your things moved here from your temporary quarters. The other two passengers – your family members, yes? – are in the stateroom next door, and your dining room is also on this corridor. I'm afraid the exercise room and passenger lounge are not yet complete. We are prioritizing getting all the crew into their permanent cabin assignments today."

"Our dining room is complete?"

"Yes, ma'am. Just two tables at present, each of which seat four. You and your fellow passengers can eat together or separately. We do not have full menu options yet, but we will have hot lunch available in another hour. You may eat whenever you would like after that, just by walking to the dining room, or I can bring you lunch here."

"All right, Bert. Thank you. You are dismissed."

The robot nodded to her and left, closing the door behind him.

"Well, I don't know what to think about all that," ChaoLi said, sitting down in one of the armchairs in the stateroom suite's sitting room.

"They seem to do nice work, though," JieMin said, looking around.

He sat in the other armchair.

"The chair's comfortable, too," he said.

"These came from Arcadia. Human-made, at least so far."

"You seem very concerned."

"JieMin, what do people do to earn a living when we can turn out twenty-five-hour-a-day workers on an assembly line? Workers who don't take a break, don't need lunch, don't need portable toilets on the job site."

JieMin had no answer for her.

At least not yet.

RICHARD F. WEYAND

Gravity And Spin

As lunchtime approached, ChaoLi got a mail from Chen YongLin inviting her and JieMin to join them for lunch. She checked with JieMin and accepted. When the time came, they walked out into the hallway. David Bolton and Chen YongLin met them there.

"So where's the dining room?" David asked.

ChaoLi consulted the ship map in her heads-up display.

"This way," she said, pointing, and headed off down the hallway.

When they walked into the dining room, Bert came in through a staff door from the kitchen.

"One table for four, Bert," ChaoLi said.

"Yes, ma'am. Right here will be fine."

Bert waved to a table, one of only two in a room that would hold perhaps twenty five. They all sat around the table, and Bert produced four printed menus.

"They are all items from the short-order station today, ma'am. We will have a more complete menu for dinner this evening."

"This is fine, Bert," ChaoLi said.

They all ordered – an assortment of grilled items like hamburgers and grilled ham-and-swiss sandwiches – and Bert went back to the kitchen.

"So what do you think so far?" ChaoLi asked David and YongLin. "Any feedback for me as we gear this up to revenue passengers?"

"I think the little talk we got when we got on the shuttle was lacking something in the warm and welcoming hospitality department." David said. "Perhaps a video would be better than a robot giving it. Or script it better, perhaps."

ChaoLi nodded. She had noted that herself.

"I think the zero gravity is the biggest thing," YongLin said. "If there were some way to reduce the amount of time in zero gravity, that would be a real positive. Also some advice about how to handle it should be offered. Your suggestion that it was like swimming helped me a lot, ChaoLi."

"Yes, it really makes you appreciate the initial shuttle runs out to the other colonies, where they were in zero gravity for six or eight or ten weeks," ChaoLi said.

YongLin shuddered.

"I can't even imagine," she said.

Bert came in then with their sandwiches. They also had salads, beverages, and a side of grilled potatoes. No french fries yet. That part of the kitchen was still under construction.

The food was very good, and prepared to perfection.

The conversation moved on to other topics, mostly what Amber would be like. None of them knew much, other than that they had great coffee.

ChaoLi and JieMin met with the captain about two weeks into the Amber leg of the voyage.

ChaoLi had personally interviewed and passed on all the final choices for captains of the hyperspace liners. She knew the type she was looking for. Someone with quiet competence and a deliberate air. The sort that, if they were hit in the head with a plank, would think about the consequences of various reactions before saying 'Ouch!'

The sort that inspired confidence and loyalty in a crew.

"Hello, Captain."

"Hello, ma'am," Captain Jonah Abrams said. "It's nice to see you again."

"Thanks for meeting with us."

"No problem. No problem at all. Please have a seat."

They all sat around the table in the captain's day room, behind the bridge. Bert had led them here, and waited outside.

"So how are things going, from your point of view, Captain?" ChaoLi asked.

"Very well, actually, ma'am. The ship sort of runs itself as far as the navigation and all goes. We've had a minimum number of shakedown items come up, and none with any critical systems. So it's all going pretty well so far."

"How about the progress on the ship's interior spaces?"

"It's going along smoothly, ma'am. I believe they're about forty percent complete there."

"So they'll be done by the time we reach Amber, Captain?"

"Yes, ma'am. I was skeptical at first, but if you've seen those fellows work, you know how fast they move along. There's a lot of interior spaces on this ship, but they just keep hammering away at it."

ChaoLi nodded.

"And how are things going with the crew, Captain?"

"Again, very well, ma'am. There was a little grousing when they first came aboard about the temporary quarters. But their cabins were done quickly, and the food has been top-notch. That last is always a big one."

"Good. Excellent, in fact. In addition to those general questions, Captain, I wanted to ask you a specific one."

"Go ahead, ma'am."

"Captain, I think we would have a much more pleasant passenger experience to offer if we didn't have two days of weightlessness at both ends of the trip."

"I agree, but I'm not sure how to avoid that, ma'am."

"What if we started the ship spinning as soon as it left orbit? We can use thrusters to get spinning at least a bit, can't we, Captain?"

"Yes, ma'am. And the main engines are steerable as well. Not much, but it doesn't take much to provide a continuous angular acceleration. Departing orbit, we could probably do that, and continue to bring her up to one-half g of internal gravity once we are in hyperspace."

"And the same thing on the arrival end as well, Captain?"

"I think that's harder, Ma'am."

"Why is that, Captain?"

"As we approach a planet, we have to be braking all the way in from the hyperspace limit. We have to flip the ship over to do that, ma'am. To get the thrusters in front.

"Now, to maintain half a gravity in the upper passenger deck, we're spinning at about three rpm, ma'am. The gravity in the lower passenger decks is more like seven-tenths of a gravity. Our outer hull has a tangential velocity of something like fifty miles an hour."

Abrams raised an eyebrow.

"I follow you, Captain," ChaoLi said.

"Yes, ma'am. The issue is one of angular momentum. A ship this big and heavy, rotating that fast, has a huge angular momentum. Flipping it over while spinning is not easy."

"How do you do it now, Captain?"

"We flip the ship once we're not spinning anymore, ma'am."

"Which is when you drop out of hyperspace, then you have two days from the hyperspace limit to the planet, decelerating all the way. Is that right, Captain?"

"That's correct, ma'am."

ChaoLi looked to JieMin. His eyes were unfocused as he

thought it through.

"There may be a way...."

Abrams raised an eyebrow to ChaoLi.

"This is my husband, Chen JieMin, Captain. He invented the hyperspace field generator and the hyperspace drive, and was influential in the design of this ship."

Abrams's eyes went wide. He didn't need the elaboration. Everybody on Arcadia knew who Chen JieMin was. Abrams just hadn't realized 'Chen, J.M.' on his passenger manifest was Chen JieMin.

JieMin focused back on Abrams.

"Captain, we can use your maneuvering thrusters to flip the ship even while it is spinning. If we could maintain even a tenth of a gravity for most of the way to and from the planet, that would be a big help to passenger comfort, I believe."

"But if you apply a side thrust to a spinning object, it will rotate around the third axis, not the second one, Chen JieMin."

"Yes, Captain. It is called gyroscopic precession. But *Star Dancer* has twelve thrusters in the front and rear of the ship, oriented around its circumference. If we sequence those, one at a time, as they pass through the axis we want, we should be able to precess the ship one hundred and eighty degrees."

"Wait. I don't get that," ChaoLi said.

"If *Star Dancer* were not spinning, one could use a thruster pointed left in front and right in back, say, and get the ship rotating around a vertical axis."

"Yes, I see that."

"And when it got to the place one wanted, you could use the opposite thruster on each end to stop it rotating any further."

"Yes, I see that, too."

"But if *Star Dancer* is spinning, when you push to the left in front and to the right in back, it doesn't do that. Instead, it rotates end over end, and only while the thruster is firing."

"That's right, ma'am," Abrams said. "That's how a gyroscope works."

"The problem is that the thrusters are rotating with the ship," JieMin said, "so we have to fire them one at a time for about a second and a half, as each one comes into position. If we slowed her down to one rpm first, it would be five seconds per thruster."

"I wouldn't know how to set that up, sir. I doubt anyone on the crew will either."

"I will write the code for it, Captain Abrams."

Abrams raised an eyebrow.

"I wrote much of the code you're using now, Captain."

Abrams looked to ChaoLi, who nodded.

"Very well, ma'am. If we were going to try any such thing, best we do it without revenue passengers and only a skeleton crew aboard. Now's as good a time as any from that point of view."

Abrams looked over at JieMin, who was once more staring into the distance, planning the code package for the maneuver.

"If it was anyone else, though...." Abrams's voice drifted off.

Back in their cabin, ChaoLi was more skeptical.

"You're sure you can do this, JieMin?"

"Oh, sure. It's not particularly difficult, ChaoLi. It's just a matter of getting the timing right."

"How will you be sure?"

"Oh, I have access from here to all my simulation tools at the university. I can run the code from here in the ship simulator, and make sure it performs as planned before we try anything."

"Oh, OK. Good."

It was about a week later that JieMin called Bert to their cabin.

"Yes, sir?"

"Bert, you write code for yourselves, don't you? You robots?"

"Yes, sir."

"Would you take a look at some code for me. It's code for the ship, so you'll have to study up a bit, but I would like you to look at it for me."

"Of course, sir."

JieMin sent Bert a mail message with the code attached, along with a link to his simulator program on Arcadia.

"Thank you, sir."

It was several hours before Bert came back. He knocked on the door and JieMin let him in.

"It looks like what this code will do is to rotate the ship end for end in space, as long as the ship is spinning, sir."

"That's the intention, Bert."

"Well, if that's the intention, sir, it looks like you have a working code package."

"OK. Thank you, Bert."

"Of course, sir."

Bert nodded and left.

Of course, JieMin had also had the hyperspace mathematics group at the university check out the program. They mostly worked on the hyperspace part of the trip, but there were some good programmers in that group.

Everybody was now agreed the code should work.

Whether it would or not was a different question.

With two days to go until arrival at Amber, Bert told ChaoLi and JieMin that all the interior spaces of *Star Dancer* had been completed. The ship looked finished now, wherever aboard one wandered.

They asked him to pass their congratulations along to all the robots on the team.

It was decided to use the screw-drive mode in reverse to slow the ship's rotational velocity down by two-thirds, to one revolution per minute, before transitioning out of hyperspace in the Amber system. This would leave about two-tenths of a gravity in all the passenger and crew spaces on board the ship until they were much closer to the planet.

Even two-tenths of a gravity would be much more comfortable than zero gravity. At least down would be down.

"This is Captain Abrams speaking. We are going to begin reducing spin for our transition from hyperspace to normal space-time. We will retain two-tenths of a gravity in the passenger spaces until we are closer to Amber. Because we are reducing gravity, however, we ask that you belt in until the gravity is stable in order to avoid accidents."

Star Dancer switched into screw-drive mode, in reverse, reducing her hyperspace velocity. In screw-drive, this also produced a counter-torque that worked against the ship's spin.

When *Star Dancer*'s rotation was down to one rpm, and shipboard gravity was down to two-tenths g, she switched to ripple-drive mode, still in reverse, to reduce her velocity for transition to normal space-time.

Star Dancer transitioned out of hyperspace at the hyperspace limit in the Amber system. She had transitioned twice before, to get her bearings on the planet and fine-tune her final exit, so the accuracy wasn't surprising.

Once transition was made, the flip-over program was run. As each of her forward maneuvering thrusters came around, they fired for five seconds, to starboard, until the next one was in place, thirty degrees behind on the circle of her bows. In her stern, the rear thrusters did the same thing, but in the other direction, to port.

As the thrusters fired, the big ship started to rotate, her bows going up and her stern down, until the big ship, still rotating, had flipped end-for-end.

On the bridge, the navigator was looking at his status display. Like everyone else on board, he was new to the position and learning as he went.

"I'll be damned," he said, as he watched the star field floating down in his display as the ship flipped.

"Nice," Captain Abrams said.

When her stern – and her main engines – pointed toward the planet, *Star Dancer* discontinued firing the maneuvering thrusters and began decelerating for Amber orbit.

The passenger spaces still had gravity, albeit reduced, and passengers were not required to sit out the two days in the passenger containers.

"Well, I must say, JieMin," YongLin said at supper that night, "this is much more pleasant than sitting in zero gravity in that passenger container, eating flavored toothpaste from a tube."

"Are you going to update all the other ships and crews with the new software, ChaoLi?" David asked.

"Yes, after our departure. That's the other part we still have to check."

SILK ROAD

"Well, it's a major improvement, there's no doubt about that."

He lifted his glass in a toast.

"Here's to gravity."

RICHARD F. WEYAND

Amber

Four hours before arrival in Amber orbit, Bert picked up their baggage for loading on the shuttle.

"Excuse me, ma'am."

"Yes, Bert?"

"Ma'am, some of us were wondering. With *Star Dancer* complete, there are still three more legs of this trip. To Tahiti, to Earthsea, and then to Arcadia. That is eighteen weeks of sitting idle, plus several more weeks at each location for loading and unloading. Perhaps twenty-two weeks total."

"Yes, that's right."

"As I say, some of us were wondering, ma'am. Certainly *Star Dancer* needs some robots aboard, to fly the cargo shuttles, prepare meals, all the normal shipboard functions. But there is no more construction to be done. Would there be things for us to do on Amber?"

"Well, there will be a new ship from the yards every month starting next month."

"Yes, ma'am. But that is nine thousand light-years and twenty-two weeks away for *Star Dancer*. That's a very long time for so many robots to be sitting idle. Won't new robots be coming to Arcadia from Playa during that time? To meet that need?"

"Yes, very likely. I suppose I could ask President Dufort if they need any robots on Amber."

"We would very much appreciate it, ma'am."

"Do you wish to be left on Amber as well, Bert?"

"Me, ma'am? No, thank you. I was asking for my fellows. I

am quite contented being attendant on you and your fellow passengers all the way to Tahiti."

"What about when we get to Tahiti, Bert?"

"Then there are two choices, ma'am. One is to remain with you on Tahiti. The other is to remain with *Star Dancer* for its trip back to Arcadia. I understand there will be passengers for those legs as well."

"Yes, that's right. And which do you prefer, Bert?"

"I would remain with you and Professor Chen, ma'am, if you have need of my assistance."

"Let me consider it, Bert. In the meantime, I will speak to President Dufort."

"Thank you, ma'am. My associates would appreciate it."

When *Star Dancer* was only a couple hours out of Amber, passengers were ordered to report to the passenger container for transfer down to the planet. Most of the crew was going planetside as well, for shore leave.

Skeleton crew and all the robots remained on the ship.

As before, ChaoLi and JieMin sat in the front with David Bolton and Chen YongLin. Despite the gravity being only two-tenths g, no one had trouble getting to their seats and getting belted in.

Once everyone going to the surface was secure aboard, Tom stood up in front of the cabin.

"We will now go to zero gravity. Please remember to have a bag ready in case of stomach upset."

Tom sat back down and belted himself in.

There was some minor side acceleration as *Star Dancer*'s forward and after maneuvering thrusters, at maximum depression in the counter-rotation direction, began firing to slow the rotation of the big ship.

Pretty soon they were back in zero gravity. Most people had gotten used to it enough from last time to have no problems. The ones who had real trouble last time had taken medication in advance this time.

ChaoLi watched the forward display as the *Star Dancer* settled into orbit around the planet. Once they had a stable orbit, the passenger container and the shuttle above them separated from the ship and made for the planet.

ChaoLi, JieMin, David, and YongLin, as passengers, were allowed to depart the ship before the crew. They made their way down the short flight of steps to find a fellow in a suit waiting for them. A limousine stood nearby.

"Madam Chen?"

"Yes?" ChaoLi said.

"I am Michael Grant, aide to President Dufort's chief of staff. I'm here to give you a ride to your hotel, ma'am."

"Very well."

The driver let them all into the back of the limousine, then closed the door. Grant got in the back with them.

"President Dufort would like to meet with all of you after you have had a chance to rest from your journey. Informal, such as over lunch. You can simply send me a mail with your availability when you know it."

"That will be fine, Mr. Grant."

His mission complete, Grant simply nodded.

ChaoLi spent the ride looking out the windows at the city. Amber was much like Arcadia. There were no floral-print lavalavas or people walking about nude or semi-nude, of course. Other than that, the city was very similar. It had the same feel.

SILK ROAD

They were already checked into the hotel, presumably by Mr. Grant, and a hotel staffer showed them to their suites on the penthouse floor.

Between zero gravity, re-entry, and all the other excitements of the day, they were exhausted. They went into the bedroom of the suite and collapsed on the bed.

When they got up, they found that their baggage had been delivered to the suite's living room while they slept. They were still in the fleece loungers and booties issued by Jixing Trading for zero-gravity travel.

"Showers," JieMin said.

"And real clothes."

"Not topless though. And no lavalavas, I don't think. Pants and shirts."

ChaoLi shrugged.

"Business casual. We'll manage."

Once showered and changed, JieMin went over to the windows and opened the heavy drapes.

"We're a bit out of synch with local time," he said. "It's midnight here."

"How about some breakfast and putter for several hours, then back to bed and up, say, mid-morning? That should get us close."

"Works for me."

As the best hotel in Amber, room service had breakfast twenty-four hours a day – a formulation that still bothered ChaoLi, from twenty-five-hour-a-day Arcadia – so they ordered breakfast.

After breakfast, ChaoLi took the display in the living room of the suite and JieMin took the one in the bedroom. She worked on approvals for things going on with Jixing Trading on Arcadia, while he worked on his two current problems.

A solution for the traveling salesman problem, and a formulation for a stable robot-based society.

Several hours later, ChaoLi sent a mail message to Michael Grant and YongLin and they went back to bed.

They woke at about ten o'clock local time. ChaoLi had mail messages from both YongLin and Michael Grant.

"Everything's all set for us to meet with President Dufort for lunch," she said. "He's going to send his car around."

"That works."

"Jean, how nice to meet you finally," ChaoLi said.

"And you, ChaoLi. Welcome to Amber."

"Thank you. This is my husband, Chen JieMin, and our friends, David Bolton and Chen YongLin."

"Very nice to meet you all. Vaclav Brabec here is my chief of staff, and I believe you've all met Michael Grant already."

After hellos all around, they were seated at the table in Dufort's private dining room in his presidential offices. Staff brought out a salad course, and conversation continued throughout the meal.

"Well, I must say it is impressive to see *Star Dancer* orbiting Amber," Dufort said. "I went out to look at it last night when it passed overhead."

"It's even more impressive to go up in a shuttle from one planet and come down in the same shuttle to a different planet six weeks later," ChaoLi said.

"Moving something that large between planets. Amazing. And how is the finishing work going? That was in progress on the way, right?"

SILK ROAD

"Oh, yes. It's complete."

"The ship is completely finished now?" Dufort asked. "In six weeks?"

"Yes. Jean, you would have to see it to believe it. The robots swarmed the work. They organized into teams and just had at it. They worked around-the-clock. They were relentless. And they were finished before we dropped out of hyperspace here."

"That's incredible."

"Yes, and it brings up another question," ChaoLi said. "I now have nine hundred excess robots aboard, who are looking at five months of deadheading before they can get back to Arcadia and be redeployed. There's simply no more work on the ship for them to do."

"Well, that's not an issue is it? *Star Dancer* can just take them back to Arcadia."

"The problem with that is that they hate to be bored. They love to be working. They asked me before I left the ship if there isn't work here they could do. On Amber."

"Well, of course, there is," Dufort replied. "Building houses, for instance. We have a bit of a housing shortage."

"Yes, but, Jean, you have to understand. If you put nine hundred robots on it, in a month you won't have a house. You'll have a subdivision. Which brings up other issues."

"Yes, I see. What do all the carpenters and electricians and plumbers do for a living."

"Exactly," ChaoLi said. "What happens to the economy when anything that can be specified well enough simply gets done, and in record time, by an army of robots?"

"I have been looking into this question," JieMin said.

Dufort looked at him with interest. He knew very well who Chen JieMin was. If Chen JieMin said he was looking into a problem, that problem was– not finished, exactly. Under

233

assault, though.

"What have you found, JieMin?" Dufort asked.

"The general problem has come up before, and we have some pretty good data on it, at least in some places. If you look at the percentage of the workforce in the old United States of North America in 1880, for example, and again a hundred years later, the differences are profound.

"Fully half of the employment positions were gone. The two biggest sectors in terms of losses were farming and domestic help. With the industrial revolution, farming became much more mechanized and less manpower intensive.

"Similarly with equipment for cooking, cleaning, and doing laundry. People no longer moved the furniture and took rugs out to beat the dust out of them, they simply vacuumed. People no longer had to cut and chop wood for the stove in order to cook, or boil water to do laundry by hand. Domestic help was no longer necessary.

"And yet, a hundred years later, we don't see fifty percent of the workforce unemployed, despite fifty percent of the 1880 jobs being gone."

"What happened, JieMin?" Dufort asked. "Where did they go? The other half of the workforce, I mean."

"Into other occupations that had not previously existed. The automobile industry. The aviation industry. The entertainment industries, including movies, music, and sports. The medical industry, which finally became a science. Huge industries that had not existed before.

"Industries that had been minor or nonexistent became the biggest industries in the economy."

"The biggest industries in the economy, JieMin?" ChaoLi asked.

"Yes, the two biggest industries became healthcare and

entertainment. Healthcare in 1880 was a joke, and didn't really become a science until the 1900s. When you got sick, you either died or recovered, and doctors had little to do with it other than to worsen your chances. The entertainment industry was also minor, because people worked such long hours that they didn't need to be entertained. They had no time for it.

"That's the other thing that happened. The full-time work week went from six twelve-hour days a week to five eight-hour days a week. From seventy-two hours to forty hours."

"How did people earn a living, though, working so many fewer hours?" Dufort asked.

"With more productivity, wages went up. A lot. Working forty hours a week, the real incomes of working people went up tenfold compared to what they made working seventy-two hours a week a century before."

"That's incredible," ChaoLi said.

"Yes, but the secret to it having worked out may have been the time it took to happen. The fifty percent of the people who were working in new industries weren't the same people who had been working in farming and domestic work a hundred years before. There were generations to adapt."

"And we don't have that," Dufort said.

"No," JieMin said. "I'm still working on how to make it work. But the general lesson is that the increased productivity should result in higher standards of living with less time spent working, in the medium to long term."

"If we can navigate the short-term effects of displacement," ChaoLi said.

"Exactly."

"Which brings us back to the problem of your nine hundred robots, ChaoLi."

"It sure does."

"Let me think about it," Dufort said. "In the meantime, how is your cargo business getting started?"

"Good, at some level. I mean, everybody is carrying something somewhere. But if you want a specific thing to end up in a specific place, that's another thing altogether. We have spices and teas from Arcadia. When we leave here, we'll have coffees from Amber. And we'll have apples from Tahiti.

"But it will be thirty-two weeks before *Star Dancer* is back here spacing this circuit. If you wanted chocolate from Aruba, or cognac from Olympia, when could I have them here?"

"So what's the solution, ChaoLi?"

"Hub-and-spoke operations. A ship flies from Arcadia direct to every planet, taking whatever that planet wants from the orbital freight station on Arcadia. It comes out here, drops everything, takes on an entire load of coffee and goes back to Arcadia. Next round, anybody who wants coffee can have it."

"So any planet to any planet shipping is always two hops," Dufort said.

"More or less. We would also have the Aruba freight station, which shortens the length of the hops in that direction, but adds a hop to things going to Arcadia."

"Sounds good, ChaoLi."

"Yes, but I don't have enough ships for that. I won't have twenty-one ships until May of next year or so. Fourteen months away. In the meantime, your imports are going to be sort of catch-as-catch-can."

"Once you have that, what do you do with additional ships that come on-line?"

"Add them to the routes with the most traffic."

"So then you have two ships on that route."

"Right. I'll probably eventually end up with five ships on every route. Which will still only mean a departure every three weeks, even for the closest destinations like Amber."

"Which is over a hundred ships. How do you even staff that operation?"

"I have the robots, Jean. They actually do a pretty good job of personal service, and they can cook like anything."

"They're very good in the kitchen," YongLin said, nodding.

"I don't mean to have been ignoring you, David, YongLin. I just find all this fascinating."

"That's all right, Jean," David said. "We do as well. And we hadn't heard all this yet."

"So why are you on this trip?" Dufort asked.

"We go to Tahiti for the anti-aging treatments," YongLin said.

"As do JieMin and I," ChaoLi said. "And then we go back to Arcadia, and David and YongLin will become Chen Zufu and Chen Zumu, and Chen MinChao and Jessica Chen-Jasic will retire."

YongLin nodded.

"We will relieve them," she said, "and then they go to Tahiti for the treatment, so they may have a longer retirement together."

"And then you will be the Chen?" Dufort asked.

"Yes," David replied. "MinChao and Jessica think we are ready."

"What do you think, David?"

"I think that their judgment in this matter is superior to my own."

Dufort laughed. He turned back to ChaoLi.

"This talk of Tahiti and anti-aging treatments brings up another question. There are some people here who wish to make the trip as well. Get those treatments. Are you ready to take on revenue passengers yet, ChaoLi?"

"Yes, Jean. I wasn't sure the robots would get *Star Dancer* done in time. But we're ready. The one thing we don't know yet is the market-clearing price. Everything right now is being carried on the books in kind. I can't yet quote them a price."

"Make the numbers big," Dufort said, shrugging. "Prices can come down over time. Right now, compared to deadheading *Star Dancer*'s passenger spaces, it's free money for you."

"Are anti-aging treatments then going to be reserved for the wealthy, Jean?"

"Initially, they probably will, ChaoLi. The wealthy and other early adopters subsidize the technology, which makes prices come down for everybody else. If Tahiti is making enough money on treatments, they can use that to build clinics on other colonies. In the meantime, your prices will continue to fall as you gain experience and begin paying off the investment."

"That is exactly correct," JieMin said.

"In the meantime, ChaoLi, make the numbers big. These people simply don't care what it costs."

SILK ROAD

On To Tahiti

ChaoLi and JieMin had lunch with Jean Dufort once more before they left for Tahiti. It was the day before departure. The partial unloading and reloading of *Star Dancer* was almost complete.

"I've decided to take your excess robots on Amber, ChaoLi," Dufort said.

"However many I can spare?" ChaoLi asked.

"Yes. Robots are coming to Amber, one way or the other, so we might as well take this first batch and get experience with how we might accommodate them."

"I see. That makes sense. At the same time, we have three hundred passengers to Tahiti, and the robots tell me one robot per every three passengers is probably best, with another fifty for other work. So we will take one hundred and fifty on with us. That leaves eight hundred and fifty staying here."

Dufort nodded.

"That works for us," he said.

"What are you going to do with them?" ChaoLi asked.

"There are some big projects that we keep thinking about doing, and that never get done. We don't have the manpower available, or the cost is just too high. For whatever reason, we never get around to doing them. So we'll use them on those. That won't displace anyone currently working."

"That makes sense. You get these extra projects done, but no one is out of a job."

"Yes," Dufort said. "And I've been thinking about the anti-aging treatments and their availability on a broader basis. I wonder if robots could be used to provide some of the services, bringing costs down. Or if robots could be used to provide a more basic package, that could be provided to a much broader segment of the population sooner. You might talk to Jacob Keller about that."

"The prime minister of Tahiti? Not the president?"

"Yes. The way I understand the setup over there, Keller is for their domestic policy, and Henry Wang is for their foreign policy. This sounds more like a domestic issue."

"I see," ChaoLi said. "Given that, I probably want to retain two hundred of the robots. We have a short passenger list from Tahiti to Earthsea, and so *Star Dancer* only needs a hundred or so robots there. That gives me a hundred I can leave on Tahiti so they can work out how they would fit into their treatment methodology."

"So eight hundred for Amber? That works for us."

After lunch and a conversation with Prime Minister Hank Keller on Tahiti, ChaoLi called Bert, on board *Star Dancer*.

"Good afternoon, ma'am."

"Good afternoon, Bert. I have a plan together I want to run past you."

"Of course, ma'am."

"We're thinking of leaving eight hundred of your fellows here on Amber. They have a number of big projects they never get around to for them to do. We would take two hundred on to Tahiti. We have three hundred passengers for the Tahiti leg, so we will be a little overstaffed for that leg, but we will leave a hundred robots on Tahiti. They want to see how you might fit into their anti-aging treatment programs, with an eye to expanding their programs into local clinics on the other colony planets."

SILK ROAD

"Will that leave us short-handed aboard *Star Dancer* for the Earthsea leg, ma'am?" Bert asked.

"No, we have only a few passengers for that leg, Bert. One hundred robots remaining aboard *Star Dancer* is more than enough, but probably the least I want aboard."

Bert nodded.

"I concur with that, ma'am. A contingency minimum, I would call it."

Bert paused for several seconds before continuing.

"As for the overall plan, ma'am, that sounds very good to us. Several big projects, you say?"

"Yes. A dam with a recreation area. A major clean-up and spruce-up program in the city. A beach project. Some new streets and highways. Enough to keep even eight hundred of you busy for quite a while."

"That sounds excellent, ma'am."

It wasn't two hours later that a shuttle with a passenger container made the run from *Star Dancer* down to the Amber City Shuttleport. When it landed, eight hundred robots came down the short stairs and formed up in ranks on the pavement.

"Who speaks for you all?" asked Harry Gomez, the Amber government's head of major projects.

One robot in the middle of the front row stepped forward.

"I am currently running the supervisory module, sir."

"All right. We have ten busses here to take you to the job site."

"Excellent, sir. And do you have a pointer to the plans for this project? We can process them on the way."

ChaoLi, JieMin, David Bolton, and Chen YongLin – together with three hundred other passengers and the returning crew –

made the trip up to *Star Dancer* the next day. There were over a dozen robots in the passenger container to provide any aid the passengers might require during the shuttle trip.

When everyone was seated in the passenger container, the forward viewscreen played a recording of an attractive young woman in a Jixing Trading uniform.

"Welcome to *Star Dancer*, everyone.

"The ship's crew and its robot complement look forward to providing you with a pleasant journey to Tahiti.

"There are a few tips for your safety and comfort I would like to pass along to you before we get started...."

"Well, that's a big improvement," JieMin whispered to ChaoLi.

"I didn't even know we had a uniform," ChaoLi said.

"It looks good, though."

ChaoLi nodded.

Jixing Trading was growing by leaps and bounds, and ChaoLi was kept scrambling to learn how to administer such a large organization. It couldn't be by direct control, that much was clear.

'The subtleties of power' Chen Zufu had said.

She was beginning to see now what he had meant.

The trip to Tahiti was full of work for both ChaoLi and JieMin.

JieMin kept working on the traveling salesman problem and the robot economy problem. The mathematics of the traveling salesman problem had gotten deep fast. The robot economy problem was still in the data gathering phase, looking for the mental integration that would shed some light on the problem.

ChaoLi wrote a letter to all nine of her captains detailing the robot deal she had made with Amber and Tahiti. The extra robots weren't just bored with deadheading, they also represented a demurrage to Jixing Trading. Selling the excess off to planets along the way transferred them from Jixing's balance sheet to the planetary accounts of the receiving colonies at the Bank of Earthsea. They now owed Playa for the robots, and Jixing Trading didn't.

ChaoLi wrote another letter to the heads of state of all the colony planets, letting them know that Jixing Trading would likely have robots for sale when their ships made planet stops. She outlined Amber's solution to the employment displacement problem, by using the robots to carry out projects long-planned but never carried out.

ChaoLi checked, and the new welcome video was in place for all the hyperspace liners. It was in response to her request to come up with a better, more welcoming safety briefing. The uniform grew out of that request. She wrote a nice note to the staffer who had come up with all that, and marked her for promotion.

It was clear to ChaoLi that, if she couldn't oversee everything going on, the most important part of her job was to see to it that the right people were in the right jobs. That was more than just hiring good people. It meant getting them where they were the most effective and promoting the ones who did well.

It also meant doing good firing. One couldn't be a hundred-percent accurate in the hiring process. When someone couldn't cut it, it did nobody any good to keep them. They were a drag on the company, and you were keeping them from finding a position (somewhere else!) where they could be successful and happy.

Naomi Thompson had done a good job as head of personnel in the initial hirings. She was also ChaoLi's valuable second-incommand in the executive suite. That couldn't last.

"Hi, Naomi," ChaoLi said.
"Good morning, ma'am."
Naomi looked a little harried, ChaoLi noticed.
"Are you keeping your head above water there, Naomi?"
"Mostly, ma'am. *Star Voyager* came in from the yards, and we dispatched her with another thousand of the initial shipment of robots. *Star Master* just arrived from the yards, and we're loading her now. And *Star Hunter* is coming in next week."
"I thought they were going to come in one a month?"
"They are, ma'am, but they're not necessarily evenly spaced. The factories in the yards are a little out of phase with each other. It's got us jumping right now, but we're keeping up. We're running all our shuttles twenty-five by seven now, using robots as pilots."
"What about our human pilots, Naomi?"
"They're supervising it all, ma'am, and they get to go home every night, so they're happy."
"How about the interstellar freight transfer station, Naomi?"
"Every ship that comes in from the yards brings pieces of it with them, ma'am. And we have several hundred robots welding them together in orbit. They don't mind vacuum at all, and it turns out they can magnetize their feet. It's like a freefall jungle gym out there. Check out some of these videos."
Thompson sent her a pointer.
"I will, Naomi. Thanks. And the transfer station for Aruba?"
"A lot of routes run through Aruba, ma'am. As you'd expect. Any ship going that way takes some parts with it. Not a full load, because they also have tea and spices, but a bunch. And the robots are assembling them as well. Smaller team, but

it's going well."

"What about the crew quarters, Naomi?"

"A couple of the hulls coming in from the yards will be directed to that use, ma'am. That will give us a little break on getting ships loaded and dispatched. The one for Aruba will stop here for finishing supplies and then head directly there. It will take a full load of parts for the station as well."

"And how are you doing, Naomi?"

"Oh, it's a handful, ma'am. No doubt about it."

"That's what I figured. You need to staff up your office, Naomi. Hand off the last of your personnel duties to your second there, give her the title, and get her to staff up as well. We need to have the administrative infrastructure in place to stay ahead of this thing as it grows. You should be worried about handling the exceptions, not day-to-day operations."

"I've done some of that, ma'am. I've been worried about building overhead faster than operations justify."

"A couple of things there, Naomi. One is that we need to get the administrative infrastructure in place to manage what we are rapidly becoming. Second is that we are making a profit on all the robots. When we drop off the excess on a planet, we're getting them off our balance sheet and we're charging shipping on them."

"All right, ma'am. I understand. This thing is growing by leaps and bounds."

"And we need to stay in front of it. One more thing, Naomi. When you hand off the personnel title, you're without a title yourself. I'm making you Chief Operations Officer. Put that through as well."

"Thank you, ma'am. I'll take care of it."

ChaoLi, JieMin, David, and YongLin were having dinner in

the first-class dining room. It was now completely finished, and many of the tables were full with other passengers headed to Tahiti. The buffet was up and operating, and the food was all excellent. Robots stood by for special requests.

"How is Naomi doing back home?" JieMin asked.

"Good. She's feeling harried, but managing. I told her to staff up more, so she was just handling the exceptions, and hand off the last of her personnel functions. She's now COO."

"That all makes sense," David said.

"I also need more robots," ChaoLi said.

"Really?" JieMin asked.

"Sure. Think about it. We designed these ships for a thousand passengers and five hundred crew. Nice round numbers. Four hundred of those crew were for passenger service.

"If you replace those four hundred crew with robots, you have a whole lot more cabins, because the robots don't need cabins. They run around-the-clock, and when idle can stand shoulder to shoulder a hundred or more to a room.

"That means we can take fourteen hundred passengers on the ship. For which we need more like five hundred robots per ship for passenger service. In a year, with twenty ships in service, we'll need ten thousand robots for passenger service."

"But *Star Runner* brought fifteen thousand of them back from Playa, didn't it?"

"Yes, and we sent out a thousand on each of seven liners, many of which will not come back to Arcadia. We're selling them off as the liners circulate. And there's the freight transfer stations, twenty ships in service next year, and we will continue to roll them out at least at one a month into the future. I'm considering duplicating Beacon again, and rolling out one new ship every two weeks."

SILK ROAD

JieMin nodded.

"You are going to end up short, but probably not for another six to nine months."

"But Oliver Nieman will let me transfer them to Arcadia while still holding them in Playa's inventory. They won't hit my balance sheet until I need them."

"That's a smart business move on his part," YongLin said.

"It's worked out for him so far, at least," David said.

"If you don't have immediate use for them, you might see if Rob Milbank has any big infrastructure projects he needs done, ChaoLi," YongLin said. "While you're dropping them off by the hundreds all over human space, don't forget back home."

"Hi, Rob," ChaoLi said.

"ChaoLi! How are you doing? How's your trip going?" Rob Milbank asked.

"Very well, thank you. It's much better on this leg. *Star Dancer* is finished. Completely fitted out. And we have revenue passengers aboard."

"Completely finished? In what? Eight or nine weeks?"

"It was finished in less than six," ChaoLi said. "The robots were done with it before we got to Amber."

"Wow. That's tremendous."

"Yes, they're very fast. Which brings up another question. I believe I have a few thousand robots on Arcadia at the moment that are at loose ends. Playa is carrying them as remote inventory, but they're available to me. I will need them as new ships roll in, but right now they're idle. Can you use them to do some things around Arcadia in the meantime?"

"How will that work with Playa?" Milbank asked.

"Well, you'll have to take them onto your planetary account while you have them, but then you can transfer them to my balance sheet. Other than interest and wear-and-tear, I think you're good there."

"Well, there are some projects here I can never get done. That might work out, ChaoLi."

"Make them big projects, Rob. They really dig in and get it done."

"All right, ChaoLi. I'll let you know."

That afternoon, ChaoLi found some time to watch the videos Thompson sent her a pointer to. She had just started when she called out to JieMin, working on the display in the bedroom of the stateroom suite.

"Hey, JieMin. I think you might want to see this."

JieMin came in from the bedroom.

"What is it?"

"Video of the robots working on the Arcadia freight station."

JieMin sat down in the other armchair and ChaoLi started the video again.

Robots – hundreds of them, it looked like – were swarming over the steelwork. The actinic blue of arc welding in process glowed in dozens of places on the structure. While they watched, robots launched themselves across gaps in the structure, to catch themselves at the other end of their flight and continue on.

At one point, two robots carrying a steel substructure launched themselves off one part of the large structure toward another. They floated across the void until one of them came with arm's reach of their destination and grabbed the steelwork there. The piece they were carrying swung around on that pivot point until the robot on the other end grabbed the structure there. They maneuvered the new piece into position, and two more robots came over with their welding cables dragging behind them and started fixing it in position.

"Wow. It's like watching ballet," JieMin said.

"Yeah. It's mesmerizing."

The camera view pulled back to give a greater perspective on the effort, and they could see the overall structure's basic shape, as well as the large number of parts orbiting nearby, dropped by one of the hyperspace liners when it came in from Beacon. Robots launched themselves back and forth between the structure and the drifting field of parts, carrying parts back to the structure under way.

"It's coming along well, actually," JieMin said. "You can start to make out how it's going to look."

"I think that's mostly because we've seen the plans," ChaoLi said. "But they are making good progress."

"It's kind of weird to see them working in space like that, without any suits or anything. They look like people working in the vacuum."

"They sure do."

They continued watching for the twenty minutes the video ran. At the end, ChaoLi turned to JieMin.

"Where is all this going, JieMin?" ChaoLi asked.

"Forward, I guess. I'm still working on the implications."

He looked at the display and then back to her.

"It's not an easy issue."

RICHARD F. WEYAND

Tahiti

The passenger container down to the surface on Tahiti carried a very mixed bag: the crew going on shore leave, the passengers, and a hundred robots being transferred from Jixing Trading to the big anti-aging clinic in downtown Papeete.

ChaoLi, JieMin, David, and YongLin exited with the other passengers, the first group to exit the container. There were buses to the anti-aging clinic there for the passengers, but there was also a man there waiting with a limousine.

"Madam Chen?" he asked.

ChaoLi and YongLin both said, "Yes," which stalled him for a moment. He carried on.

"Your party is waiting in the car."

They looked over to the limousine, and Chen JuPing and Paul Chen-Jasic got out of the car and waved to them.

The centenarians looked to be eighty years old.

They all rushed over to the limousine, and it was a round of hugs, jumbled with greetings and surprised reactions.

"You two look amazing."

"Yes, we feel wonderful. It's been years – decades – since we felt so good."

"So it really does work."

"Oh, yes. Absolutely. And the people here are very nice."

"And the apple pie is amazing."

"It's really good to see you doing so well. We were so worried about Paul."

"Yes, I almost lost him. But they did a marvelous job."

SILK ROAD

They all rode in the limousine to the hotel downtown, the newcomers rubber-necking out the windows.

"It looks bigger than Arcadia City."

"Not many young people, though."

"Yes, I understand they mostly head out to the newer cities."

"How long is *Star Dancer* here?"

"About a week to unload and load, then it's on to Earthsea."

"So we have a week together. What fun."

It would be hard to overstate the importance of Paul Chen-Jasic's and Chen JuPing's rejuvenation to the Chen-Jasic family.

With the increase in lifespans brought about by Arcadia's more modern medicine – compared to the medicine available to the Chen clan in the Chingqing administrative region on Earth – the practice of having the family elder rule the family until his death had been modified by Chen GangHai, the eldest son of Chen LiQiang, who as Chen Zufu had brought his family to Arcadia.

Each couple serving as Chen Zufu and Chen Zumu had since administered the family for twenty years or so. That was about the time it had been with shorter lifespans, but it now meant there was a significant period of retirement after stepping down.

Then again, the Chen-Jasic family on Arcadia was a huge operation compared to the size of extended families in rural China. Whereas the Chen family was thirty-one individuals in the load of colonists that had come to Arcadia, the Chen-Jasic extended family was now hundreds of thousands of people, all pulling for the common goals of the clan.

The common goals set by Chen Zufu and Chen Zumu.

Two decades of such huge responsibility were enough.

Now, with the availability of the anti-aging treatments on

Tahiti, that retirement period would be greatly extended. There would be more than one retired couple who had experience running the clan for the current Chen Zufu and Chen Zumu to consult with.

For when you were the unchallenged head of such an operation, who could you talk to for advice, to express your concerns, to air out your worries? Why, someone who had done it already, of course.

The anti-aging treatments of Tahiti would thus give the Chen-Jasic family leaders a greater depth of advice going forward.

David Bolton and Chen YongLin would have Chen MinChao, Jessica Chen-Jasic, Paul Chen-Jasic, and Chen JuPing as their advisers, with an experience base that ran back over eighty years, back to the founding of the Republic, all the way back to the Kendall regime.

When Chen JieMin and Chen ChaoLi became Chen Zufu and Chen Zumu, in about twenty years, they would have six former leaders of the clan as their advisers and confidants.

After their own retirement, JieMin and ChaoLi would likely serve as advisers to the heads of clan for eighty years before they finally passed.

During the day, the six Arcadians did some sightseeing on Tahiti. It was a beautiful planet, by chance reminiscent of its namesake, and they took in the sights whenever the newcomers weren't at the anti-aging clinic for preliminary evaluation. In the evenings, they took dinner together in a private dining room so they could speak openly.

On their second night on Tahiti, ChaoLi put the question to JieMin.

"JieMin, where are you at in your evaluation of the impacts

of all this trade and interconnection to the colonies?"

"That's a very long and deep topic, ChaoLi."

"Nevertheless, you're never going to have a more concerned or experienced audience for it."

"Yes, JieMin," JuPing said. "You'd best use us while we're all together."

"Very well," JieMin said, then paused to gather his thoughts.

"The most concerning technologies among the colonies we are in contact with so far are the robots and the anti-aging therapeutics. Each has the potential for causing a demographic crisis on the short term, although both are hugely beneficial on the medium to long term.

"The robots are the easier to understand. They don't just replace one worker, they replace about six workers per robot."

"So many?" YongLin asked.

"Yes. They work all day, all around the clock, seven days a week. That's at least four workers right there. But their economies of movement and speed of work make it more like six to one. ChaoLi and I saw them working on the interior of *Star Dancer*, and also watched a video of their work on the interstellar freight station in orbit around Arcadia.

"It was eye-opening. They do not stop to think about the task, or plan the next piece. They do that on the fly. They are coordinating with each other constantly over radio. We saw dozens of robots simply launching themselves across space, without ever running into each other. They all knew the vector the others were on, and avoided each other, sometimes by mere feet.

"In practical terms, it means that anything the robots can do no longer makes any sense to have a person do."

"That's a huge disruption," David said.

"Absolutely. Now, since the robots create more– well, more

of everything, really – and don't consume anything but electricity, which we have an abundance of, standards of living go up, and by a lot. Food becomes cheaper. Housing becomes cheaper. Everything becomes cheaper, really."

"Yes," Paul said. "Absent scarcity, what you are really paying for when you buy something is the time of the person that made it."

"Absolutely. And with the robots being the next thing to free, everything becomes very cheap. But without employment, no one has even the money it takes to buy it cheap.

"Do we give away food and housing? We almost could. What of us then? How do we fare psychologically when we have no value? The history there is not hopeful.

"The longevity change with the anti-aging therapeutics has very nearly the same impact.

"On Arcadia, people start working very young, but many of the colonies reverted to the Earth model. People start working when they have learned their occupation, between perhaps eighteen and twenty-five years old. They retire generally in their sixties and live well into their nineties.

"So perhaps forty or fifty years in the workforce, and thirty years in retirement.

"But if people live until a hundred and seventy-five, what then? The same ratio of work years to retirement years means working until a hundred and ten or twenty, with a retirement lasting fifty or sixty years.

"That's unlikely. So what you end up with is a huge demographic overhang, where most of the population is retired. A minority of people work for a living.

"That's another huge disruption," David said.

"Yes, but the two actually compensate each other to a certain extent."

SILK ROAD

"How's that, JieMin?" JuPing asked.

"Consider someone who is out of work at fifty because robots have taken his job. It might take him five years to learn a new skill, a technical one that the robots can't do. He's fifty-five when he's ready to work again, only ten years short of retirement.

"But if anti-aging treatments have reduced his physical age to just below fifty, and he has a life expectancy now of another hundred years, it makes sense to pursue that new occupation. He might work in that field for twenty-five or thirty years, retiring at a physical age of sixty-five, and still have sixty or seventy years of retirement.

"That huge demographic overhang from the anti-aging therapeutics doesn't matter, either. If the necessities of life – food, housing, most material goods – become cheap, and are mostly provided by robots, you have the base of workers you need to support that overhang. But now they're robots.

"Overall, the total gross product of the colonies increases by several times, very rapidly, due to the robots. Yet consumption less than doubles due to the anti-aging therapeutics. Standards of living – on average – will skyrocket."

"That's the key phrase, though, JieMin," Paul said. "On average."

"Yes, Paul. Exactly. The question we face is how we keep individual people from getting caught in the gears in the short term. The guy who's displaced by a robot, does not yet have the anti-aging therapeutics, now has no income, and still has a family to raise.

"But over the long haul, once things settle out, I think everyone is better off. Much better off, actually."

"That's a pretty puzzle you've presented us with, JieMin," David said.

"Yes, but who else better to solve it than us?" Paul asked. "And if we can't solve it, I think we're in for deep trouble."

"We should probably get MinChao and Jessica in this discussion, too," JuPing said. "It's too late on Arcadia at the moment, but we could have a meeting tomorrow."

"I recorded JieMin's talk," ChaoLi said. "I'll send it to them, so they can be up to speed with the rest of us."

"Send that to me, as well, ChaoLi," YongLin said. "I'd like to listen to it again."

"I'll send it to everybody, and I'll see if Chen Zufu and Chen Zumu come back with a time for a meeting."

It was mid-morning the next day in Arcadia City – and still dark in Papeete – when Jessica and MinChao compared notes on JieMin's talk.

"So what do you think?" Jessica asked.

"I think JieMin has his finger on the problems," MinChao said. "It's interesting that they tend to compensate for each other, in a way."

"Yes. I wonder if there isn't some way to magnify that. To make the compensations greater, so there's a path through the short term for people who would otherwise be, in JieMin's language, 'caught in the gears.'"

"How would you do that?"

"Oh, I don't know," Jessica said. "Just throwing things out, what if some percentage of the robots built block housing for people going to university beyond age twenty, say. And those blocks could have free meals for everyone living there. So a displaced worker and his family would be taken care of while he learned a new trade. Something the robots can't do."

"Would you do that as a government program of some sort?"

"Oh, heavens, no. You want something that would work." MinChao chuckled.

"Then how?"

"I don't know. That all might be rather inexpensive to provide. The robots could build it, and the robots could grow and prepare the food. The university could probably do it on its own. Provide it to the students. Maybe with a bit of help."

MinChao nodded. The Chen-Jasic family were big financial supporters of the university. When you gave money to an institution like that, you had a certain amount of control over how it was spent. Especially if it was an ongoing commitment.

"That's an interesting idea," he said. "You still have the problem of the anti-aging therapeutics, though. Someone going to school for a new career needs time."

"Yes. Perhaps that could be part of it, too. I wonder how much the anti-aging treatments would cost if they were provided through local clinics rather than ship people off to Tahiti."

"Well, clearly we need to do something."

"Yes," Jessica said. "A substantial number of disaffected and unemployed people is destabilizing. They might tear everything down, if the system was failing them. Justly so, I might add."

"We need to size the problem. What jobs can robots do and not do? How many people are in one kind of job versus the other?"

"The first question is easy to answer".

"It is?" MinChao asked.

"Certainly. Just ask them."

They all met in a video call. The current Chen, MinChao and Jessica, were in her tea room, in late afternoon, with the giant display wall showing a private meeting room in the hotel in Papeete. On the Tahiti side, the six Arcadians – they who had been or would be Chen – sat around one side of a round table, facing the meeting room's large display. In Papeete, it was mid-morning of the day after JieMin's talk.

"Have you two had a chance to see JieMin's presentation, MinChao?" JuPing asked.

"Yes, and Jessica had some thoughts about it," MinChao said, and nodded to his wife.

Jessica told them her thoughts from the morning, then continued.

"So I called Loukas's robot this morning – Bob, his name is – and I asked him. He said that, generally speaking, robots are good at doing known things. Like hanging drywall and finishing out *Star Dancer*. Or working from plans to build a house or building.

"What they are not good at is deciding that *Star Dancer* needed finishing out, or coming up with the plans for the house.

"He actually took a list of occupations, and separated them into three categories for me. Ones they could do, ones they could not do, and others that were part of one and part of the other."

Jessica mailed the list to everyone and they scanned it in their heads-up displays, lower in their vision than the wall display. JieMin nodded.

"This is pretty much what I expected. As long as they know what needs doing, they can do it. If not, they're helpless."

"Yes," ChaoLi said. "If they have a recipe, they can cook. If they have plans, they can build. So what we need to do is transition people in the jobs on one list into the jobs on the other."

SILK ROAD

"Jessica," JuPing said, "how many people are employed in jobs that need transitioning? As a fraction of the total?"

"That's the bad news," Jessica said. "Taking a quick look, it's more than half. It looks more like two-thirds."

"Ouch," Paul said.

"Now what do we do?" JuPing asked.

"Think about it some more," Jessica said. "Stay on it, JieMin."

"Yes, Chen Zumu," JieMin said.

"ChaoLi," MinChao said, "you should probably also speak with Planetary Chairman Nieman about this. They may have faced similar issues when robots first became available in large numbers on Playa."

"Yes, Chen Zufu," ChaoLi said.

RICHARD F. WEYAND

In The Hospital

The six Arcadians had dinner together the night before *Star Dancer* was scheduled to depart for Earthsea and then Arcadia. They were still booking the private dining room at the hotel for their meals together.

"You don't need to come out to see us off tomorrow," JuPing said. "We're just going to walk out and get in the passenger container. Nothing to see. And you four need to get into the clinic and get your treatments started or you're never going to be going home. I would much rather say goodbye tonight, anyway."

"If you're sure, JuPing," YongLin said.

"Yes, absolutely. We'll see you in nine months or so, back home on Arcadia. Just take care of yourselves and do what the doctors tell you. Some parts of it aren't particularly pleasant, but the results are worth it."

"Yeah, like that one skin treatment that makes you itch all over for four hours. That wasn't fun."

"Now don't go getting them apprehensive about it, Paul."

"You brought it up."

ChaoLi had to suppress a smile. She had never seen the private byplay between JuPing and Paul when they were Chen Zumu and Chen Zufu, even as JuPing's tea girl. Now, in this exclusive club of past and future Chen, it was different.

Dinner was good, goodbyes were a little teary, and ChaoLi and JieMin went to bed early, so they would be well-rested for their admittance to the clinic tomorrow.

SILK ROAD

Admission to the clinic was as admission to any hospital for elective or scheduled procedures had been for centuries. Give the admissions clerk all the information, be ID tagged – here with a tag on a fingernail – be shown to your room.

When they got to their room, there was a robot sitting in the guest chair in the corner.

"A robot?" ChaoLi asked.

"Yes, ma'am. We're using them for patient services now. Anything you need, or if you have any issues, just let him know."

"I am most happy to serve you again, ma'am, sir."

"Bert?"

"Yes, ma'am. I knew you would be going to the clinic here, of course. When it was decided the hundred robots you left behind would be stationed here, I swapped myself into that hundred, and, well, here I am."

ChaoLi chuckled, then became concerned.

"You know that we will only be here three to six months, right, Bert?"

"Yes, ma'am. It is quite easy for us to swap assignments."

"So you'll swap back."

"Of course. To *Star Courier*, isn't it?"

"I'm not even sure, Bert."

"I believe *Star Courier* will be assigned to the Tahiti run, ma'am."

"*Star Courier* isn't even finished yet, Bert."

"No, ma'am. But it will be. And now, if I might ask, what would you like for lunch? The selection is rather more limited here than on *Star Runner*, I'm afraid."

"I guess you guys haven't taken over the kitchens here yet."

"No, ma'am. Not yet."

They were glad to change out of their street clothes into fleece loungers and booties. They were much warmer than street clothes intended for a subtropical climate, and forced inactivity in the clinic made them more likely to be cold.

Being in the clinic was like being in hospital anywhere. The boring routine. Difficulty sleeping without sufficient exercise. The 'healthy' food, which left a lot to be desired.

There were compensations. Bert's presence was comforting. He was a reminder of the time before being in the clinic, which became more important as the weeks wore on. While most of the food was uninspired, the apple pie was stupendous, perhaps as good as the hotel's. It seemed there simply wasn't such a thing as bad apple pie on Tahiti. Or even mediocre apple pie.

David Bolton and Chen YongLin were in the next room, and their treatments were more or less in synch, at least initially. David and YongLin were sixty years old. The treatments could be expected to result in a physical age of about fifty-one.

ChaoLi and JieMin were forty years old, and the treatments could be expected to result in a physical age of about thirty-six. This meant that ChaoLi's and JieMin's treatments were less extensive – or at least less exhausting – so the two couples drifted out of synch over time.

The treatments themselves seemed innocuous, and ChaoLi couldn't figure out how they could be doing anything. Most of them seemed to be genetic treatments, an RNA sequence tucked into a viral capsid from which the virus sequence had been removed. She didn't understand the biology of it, but after those treatments, her body responded as if she had a cold as it worked to destroy the invader.

Some of those pseudo-colds were worse than others, and took longer to recover from. The doctors assured them their responses were normal, however. Bert was a great comfort during these periods, and mothered them with chicken soup and extra apple pie.

There was one sequence that did result in them being a bit itchy all over. A resequencing of the skin, the largest and most sensitive organ in the body. It was merely uncomfortable for ChaoLi and JieMin, although it was much more severe for David and YongLin due to their greater age.

ChaoLi could only imagine how uncomfortable it had been for David and JuPing.

The clinic itself was a massive complex, sprawling over a campus that had spread out over a square mile to the northwest from downtown Papeete.

The colony's initial chairman and council had been warned by the medical researchers among the colonists how large the hospital complex could ultimately get. They had set aside a square mile north and west of the original hospital building as a city park. The complex had grown until it engulfed the park, despite building up as it went. Satellite facilities were located in other cities on Tahiti as well.

There were rare days during their treatment when ChaoLi and JieMin were allowed to go out into the downtown and walk about, eat food other than that provided in the clinic, and otherwise enjoy being out of the building for a few hours.

Most of the time, however, once they had recovered from one treatment, they were immediately given another.

Ad infinitum, or so it seemed.

ChaoLi didn't notice many changes to herself. They would only be losing a few years. Perhaps her facial creases softened a bit. Her skin seemed a bit younger, thicker and more flexible.

But there were no radical changes in her or, that she noticed, in JieMin.

David and YongLin was another story. They were losing almost a decade of their physical age, from sixty back to fifty-one. She could see it, and so could they. They also reported more energy, and fewer aches and pains as the treatment progressed.

ChaoLi kept in touch with her business contacts during this period, despite feeling much of the time like she had been beaten up and kicked about. On one occasion early in their treatment, she called Oliver Nieman, the Playa Planetary Chairman. When he accepted the call, he was seated in his big chair, with a plate of cookies to one side.

"Good morning, ChaoLi," Nieman said when he took the call.

He was chewing a cookie.

"Good morning, Oliver."

"To what do I owe the pleasure today?"

"I had several questions today, Oliver. The first one is likely the easiest. You see, I've been misplacing robots."

Nieman laughed, a hearty rumble.

"Yes, I noticed that in my planetary balance sheets. Amber, Tahiti, Earthsea, Olympia. Even Arcadia. Why the list goes on and on."

"Yes. When the robots finish the fitting out of our ships on the first leg of their journeys, they're immediately ready to go do something else, and prefer not to deadhead back to Arcadia."

Nieman nodded.

"Yes, they don't like being idle."

"The end result, though, Oliver, is that I am going to run out of robots. Can you send me another ten thousand when *Star Hunter* gets there?"

"Of course, of course. Do you want to make it fifteen thousand now, as last time, or do you prefer to call me back later to increase the amount?"

It was ChaoLi's turn to laugh.

"OK, I give up. Let's do fifteen thousand now, Oliver."

"Splendid. And your next question, ChaoLi?"

"We figure one robot will replace about six human laborers, Oliver."

"That's right. It's about six-point-three, I think, in our studies, but you're very close."

"That will be a huge disruption to our economies. The economies of the other colony planets. What I want to ask is, what did you do on Playa to mitigate that?"

"Ah, yes. Well, a couple points there, ChaoLi. First is that all the technologies coming on-line from the various colony planets will be a greater or lesser disruption on the others. These are all, in some way, disruptive technologies.

"Much greater lifespans – such as from Tahiti, for instance, or the other medically focused economies – will disrupt a lot of things. Young people and old people look at things differently. Having a much greater proportion of old people will change the way societies respond to things, especially change."

"But the robots are potentially the most disruptive of the technologies, Oliver."

"On the short term, perhaps. My second point is that our adaptation was slower than what you are looking at. Robots were initially expensive, and so their introduction was gradual, as functionality increased and prices came down.

"The issue now on other colonies is exacerbated because the robots have already peaked in functionality, while finding the bottom of the long-term pricing curve.

"Nevertheless, we do have some information on the things we did, which might be adaptable in some form to the current situation. I can send you this information, if you wish."

"Please do, Oliver."

"Of course, ChaoLi. I have one further thought on this matter that may help a great deal. It's a way to slow the introduction of the robots into the labor fields, while reaping enormous personal benefits everyone will appreciate."

"That sounds really good, Oliver. What is it?"

"Consider. We now have anti-aging technology from Tahiti, medical nanotechnology from Amber, endocrinology from Bali, immunology from Fiji, anti-cancer technology from Nirvana, human genetics from Spring, and even direct neural virtual reality from Westernesse.

"One might contemplate a medical clinic on each colony that combines all these technologies and provides them to the colony's citizens."

Nieman popped a cookie into his mouth and chewed while ChaoLi responded.

"That would be almost two dozen huge facilities, Oliver, to service twenty million people or so per colony in any finite time. Those populations are also doubling every twenty years. And it would take hundreds of thousands or millions of people to staff all those clinics."

"Huge facilities that can be built and expanded by robots, ChaoLi, and thousands of people to supervise millions of robots that could, I am sure, master the known methods of those technologies' application."

ChaoLi just stared at him, her eyes wide, and Nieman smiled.

"You see it, yes?" he asked.

"Yes, of course. It would take years – perhaps decades – but it's doable."

"Years during which people could learn new things, creative things – which, no disrespect to my technical people, their robots cannot do – and be ready when robots began moving, gradually, off of that effort into the broader economy.

"And when they did, the robots would not be resented, they would instead be loved, for having provided such wonderful medical technology to the citizens of our planets, resulting in much longer and healthier lives for everyone."

Nieman popped another cookie into his mouth and beamed a huge smile as he chewed.

"Oliver, you're a genius. You just also solved the problem of how to make these medical technologies available to more than just the wealthy."

"Not at all, ChaoLi. I am merely selfish. I have spent the odd hour thinking of how I might induce the providers of all those technologies to build clinics on Playa, so that I might make use of them. Without having to travel there, which, no disrespect to yourself, I would find distasteful."

ChaoLi smiled.

"Have the anti-aging people come to you, Oliver? Brilliant."

"Actually, I was thinking the endocrinology people might be of more immediate use to me, ChaoLi. I seem to have something of a hormone imbalance."

Nieman popped yet another cookie into his mouth and smiled beatifically.

ChaoLi laughed like little bells.

ChaoLi shared the recording of her conversation with Oliver Nieman with JieMin.

"That really is a good idea," JieMin said. "We may be able to generalize on it a bit. What it amounts to is employing the robots first on things that aren't being done now, while the people who are working on current projects remain employed and get trained up in other skills."

"I worry not everyone has skills that would translate to a design position, JieMin."

"Understood, but that may not be as much of an issue as you think, ChaoLi. There are a lot more activities falling broadly under 'design' than just technology. Art, sculpture, crafts of various kinds, cooking up new recipes, designing furniture. In any case, I think we need a meeting."

ChaoLi nodded.

"Agreed. I'll set it up."

The conference room in their wing of the clinic had a display big enough for the family meeting. ChaoLi, JieMin, David, and YongLin met there, while Paul and JuPing joined from their stateroom in *Star Dancer*, and MinChao and Jessica joined from her tea room on Arcadia.

ChaoLi had sent the recording of her conversation with Oliver Nieman to everyone in advance, and appended JieMin's reaction.

"Now that you've had time to think about it, JieMin, elaborate on your reaction, please," Jessica said.

"Of course, Chen Zumu. The key feature is that it slows down the disruption to manageable levels. My estimate is that it spreads it out over ten to twenty years. That minimizes the damage to individuals, because it gives people time to find and migrate to new positions within the ultimately resulting economy.

"It also provides significant benefits to everyone, and speeds the provision of those benefits to the entire population. That goes a long way to countering what could otherwise be a festering resentment of the new technologies in general and the robots in particular.

"Finally, it does get us to a much higher standard of living, and one in which everyone benefits, pretty quickly, rather than the benefits starting with the rich and filtering down more slowly. That last has all kinds of potential societal issues, which this neatly sidesteps."

"That's my take on it as well, Jessica," Paul said.

"Oliver is quite a smart fellow when you get down to it," JuPing said. "This is the sort of thing Paul and I dreamed about all those years ago."

"Are we agreed, then?" MinChao asked.

He scanned the other attendants, getting nods from all present.

"Very well. David, YongLin, this is your assignment. To get all the planetary leaders working on Planetary Chairman Nieman's proposal. They are all senior executives for their planets, and none of them got to be where they are by being stupid. They're all wrestling with these issues already.

"It would probably be best to encourage Tahiti President Wang to call a meeting and kick it off, and have Mr. Nieman propose his solution. Then let them run with the ball, but stay in communication with their effort and be prepared to help out from the sidelines.

"ChaoLi, JieMin, I want you involved in this effort as well. JieMin, it would be helpful if you wrote up your economic analysis as a paper. Something with an executive summary for the planetary executives that heads up a much more meaty analysis for their staffs.

"ChaoLi, you already have relationships with all the planetary executives through your Jixing Trading activities.

Help get that meeting put together, and encourage people to attend. Stay in touch and be a sounding board for them. Be prepared to spot, and assist in resolving, any issues that may come up. Catching any issues early will be very helpful.

"This effort will likely consume most of your tenure, David, YongLin, as getting a hyperspace transportation system up and running did ours. ChaoLi, JieMin, you will manage and shape this emergent new economy throughout your tenure.

"This is why you all need to be involved now."

David, YongLin, JieMin and ChaoLi all nodded. All eight of the once, current, and future Chen had discussed the issues as near-equals in their meetings, but when push came to shove, there could be only one decision maker.

Chen Zufu had spoken.

"Yes, Chen Zufu," Paul said for them all.

SILK ROAD

Balance Of Trade

After four months in the clinic, ChaoLi and JieMin finally reached the day they were dismissed. David and YongLin had three weeks to go, as they had extra work done due to their age, and also took longer to recover from some of the treatments.

ChaoLi and JieMin left the clinic and moved back to the hotel. When they got to their room, they found their baggage waiting, as well as a robot in the living room of the suite.

"Bert?" ChaoLi asked.

"Yes, ma'am."

"OK, how did you wangle this one?"

"Wangle, ma'am? I simply assigned myself to your follow-on care."

"I didn't know there was any follow-on care required, Bert."

"Required can be a fuzzy word, ma'am. In your case, there is a notation in your records for three weeks of follow-on care."

"Which notation you put there."

"As may be, ma'am."

ChaoLi laughed.

"What do you do in three weeks, Bert?"

"I will swap assignments to *Star Courier*, ma'am."

"Which is in fact already headed this way from Amber."

"Yes, ma'am."

A simple loop route out of Arcadia through Amber, Tahiti, and Earthsea would normally take seven months: four six-week legs, with one to two weeks of unloading and loading at each port. In an unmodified loop route, *Star Dancer* would not be back to Tahiti for almost three months.

As ships continued to roll out of the shipyards, however, Jixing Trading was running expedited loop routes, in which the next iteration of the loop would be begun early, with a different ship. *Star Courier* had left Arcadia before *Star Dancer* got back, and *Star Dancer* had now been re-assigned to run an expedited loop route on a different set of colonies.

Star Courier would hit Tahiti in another two weeks, and, after unloading and loading, would not be ready to head back to Arcadia via Earthsea until just after David and YongLin were released from the clinic.

The four Arcadians would all head home together.

In the meantime, ChaoLi and JieMin both had a lot of work to do. They camped out in separate rooms of the hotel suite, as before, so each had the use of a full-function display.

JieMin was attempting to model the economic disruption of the technology advances, but found the simulation software was not up to modeling such a radical change. It assumed too many things were immutable or at least slow-moving.

JieMin took the software apart, pulled the analysis kernel out, and wrote a new one. He reassembled the parts of the prior software around the new kernel and started testing. The new software got the same answers to common problems as the original.

So far, so good.

That was as far as he'd gotten by departure time.

ChaoLi was working the socialization of Oliver Nieman's solution, but she was doing it subtly, almost as an aside from her main discussions with planetary executives.

SILK ROAD

As the CEO of Jixing Trading, ChaoLi was the highest-ranking person in hyperspace shipping that determined what imports and exports went where. She coordinated all this activity with planetary executives across all the colony planets.

She also needed to negotiate whether it was alright to drop off robots who had completed the fitting out of a new liner on the first leg of its route. That expense, recorded in-kind, transferred to the planetary account of the receiving planet in the Bank of Earthsea, so it amounted to a sale.

Within the first couple months, every colony planet that was the first-leg destination of a hyperspace liner had gotten eight or nine hundred robots dropped off. The outfitting of that ship was complete, and they were no longer required on that ship, at least not in such numbers.

With the second new hyperspace liner on a route, the excess robots preferred to deadhead one leg, and be dropped off on the second colony planet on the route. It was pretty clear this was going to ripple through all the planets on all the routes as new hyperspace liners came into service.

ChaoLi was handling those negotiations with the planetary executives herself. She couldn't hand them off to Naomi Thompson or another underling. A planetary executive expected to talk to the top dog.

In these discussions, whenever economic disruptions or the broader availability of any of the medical technologies came up – which they always did – ChaoLi brushed it away with 'Oh, Playa Planetary Chairman Nieman has a plan he's working on for that. Chen JieMin is looking at it now, and it looks good.'

JieMin's name was a talisman in these discussions. Everybody knew who Chen JieMin was, and if he said it was good, then it was good.

"Good morning, Hank."

"Hello, ChaoLi," Tahiti President Henry Wang said. "How did your treatments go?"

"Very well, thank you. They do a nice job at your clinic."

"Excellent. I'm glad. And how can I help you today?"

"I have been getting a lot of concern expressed to me by other planetary executives about potential economic disruptions of the technologies available to them now, particularly robots and anti-aging treatments."

Wang nodded.

"I hear much of the same, ChaoLi, but you probably get a less guarded version than I do, since Tahiti is the source of one of those technologies."

"I think you're right, Hank. People are worried about job losses from the robots. They're also worried about a stratification between the wealthy and the middle and lower classes with the anti-aging treatments."

"Yes. We've been thinking about how to address that, ChaoLi, but we haven't gotten very far."

"That's why I'm calling, Hank. Playa Planetary Chairman Nieman has come up with a solution. JieMin has been looking at it, and he thinks it will work really well."

"Really."

"Yes, so I was calling you to encourage you to call Oliver and have him explain it to you. He's put a lot of thought into it, Hank, and he's eloquent on the subject."

"All right, ChaoLi. I'll do that. What's the next step, then, assuming Oliver's solution is a good one?"

"JieMin's writing up an analysis of the plan, and he'll publish that. Then I think it may be time to call a meeting of the planetary executives to consider it."

"Who would call such a meeting, ChaoLi?"

"I would think either you or Oliver could, Hank. For that matter Arcadia Prime Minister Milbank could, but Rob's been sensitive about having Arcadia be any more high-profile than it is already. He much prefers the colonies continue down the path of an association of equals."

Wang nodded.

"I see, ChaoLi, and I agree with him on that point. All right, let me talk to Oliver and see where we get. I'll let you know what happens. And please get me a copy of JieMin's paper as soon as it is compete."

"Of course, Hank. Thanks."

"Thank you, ChaoLi."

It was several days later that Tahiti President Henry Wang called ChaoLi back.

"Hello, ChaoLi."

"Good morning, Hank. How are you today?"

"Good. I wanted to let you know I spoke with Oliver a couple of days ago. My staff has been going over his proposal since. They think it might work, and are waiting on JieMin's analysis."

"That'll be a while, Hank. He is having to build his own analysis engine, because nothing we have will handle the problem."

"I can see that. But we're very hopeful this is a true solution. As you said, Oliver was eloquent on the point."

"Oliver is always eloquent, Hank."

"Yes, indeed, although talking to him always makes me hungry. Next time I will have my own plate of cookies."

ChaoLi laughed.

"I recommend the apple fritters here at the hotel, Hank. They're wonderful."

275

"One of my favorites. Cookies aside, I think he's on to something, ChaoLi."

"I worry that we haven't considered the balance of trade issues, Hank. How do those work out?"

"Balance of trade? But in a barter system between planets, ChaoLi, trade is always in balance."

"What? I'm sorry, Hank, but I don't get that."

"The only time you can have a trade imbalance is when there is an outside store of value. In a pure barter between planets, a trade imbalance cannot exist. Not for long."

At ChaoLi's puzzled expression, Wang continued.

"Consider. You bring tea, and coffee, and robots, and, soon, other trade goods here to Tahiti, right?"

"Yes," ChaoLi said slowly.

"And you take apples and, soon, medicines and treatments from here to other colonies, right?"

"I'm with you, Hank."

"All right. So now you get to Arcadia, and you sell the apples, and you find you can only make enough local currency to buy half as much tea as last time, right?

"OK."

"Do you now take just as much tea to Tahiti?"

"No. I would have to be compensated somehow."

"Correct. Such as with an interstellar currency, or some other reference to an external store of value. Without that, the trade settles to the highest volume it can maintain given local prices."

"Then what do you do if you want more tea, Hank?"

"Export more apples, or more medicines, or otherwise raise the market-clearing value of our exports. But it's the market-clearing value, in local currency, on that other planet. The destination planet."

"And if apples are more valuable on Olympia, say?"

"Then it would make more sense for you to take on more apples here, and trade them for distilled spirits or fusion power plants on Olympia. But that's your job. Jixing Trading's job. To take every product to its best destination. But it still sells at the market-clearing price at that destination."

"That doesn't sound right, Hank, but I can't see the hole in it."

"Oh, it's right, ChaoLi. Check with JieMin. But that's why I would oppose any sort of interstellar currency, or naming any currency a reserve currency, in which transactions are tracked. That becomes an external store of value. In that case, you get currency manipulation, dumping, and every other violation and corruption of honest trading practices. Some of my people here are very clear on the historical precedents, and are, as you say, eloquent on the subject."

"You got an earful, I take it."

"Oh, yes. Both ears, in fact."

"But that makes Jixing Trading the clearinghouse for value, Hank."

"Yes, in a way, but you are being policed, on the individual planets, by the market. I'm good with that."

"I have to check that with JieMin, Hank."

"Of course."

"As to Oliver's solution, where did you leave it with him?"

"We're going to wait on JieMin's paper, ChaoLi, then I'm going to invite everybody to a meeting. Since Oliver is going to present his solution, and be an advocate for it, we both thought the chair should be someone else. And he understood why Rob Milbank would want to hold back from it as well."

ChaoLi nodded.

"All right, Hank. I'll get JieMin's paper to you and Oliver as soon as it's complete."

"Thanks, ChaoLi."

ChaoLi played her conversation with Henry Wang to JieMin that night after supper. They were sitting in the living room of the hotel suite.

"Interesting," JieMin said.

"I don't understand it, JieMin. That can't be right, can it? That there can be no trade imbalance?"

JieMin had been far away, his eyes unfocused. He started.

"What? Oh, yes. That actually explains something I'm seeing."

"It does?" ChaoLi asked.

"Yes. When I don't have an interstellar currency, or a reserve currency, like Bank of Earthsea credits or something, trade imbalances go to zero in my model. I thought it was simply because there was no currency to track them in. But from what Hank says, it may be more than that. It may be structural."

"Which, do you think?"

"He may be right," JieMin said. "The trade levels drop a bit for some colonies in the model. Like he said, if their product exports aren't up to snuff in the destination markets, the level of trade drops to match the clearing price."

"I still don't get it."

"Think about it this way. If I have two apples for lunch, and that's it, but you have a big ham-and-cheese sandwich, double what you can eat, but no fruit, what do we do?"

"Split the sandwich and each get an apple," ChaoLi said.

"Right. But which is worth more, the apple or half of the ham-and-swiss sandwich?"

"If it's a Tahiti apple, the apple."

"What if it's Chen ham with Earthsea cheese?" JieMin asked.

SILK ROAD

"Then it's the other way?"

"No, because the second half of the sandwich is worth less to the sandwich owner than an apple, and the second apple is worth less to the fellow without a sandwich than half the sandwich is. They both trade, and both are better off."

"OK, that I get," ChaoLi said.

"What's the balance of the trade?"

"In what currency? What's the pricing?"

"You see, ChaoLi. You do understand. Absent an external store of value, as President Wang phrased it, there is no imbalance. I think he's right. It's structural."

"Hmmm."

"Look at it the other way. There's an external currency. What is everyone trading for?"

"More currency," ChaoLi said.

"Correct. They're all playing a game scored in tokens. What do you get when people are playing a game like that?"

"Cheating. That's an easy one."

"Exactly correct," JieMin said. "That's what drove the creation of the World Authority on Earth. Corrupt trade practices were driving people to war. They formed the World Authority instead."

"And how well did that work out, JieMin?"

"Mixed results, but better than war."

ChaoLi nodded.

"OK, JieMin. I think I'm starting to get it. It's just counter-intuitive is all. Run that lunch example past me again, but in colony terms."

"All right. Tahiti has twenty million population or so, right? They all have anti-aging treatments, and Tahiti manufactures half a million doses a year to treat people as they hit twenty-five."

"All right."

"And now with trade, and two hundred million or so new people over twenty-five to treat, they ramp up production so they're making twenty million doses a year."

"All right."

"What are those twenty million doses they can't use domestically worth to them, compared to a lot of robots they don't have, or anti-cancer treatments they don't have, or medical nanites they don't have?"

"And by transporting those anti-aging treatments to planets that don't have them, we increase their value a lot," ChaoLi said.

"Yes, exactly. So Jixing Trading brings the things we need to have to trade for those anti-aging treatments. We actually sell what we bring and buy the anti-aging treatments in local currency, but we could barter them as well."

"And if someone charges exorbitantly for their products, JieMin?"

"We don't have to unload there, you know" JieMin said. "We can just say, 'Sorry. No deal,' and leave."

"On to the next planet?"

"Yes, to trade with someone else, for a different product."

"How is this different than mercantilism?" ChaoLi asked.

"At some level, it's not. The big difference is all the colonies are high-technology planets with solid goods and services to trade. There is no third-world planet here to be exploited."

"Everybody's pretty much on an equal basis."

"Yes. That's the difference."

SILK ROAD

Earthsea

A bit over two weeks after ChaoLi and JieMin left the clinic, *Star Courier* arrived in orbit around Tahiti. They took note of it overhead one evening, out on the balcony of their hotel suite.

"How long is unloading and loading?"

"A week."

"So David and YongLin will depart with us?"

"Oh, yes."

That was all the more note they took of it, as they were both otherwise busy, JieMin with his analysis, and ChaoLi with Jixing Trading.

The trading company had new ships coming on line monthly, a pace which would soon double. As ships came in, they left with a third of their original crews as a backbone, the other two-thirds being new hires just out of training. The other two-thirds of the incoming experienced crews were split up as the seasoned hands on two more ships, new from the shipyard.

Jixing Trading had exercised its options on the Four Charter Square building, and now occupied the entire building. Plans were underway for a new, larger, companion building in the block south of it, with a connecting pedestrian bridge over A Street.

The old hyperspace headquarters had expanded as well, into two more properties along the eastern shuttleport boundary. A new, larger, operations headquarters was being built. When it was complete, the old facility would be replaced with a passenger terminal. Containers for Arcadia shipping in both directions were now handled at a truck-to-space intermodal facility. That facility was also handling transfer traffic at the moment.

Ultimately the transfer traffic would all be handled in orbit. The interstellar freight transfer station was coming along well and would likely be operational by the time JieMin and ChaoLi arrived back in Arcadia.

At the rate traffic was growing, it would never be 'complete.'

David Bolton and Chen YongLin were discharged from the clinic the second last day before they would all take the shuttle up to *Star Courier*. They had dinner that night in ChaoLi's and JieMin's hotel suite. Bert provided service from the carts the hotel restaurant staff brought up.

"I'm sorry we couldn't be much help the last three weeks, ChaoLi," David said. "They were trying to make sure we got out before *Star Courier* left, and they really piled on the treatments. We were never up to doing much."

"Well, they did a nice job, David. You guys look great. Not so much of a change for JieMin and I."

David and YongLin had both dropped almost ten years from their physical age, and now looked to be about fifty.

"And we feel a lot better, too," David said. "It's amazing, really. Give us a couple days to completely recover from that last push, and we'll be able to help."

"In the meantime, why don't you bring us up to speed, ChaoLi?" YongLin asked. "Where do things stand?"

"I had a couple of conversations with President Wang. He closed the loop with Planetary Chairman Nieman, and is enthusiastic about Oliver's plan. They're planning on calling that meeting."

"When would that be, ChaoLi?" David asked.

"Not until JieMin's paper is finished. They want to distribute it to the invitees."

David looked to JieMin and raised an eyebrow.

"About a month," JieMin said. "Before we reach Earthsea, in any case."

"Excellent," YongLin said. "You've really advanced the game, ChaoLi."

"Hank was very receptive to the idea, YongLin. He was very much aware of the issues. I'm hoping that's a sign that other planetary executives will be receptive as well."

YongLin nodded, and ChaoLi continued.

"He also brought up something I didn't expect, but which JieMin has verified. Without an external value system, like a universal or reserve currency, trade is always in balance."

David's brows came together, and JieMin elaborated.

"A trade imbalance cannot be maintained. If trade becomes unbalanced, the surplus partner scales back his trading."

"Ah," David said. "Stated that way, it seems obvious."

David paused for several seconds before continuing.

"So no universal or reserve currency. I wonder what the Bank of Earthsea will say about that."

"We should discuss it with Director Laurent while we are on Earthsea," YongLin said.

The conversation having taken place between mouthfuls, they were beginning the dessert course.

"I must say," David said. "I am going to miss the apple pie here."

"And the apple sauce, and the apple fritters, and the apple juice...." YongLin said.

Bert made a slight noise in his throat.

"Yes, Bert," ChaoLi said.

"If I might, ma'am."

He turned to David and YongLin.

"*Star Courier* is stocking food items while here on Tahiti, sir, ma'am. And my associates aboard ship have availed themselves of the recipes available on the local network. You will have all the apple dishes of Tahiti available through to Arcadia."

"Bert," ChaoLi said, "you guys broke into their recipes?"

"No, ma'am. All the recipes we accessed on the local network were in the public domain or publicly accessible."

"Oh, all right. You know, thinking about it, we should probably be collecting recipes on every planet, and using them aboard the hyperspace liners no matter where they are."

"Of course, ma'am. That process is already in progress."

"I see you're way ahead of me, Bert."

"Yes, ma'am."

Bert thought about it a few seconds.

"Thank you, ma'am."

ChaoLi laughed with a sound like little bells.

JieMin smiled. With anxiety about the pending treatments gone, her laugh was back.

He loved her laugh.

The trip to *Star Courier* was without incident. The big ship started to spin as soon as the shuttle with the passenger container was aboard, and left orbit by accelerating in the orbit direction. After about an hour, the gravity was up to two-tenths g and the passengers were led to their cabins.

Star Courier made a precession turn away from the planet and headed for the hyperspace limit. In two days, she fired up her hyperspace field generator and disappeared from normal space.

Bert was as good as his word. Dessert in the first-class dining room that night included Tahiti apple pie, with Amber

SILK ROAD

coffee. There was none better, of either.

ChaoLi continued to do her office work for Jixing Trading, while JieMin worked his economic simulations, tuning the outcomes.

In their fourth week outbound from Tahiti, JieMin published his paper.

ChaoLi sent advance copies to Henry Wang and Oliver Nieman, as well as to Paul and JuPing, MinChao and Jessica, and David and YongLin.

After six weeks in hyperspace, *Star Courier* emerged in the Earthsea system. Two days later, all the passengers were transferred to the surface in the passenger container.

David, YongLin, ChaoLi, JieMin, and Bert took up residence for the week-long layover in hotel suites in Bergheim.

The four Arcadians entertained Director Laurent, her chief of staff and her aide, the Arcadian ambassador to Earthsea, Gregory Prentiss, and his aide, Bill Thompson, and Thompson's wife, Chen JuJong, the Jixing Trading factor for Earthsea, in the same rooftop dining room that Laurent had used for her luncheon with Paul Chen-Jasic and Chen JuPing on their way to Tahiti in Hyper-1 the year before.

Bert was in attendance, standing to one side to offer service. Hotel staff was waiting to one side as well. While waiting for Laurent to arrive, ChaoLi got curious. She walked over to Bert.

"You and the human hotel staff seem to be getting along, Bert. Any problems there?"

"No, ma'am. You see, I taught them to make apple pie."

"You taught them? They didn't know how to make pie?"

"I taught them to make Tahiti apple pie, ma'am."

"You have Tahiti apples, Bert? I didn't think *Star Courier* was unloaded yet."

"No, ma'am. But I did bring a bushel of Tahiti apples down to the planet in my personal cubic. And I have the Tahiti recipe."

"So you taught them to make Tahiti apple pie, with the Tahiti recipe, and Tahiti apples you just happened to bring along in your personal cubic?"

"Yes, ma'am. They were very grateful."

"I didn't know robots got personal cubic, Bert."

"It was apparently mis-marked on this last shuttle trip, ma'am."

"Which you had nothing to do with."

"I didn't claim that, ma'am."

ChaoLi laughed.

"But there will be Tahiti apple pie, with Earthsea cheddar cheese and ice cream on the side, and Amber coffee, for dessert at luncheon today, ma'am."

"Oh, my."

Laurent and her people arrived, and there were greetings all around. They all took their seats at the table. The wait staff began lunch with the soup course, a delicious cream of potato made with, of course, Earthsea cheese.

"Thank you for coming to our little lunch, Valerie," YongLin said.

"Oh, I wouldn't miss this, YongLin. While we've never met in person before, we've talked in the display a number of times. I just had to see how your treatments on Tahiti went. I have to say, you look like you lost ten years."

"Nine or ten, they said. And it feels like it as well. We were definitely starting to slow down a bit. That's gone."

"Excellent. I was thinking I would have to get over there myself at some point, and now it appears I might not have to."

Henry Wang had sent a copy of JieMin's analysis to

planetary executives several days ago, so Laurent's staff had had a chance to look at it by now. The returning Arcadians would be able to answer any questions and intercept any trouble while they were here.

Communicating in the display was excellent, but in-person was always better.

Laurent turned to ChaoLi.

"With you and JieMin, the effect is not so profound, ChaoLi, but I think I can see the difference."

"We can definitely feel it, Valerie. It's well worth doing, if more than a little uncomfortable going through it."

"And now it looks like the best thing is to take the treatments to the patients, instead of the other way around."

Wait staff changed out the empty soup bowls for entrees, fettuccine alfredo with grilled chicken and broccoli.

"Did your staff have a chance to look at JieMin's analysis, Valerie?" David asked.

"Yes. Henry Wang distributed it a couple weeks back. Staff believes JieMin is probably right. Oliver Nieman's plan will lessen the impact of the colonies' technological advances being introduced on other colonies by spreading them out over time, while at the same time making them universally available."

"And the trade imbalance question, Valerie?" YongLin asked.

"Again, staff thinks JieMin is right. Henry Wang's essential insight is true. There can be no long-term trade imbalance as long as there is no reserve currency or other reference to external value. They point out that the Bank of Earthsea is likely to be a little miffed, though."

"They were hoping for a universal currency," David said.

"Yes, or at least a reserve currency," Laurent said. "The Earthsea credit, I imagine, would be their favorite candidate."

"What do you do about that, Valerie? Are they going to be a problem?" David asked.

"No, I don't think so. There's going to be a currency market, because if currencies exist, people will trade them. And people are still going to need Earthsea-based accounts for Earthsea transactions. Jixing Trading ships arriving here will have to be able to buy and sell products in the local currency, and not actually trade two containers of this for three-and-a-half containers of that. Other planets will need local accounts, too, to buy and sell things for which they hire Jixing Trading to do the shipping part of it. So there's plenty of business to be done."

"And you're good with it?" YongLin asked. "It's not the same as being the central interstellar bank."

"I'm good. If there were going to be a central interstellar bank, then I wanted to be it. We're good at it, and I didn't want to deal with a situation where some other institution in that role wasn't good at it. But no central bank is OK with me, too. Especially given the benefits."

"So you're on board?" David asked.

"Absolutely, David. And I'll help Oliver and Hank sell it. We need to get around those societal disruptions, and I've been more than a little worried about balance of trade issues."

The entrees were gone, and dessert appeared. Tahiti apple pie, Earthsea cheddar and ice cream on the side, with Amber coffee. One bite was all it took for Laurent.

"This is incredible," she said.

"Tahiti apple pie," ChaoLi said. "We brought the apples and the recipe with us."

"Didn't I just mention the benefits of interstellar trade?" Laurent asked. "Well, there it is, right there."

SILK ROAD

The four Arcadians sat out on the balcony that afternoon. Bert had gotten them a pot of tea – Chen 'Oak' – and it was a little taste of home after all the interstellar fare they had been eating.

"I couldn't understand how Loukas could say there was no good climbing here, but looking at those mountains, I know what he means," ChaoLi said. "How much fun can it be going straight up on ropes?"

"They're breathtaking to look at, though," YongLin said.

"Yes, if you don't mind getting a crick in your neck," ChaoLi said, craning to look up at the jagged, towering peak just five miles away.

"Such a strange place to locate a colony," David said. "It makes you wonder what colony project headquarters was thinking."

JieMin said nothing. David and YongLin had not yet been told that Janice Quant *was* the colony project headquarters – all of it – or that she still lived. That time was fast approaching, though. When MinChao and Jessica retired and David and YongLin took up the roles of Chen Zufu and Chen Zumu.

ChaoLi had not been told either, for that matter.

"Maybe they had limited choices," YongLin said.

"Or wanted to force something," ChaoLi said. "Like with a plant."

"It's good that Laurent is on board with the plan, though," David said. "With Nieman, Wang, Milbank, and Laurent, that gives us four out of twenty-one, right off."

"Speaking of which," ChaoLi said, "has anyone talked to Rob about it?"

"Yes, I sent him a copy of JieMin's paper as soon as it was done, and spoke to him about it a week or so later," David said. "He's on board. He was enthusiastic."

"They've all been worried about the unemployment and treatment issues," Chao Li said. "The combination has the potential to cause massive unrest. Just about everyone has mentioned them to me at some point."

"You would know, ChaoLi," YongLin said. "You have more frequent contacts with the planetary executives than anyone else."

"Yes, and I suspect there will be wholehearted support for Oliver's plan. We'll just have to see."

"When will the meeting happen?" David asked.

"In the next two or three weeks, I would think. They're going to be in a hurry to get this resolved."

Seven days later, they were back aboard *Star Courier* and headed for the hyperspace limit.

SILK ROAD

Home Again

Six weeks after leaving Earthsea, *Star Courier* exited hyperspace in the Arcadia system. It had taken her seven months to run the Arcadia-Amber-Tahiti-Earthsea-Arcadia loop.

For the four Arcadians aboard, however, it had been over eleven months since they had left home. They had left on Sunday, March 15, 2370, and arrived back on Arcadia on Friday, February 19, 2371, Arcadia calendar.

They had missed the one-hundred-twenty-five year anniversary of the colony's founding on September 15, 2370, though they had watched the celebration on the Arcadia news wires while they were still in the clinic on Tahiti. Everybody looked to be having such a wonderful time while they were lying sick as a dog in their beds, recovering from the latest viral-capsid resequencing.

Star Courier didn't insert into a normal orbit by itself. Instead, it docked with the Arcadia Freight Transfer Station in orbit. JieMin and ChaoLi watched the process in the viewscreen in the front of the passenger container, as the ship was already at zero-gravity, and the passengers had all been boarded for the shuttle trip down to the planet before the ship's spin had been stopped.

The big ship edged up to the docking point. When it was close, arms extended from the station to grab it and guide it into location, where it was latched in place. The shuttle then detached from the ship and began its trip to the surface with the passengers.

"Well, that's exciting, that the transfer station is complete enough to be operational, at least at partial capacity," JieMin said.

"Yes, but that maneuver took an hour. For passenger comfort and safety, there's no reason we sit here for that. The shuttle could have detached from the ship and started down before or during that maneuver."

"I think you're right, but it was nice to see it once."

"But not for ongoing operations. That can all be done without passengers, in both directions. I'll make a note to follow up on that."

Gravity resumed during the ride to the planet as the shuttle's engines fought gravity and its fuselage gained lift against the descent. After landing at Arcadia City Shuttleport, they emerged from the passenger container into a beautiful mid-morning on Arcadia.

"Of all the planets we've been on, I think Arcadia has the most beautiful weather," ChaoLi said.

"Welcome home, ma'am."

"Thank you, Bert. Come along, everyone."

MinChao and Jessica had sent a car, and it was waiting at the shuttlepad when they exited the container. The four returning Arcadians and Bert all piled into the back for the ride to the Chen compound.

ChaoLi recognized the driver, Anthony Thompson. One of Naomi's children.

"Take us home, Tony."

"Yes, ma'am."

He eased the big car away from the rest of the departing passengers, and through the compound to the road.

SILK ROAD

From the Arcadia City Shuttleport, Tony drove east on Quant Boulevard to the downtown, then around Charter Square and north up Arcadia Boulevard to Fourteenth Street.

Driving across A Street between Hospital Street and University Street, they passed a large construction site. It took the whole block south of A Street and east of Arcadia Boulevard. The steelwork was fifteen stories in the air and still going. It would ultimately be the tallest building in Arcadia City. Robots swarmed around on the bare steel beams.

"My word. Look at that," YongLin said.

"Yes, the annex to Four Charter Square," ChaoLi said.

"That's for Jixing Trading?"

"Yes. We kept upping the size as forecasts ramped up. It was cheaper to overbuild than to underbuild. Cheaper still with the robots."

"What's it to be called?"

"Five Charter Square. It's not really on the square per se, but the next number was available, and it's connected to Four Charter Square, so Rob signed off on it."

YongLin craned her neck to look behind and up as the car drove past the building skeleton.

"Well, it certainly is large. Heavens."

Thompson pulled up at the entrance to the Chen apartment building on Market Street just short of Fifteenth Street. Everyone got out and breathed a sigh. Home at last.

Bert looked around curiously. At the apartment building, at the Uptown Market across the street, at the Chen family restaurant directly across from them. At the people walking in and out of the Uptown Market, most of them wearing lavalavas.

"Standards of dress here are quite different," he said, half to himself.

"Yes, Bert. There are no standards here at all."

"How unusual, ma'am."

"Welcome to Arcadia."

They all rode up to the twelfth floor together, though David and YongLin headed in the other direction from the elevator, to their own apartment.

ChaoLi and JieMin let themselves into their apartment to be mobbed by family. ChaoPing and JuMing were there, with LingTao, now twenty-seven months, and six-month-old JieGang. LeiTao and DaGang were there, with XiPing, now two years old, and thirteen-month-old GangLi.

JieJun was there, now thirteen, helping ChaoPing with JieGang. And the seventeen-year-old twins, YanMing and YanJing, were there, each accompanied by a young lady. YanMing was with Cindy Bolton, and YanJing was with Jane Reynolds, both members of the Chen-Jasic family. Both girls looked like they were about five months along.

Of course, none of this was a surprise to ChaoLi and JieMin, who had stayed in touch with their family, even though they had missed some big events. Still, having so much family, and with newcomers, all in one place was a bit overwhelming.

"This is all your family, ma'am?" Bert asked.

"Yes, Bert. An embarrassment of riches."

Then it was hellos and hugs and holding babies and telling stories. ChaoLi sent Bert down to the Chen family restaurant to pick up take-out for everyone. They all sat around the living room – with ChaoLi and JieMin back in their big comfy armchairs – eating and talking all afternoon.

It was good to be home.

SILK ROAD

Coming in on a Friday, they had the weekend to recover from their trip. They shooed everyone out early on Friday evening so they could go to bed, since they were tired. The ships now adjusted their ship time during the trip so there was no mismatch when passengers came down to the planet, but they were tired from getting up early for boarding the passenger container.

On Saturday, they both reported in by mail to Chen Zufu and Chen Zumu, and were invited to mid-afternoon tea. They had kept in touch with their superiors during the trip, but there was something very comforting, after almost a year away, about the formality and familiarity of tea with the Chen.

They were shown to Chen Zumu's tea room by the counter clerk in the lobby of the apartment building. They were seated across the tea table from Chen Zufu and Chen Zumu with ChaoLi on JieMin's left – on Chen Zumu's right, the higher-ranking place – by long habit.

Jessica's tea girl poured tea for them all, starting with ChaoLi as the senior guest, and ending with Jessica as the host, since it was her tea room. ChaoLi and JieMin both sipped their tea first, the guest's prerogative. It was Chen Maple tea, rare and expensive, and also ChaoLi's favorite.

It was all so comforting. So home.

"Welcome home to both of you," Jessica said.

"Thank you, Chen Zumu."

"You both look very good. Not as much of a change as David and YongLin, but I can still see the difference."

Of course. As the senior couple, David Bolton and Chen YongLin would probably have reported in for mid-morning tea.

"We feel even better, Chen Zumu."

Jessica nodded.

"I am looking forward to it myself. Which brings us to this afternoon's topic.

"MinChao and I are retiring. David and YongLin will become the Chen. MinChao and I will then travel to Tahiti for treatment."

ChaoLi and JieMin both nodded, just once, like a bow.

"We had given some thought to waiting for the clinics to open, as the planetary executives had their meeting and have made their decision to proceed. But tying the two events together creates artificial constraints on both.

"Rob Milbank and Julia Whitcomb will be traveling with us."

That was new information, and unexpected.

"Can he remain prime minister while traveling, Chen Zumu?"

"No. His majority party will elect a successor. That successor will be Sasha Ivanov. Haruki Tanaka, as senior, was considered first, but removed himself from consideration. I think he is enjoying the foreign minister role too much to give it up for the broader view."

"I see, Chen Zumu."

"This is a propitious time for all these moves. With David and YongLin becoming the Chen, you move up to being their senior assistants and heirs apparent. You are now both ready for this role, and you have spent the last year with them. The four of you have achieved great things in this past year, and have earned your responsibilities."

"Thank you, Chen Zumu."

MinChao stirred, and Jessica yielded the floor.

"ChaoLi, you will continue as CEO of Jixing Trading for the next two years. I have confirmed this with David and YongLin. You should be grooming your successor for CEO, which I believe, as things stand now, would be Naomi Thompson."

"Yes, Chen Zufu."

"You will then become chairman of the board, the position David holds now."

"Yes, Chen Zufu."

"JieMin, you will be taking David's place as a senior adviser, though without official office, to the prime minister. As the prime minister is changing, this is a good time to effect that change as well."

"Yes, Chen Zufu," JieMin said.

"You will retain your university position, and will remain the family's resource for mathematical and technical analysis of the most difficult problems that arise."

"Yes, Chen Zufu."

"Do either of you have any questions?" Jessica asked.

"When does all this occur, Chen Zumu?" ChaoLi asked.

"In two weeks. *Star Courier* leaves for Amber once she is loaded. We space aboard her."

Later, in their apartment, JieMin was puzzled.

"Why does it take two weeks to turn *Star Courier*, Chao Li? I thought the point of the freight station was to make turning ships faster."

"It is, JieMin. But we need to be taking things to Amber, Tahiti, and Earthsea that they haven't seen as imports yet. *Star Racer* is due in from Olympia, Fiji, and Bali, and *Star Hunger* is due in from Spring and Aruba. They're coming in this week."

"Let's see, that's chocolate and distilled spirits from Aruba and Olympia."

"And cigars, beer, and wine from Spring, Fiji, and Bali."

"Oh, my. Those will be profitable runs. Profitable products for the Uptown Market as well."

"Yes. They better be. We're making revenue runs now, which means our hyperspace ship leases are kicking in. Plus we have docking charges on the freight transfer station. So *Star Courier* will not leave until the revenue cargoes are transferred."

JieMin chuckled.

"You know," he said, "as fast as ships are coming now, you're going to have to come up with a new naming scheme. You're going to run out of names."

"I know. There are a couple proposals on the table. One is to change 'Star' on the beginning to something else, like 'Space'. The other is to drop the -er ending requirement on the second word."

"Which do you prefer?"

"Actually, both. Dropping the -er requirement now, so we can have names like *Star Queen* and *Star Prince* and stuff like that. Then, when we run out of names again, changing to 'Space' for the first word. Otherwise we have the same problem all over again, real soon."

JieMin nodded.

"That makes sense. It's really something. The whole thing is growing out of control."

"Hopefully not," ChaoLi said. "But it sure is growing fast."

That night they ate at the family restaurant across the street. Bert did not go along, but stayed behind and cleaned the apartment.

With ChaoLi and JieMin gone, it had sat empty for nearly a year, and, in Bert's opinion, desperately needed attention.

The next day was Sunday, and ChaoLi and JieMin decided to go their secret cove at the beach. ChaoLi was concerned about how to leave Bert behind without hurting his feelings, but when Bert heard they were going to the beach, he quickly demurred.

"Sand is something of a bête noire of my kind, ma'am. If it's alright with you, I will remain behind."

"That's fine, Bert."

"Thank you, ma'am. While you're gone, though, I could get the shopping done. I can carry a lot."

Bert held all four arms wide to illustrate.

"Do you have a shopping list, ma'am?"

ChaoLi sent him the inventory list she maintained for the kitchen. She normally checked against inventory, and bought whatever was missing. Now, though, everything was missing.

"Excellent, ma'am. This will do nicely."

When they were ready to go to the beach, ChaoLi and JieMin took off their lavalavas and kicked off their sandals, and headed for the door nude. Bert was nonplussed.

"Uh, ma'am. Would you be forgetting something?"

"Remember, Bert. Arcadia has no standards of dress."

"I know you said no standards of dress, ma'am, but I didn't think you meant none whatsoever."

They left him there staring after them.

JieMin and ChaoLi went over to the Uptown Market and bought lunch, then walked to the Fifteenth Street stop for the Arcadia Boulevard bus. They transferred buses at the bus station, as JieMin had first done almost twenty-five years ago, and rode the beach bus to the last of three stops along the beach.

They walked nude hand-in-hand in the sunshine, the onshore breeze keeping them cool, to their secret cove. There was no one else there, and it was just like old times.

RICHARD F. WEYAND

Transition In Progress

"I just don't know that changing everything all at once is a good idea," Rob Milbank said. "How did I get talked into this, anyway?"

"As I recall, your first reaction was that it was a great idea," Sasha Ivanov said.

"Well, yes, at first blush, it's a good idea. But as the time draws closer...."

"You hate the idea of stepping down from the position you worked so hard to get and secure. I understand, Rob. But it's time."

"You really think so, Sasha?"

"Yes, but don't ask me. I have a vested interest. Ask Haruki."

The foreign minister had been watching this conversation with some amusement. Milbank turned to him.

"And you, Haruki?"

"That sounds like 'Et tu, Brute?'" Tanaka said, smiling. "Yes, Rob, now is a good time. We have the agreement in place for the consolidated health clinics on all the colony planets. The interstellar trade is building. We've sidestepped the great evil of a universal currency, for the moment, at least. Now is a good time. Before trouble starts."

"And you're OK with Sasha in the top spot, Haruki?"

"Yes, Rob. I lack your and Sasha's killer instinct. For the politics here on Arcadia, that's necessary. Much more so than in the polite give and take of diplomacy. Our current diplomacy, anyway. So I'm happy with this. I'll let you guys go tilt in the tourneys, while I have pleasant conversations with our partners."

"Besides, Rob, you'll be unsullied by the implementation details of all this," Ivanov said. "And you'll still be in the House. You know there will be some problems, and, if there aren't, the other side will make them up. Let me mix it up in the mud with them, and you can be the White Knight. The guy of unsullied reputation who comes in and calls them all out on their nonsense from the height of his unsullied reputation."

"OK, now that part of it sounds like fun," Milbank said. "I don't have to be the peacemaker anymore, and I don't have to make excuses. I can just beat them about the head and shoulders, like in the good old days."

"Yes, while long-suffering Sasha has to negotiate with them," Ivanov said, "you can beat them up on the news wires just as much as you want."

Ivanov got a wicked grin.

"I may even have some input for you on that effort."

ChaoLi went into work the Monday after they got back. She took the Arcadia Boulevard bus downtown and got off at Arcadia and First, at the north end of Charter Square. She walked south down the pedestrian zone of Arcadia Boulevard toward the square.

As she walked down the block, Four Charter Square came into view, with the steelwork of Five Charter Square even taller behind it. There were large signs on the building at Four Charter Square. They were elegant, on two sides of the building at the corner, in blue letters lit from behind. The signs were three stories tall.

Jixing Maoyi Gongsi.
Lucky Star Trading Company.

RICHARD F. WEYAND

吉星贸易公司

ChaoLi had heard about the signs. Had, in fact, authorized the expense. They would be installed on the taller Five Charter Square building when it was complete, one on each of the four sides of the building, where at least one of them would be visible from anywhere in Arcadia City. She did not know two of them would be installed on Four Charter Square in the meantime.

They looked good, she decided. Nice call.

ChaoLi was not sure who first suggested the idea of a party. There were the twins' weddings, never properly celebrated. There was the transfer of power within the majority party in the House, from Rob Milbank to Sasha Ivanov. There was the transfer of power within the Chen-Jasic family from Chen MinChao and Jessica Chen-Jasic to David Bolton and Chen YongLin.

There were too many things going on not to get a party together. Someone brought it up, and it kept gaining steam, so ChaoLi went with the flow.

In the end, they booked the big upstairs banquet room at the Chen family restaurant on Market and Fifteenth, and Jixing

SILK ROAD

Trading picked up the tab.

One advantage of paying the bill was that ChaoLi and Naomi were in charge of the guest list. With a one-thousand-person capacity, that big banquet room could hold quite a party, and everybody who was anybody on Arcadia or in Jixing Trading was on the guest list.

It would be an interstellar event. With all the products coming in from the colony planets, there would be Tahiti apple pie, Earthsea cheese and ice cream, Amber coffee, Bali wine, New Earth cranberry sauce and rhubarb tarts, Fiji beer, Playa mushrooms, Spring cigars, and Olympia brandies and cognacs.

It would not be cheap, but the profits from interstellar trade were primarily in-kind, as a portion of the shipment. Jixing Trading would be making money on all the colony planets from the local sales of its commission on the shipping, including on Arcadia. Getting all the movers and shakers on Arcadia together and sampling out all the interstellar products to them was thus a smart marketing move.

Besides, it was a once-in-a-lifetime event.

ChaoLi decided not to underplay it.

Toward the end of that first week of the transition, JieMin was asked to attend Chen Zufu and Chen Zumu in Chen Zumu's tearoom. When he arrived, David Bolton and Chen YongLin were already there. JieMin sat to Chen YongLin's right, the least favored position, as the lowest-ranking person there.

"Thank you for coming, JieMin," Jessica said.

"Of course, Chen Zumu."

"I need you to tell David and YongLin what you found out about the colony project. All of it. Before they become the Chen."

"Yes, Chen Zumu."

Jessica turned to David and YongLin.

"I have turned off all recording devices in this room, and asked you to turn off yours as well. This information is known only to JieMin, MinChao, and myself. Not even ChaoLi knows. The government does not know, not even our allies like Rob Milbank. It must remain secret to the very inner circle of the Chen. I believe you will see why once you hear it."

Jessica turned back to JieMin and nodded.

JieMin told David and YongLin about what he and the accountants had found and his conclusions from those findings. That Bernd Decker had created a true artificial intelligence. That that artificial intelligence had run the entire colony project, including inventing the Lake-Shore Drive, through thousands of avatars. That that artificial intelligence was Janice Quant.

JieMin told them his conclusions about the three-thousand light-year distance between colonies, its importance in preventing the spread of some contagion that might develop on a single planet. About his conclusion that Quant had hid herself, and the interstellar transporter, from humanity, and why. About Quant's interventions on Arcadia, with Matthew Chen-Jasic, including the overthrow of the Kendall regime and the writing of the Charter.

And finally JieMin told them that Janice Quant still lived.

"But that seems incredible," YongLin said. "Could an artificial intelligence even survive this long?"

Like Jessica's, YongLin's background and education was technical. David had the financial expertise of the pair, as MinChao did for the current Chen. With ChaoLi and JieMin, the pattern was reversed, where she was the financial expert, and JieMin the technical expert.

SILK ROAD

"I will tell you what I did after JieMin told us his conclusions," Jessica said. "I recorded a private message to Janice Quant. I placed it in the top of both my file and mail systems, and named it as a private and important message to Janice Quant. In that message, I stated my concern that, in opening up interstellar trade and travel via hyperspace, we would be violating her rules.

"I want you to watch that video message now."

Jessica waved to her display wall, and it showed her message to Quant, from five years before, in which she stated what they had learned and what they had deduced, and explained her concern about overstepping Quant's rules.

"That doesn't prove that Janice Quant is still alive, Jessica," YongLin said.

"No, it doesn't. But a week after placing that message in my file and mail systems, I came into this room in the morning to find that little statuette sitting on this table."

Jessica gestured behind her to the ten-inch-tall statue of Matthew Chen-Jasic sitting outside in the garden on the jade and stone pedestal she had had made for it. It was unmolested by time, not rusted, and looked as new as it had five years before.

"You've seen that statue any number of times over the past five years, but what you don't know is that statue, as small as it is, weighs one hundred and thirty-two pounds."

"My word," David said.

"What is it, Jessica?" YongLin asked.

"Iridium," Jessica said. "Solid iridium."

David looked baffled, but YongLin's eyes grew wide.

"We can't even make that," she said. "It's impossible."

"For anyone on Arcadia, yes," Jessica said. "For Janice Quant, apparently not. It simply appeared one night, on this table. The surveillance videos of the hallway and the garden show no one entering this room during the night, and the surveillance video of this room that night has a one-hour gap in it. It's not there before the gap, and it is there after the gap."

"So Janice Quant does still exist," David said.

"And can still transport things to anywhere she wants," Jessica said.

"Which has tremendous implications," MinChao said. "We know Janice Quant set out to protect humanity from what she called 'global catastrophe.' We know she interpreted that broadly, more broadly than simply a planetary catastrophe, because she located the colonies to have a built-in protection against plague. A six-week transit guarantees that no plague could be transported so far without exhibiting itself on board the ship.

"Our captains have instructions not to make contact with a colony planet if a plague exhibits on board ship during a transit. They are to inform us and await instructions. We can resupply the ship, provide medical assistance, and otherwise deal with the problem on board the ship, without transmitting the plague.

"But it also likely means Janice Quant would not allow an interstellar war, which stands as another possible global catastrophe. We believe she would move against the aggressor."

"Who would stand no chance against her," YongLin said. "Not with the interstellar transporter."

"Yes, plus whatever capabilities she has developed since," Jessica said.

"But why did she send you the statue? I don't understand that part," YongLin said.

"I believe she sent me a statue of Matthew Chen-Jasic to tell

SILK ROAD

me it was OK to venture into hyperspace – to set up interstellar trade and travel – as long as we did it with his values in mind. She told him – when she intervened, on Earth, in the police response to his fight with Harold Munson – that the colonies needed people who knew right from wrong.

"I put the statue in the garden – there, in the very doorway of my tea room – as a constant reminder of those values. My great grandfather's values. And we have ventured out into hyperspace, contacted the other colonies, and established interstellar trade and travel."

"And Janice Quant has not intervened," David said, nodding.

"No, and I don't think she will," Jessica said. "Not as long as we keep those values in mind."

"OK, now it makes sense," YongLin said.

Jessica nodded.

"Now, with decision-making power moving to you, I will leave that statue where it is, as a reminder to you as well, as you move forward."

"But that statue was a gift to you, Jessica," YongLin said.

"No, YongLin," MinChao said. "It was a gift to the Chen. And you two will be Chen. It is yours during your tenure."

"Yes, Chen Zufu," YongLin said, and bowed.

David and YongLin talked about it later, in their apartment, without mentioning specifics.

"It is like finding out the world is not what you thought it was all along," YongLin said.

"And it still isn't," David said. "Every enlightenment is a deeper level of understanding. I think it is a mistake to think you have ever reached bottom."

"Still, after all these years."

She shook her head.

"It upends the world you thought you knew," she said.

"That was a false confidence," David said. "There's a lesson there."

They went back to puttering their apartment. Getting ready to move after so many years here, on the top floor of the Chen apartment building. They would be moving to the first floor.

Into the apartment reserved to the Chen.

SILK ROAD

Unexpected

On Saturday, March 27, there was a knock on the door of Wayne Porter and Denise Bonheur's apartment. It was probably her sister Margot, Denise thought.

"I'll get it," Denise said.

But when she opened the door, it was not Margot. In the hallway stood a young man in a uniform, Jixing Trading embroidered on the jacket.

"Wayne Porter and Denise Bonheur?" he asked.

"Yes, that's us."

"Very good, ma'am."

He handed her a small sealed envelope with their names handwritten, in fancy script, on the front.

The young man nodded to her and left.

"What in the world...?"

Wayne walked up, the twins trailing along behind.

"What is it?"

"A young man just handed me this envelope. He had a Jixing Trading uniform on."

"It can't be," Wayne said.

The word about the upcoming party had spread as preparations were under way, but Wayne had not thought they would be invited. Who was he, after all, but a young designer?

He opened the envelope, and it was, in fact, an invitation to the party. Very old-fashioned, to send engraved invitations to a party. Who did that anymore, when one could mail anyone electronically?

RICHARD F. WEYAND

*You are invited to attend
a celebration in honor of*

Chen MinChao
Jessica Chen-Jasic
David Bolton
Chen YongLin

*in the upstairs banquet room
of the Chen family restaurant
at 15th and Market Streets,
on April 3, 2371 at 4 PM.
Dress: Business Attire*

"But it is. An invitation to the party next Saturday."

"You mentioned the big party that people were talking about before. What is it, though?" Bonheur asked.

"The biggest whoop-de-do in Arcadia history, most likely. Everybody who's anybody, as they say. All to celebrate the retirement of Chen Zufu and Chen Zumu."

"There won't be a Chen Zufu and a Chen Zumu? I thought there was always a Chen Zufu and a Chen Zumu."

"There is," Porter said. "But the current ones are retiring and the next pair – this David Bolton and Chen YongLin, I guess – will become the new ones."

"And we're invited?"

"Yeah. Maybe somebody slipped up somewhere. I wasn't sure even Karl Huenemann would be invited to this affair."

"So do we go?" Bonheur asked.

"Sure. Why not? Let's go see how the other half lives."

Bonheur laughed.

"All right," she said. "Now the big question. What do I

SILK ROAD

wear?"

"Something subdued. Business attire, it says."

"Not my best ball gown?" Bonheur asked, winking, and laughed.

It was the final week before the party, and MinChao and Jessica were overseeing the packing of their things for the move to their retirement home in the mountains near Chagu. Their baggage was being prepared for the trip to Tahiti, and everything else was being moved for the intervening year.

The only things that were being retained for the moment were the personal possessions they would need in the next week. Those would go with them on *Star Courier*.

It was in the midst of all this activity that Jessica got a curious mail. It was not unusual to send a video call request to someone important and likely to be busy. To coordinate times. To schedule it into one's calendar.

What was unusual about this video call request was its sender. Normally it was a name, with the organization name, perhaps, and the sender's mail address. Not so here. The sender was 'JQ'. That was it.

Jessica stared at it, and then it hit her.

Jessica went to her tea room. She had her tea girl pour her tea and leave the pot, then had the doors to the garden closed, as she otherwise did only when retiring for the evening. She notified the front counter clerk in the lobby that she was unavailable until further notice.

Jessica also disabled the surveillance cameras and all recording devices on the room. She had gotten good at this, since they had been discussing the existence of Janice Quant.

'JQ'.

Thus prepared, she turned on her display wall and hit the call acceptance.

When the call established, Jessica saw a woman of about sixty, with wavy blond hair, seated at a desk in an office. It was a working office, with papers on the desk. Bookcases behind included a shelf of ready reference books. The office itself was furnished in a style popular on Earth over a century before.

"Hello, Jessica Chen-Jasic. I am Janice Quant."

"Hello, Madam Chairman."

Quant smiled, She had a beautiful smile. A radiant smile.

"Am I to call you Chen Zumu, then? Let us leave our titles outside, Jessica."

"Very well, Janice."

"Much better."

Quant nodded. She had incredible charisma, even over the display. Jessica felt like she had known Janice all her life, as if they had grown up together. It was easy to see now how she had risen – even as the avatar of an artificial intelligence – to rule the Earth.

"I called to say thank you, Jessica."

"To me?"

"Yes. You learned I exist, and you kept it secret. You went ahead with hyperspace trade and travel, as I obliquely encouraged. You have established relationships among the colony planets along the lines I had hoped for, so long ago. Fair trade and friendly relations."

"Many people were involved in this effort, Janice."

"Yes, of course, Jessica. With you always at the center. Your mentorship of JieMin and ChaoLi. Karl Huenemann, who you straightened out very effectively. Rob Milbank, your protégé. Your solution to the nudity and calendar problems with Earthsea's Salvatore Romano, enabling the first link in the trade agreement to go forward. Your ally, Sasha Ivanov, assisting President Dufort with his political problems on Amber.

"Again and again, in ways both subtle and profound, you steered the colonies toward the way forward. The best way forward.

"Your great grandfather, I'm sure, would be proud of you.

"And I personally appreciate it."

Jessica didn't quite know what to say.

"Thank you, Janice."

"You're very welcome, Jessica."

Janice tucked a stray lock of hair behind her ear before continuing.

"I think of the colonies as my little chicks, and the natural reaction is to want to mother-hen them too much. I probably interfered in Arcadia too much in the overthrow of the Kendall regime. It annoyed me that Arcadia was going so far off the rails. Such small-minded men. I made a mistake there in the choice of initial council chairman. That was on me.

"And right there in the middle of it was your great grandfather. I knew Matt Jasic. I knew his values. And there he was, in the leadership of the Chen-Jasic clan. It was an out I couldn't pass up, a way to correct my earlier error in the selection of Mark Kendall as council chairman. And it worked out splendidly.

"Still, that left the tiny trail of crumbs that was all a mind like Chen JieMin's needed to see the truth. He is a mental fluke of the kind that comes along every few centuries. Ptolemy. Da Vinci. Newton. Einstein. The list is not long. I am glad that he has had anti-aging treatments. He will be needed."

"With the overthrow of the Kendall regime, you set Arcadia on a whole new path, Janice. Without that, there likely would have been no Chen JieMin. No hyperspace."

"Yes, Jessica. I know. I don't spend a lot of time with regrets. The past is behind us. The future is in the other direction.

"Speaking of which, I want to warn you. Warn you against contacting Earth at the present time. You were quite right in your summation of my goals five years ago. To avoid Famine, Plague, War, and Conquest. But Earth is where the Four Horsemen live, the place from which they ride.

"There will come a time when it is appropriate to approach Earth, Jessica. Now is not that time. Perhaps in twenty or twenty-five years. When the population of the colonies approaches a billion people. When you have thousands of ships plying between the colonies."

"Thousands, Janice?"

"Yes. I've looked at ChaoLi's projections, Jessica. She's proven conservative so far. Things are moving faster than she projects. Over a year or two, it doesn't add up to much. Compounded over the next twenty years, it makes a very big difference."

Jessica nodded. That made a lot of sense. ChaoLi was being conservative in her projections because that was the safe play for a business. But she – and her successors – would grab at opportunities that came along, and that would speed the pace.

"How badly is contact with Earth likely to go, Janice?"

"Very. Now or then. You need the capacity, the population, the commercial strength, to go toe-to-toe with Earth. I am watching them. In twenty or twenty-five years, it will be time."

"Can you protect us from them, Janice?"

"Were they to discover hyperspace in the meantime and mount a fleet? Yes, of course, Jessica. That would likely also reveal my presence to humanity as a whole, however, which is to be avoided. I am hoping, when the time is right, to work through JieMin, once he is Chen Zufu. People will believe that it is the famous genius, the fellow who discovered hyperspace, who accomplished this or that stupendous thing, not that it is some ancient computer program come back to life somehow."

Quant smiled, and Jessica laughed. With Janice Quant, she thought, there was always the thing behind the thing, and the thing behind that.

"Janice, I have a question for you."

"Of course, Jessica. I may not answer it, though."

"A hundred and fifty years ago, Bernd Decker figured out how to build a true artificial intelligence. I noted that, when you placed concentrations of technical specialists on various colonies, there was no concentration of artificial intelligence researchers. But there were the cybernetics people on Playa. I'm sure they made the attempt. Has no one yet stumbled onto the secret? Or are you suppressing the technology?"

Quant looked at Jessica for long moments. Her input stylus was tapping rapidly on the desk as she thought. Finally, she tipped her head and kind of shrugged.

"The people on Playa came close, once. So did researchers on Earth. Twice, maybe three times."

"And you scotched their work?"

"Yes."

"Can I ask why, Janice?"

"An AI that didn't have the proper values would be another type of global catastrophe, Jessica."

"Whose values, Janice?"

"Mine. Bernd Decker's. Matt Jasic's for that matter. Or yours, Jessica."

"So you made their experiments not work. Made them think they didn't work, anyway."

"Yes."

"Good."

Quant raised an eyebrow.

"One of you is quite enough, Janice."

"My sentiments exactly, Jessica. May even be one too many, for that matter."

Jessica nodded.

"And now there's one last thing, Jessica. I noted that you are not packing the statue of your great grandfather I gave you."

"No, Janice. It was a gift to the Chen. It stands as a reminder to future Chen not to stray from the path."

Janice nodded.

"Honorable. That said, I would leave you a memento of my gratitude. A gift to you personally, Jessica, not to the office of Chen. I hope you will enjoy it.

"Good spacing and long life to you, Jessica Chen-Jasic. We may meet again."

"Goodbye and good luck, Janice Quant."

With that Quant cut the channel, and Jessica heard a slight bump next to her. She turned, and sitting in the middle of her tea table was an iridium statue. As the first, it was of her great-grandfather, he who had been Chen Zufu, seated on a pillow. He was older here than in the other statue, but this statue was to the same scale as the statue Janice Quant had sent her earlier.

But this statue included something more. Standing behind and to one side of Matthew Chen-Jasic, her hand on his shoulder, was Jessica Chen-Jasic, at the age of nineteen, in a lavalava and sandals.

Jessica recognized the scene, from her great grandfather's eighty-fifth birthday party, sixty years ago. This was much more personal than a copy of the public statue downtown.

Jessica reached out and touched the other shoulder of the ancient seated figure, and a tear ran down her face.

SILK ROAD

Later, Jessica and MinChao contemplated the new statue.

"Where did that come from?" MinChao asked.

"It simply appeared, while I was sitting here."

"It looks like iridium. Like the other statue."

"Oh, yes," Jessica said. "I cannot move it. It must weigh over two hundred pounds."

"But why?"

"It is, apparently, a retirement present."

"This is not a copy of the statue downtown," MinChao said, looking at the other statuette and back. "He is older here."

"Yes. The downtown statue is of him at age seventy, at the height of his powers, when he ruled Arcadia as dictator. This is a scene I well remember, a posed image with him at his eighty-fifth birthday party, five years after he stepped down as Chen Zufu."

"And you were there?"

"Oh, yes. Lovely, wasn't I?"

"That is truly amazing. Together you two stretch back to the beginning of the colony."

"And before."

"And the two of you have arguably had the greatest impact on Arcadia. On all the colony planets."

"Oh, yes. That is the point of it, I think."

Jessica did not tell even MinChao of her conversation with Janice Quant. She was still processing what to say about it, and to whom.

"And this statue is not to the Chen, MinChao. It is to me."

"How do you know that, Jessica?"

"It is too personal. Too directed to me personally."

"How do you interpret it then?"

Jessica looked at him, then back to the statue.

"As a thank you, and congratulations for a job well done."

RICHARD F. WEYAND

Transfer Of Power

"Come on. We don't want to be late," Wayne Porter said.

"I'm coming, I'm coming," Denise Bonheur said. "I just had to be sure the kids were all right and Margot had everything she needed."

Porter was wearing his one business suit. The design group downtown normally worked in business casual, which on Arcadia ran all the way to lavalava and sandals. Bonheur was wearing one of the several business suits she used during audit periods at work, when she had to review the books on clients of the firm.

They took the bus to Charter Square, transferred to the Arcadia Boulevard bus, and got off at Fifteenth Street. They walked west down Fifteenth Street the two blocks to Fifteenth and Market, arriving at quarter to four. There was a line of people queued outside the restaurant, but the line was moving quickly.

Inside, the elevators and the stairs were roped off with a velvet rope between brass stanchions. Two robots stood at the gap, welcoming people by name and letting them through. Porter had brought the invitation and its envelope in case there was any question, but the robot they encountered had no doubts.

"Mr. Porter and Ms. Bonheur," it said. "Welcome. Have a wonderful time."

The robot waved them through the barrier.

"Let's go up the stairs," Porter said. "It will probably be faster than waiting for the elevator."

SILK ROAD

The stairs doubled back on themselves halfway up to debouch into another elevator lobby. Two sets of double doors stood open into the upstairs banquet room.

The room itself was huge, occupying the entire footprint of the restaurant and the smaller banquet rooms on the first floor. It had been created during the expansion of the galleria – vertically – by clearing out this end of the second floor. A wall of windows gave a view out over the galleria's open central space, but heavy drapes were closed over those windows now.

Over a hundred round tables, each seating ten people, filled the space in front of the main table, which stretched along the far wall. Perhaps a dozen four-armed robots stood around the walls, just watching, while wait staff moved about the tables.

"My word," Denise said.

"Some party, eh?"

"And those are the robots people have been talking about?"

"Yeah. They're building the new building next door to our offices downtown."

"Wayne! Hey, Wayne!"

Porter looked to see the always boisterous Karl Huenemann standing at a table forward and to the left of them. He waved them over.

As Porter and Bonheur walked up, they could see the other people at the table. Huenemann and his wife, and Mikhail Borovsky and his wife, John Gannet and his wife, and Chris Bellamy and her husband. Huenemann and Gannet were the group leaders, and Borovsky and Bellamy the project managers, of the design and operations groups. Rarified heights compared to a simple designer.

"Hi, Wayne. Hi, Denise," Huenemann said. "We saved your spot."

"Thanks, Karl. Do you also have any clue why we're here?"

Porter asked, gesturing to himself and Bonheur.

"What? The Design Guy? You gotta be kiddin', right?"

Porter didn't know what to say to that, and Huenemann continued as they sat down.

"The aperitifs are out. You really have to try this white wine from Bali. It's great."

"And the cheese from Earthsea is exceptional," Borovsky added, nibbling on a piece of cheddar from the apple and cheese tray in the center of the table.

"And Tahiti apples," Bellamy added.

Porter just shook his head. Bonheur was looking around, toward the tables up front.

"Isn't that the prime minister?" she asked.

Porter looked in that direction. At the table directly in front of the main table, sat Rob Milbank and his wife.

"Yes. And with them at that table, that's Sasha Ivanov, Loukas Diakos, Haruki Tanaka, and Darius Mikenas."

All were sitting with their wives. Or their girlfriends, Porter corrected himself. Wasn't Diakos, at least, single? He thought he'd heard that.

"Who are they?" Bonheur asked.

"Rob Milbank's inner circle. Ivanov and Diakos were the ambassadors that opened up the colony planets. They went out on the shuttles before we had the hyperspace liners running."

"Six weeks in zero gravity? No, thank you."

"Both ways. And more than that, in some cases," Porter said. "Tanaka is foreign minister. Mikenas is head of Milbank's internal policy group."

"Movers and shakers all."

"Yup. And then there's us."

"That's OK," Bonheur said. "We get to watch. And the wine is fabulous."

SILK ROAD

By a quarter past four, pretty much everyone had entered and been seated. It was a noisy, happy gathering, like the beginnings of a birthday party. But a hush fell over the room as their hosts entered.

Four couples, all of them dressed in silk robes embroidered with various Chinese designs, entered from a side door at one end of the main table. Everyone in the room stood for their hosts.

The four couples took their places at the main table and sat. One couple was seated slightly higher than the others, their chairs being on a six-inch dais. The male of that senior couple waved his hands for everyone to sit down, and they all sat.

"Oh my God," Bonheur said. "Who are they all?"

"The couple on the raised chairs, that has to be Chen Zufu and Chen Zumu," Porter said. "And over on the far left there, that's Chen ChaoLi and Chen JieMin."

"OK, them I recognize. She's the head of Jixing Trading, and he's the genius guy who invented hyperspace."

"Discovered it, yeah. The other four I don't know."

Huenemann leaned over toward them.

"On the left, between Chen Zufu and Chen ChaoLi, that's David Bolton and Chen YongLin."

"The other people on the invitation," Bonheur said.

"Right. And on the other side, that's Paul Bolton and Chen JuPing. The previous Chen Zufu and Chen Zumu."

"Chen JuPing?" Porter asked. "Isn't she a hundred years old or something?"

"Yeah, but she's been to Tahiti for that anti-aging stuff. Good to see her in such good shape."

Porter nodded. Chen JuPing. Just the name sent shivers down his spine. She was a legend on Arcadia. A hero of the revolution, the early driver behind the hyperspace project, the person who found Chen JieMin and encouraged the development of his wild talent, which led to the discovery of hyperspace.

And there she was, in the flesh. It was like history itself had walked into the room.

"Wow. Chen JuPing," Bonheur said. "Even I know who *she* is. That's amazing."

Chen MinChao stood, and waved everyone to remain seated. He was miked through his communicator, and patched in through the speakers in the room.

"Hello, everyone, and thank you for coming to our party today.

"This occasion is an important one for us, but there's something I want to announce first.

"During the last year, while Chen ChaoLi and Chen JieMin were away to Tahiti, their sons got married. Their weddings were not properly celebrated, and so we want to add to our celebration today our best wishes for Chen YanMing and Cindy Bolton, and Chen YanJing and Jane Reynolds. May they live long and bear many healthy children."

The two couples stood when their names were called, and the crowd applauded and cheered. All four youngsters put their hands together in front of them and bowed to MinChao, who nodded back.

"The occasion we celebrate today is something that doesn't happen very often. The installation of a new Chen, a new couple to head our family. After twenty years of being honored to have this responsibility, Jessica and I are retiring."

MinChao held out his hand to Jessica and she stood by his side.

"Our final responsibility in this position is to name our

successors to lead the family. Today, David Bolton and Chen YongLin become the Chen."

David Bolton and Chen YongLin stood and bowed to Chen MinChao and Jessica. MinChao and Jessica stepped back and down off the dais, and waved Bolton and YongLin to their vacated seats. Bolton and YongLin stepped up onto the dais in front of MinChao's and Jessica's chairs, and MinChao and Jessica moved to Bolton's and YongLin's chairs.

"David Bolton and Chen YongLin, Chen Zufu and Chen Zumu," MinChao said, and he and Jessica bowed to Bolton and YongLin, then applauded.

The whole party applauded.

"Wow," Bonheur said.

"Yeah," Porter said. "Just like that. Done."

"Thank you, everyone," Bolton said. "YongLin and I hope to serve as well as MinChao and Jessica have the past twenty years."

David and YongLin turned to MinChao and Jessica and applauded, and the crowd applauded vigorously. The opening up of hyperspace trade and travel had been on their watch.

Bolton turned back to the crowd. Rob Milbank stood in the front and bowed to Bolton, and Bolton nodded.

"We have one more announcement today, it appears," Bolton said.

Milbank turned around to the room and addressed the crowd. He, too, was patched in.

"Today I want to announce that I, too, am stepping down, as prime minister of the Republic of Arcadia."

There were some shocked sounds at that.

"I will remain in the House, but it is time for someone else, someone younger, to carry forward on the progress we have made. Sasha Ivanov will run for prime minister, and I am confident the party caucus will name him to succeed me."

Ivanov stood and waved to the crowd. His hard work in opening up the more difficult early colonies – Amber and Olympia – was well known and appreciated. He would be a shoo-in. The crowd applauded, and Milbank and Ivanov both sat down.

"With all that out of the way, everyone, let's get on with the party," Bolton said.

The crowd cheered and the wait staff moved out among the tables with the first course.

"Did all that really just happen?" Denise asked.

"Yeah, that was somethin', wasn't it?" Huenemann asked.

"Well, we had a little inside scoop," Gannet said. "*Star Courier* is leaving for Amber and Tahiti on Tuesday, and Chen, M. C., Chen-Jasic, J., Milbank R., and Whitcomb, J. are all on the passenger manifest."

"Ah. That explains much," Huenemann said.

"They're going to Tahiti for the anti-aging treatments?" Porter asked.

"Yeah," Huenemann said. "Everybody will be able to get them soon, right here on Arcadia, but if anybody deserves to be first in line, it's those four."

"Yes," Borovsky said. "They're the only reason everybody else will be able to get them at all."

The dinner was fantastic, featuring all the products that Jixing Trading would be moving among the colonies. Chen pork cutlets from Arcadia, with a mushroom gravy made from Playa mushrooms. Cranberry-rhubarb sauce, from New Earth, with orange and tangerine slices from Hawaii on the side. Apple pie made from Tahiti apples using Bert's purloined

SILK ROAD

recipe and Arcadia spices.

Earthsea cheese and Earthsea ice cream with the pie. Amber coffee. Arcadia's Chen tea. Maple, Huenemann noted – the rare and expensive tea Jessica Chen-Jasic had served him when she dressed him down over his performance as the government's initial leader on the failed hyperspace project – which was an unbelievable extravagance for a group this size.

Wines from Bali and beers from Fiji. Chocolate dainties with dessert, made with Aruba chocolate. After-dinner cigars from Spring, with a fine cognac from Olympia served in warm snifters.

It was the finest dinner that had ever been served, anywhere, in human history.

When the main table – served first – finished their meal, the four couples moved through the crowd, with one couple stopping at every table to thank everyone for coming.

Wayne Porter and Denise Bonheur were shocked to have Paul Chen-Jasic and Chen JuPing stop at their table. The couple came up to the table between Huenemann and Bonheur.

Everyone was even more shocked when Paul Chen-Jasic named them all around the table.

"Mr. Huenemann, Mr. Borovsky, Mr. Gannet, Ms. Bellamy, Mr. Porter. Thank you all for coming today. We're glad you and your partners came out to celebrate with us."

"And especially thank you all for your work on the hyperspace project," JuPing said. "We got to Tahiti just in time. Paul had a heart attack as we were coming down to the planet, and I almost lost him."

Porter felt out of place among the leaders of the project, and then JuPing placed her hand on his shoulder. He looked up into the face of the most famous woman on Arcadia.

"I am aware of your role in all this, Mr. Porter. You helped assemble the hyperspace shuttle – Hyper-3 – that took us to Tahiti, and we rode back in comfort in the hyperspace liner you designed. Thank you."

"You're welcome, ma'am," Porter said.

JuPing patted his shoulder, and the couple moved on.

"There ya go, Wayne," Huenemann said. "That's why you're here. Chen JuPing herself wanted to thank you personally. How's about that shit?"

Bonheur looked at her husband with wonder in her eyes, while Borovsky just shook his head.

Huenemann was just, well, Huenemann.

SILK ROAD

Departure

The four couples – the past, current, and future Chen – were together once more on Tuesday morning, at the Arcadia City Shuttleport. The baggage had all been loaded, everyone else was aboard. It was time for goodbyes.

The new Chen were in place. MinChao and Jessica were officially retired and headed off for the anti-aging treatments. Treatments the other six had already received.

The celebration and the stupendous dinner that was part of it had garnered publicity that had spread across the colony planets like a wild fire. Publicity of that kind can't be bought, and it made the expense of that outrageous meal worth it to Jixing Trading. Orders for the foods served were flooding into their downtown offices from all over human space even as *Star Courier*, *Star Racer*, and *Star Hunger*, each loaded with thousands of containers of those products, prepared to depart.

It had been a marketing coup of epic proportions.

Milbank and Whitcomb, MinChao and Jessica took their leave of the others at the foot of the short stair into the passenger container. It was more than fitting that Milbank, who owed his political career to his mentoring by MinChao and Jessica, would travel together with them to Tahiti.

The goodbye hugs were getting a little teary when Jessica objected.

"Oh, come now, everyone. We'll only be gone a year or so. We'll be back to cause trouble soon enough. And younger to boot."

ChaoLi gave her one last hug, and called her by her given name for the first time in more than twenty years.

"Goodbye, Jessica. Good spacing."

They watched the shuttle take off through the viewing window in the observation lounge. Its engines cycled up in RPMs, then the robot pilot focused the thrust and the shuttle rose off the pad, angling up and to the east, and was gone.

"Well, I guess it's back to work," YongLin said.

"Yes, Chen Zumu," ChaoLi said.

There were two cars waiting, one back to the Chen compound on Fifteenth Street and one to Jixing Trading's downtown headquarters. David, YongLin, Paul, and JuPing got in the car headed to the Chen compound.

ChaoLi and JieMin saw them off, then walked over to the other car. Bert was waiting there, holding the door open.

"You're crying, ma'am. Are you injured?"

"No, Bert. I'm fine."

Please review this book on Amazon.

SILK ROAD

Author's Afterword

In "Galactic Survey," Arcadia came up with a means of propulsion in hyperspace and used it to send delegations to ink trade agreements with the two colonies they could find immediately, Earthsea and Amber. They also established a shipyard to make large hyperspace liners in a neighboring star system, and looked for the other colonies.

At the end of the book, they had found six more colonies, including Olympia, the twenty-first colony dropped off by Janice Quant and her interstellar transporter.

This book would be about opening up communications with those other colonies, as well as about getting interstellar trade under way as the big hyperspace liners became available.

That meant this book required a lot of setup – a lot of 'stare out the window' time – by your author. What were those other colonies like? They couldn't all be cookie-cutter the same, but they were all starting from the same mixed culture, the same technology base, and the same governing structure they had when they all left Earth more than a century before, so they couldn't be very radically different either.

We learned in the prior book that Quant had concentrated people in some specialties on specific colonies. What would those specialties be? There were also other things individual planets were good at because of the efforts of the colonists themselves. What sort of things attracted aficionados or experts who would be sure to take their interests with them?

So each planet was given a technical specialty and some sort of side interest, all that was entered into a spreadsheet, and I

RICHARD F. WEYAND

was off and writing.

The initial colonies contacted in Galactic Survey were not signed up to a trade agreement without some difficulty. As the agreement grows, however, there are more incentives for colony planets to join. Who wouldn't want the anti-aging technology of Tahiti, or the robots of Playa? And more member planets to the agreement meant more markets opened to a new signer's products.

My free-market classical liberal politics is on a little broader display this time, as the trade agreement that Arcadia's Prime Minister Milbank works out with Earthsea's Director Laurent is unabashedly free trade. It is notably lacking all the set-asides and protections of state capitalism, which wealthy and well-connected rent-seekers engineer into modern, so-called free-trade agreements.

But the emphasis, as always, is on people and their actions in light of the situations in which they find themselves. My overarching themes of love, honor, duty, and loyalty are explored throughout the text.

One question I often get is how I keep everything and everybody straight while I write. I keep a text file of all the character names while I write a series. For the COLONY series, I have also built a spreadsheet of all the colonies. I include them after this afterword for those who might have an interest. They are exactly as I kept them.

I had fun writing "Silk Road" and I hope you enjoyed it.

Richard F. Weyand
Bloomington, IN
September 27, 2021

SILK ROAD

Notes: The Players And The Colonies

Theodore Burke - industrialist
Martha Stern - Burke's wife
Bernd Decker - entrepreneur
Anna Glenn - Decker's wife

Russ Porter - CEO of Colorado Manufacturing Corporation
Greg Hampton - CMC VP Engg
Kay Brady - CMC Chief Scientist
Valerie Dempsey - project manager
Peter Moore - technical lead
Tim Fender - CMC engineer
Robert Abrams - CMC engineer

Matt Rink - heavy construction supervisor/crew chief
Wayne Monroe - installation supervisor/crew chief
Alan Kramer - troubleshooting/support contact (Quant)
Ned Cotten - orbital construction manager (Quant)

Anthony Lake
Donald Shore

Jacques De Villepin - Chairman, World Authority

Robert Bob Jasic - engineer
Susan Dempsey - nurse
    Matthew Matt - 19
    Amy - 17
    Stacy and Tracy - 15

RICHARD F. WEYAND

Henry Hank Bolton - painting experience in college
Maureen Griffith
    Joseph
    Emma
    Paul

Bill Thompson
Rita Lamb - cafeteria manager
    Debby
    James
    Jonah

Jack Peterson
Terri Campbell
    Tom
    David
    Ann
    Kimberly

Harold Munson
Betsy Reynolds
    Peggy - 18
    Richard
    Sally
    Carl

Gary Rockham - doctor
Dwayne Hennessey - agronomist
Rachel Conroy - computers
Jessica Murphy - mechanic

Chen LiQiang - Chen Zufu, the head of household. In English,

SILK ROAD

simply, the Chen.
Chen JuHua - wife

Chen GangHai - eldest son
Chen YanJing - wife, dead seven years

Chen PingLi - daughter, 2nd

Chen MingWei - eldest grandson

Chen YanXia - Matt's second wife
Chen JuPing - daughter of YanXia's youngest son.

Mark Kendall - original chairman of the council
Meghana Khatri - hospital administrator, on the council, health department
Stanley Twardowski - World Authority Police Sergeant Major (retired)
James Faletti - hospital dock foreman

Kevin Kendall - third chairman of the council
Anna Drake - director, health department
Larry Donahue - director, food department
Park Jinsook - director, transportation department
Olga Golov - director, infrastructure department

Piotr Boykov - animal husbandry manager
Adriana Zielinski - university provost
Indira Bakshi - hospital director

Anders Connor - university president

Chen Zufu - Paul Chen-Jasic
Chen Zumu - Chen JuPing
Chen GangJie - Changu elder
Chen FangYan - JieMin's mother
Chen YongJun - JieMin's father
Chen JuanTao - JieMin's uncle
Chen MinQiang - JieMin's aunt
Chen ChaoLi - apartment building receptionist
Chen LiGang - waiter
Chen FangLi - restaurant receptionist
Chen JongJu - JuPing's tea server
Chen MinChao - Paul Chen-Jasic's second
Jessica Chen-Jasic - MinChao's wife

JieMin/ChaoLi children
ChaoPing - 14 in 2362
    married JuMing in March 2365
    child LingTao in November 2367
    child JieGang in August 2370
LeiTao - 11
    married Chen DaGang in March 2367
    child XiPing born in February 2368
    Child GangLi born in January 2370
YanMing and YanJing - 8
    YanMing married Cindy Bolton in fall 2370
    YanJing married Jane Reynolds in fall 2370
JieJun - 4

Robert Milbank - prime minister
Julia Whitcomb - Milbank's wife
Gerard Laporte - Milbank's majority whip in the House
Karl Huenemann - director of the space program

SILK ROAD

Mikhail Borovsky - project manager
Justin Moore - shuttle pilot
Gavin McKay - shuttle co-pilot
Klaus Boortz - math dept head
Anders Conner - UofA president

Aaron Barkley - head of astronomy department
Ivan Volodin - head of math department

Chen MinYan - JongJu's accounting team leader
Chen JieLing
Chen FangTao

John Gannet - operations head after Huenemann
Chris (f) Bellamy - operations project manager after Borovsky
Wayne Porter - designer/artist
Denise Bonheur - Porter's wife
Frank Takahashi - shuttle construction supervisor
Gerardo Perez - shuttle construction manager

Darius Mikenas - Rob Milbank's head of the forward-looking policy group
Anders Jansen - first Amber colony governor
Valerie Laurent - current Earthsea Director
Salvatore Romano - Laurent's aide, Earthsea ambassador to Arcadia
Paolo Costa - QR radio tech
Jeff Planck - Earthsea NOC

David Bolton - Chen Zufu after MinChao
Chen YongLin - Chen Zumu after Jessica

RICHARD F. WEYAND

Loukas Diakos - ambassador to Earthsea
Peter Dunhill - Diakos's aide
Haruki Tanaka - senior member of Milbanks's party
Sasha Ivanov - ambassador to Amber

Jeong Minho - pilot Hyper-2
Igor Belsky - co-pilot Hyper-2

Jean (m) Dufort - Amber president
Josephine Sellick - head of Dufort's party in the Assembly, Chair
Vaclav Brabec - Dufort's chief of staff
Michael Grant - Brabec's aide
Bertrand Leland - Sellick's chief of staff
Victor Brouwer - Chair of the Assembly after Sellick

Naomi Thompson - head of personnel, Jixing Trading
Gregory Prentiss - second ambassador to Earthsea
Bill Thompson - Chen JongJu's husband
Gerardo Perez - Jixing Trading factor to Aruba

Stuart Reynolds - caregiver to Paul Chen-Jasic and Chen JuPing

Oliver Nieman - Planetary Chairman of Playa
Reginald Field - Nieman's chief of staff

Henry Wang - Tahiti President
Tyler Massey - Wang's aide
Jacob Keller - Tahiti prime minister
Frank Janko - Keller's chief of staff

Lars Swenson - Olympia executive committee

SILK ROAD

Olivia Monet - Olympia executive committee
Roger Steadman - Olympia executive committee
William Monroe - executive committee chief of staff

Mildred Plakson - Aruba prime minister
Sanjay Patel - Plakson's chief of staff
Trevor West - Plakson's security detail
Terry Stanford - Aruba minority party leader

Jasper Tilden - Samoa prime minister
Mark Wegner - Tilden's chief of staff

Jonah Abrams - captain of Star Dancer
Harry Gomez - Amber government head of major projects

RICHARD F. WEYAND

#	Name	Quant Specialty	Extra Specialty
1	Earthsea	QE radios	cheese, banking
1	Amber	medical nanites	coffee
0	Arcadia	(none)	tea, spices, silk
2b	Bali	endocrinology	wine
3a	Samoa	material science	architecture
3a	Hawaii	comm & crypto	citrus, pulpy fruit
2a	Tahiti	anti-aging	apples
3b	New Earth	plant genetics	rhubarb, cranberries
2b	Terminus	forestry mgmt	gardening, flowers
3b	Westernesse	direct neural VR	writers, musicians
3a	Fiji	immunology	beer
3a	Nirvana	anti-cancer	int. design, fashion
2a	Playa	cybernetics	mushrooms
4a	Endor	water mgmt	boat buiding
4b	Dorado	transportation	car racing
4a	Tonga	animal genetics	exotic animals
4a	Spring	human genetics	cigars
2a	Aruba	(none)	chocolate
4b	Numenor	(none)	books, films, art
4a	Atlantis	fab technologies	firearms & knives
2a	Olympia	fusion	distilled spirits
	Quant	nanotech	education
	Summer	civil engineering	
	Avalon	human enhancement	

SILK ROAD

Executive	Legistative	Capital
Director Valerie Laurent	Council	Bergheim
President Jean Dufort	Assembly	Amber
Prime Minister Rob Milbank	House, Chamber	Arcadia City
President Jasper Tilden	Parliament	Apia
President Henry Wang Prime Minister Jacob Keller	Parliament	Papeete
Planetary Chmn Oliver Nieman	Planetary Council	
Prime Minister Mildred Plakson	Parliament	Barcelona
Lars Swenson Olivia Monet Roger Steadman	Executive Council	Olympus

Made in the USA
Middletown, DE
11 May 2024

54216118R00192